BWK

KT-231-205

THE THREE WEISSMANNS
OF WESTPORT

THE THREE WEISSMANNS OF WESTPORT

Cathleen Schine

WINDSOR
PARAGON

First published 2010
by Corsair, an imprint of
Constable & Robinson Ltd
This Large Print edition published 2011
by AudioGO Ltd
by arrangement with
Constable & Robinson Ltd

Hardcover ISBN: 978 1 445 85754 1
Softcover   ISBN: 978 1 445 85755 8

Copyright © Cathleen Schine, 2010

The right of Cathleen Schine to be identified as
the author of this work has been asserted by her in
accordance with the Copyright, Designs and
Patents Act 1988

All rights reserved.

British Library Cataloguing in Publication Data available

ROTHERHAM LIBRARY &
INFORMATION SERVICES

B49097472 8
R0005 4679

Printed and bound in Great Britain by
MPG Books Group Limited

To the indelible memory of

Bertha Ehrenwerth

The fruit does not fall far from the tree

CHAPTER ONE

When Joseph Weissmann divorced his wife, he was seventy-eight years old and she was seventy-five. He announced his decision in the kitchen of their apartment on the tenth floor of a large, graceful Central Park West building built at the turn of the last century, the original white tiles of the kitchen still gleaming on the walls around them. Joseph, known as Joe to his colleagues at work but always called Joseph by his wife, said the words 'irreconcilable differences', and saw real confusion in his wife's eyes.

Irreconcilable differences? she said. Of course there are irreconcilable differences. What on earth does that have to do with divorce?

In Joe's case it had very little to do with divorce. In Joe's case, as is so often the case, the reason for the divorce was a woman. But a woman was not, unsurprisingly, the reason he gave his wife.

Irreconcilable differences?

Betty was surprised. They had been married for forty-eight years. She was used to Joseph, and she was sure Joseph was used to her. But he would not be dissuaded. Their history was history to him. Joseph had once been a handsome man. Even now, he was straight, unstooped; his bald head was somehow distinguished rather than lacking, as if men, important men, aspired to a smooth shining pate. His nose was narrow and protruded importantly. His eyes were also narrow and, as he aged, increasingly protected by folds of skin, as if they were secrets. Women liked him. Betty had

1

certainly liked him, once. He was quiet and unobtrusive, requiring only a large breakfast before he went to work, a large glass of Scotch when he arrived home, and a small, light dinner at 7.30 sharp.

Over the years, Betty began to forget that she liked Joseph. The large breakfast seemed grotesque, the drink obsessive, the light supper an affectation. This happened in their third decade together and lasted until their fourth. Then, Betty noticed, Joseph's routines somehow began to take on a comforting rhythm, like the heartbeat of a mother to a newborn baby. Betty was once again content, in love, even. They traveled to Tuscany and stood in the Chianti hills watching the swallows and the swift clouds of slate-gray rain approaching. They took a boat through the fjords of Norway and another through the Galapagos Islands. They took a train through India from one palace to the next, imagining the vanished Raj and eating fragrant delicate curries. They did all these things together. And then, all these things stopped.

'Irreconcilable differences,' Joe said.

'Oh, Joseph. What does that have to do with divorce?'

'I want to be generous,' Joe said.

Generous? she thought. It was as if she were the maid and she was being fired. Would he offer her two months' salary?

'You cannot be generous with what is mine,' she said. And the divorce, like horses in a muddy race, their sides frothing, was off and running.

*   *   *

2

The name of Joe's irreconcilable difference was Felicity, although Betty referred to her, pretending she could not remember the correct name, sometimes as Pleurisy, more often as Duplicity. But that was later, when Betty had surrendered the apartment on Central Park West. During the negotiations leading up to that move, Betty and her daughters were left to speculate, to surmise, and to suspect the existence of a Felicity to whom they had never been formally introduced.

'I will be generous to my wife,' Joe told Felicity. 'After all, I did spend almost fifty years of my life with the woman.' When he said the words 'my wife', it made Felicity glare at him. But he didn't notice, for when he said the word 'fifty' it made him sad and confused. That was more than half his life. What was he doing? He was too old to be starting out fresh. But when the word 'old' passed through his thoughts, that heavy, gloomy syllable, followed so closely by the word 'fresh', his doubt passed and he uttered the word 'woman' as if Betty were a rude ticket taker at a tollbooth, a stranger with her unmanicured hand out, and Felicity's glare softened.

'Of course you'll be generous,' Felicity said. 'You are a generous man. Anything you do will be generous, Joe.' She took his hand and kissed it. 'And I will help you, Joe,' she said. 'I'll help you be generous.'

'Naturally I'll give her the apartment,' Joe said. 'It seems only right. We've lived in it all our lives. She's put so much work into it. It's her baby.'

Felicity had seen the apartment. In a magazine. It sparkled and gleamed with a comforting Old World charm. Or so the magazine said. To Felicity,

3

it just looked big and luscious, though the various shades of cream could do with a little splash of color, and some of the furniture seemed a bit rickety, antique or no antique. She would like to live in such an apartment. But she said, 'Naturally.' Then she looked thoughtfully at Joe, who sat on her own sofa in her own living room, a perfectly respectable place in Lincoln Towers that had once had a view of the Hudson River. She stood up and peered out the window at the Trump Towers that now blocked that view. 'You bought that place for a song, didn't you?' she asked.

Joe smiled. 'We did. We never missed a mortgage payment, either.'

'*You* never missed a mortgage payment,' Felicity corrected him.

'Yes, of course. That's true.'

'Paid it from your salary?'

'Well, who else's salary would there be?' he asked. 'Betty never worked a day in her life. Never had to. You know that.'

Felicity did know that. She, on the other hand, had worked many days in her life.

'But it was her money that made the down payment,' Joe added. He thought of himself as a fair man.

'A mere song,' Felicity said. 'You said so yourself.'

Joe considered this. 'Yes. Five thousand dollars down. Can you imagine?'

'And now the apartment is worth—what? Three million?'

'Oh, at least.'

Felicity was silent, letting the implication sink in.

'That's quite a return on a five-thousand-dollar

investment, isn't it?' he said.

'I suppose the upkeep is very high these days.'

Joe nodded.

'It's really a burden, that big old place,' Felicity said. 'Poor Betty. I don't envy her. At her age.'

'She ought to downsize,' Joe said. 'We should sell the place, and she can take her share and buy something a little more realistic.'

'Joe, you really are a generous man,' Felicity said. 'And self-sacrificing, too.'

He looked at her blankly. He knew he was generous and self-sacrificing, but just for a moment he could not quite make out how this act of taking half the proceeds, rather than none, fit that description. Then Felicity said, with some alarm, 'But what about the taxes? There will be hardly anything left from the sale after taxes. Poor Betty.' She saw it was six o'clock and made him his drink. 'It really will be a burden on her, much more than on you. You have so many deductions. She doesn't. Not having a business.'

Joe was not a stupid man, and he liked to think of himself as a generous man; but he loved the big, airy apartment Betty had made so comfortable for him, and he loved Felicity. Obviously the apartment would be too much for Betty to handle, he told himself. How could he have been so thoughtless, so insensitive?

'At her age,' Felcity murmured again, as if reading his thoughts.

The apartment was far more suitable for him and Felicity. She was young and energetic. He was neither, but he was so used to the place. Was it fair that he should be thrown out of his own home just to pay good money to the government? It would be very bad judgement. It would bankrupt Betty with taxes. It would be cruel.

And so it was decided. Joe would be generous and keep the apartment.

*   *   *

Betty had been married before she met Joseph Weissmann. Her first husband had died suddenly and young in an automobile accident, leaving her with two little girls, Annie, age three, and Miranda, two months. Joseph came into their lives not quite a year after the accident. He married Betty, and though they ate dinner in the kitchen before he came home from work and never saw him on the Saturdays when he went to the office, the girls took his last name, called him Josie, considered him their father, and loved him as if he were.

When Annie got the phone call from her mother announcing Joseph's discovery of irreconcilable differences after almost fifty years, she immediately urged a visit to a neurologist. Had Josie been complaining of headaches? Erratic behaviour, headaches, dizziness: Of course it was a brain tumour. Did her mother remember her friend Oliver from graduate school? He died just like that. Betty had better get him to a doctor that day. Poor Josie.

'It's not a brain tumour,' her mother said. Joseph was feeling better than he had in years. 'And you know what that means.'

Annie grudgingly accepted what her sister, Miranda, understood immediately.

'He is in love,' Miranda said when Betty called her to tell her the news.

6

'I'm afraid he must be,' Betty said.

The two women were silent. They were both believers in love. This love was heresy.

'What does Annie say?'

'She's going to speak to him. And she suggested I get a lawyer.'

'A lawyer?' Miranda's voice was disapproving. 'What does Josie say about *that*?'

'He suggested we use a mediator.'

'This is not really happening,' Miranda said.

And she, too, decided to see Josie.

*　　　*　　　*

'I am entitled to live my life,' Joseph told them when they appeared together at his office. But there were tears in his eyes. 'I am entitled to my life.'

Both women were moved by the tears. And both agreed that he was entitled to his life, but with these provisos: Annie explained that the life Josie was entitled to was the life he had always lived, the one with their mother; Miranda, a more romantic soul, pointed out that while life must be lived to the fullest, Josie was no longer young, and his present life was surely full enough for someone his age.

'This is difficult for me, too,' Joseph said. He squeezed his fists into his eyes like a child. The two women put their arms around him.

'Josie, Josie,' they said softly, soothing the distinguished man in his pinstriped suit. They had never seen their stepfather cry.

He stood back and looked down at his two daughters, his 'girls', and he saw that his girls were

7

no longer girls. Miranda was as lovely in her skittish, eye-flashing way as ever, her light brown hair shining, grazing her shoulders, the style not much different from what she wore as a teenager. But now in her still-youthful beauty there was something willed and hard. As for Annie, she had never looked youthful, always so serious, her dark eyes taking everything in and giving nothing back. He could see a faint line of gray where her hair parted. She watched him anxiously. What could he do for her, his sad little girl? Decades ago, in his youth, a man in his position might have handed her some bills and told her to buy herself a hat to cheer herself up. He imagined her in a little velvet cocktail hat, inclined rakishly to one side. The incongruity of it made him want to shake her.

'I will be very generous to your mother,' he said. 'You can count on me for that.'

And the daughters left the office, angry, disappointed, but hopeful for their mother's material comfort, at least.

'Hi, Felicity,' they said with forced cheerfulness to the pretty VP who had initiated the increasingly successful online side of the business. There was no point in letting their misery show. Perhaps the whole thing could be patched up before Felicity and the others in the office knew anything about it.

*   *   *

'Well, at least they're not getting lawyers,' Miranda said. 'Lawyers are parasitic vultures.'

'You're mixing unpleasant species characteristics.'

'Vermin,' Miranda said defiantly. Miranda was a literary agent and resented the legal profession on

8

principle for interfering in matters that ought not to concern them, like her clients' contracts, but her experiences with lawyers had been particularly painful in the last six months. 'They should mind their own business.'

'Unfortunately, divorce sort of is their business. Some of them anyway.'

Miranda had never been divorced herself. This, she knew, was only because she had never been married. She fell in love too easily, too frequently, too hard, to get married. Miranda loved to be in love. It was a pleasure she was willing to suffer for, but not give up. Right now she was in love with a ne'er-do-well day trader. She thought of him and felt a flutter of giddy admiration: his bare back bent over her computer in her dark bedroom late at night, the pained expression on his face illuminated by the big, bright monitor.

Love was one of the reasons she gave for never getting married, the primary one. But there was another. She had always been too busy, constantly on the phone, barking out orders to her harassed assistant, flirting with a publisher on the hook, raising the spirits of a disappointed author. She specialized in the genre of what Annie dubbed the Lite Victory memoir. Her clients, the Awful Authors, as even Miranda called them, had always overcome something ghastly and lurid, something so ghastly and so lurid they had to write a ghastly and lurid book recounting every detail of their mortification and misery. At the end of the book, there was a nice epiphany, and since no one could really object to an epiphany, not even Annie, the books were very popular and Miranda had built a thriving agency that required her constant attention.

Until the lawyers got to it, she thought. 'Vermin,' she said again. 'Ha! No divorce lawyer will ever dine on my flesh.'

Annie said nothing. Miranda's antipathy to marriage was a point of contention between them. Annie had always maintained that Miranda simply lacked the imagination to get married.

'Marriage is too much like fiction for you,' she once told Miranda. 'Too unpredictable, too influenced by idiosyncratic characters.'

Miranda, who considered herself a hopeless romantic, had replied, 'Fiction has a plot, the same old plot. In what way is that unpredictable?'

'Because it all hangs on temperament, on personality, on serendipity and happenstance. On chance. Your books, and all your love affairs, are about control, losing it and then reasserting it.'

To which assessment of the genre of memoir and the miracles of the heart Miranda would shake her head, smile pityingly at her benighted older sister, contemplate her puzzling insistence on always wearing such drab colors, and say gently, 'I want to be free, Annie. And I am.'

Then, invariably, the sisters would quote Louisa May Alcott at each other—'She is too fond of books, and it has turned her brain'—and move on to other things.

Now, as Miranda walked beside her sister, she wondered if Josie wanted to be free, free of Annie and herself. As well as their mother, of course.

'It's so sad,' she said. 'Lawyers would make it ugly, too.'

She felt her phone vibrating. When she saw who it was, she didn't answer.

10

'Christ,' she muttered, but Annie didn't hear her.

'And expensive,' Annie was saying. 'They make it so expensive.' That had certainly been her experience. She had been married, many years ago. She had two grown children to prove it. But her husband, such an intense, driven young man, had turned out to be a gambler. Annie hadn't seen him after the divorce, eighteen years ago, nor had he kept in touch with his children. She had been informed of his death, of leukaemia, two years ago. 'Nothing lasts,' she said now, thinking of the waste that was love.

Miranda said, 'You're so literal minded.'

And the two sisters continued down the street, arm in arm, affectionate and indulgent, each smiling a small, comfortable smile at her superiority to the other.

*　　　*　　　*

On leaving her stepfather's office, Annie had given Felicity Barrow a brave, friendly hello, yet she had never liked Felicity. Felicity had round, oversized eyes, bright blue eyes, like a child actor who knows how to act like a child. Annie respected her stepfather's colleague. She knew how hard Felicity worked and how much she had contributed to the company, but she knew of Felicity's accomplishments by way of Felicity. It was not that the woman boasted. Quite the opposite. She was modest to a fault, the fault being that she insinuated her modesty, deftly, into almost any conversation, proclaiming her insignificance and ignorance, thereby assuring a correction.

11

Even so, under other circumstances, Annie would have stopped for a more extended greeting, for Felicity's older brother was the distinguished novelist Frederick Barrow, and through Felicity's generous intervention he had been induced to speak at the library where Annie worked. It was a small, private, subscription library started in the nineteenth century by wealthy furriers hoping to help promote literacy and thus good citizenship among aspiring young men entering the trade. It was endowed with funds not quite sufficient to keep it going, and among her other duties as deputy director, Annie arranged readings there. They had become something of an event in the Upper West Side neighbourhood where the library was located. The tickets were sold for twenty-five dollars apiece, and after a rocky start, they had gotten audiences of over two hundred people for three years running.

One of Annie's talents was convincing writers to participate. At first she had simply kept abreast of who had a book coming out and might therefore be eager to promote it. But after a few years, she began giving the authors a percentage of the take, something she had observed at readings she'd attended in Germany. It seemed to excite the writers when she handed them a wad of smooth, worn bills, far more than an honorarium cheque would have done. They were like children receiving shiny coins. Annie had no illusions about authors. On the one hand, she admired them, for they created the books she admired. But, too, she felt most of them were rather sad, desperate people who couldn't hold down a job, and she counted out the money into their open palms with

12

the same expression she wore when tipping the doorman.

But even with the inducement of a pile of twenty-dollar bills, it was unusual for her to get a writer like Frederick Barrow to read at her library. He was not only revered and rich, he was also reserved, and he rarely appeared in public. Felicity's offer had been a welcome one.

Annie had first met Felicity one evening a year ago when Annie went to the suite of offices to surprise her stepfather and join him on his walk home. Joseph walked home every day, rain or shine, and Annie liked to join him sometimes. It was not far from his office to the apartment, eighteen blocks, it was on her way home, and that night had been a lovely, cool spring evening, the sunlight lingering and the finches warbling gloriously from the light poles.

The receptionist was not there when Annie stepped out of the elevator. Felicity, who was just leaving Joseph's office, appeared to be the only other person around, and Joseph introduced the two women. It was then that Felicity had offered up her brother. Annie, though excited at the prospect, did not take her seriously and forgot all about it. But a month later, an email appeared in her inbox from Felicity with Frederick Barrow's phone number, email address, and pledge that he would participate.

The reading promised to be a huge success. They had sent out the announcements, and one hundred tickets had been ordered already. Frederick Barrow himself, though he wrote turbulent, wrenching books, turned out to be as tranquil a man as Annie had ever met. They went

13

for drinks to discuss the event, drinks somehow became dinner, and dinner led to after-dinner drinks at Bemelman's Bar. They walked together up Fifth Avenue past the closed museums and the dark forest of Central Park at night. They walked and walked in the windy night, quoting Shakespeare like undergraduates and holding hands.

Never, Annie thought, have I regretted an evening as a librarian less. This mood lasted for weeks. Then Frederick Barrow joined the library and began to use it for his research, which led to more lunches, more dinners, and considerably more quotation. Indeed, on the day that Annie and Miranda left their stepfather in tears and retreated to a café to drink tea, Annie was planning to have dinner with Frederick.

'He's so handsome in his author photos,' Miranda said.

'They're not terribly recent. His hair is almost white now. I think writers should keep their photos up-to-date. When he does finally use a new one, it will be a terrible shock to his readers. They'll think he's been ill.'

'Good God, Annie.'

Miranda's cell phone gave a plaintive cry, and she checked a text message, frowned, and swore beneath her breath. 'Where does he live, anyway?' she said as she typed into the cell phone. 'These fuckers.' She put the phone away. 'So? Where?' It was important to Miranda that Frederick Barrow be a New Yorker. It would not do anyone any good if he lived in San Francisco or taught at the University of Iowa.

'He's been in Berlin for the past year—that's

where I first got in touch with him.'

'Oh, Berlin!' Miranda, in her enthusiasm for a city she found endlessly fascinating, forgot for a moment that she wanted Frederick to live nearby. 'Wonderful.'

'But I think he actually lives in Massachusetts. Cape Cod? He's been staying with his kids in the city.'

Massachusetts was not bad. Miranda nodded in approval. She'd had a boyfriend in college who went to Harvard while she went to Barnard. There was a good train, and Miranda liked trains. A train felt fast, faster than a car, faster even than a plane, and the illusion of speed was almost as important to Miranda as was speed itself. She became bored and impatient easily, but had found that anything framed by a train window could hold her attention, as if the undersides and back ends and rusty corners of dying cities were episodes of a rough, rousing life flashing by. She had ended up detesting the Harvard boyfriend, Scarsdale Nick, as she used to call him, but the train had never disappointed her. No, Frederick Barrow in Massachusetts was not bad at all.

'He *is* still pretty good-looking,' Annie said. 'He wears nice old tweed jackets.'

Annie's tone was serious and full of warmth. Miranda gave a snort.

'What?' Annie said.

'Ha!'

'You're crazy.'

'I know what I know,' Miranda said.

*　　　*　　　*

15

As the weeks wore on, the marriage mediation sessions began. Betty and Joseph went to an office oddly situated in Chelsea.

'Where did you find out about this woman?' Betty asked.

'Referral.'

'This is a very dumpy office,' Betty whispered. They had walked down the narrow stairs of a decrepit brownstone to what was the basement level. 'This was called the English basement when they first started doing them in New York. Nineteenth century. Very *Upstairs, Downstairs,* don't you think? Do you remember when Annie hired a carpenter she found in the *Village Voice* classifieds? Did you find this woman in the *Village Voice* classifieds, honey? Those bookcases tilted terribly.'

A small dumpy woman appeared at the door to an inner dumpy office. She had full, poorly cut salt-and-pepper hair. She was, Betty noticed, wearing space shoes.

'Are those back?' she asked the woman. 'They were very popular in the fifties. Our dentist wore them.'

The mediator did not smile. But she did hold out her hand and introduce herself. Her name was Nina Britsky. A *matzoh-punim,* Betty thought, feeling sad for her.

The office was small and crowded with piles of bulging folders. It resembled a closet, really—the bulging file closet. The mediator sat on a complicated ergonomic chair and placed her feet on a small stool that was on rockers. So much specialized equipment, Betty thought, just to listen to Joseph and me disagree.

16

Nina Britsky opened her laptop and began to type and speak.

Betty did not hear much of what she said. The initial barrage of New Age pop-psychological platitudes delivered in a hoarse Bronx accent immediately told Betty that daydreaming would be the most polite response. And Nina Britsky looked so much like a chimpanzee curled on her ergonomic chair: her coarse cap of hair; her lips pursed in contemplation, then opening wide to reveal large teeth. Betty imagined herself in a dark chimpanzee cave, though she did not believe, now that she thought of it, that chimpanzees slept in caves. Surely they slept in trees. But the room was almost as dark as a cave. Perhaps there was a divorce mediation lighting theory: if the two people could no longer see each other, they would leave each other more easily. The woman was probably just trying to keep her electricity bills down, and who could blame her? Betty had just begun changing over to the new energy-saving bulbs herself. They were so pretty, twisting and turning, like old-fashioned filaments . . .

'It's good there's no child custody involved,' the woman was saying. She typed importantly on her laptop. 'In these cases, that can get pretty ugly.'

'These cases?' Betty said. 'In all cases, I would think.'

'Well, it can be much worse in same-sex cases.'

'But Joseph and I are not the same sex,' Betty explained gently.

Joseph was squirming a bit, she noticed.

'Are we, Joseph?'

'I was referring to the third party,' Nina Britsky said.

17

'There is no third party,' Joseph said hurriedly.

'And if there were, I don't think it would be a man,' Betty said.

'Well, I assumed it was a woman,' Nina Britsky said, throwing Betty a pointed look. 'A same-sex woman,' she added, to Betty's further confusion. 'Why else would you come to me?'

It was only after they had been handed pamphlets inviting them to a support group—My Spouse's Closet Anonymous or MYSPCL, pronounced like bicycle—and left the office in a dull daze that Betty asked Joseph exactly who it was who had referred the ergonomic chimpanzee.

'Because, Joseph, she seems a rather specialized mediator.'

Joseph said, 'That was a disaster. Let's go get dinner.'

'Look at her card: *For couples seeking divorce when women seek women.* It could be a classified ad in *The Village Voice,* couldn't it? Maybe she'll build us a crooked bookcase.'

Joseph couldn't help laughing. Betty had always made him laugh.

'You're so funny,' he said.

Betty burst into tears.

CHAPTER TWO

It was around this time that Miranda made her infamous appearance on *Oprah*. It was all a blur at the time—being led from a room full of snacks she was far too nervous to eat, stepping over cables, stepping onto a stage, sitting on a sofa, the sound

18

of applause, the radiance and confidence of the woman across from her, some questions, some answers . . . *How could she have let this happen? Didn't she check up on the stories the writers told her? Couldn't she see? Didn't she care? . . .*

She felt like a corrupt politician stonewalling the press, like a criminal, like one of her disgraced writers. But Miranda knew that what she was saying to this woman, who hardly seemed real she was so very Oprah-like, was not only true, it was profound. Why did no one understand when she tried to explain? When she told them that her writers' stories were real-life stories even when they were lies?

'Because in real life people make things up,' she said to Oprah.

But Oprah shook her iconic head, and Miranda was overwhelmed with shame.

She stayed in her loft for weeks after that, not answering the phone, not picking up calls from the clients whom she had tried to defend, ignoring the chorus of pleading voices on her answering machine: her mother, her sister, even the lawyer who was trying to defend her, for several publishers were now coming after her for fraud.

She lay in bed, tangled in her sheets, asking herself and her four walls in a loud keening voice: *Why?*

And then imagining, in the ironic voice with its Yiddish lilt that she had always playfully bestowed on God, a voice that answered by raising its shoulders and helplessly holding out its hands: *Why not?*

This is Miranda Weissmann, the answering machine said. *This is your lawyer,* the answering

19

machine answered, *and there is a lien on all your property until the lawsuit is settled, so couldn't you please call me back?*

In real life, people don't call back, Miranda explained to the pillow. In real life, people have tantrums.

Annie and Betty both tried to visit her, but even they were left standing in the hallway banging on the door, Annie calling in, 'Oh, don't be such an ass.'

It wasn't until Annie left a message on the answering machine describing their mother's unhappy state in gruesome detail that Miranda felt she actually had to answer the phone.

'She's really suffering,' Annie said when Miranda finally picked up. 'She needs you.'

Miranda showered and dressed and headed uptown. Though she was acknowledged even by herself to be extraordinarily self-absorbed, no one had ever accused Miranda Weissmann of being selfish.

The apartment was on the tenth floor, just high enough for a spacious view of the park, just low enough for a human one. Central Park was their front yard, Joseph liked to say. Their grounds. He and Betty had tried living in the suburbs when the children were little, in Westport, Connecticut. Dull and lonely there, they agreed, and after only one year, when so many other young couples were leaving the city, they found the big apartment on Central Park West and bought it for a song. That was the word Joseph had used, a 'song', and Betty still recalled that day when they signed the papers and went to look at their new home. That sickly ambience of someone else's old age had surrounded them—the filthy fingerprints around the light switches, the greasy Venetian blinds, the grime of the windows, and an amber spiral of ancient flypaper studded with ancient flies. But all Betty could think of was that they bought it for a song, and she had looked so happy and so beautiful in the weak silver city light that Joseph had not had the heart to explain the expression, to tell her they had paid the song, not received it.

Now they both stalked the premises like irritable old housecats, watching each other, waiting.

'You are leaving me,' Betty said late one morning. 'Hadn't you better leave, then?'

'Hadn't?'

'I think a certain formality of address is required under the circumstances, don't you? Unless you want to call the calling off off, of course.'

There were times when Joe did want to call the calling off off. But that day was not one of them. Betty was being insufferable. She was vamping mercilessly, wearing her bathrobe, speaking in an arch yet melodramatic voice, and, perhaps most alarming of all, drinking shots of single malt in midmorning.

'That's a sipping whisky. Not a gulping whisky.'

'I'm distraught.'

'You're being ridiculous, Betty. You look like something out of *The Lost Weekend*. This is not healthy, moping around the apartment, drinking.'

'My husband of fifty years is leaving me,' she said.

Forty-eight, he thought.

As if she'd heard him, she said, 'Bastard.'

She threw her glass at him.

'All right, Elizabeth Taylor,' he said, getting a

towel from the bathroom.

'Wrong movie,' she screamed.

'It's not a movie, Betty,' Joseph said. 'That's the point.'

'Bastard,' she said again. She sat down on the couch.

The buzzer rang, and Betty stayed where she was, staring straight ahead at the fireplace. She had discovered the mantel with its towering mirror and decorative gesso detail at a salvage yard decades ago. How could Joseph expect her to leave her Greek Revival mantel? Her *hearth*, as it were? She saw her reflection, sullen, in the mirror. The matching busts of impassive Greek Revival women adorned with gold leaf gazed back at her from either side of the mantel. She heard Joseph's footsteps. What a heavy tread he had. How she would miss it when he was gone, when she was alone with the mantel's two white wooden busts. Through the intercom, she heard the doorman announcing Miranda. As a child, Miranda had talked to the fireplace ladies, sometimes staging elaborate tea parties with the disembodied heads as her guests.

'Do you want her to see you like this?' Joe said when he returned to the living room.

For a moment Betty thought he was addressing one of the busts. Then she understood.

'Do you want her to see you at all?' she said. She heard and hated the sound of her voice. Oh, Joseph, she wanted to say. Let's stop all this nonsense now.

They could hear Miranda's key in the lock. Joe thought, I have to get that key back. Annie's, too. He glanced at his wife. She was wearing her old

22

white bathrobe, and curled in on herself on the couch, she looked like someone's crumpled, abandoned Kleenex. Joe winced at his own word, the word 'abandoned'. No one was abandoning anyone. He would be generous. He was generous. She was being irrational. It wasn't like her. She didn't even look like herself, her face puffy from crying. If she would just be reasonable, everything would be fine: she would be so much happier once she moved into her own place.

'This situation is becoming sordid,' he said.

'Squalid even.'

Miranda came into the living room, walked to the couch, and gave her mother a kiss.

'Whew,' she said, sniffing. 'Someone got started early.'

'I'm suffering.'

Miranda sat down and put her arms around her mother.

'My poor darling,' Betty said. 'So are you, aren't you? There, there, Miranda darling. There, there.'

Joe looked at the two of them patting each other's back and murmuring, 'There, there.' He felt awkward, an oger standing with an enormous white bath towel. But what had he really done? Was it so wrong to fall in love?

'This is a very unhealthy situation,' he said.

The two women ignored him.

He threw the towel down at the spill and stared at it. 'Your mother never drinks,' he said. 'You have to talk to her, Miranda. I'm worried about her.'

There was withering silence. The warm perfume of Scotch whiskey hung in the room.

'I'm not an ogre,' he said.

23

*   *   *

The next day, Joseph packed his bags and left for Hong Kong on a business trip.

'You must be relieved,' Annie said to her mother on the phone.

But Betty was not relieved. She was even more miserable than before.

And, too, there was the problem of money. An immediate, acute problem. Unaccustomed, unaccountable. Undeniable. On the advice of Joseph's lawyers, Joseph's lawyers now informed her, Joseph was cutting off all credit cards. The joint bank account, which Betty used for household expenses, would not be replenished until a settlement had been reached.

'I thought Mr Weissmann didn't want to use lawyers,' Betty said to the lawyers. 'We have a mediator.' The lawyers replied only that they supposed, judging by the evidence of their employment, that Mr Weissmann had changed his mind.

'I'm awfully sorry,' Joseph said when he called. 'It was on the advice of my lawyers that I got lawyers.'

'Do they advise me to get lawyers, too?'

'We can work this out equitably. It just takes a little time. I'm prepared to be generous.'

'Joseph, you're squeezing me out of my own home.'

'Well, maybe that would be best. While we settle things.'

Just hearing his voice made Betty feel a little better. It was a voice she had heard every day.

24

After the conversation, she felt more herself.

'That's crazy,' Annie said when her mother explained this to her. 'He's behaving horribly. And you can't move out. That's Divorce 101.'

'The co-op is in his name. Legally, it's his. So he just has to straighten things out—legally. Then we'll work it out between us. Until then, he's not really free to let me have the apartment. Legally.'

'Mother, you know that makes no sense, don't you? I mean, you do know that?'

'And of course I don't have the money to keep it up just now. Do you know what it costs to maintain a place like this? I'm sure it's a fortune. But I don't really know. Joseph always took care of that part of it. He's always taken such good care of me . . .' she said with a wistful sigh that was soft with gratitude and comfortable memories.

Annie thought of the little bag with money in it her great-grandmother had always kept hanging around her neck, for emergencies. 'Don't you have anything in your own name?' she asked.

'A little *knipple* like my grandmother? Why should I?'

'Well, in case something like this happened.'

'Something like this was supposed to happen thirty years ago, when you girls went off to college, when women were unprepared for something like this.'

'But you're unprepared *now*.'

'But it wasn't supposed to happen now,' Betty patiently explained yet again.

*   *   *

It was soon after Joseph left that Betty heard from

25

her cousin Lou. Cousin Lou was an elegantly dressed man with a pink face for whom the description open-handed might have been invented. He had, to begin with, disproportionately large hands that burst from his sleeves and were constantly slapping the backs and patting the cheeks and enfolding the helpless smaller hands of the many people he liked to have around him. Lou had come to the United States as an evacuee in 1939, an eight-year-old boy from Austria bringing nothing with him but his eiderdown and a copy of Karl May's first Winnetou novel. Betty's uncle and aunt had taken him in for the duration of the war, but he stayed on after the war ended, for he had lost everyone in the camps. The loss of his family was something he never mentioned. In fact, the only topic from that time that he did talk about was someone named Mrs James Houghteling.

Mrs H., as he called her, had been the wife of the Commissioner of Immigration when the eight-year-old refugee had arrived at Ellis Island.

'Now, that same year there was a bill before Congress,' he said, the first time he discussed Mrs H. with the little Weissmann girls. 'Do you know what Congress is?'

They nodded yes, though they had only the vaguest idea of men seated in a horseshoe arrangement from a poster in school.

'Then what, Cousin Lou?' Annie said, adding, 'Don't worry,' for in spite of the parties he always gave, Cousin Lou always did look a little worried.

'That same year,' Cousin Lou continued, 'someone thought it would be a good idea to allow twenty thousand refugee children to come here, to the United States. Children just like me. Did you

26

know I came here on a boat when I was little?'

Annie nodded again. Annie knew about World War II. She knew about the Holocaust. She had seen a terrifying documentary on Channel 13.

Miranda began to rock on her heels.

'Twenty thousand! That's a lot of little boys and girls, isn't it? So they asked the Congress, which is in charge of things like that. But the Congress, it said, No, we don't *want* those twenty thousand children. What would we do with twenty thousand children? We have our own children!'

At this point in the story, Annie took Miranda's hand. What if Miranda had heard of the Holocaust, too? Was that why she was rocking back and forth?

'Their own children,' Annie repeated, trying to move things along.

'Now, I never actually met Mrs H., but I feel as if we're old friends. And one night Mrs H. was at a party, and at this party she said that the trouble with the Wagner-Rogers bill—that's what it was called—the trouble with bringing in these twenty thousand children was that they would all too soon grow up into twenty thousand ugly adults!'

Miranda began to sob, not because she knew of the Holocaust as Annie feared, but at the thought of so many ugly people. She had nightmares for a week afterwards, but no one blamed Cousin Lou. It was impossible to blame Cousin Lou for anything. And in time the story of Mrs H. became a welcome ritual for the girls whenever they visited Cousin Lou or he visited them.

Lou would pause on those later occasions. He would narrow his eyes and purse his lips, as if he were thinking, thinking, thinking. 'Mrs

27

Houghteling,' he would then say, pronouncing both the *H* and the *gh* with a hard, exaggerated Yiddish *ch*, as if he were clearing a hairball from his throat. It was only years later that Annie and Miranda discovered the proper pronunciation was Hefftling. 'Mrs *Chech*tling,' the girls would chant back at him, feeling the word, an ugly word for an ugly soul, vibrating deliciously in their throats. Then Lou would shrug and say, 'Well, I must have been a beautiful baby.' And Miranda and Annie would always respond, like good congregants, ' 'Cause, baby, look at you now.'

They had heard the story so many times that 'chechtling' had become a Weissmann family verb for snobbish behaviour. 'Stop *chechtling*, you big prig,' Miranda would say if Annie turned up her nose at some outlandish adolescent style Miranda was affecting. 'You're just a selfish bourgeois *chechtler*,' Annie would say when Miranda made fun of her brief eighth-grade Maoist phase.

Cousin Lou, who insisted that everyone call him Cousin Lou, was not a subtle man, but he was a sincere one. He had made a great deal of money as a real estate developer, but his true business seemed to be providing food and drink for as large a number of guests as he could manage. Passionately devoted to his adoptive American family, his definition of that family had grown so prodigiously over the years that he could no longer fit all of his family into his house at one time, or even two. 'You're like family!' he would say, embracing freeloaders, friends, hangers-on, acquaintances, in-laws, and stray children from the neighbourhood. Like many immigrants, he was a patriot, and the frenetic magnanimity of his social activity was, as he saw it, his patriotic duty.

His first solution to convivial overpopulation had been to build ever bigger houses for himself. He now lived in a sprawling modern house of glass on a steep hill overlooking Long Island Sound. But even this would not accommodate his guest list. The teeming friends who were 'like family' multiplied like fruit flies in a jar, and Lou had finally begun to rotate them in shifts, one swarm at a time.

One of Betty's times, an exalted one, was Labor Day. When Lou called this year to invite her and Joe and the girls to his usual Labor Day party in Westport, Betty said, 'Oh, what a shame. Joseph would have loved to come, but he's divorcing me. Well, maybe next year,' and hung up.

It was this kind of behaviour, fey and satirical and so unlike their normally open, cheerful mother, that filled Annie and Miranda with despair and, when they were honest with themselves, outrage not just at Josie but at Betty as well.

'She's insane,' Annie said when Lou called to ask what was going on. 'He's driven her mad. You can't tell her anything. She won't listen. All she does is watch black-and-white movies all night and quote them all day. She's paralyzed, she's broke, she sits by the phone and waits for him to call. I know she does. She answers on the first ring. Did you notice? And she might have been drunk, too. My mother! Drunk! Was she? God, I hope not. Was she?'

'Well now, let me think—'

'—and I had to force her to get a lawyer—she wasn't even going to get a lawyer! She can't pay the

29

bills. The bastard has somehow cut her off, and he says nothing can go forward until the apartment is empty and . . .'

But by now Cousin Lou had gotten the picture, and to him it was a picture of a refugee, and he never could resist a refugee. Within minutes he had called Betty and invited her to come and stay in Westport, as long as she liked, in a cottage he owned at Compo Beach.

Betty knew the property was extremely valuable. It stood in a little cluster of little streets among what had once been other little beach cottages. Small, cheek-by-jowl, with tiny front yards, no garages, the cottages had not been fashionable during the heyday of the suburban house and showy green lawn, when she and Joseph and the children had briefly lived in the town. Schoolteachers rented them in those days. A few divorced mothers or widows fallen on hard times. Like me, Betty thought. Somewhere in the late 1980s all this changed and the cottages were snapped up and vigorously renovated. They were now a huddle of self-consciously and charmingly designed 'vacation homes'—McCottages, Annie called them. Lou's bungalow was the sole survivor from the old days. He had been renting the place out to the same woman and her son for years— 'They're like family!' But now the son had grown up and moved away, and the old lady had finally died.

'Don't you want to beautify it?' Betty asked, using Cousin Lou's code for demolition.

'Time enough for beautification,' he assured Betty. 'Just your presence will be beautification.'

Betty tried to remember Lou's cottage. A little

boy had been swinging from a rope swing, she was sure. From an apple tree in bloom. Or was that in a movie she'd seen? Well, never mind. It was a charming place, it had to be; it was a cottage, after all. Cottage. Such a charming word. She imagined rose-patterned wallpaper. She would take long, lonely walks by the sea. It was only Long Island Sound, not the sea, really, but there were sure to be gray, windy days nevertheless. She stared out the window at the nighttime view she'd known for so long. The park was black and deep, the yellow pool of a streetlight puffing out of the darkness here and there, a taxi's red taillights just visible, then gone. Could Joseph really mean for her to abandon her life, just as he had abandoned her? Well, then. What did she have to lose? It was all gone already.

'You're very generous,' she said. She shook off an uncomfortable echo of Joseph's voice—*I'll be very generous . . . very generous . . .* 'Thank you, Cousin Lou. What would I do without you?'

'Ha!' cried Cousin Lou. 'I think we should ask Mrs James Houghteling that one!' And he chuckled, invoking that long-gone lady's name three more times before hanging up.

And so it was, against the advice of the divorce lawyer Annie insisted her mother hire, and in direct refugee defiance of the spirit of the wife of the former Commissioner of Immigration, that Betty Weissmann decided to emigrate to what Cousin Lou newly dubbed Houghteling Cottage.

CHAPTER THREE

Miranda Weissmann was terrifying. This judgement had been passed in an earlier time when, following a briefly fashionable craze for eye exercises, she refused to wear either glasses or contact lenses, consequently sweeping past people she knew without recognizing them. When this seemingly aloof, grand manner was added to a tendency to ask her assistant to retrieve various items that were sitting right in front of her and a habit of inviting editors out to lunch and then not noticing when the bill came and so leaving them with the tab, her reputation was complete. Myopia had established Miranda as irrational, high-handed, sly, and demanding. Myopia made her reputation.

This was at the beginning of her career. A year later, her interests switched first to inversion therapy and then marathon running, at which point she popped in contact lenses and her warmth toward newly visible old friends and acquaintances, so sudden, was that much more pronounced. People were flattered, they were touched. The word around town among young writers was that Miranda Weissmann was unpredictable, but once she turned her attention to you, she would never turn away. The word around town was surprisingly accurate, and the Miranda Weissmann Literary Agency was on its way.

'I am a nightmare,' Miranda had always said to her latest assistant, smiling innocently.

And it was quite true. Her bullying was both

caustic and disarmingly kindhearted. Half the time, she was harsh toward her assistants, demanding order and obedience to compensate for her own natural disorder and rebellious confusion. The other half, she spoiled them like a coddling mother. They never knew if she would snap or stroke. Her assistants trembled, preened, adored and loathed her. They came and then went as quickly as they could extract themselves, but it was she who always made certain they got wonderful new jobs. People called Miranda many things—a horror, a wild woman, and, following her example, a nightmare—but never in all the annals of gossip and slander in her small world had anyone ever doubted her loyalty or, finally, her goodwill. She specialized in melodrama, in her life and in her work, but in both areas, Miranda Weissmann insisted on a happy ending.

For the members of Miranda's family, her unpredictability had become predictable. There were tantrums when she was young; when she was older, a combative dedication to whatever it was to which she was dedicated at the moment, and, at every age, the demands and the drama. But with Miranda's bombast and theatricality, always, came an almost fanatical tenderness. Miranda was manipulative, Josie once whispered to Betty, late at night in bed when he'd been thinking about how lucky he was to have inherited his little family: Miranda was manipulative, but who better to be manipulated by?

Manipulanda, Annie called her.

Now Manipulanda was terrified. Betty and Josie's divorce was shattering, far removed from any conceivable happy ending for anyone involved.

Miranda knew her mother needed her now—an unnerving realization for the baby of the family. Worse, she knew that she also needed her mother more than she ever had before.

Sometimes Miranda could not sleep at night, staring in rigid fear at the ceiling as she had as a child after a bad dream.

But she was forty-nine years old. That ought to have made the divorce easier to accept. Or so she was told.

'It's like that old joke, the old Jewish couple in Miami, they go to the rabbi and say we want a divorce, and he says you've been married for seventy-five years, why now? And they say, We were waiting for the children to die.' That was what Miranda's current beau, the day trader, had said a week or so before the *Oprah* debacle.

'I'm not dead,' Miranda replied. She'd looked at the day trader with distaste and realized what she had always known but somehow hadn't seen: he was actually a retired professor of economics who now spent his days in front of the computer losing money in the stock market. 'I'm not dead,' she repeated. And why, really, should the long marriage and her age make it any easier to accept this divorce? Surely that made it worse. She was going to be fifty, a traumatic moment for any woman. Joseph and her mother had been together for as long as she could remember. Another way of saying forever. And Joseph was her father, she had always considered him her father—the only father she had ever known.

Sometimes she cried at night. She wanted to be near her mother: to comfort and to be comforted.

That night, the night the day trader told her the

joke, she tossed and turned, unable to sleep. When she finally drifted off, the day trader poked her and asked her to stop snoring. She didn't like his unsympathetic tone of voice and snapped, 'Why don't you stop being a fucking asshole?' The next morning, he left in a huff, never to return, and Miranda cried and flung herself around her loft for the rest of the day, then took two Ativan and went back to bed.

She began to refer to herself as the product of a broken home.

'Don't be ridiculous,' Annie said. 'Your expiration date has expired, Miranda.'

*   *   *

Separation is a positive thing, Felicity explained to Joseph. He heard her, but pretended not to. He waved the waiter over. He was tired of getting divorced. If everyone would just get down to business and do what was right, it would all be taken care of. When he thought of Betty, he thought of her in the apartment. That was where she belonged. For him, Betty was suddenly but utterly in the past, but so was the apartment, parts of the same memories, a different life, a life he was leaving behind. So, yes, separation was a positive thing. Yes, yes. But now it appeared he would not only have to separate from Betty, he would also have to separate Betty from her apartment.

'How are the stepdaughters doing?' Felicity asked when they'd ordered.

Joseph never called them his stepdaughters. They were his daughters. He must have shown his distaste for the word. Felicity's wide eyes opened

35

just a bit wider. Her lips parted. She said quickly, 'I haven't seen them around the office. I miss them.'

'So do I.'

'Poor Miranda. What a scandal.'

'Double whammy.'

'It's no wonder she doesn't come around. The poor woman is probably afraid to leave the house.'

For a moment, Joseph did not connect the word 'woman' with Miranda. She was a girl, always had been, always would be. If she were a woman, what did that make him?

'Time flies,' he said, pouring himself another glass of wine. 'I used to read them their bedtime stories. Now they're women with scandals.'

'Well, not Annie. Nothing scandalous about that one.'

Felicity was right about Miranda being afraid to leave her apartment. She had always spent as little time as possible in her loft, an overpriced, underfurnished rental, always at her office or out to dinner or just out. Now she ordered her meals from every Tribeca restaurant that delivered, answered the door in her nightgown, paid with a credit card, and shuffled back to bed. Her slippers slapped disconsolately against the highly polished wood floors. The world droned on, uninterested and uninspiring, beyond her tall windows. She did not hear the car horns or the shouts of the drivers stuck behind double-parked delivery vans. She did not hear the helicopters. She did not have the energy. She heard only what followed her closely— her slippers and the murmur of the television, the creak of the platform as she settled back into bed, the sickly clatter of the plastic tops hitting the floor as she opened her containers of gummy food, her strong, unhappy heartbeat.

Felicity was right about another thing: it had been a bad year for the Miranda Weissmann Literary Agency, a terrible year, a year of queenly *annus horribilis* proportions. The Scandal of the Scandals, the blogs called it. All involving Miranda's highest-profile clients. First, Rudy Lake, whose best-selling, wrenching prison memoir had won him a parole for the murder of his first wife, turned out to have plagiarized the better part of his book from an obscure Hungarian novel of the 1950s; then the elusive Bongo Ffrancis had turned out to be a middle-aged Midwestern housewife, not the seventeen-year-old Welsh heroin addict his memoir had described; and finally, the Midwestern housewife Sarah-Gail Laney, who wrote about her painful search for normality after being raised by sexually abusive missionaries who poisoned each other in Uganda, had actually been raised in Hoboken, where her parents, sharing in the profits of her book, still lived in the quiet two-bedroom apartment in which she'd grown up.

Miranda had greeted these developments with her typical high-volume, inefficient ferocity, berating the press and the world in general; and simultaneously with a quick, irritable tenderness for her clients. When the scandals first broke, six months ago, she had busied herself arranging lawyers and interviews and excuses. She had been indefatigable. Now the publishers were after their advances, her other writers had fled, and the lawyers, interviews, and excuses were as much for herself as for the fraudulent memoirists.

Before the scandals came, Miranda had been the agent who could spot the flash of memoir gold in the barren hills of anecdote, who could meet someone on an aeroplane one day and sign a deal on the book they had never before thought of writing the next. She found talent and excitement everywhere. In the beginning, there had been two beautifully written, deeply moving memoirs—the Rhodesian childhood, the Egyptian one—that won prizes. Miranda had discovered them, had cherished them and shepherded them into their rightful place in the world, had made a great deal of money from them, too.

In the following years, she uncovered originality and authenticity with such regularity that her little agency was dubbed the Memoir Mill on Gawker. Now, suddenly, some of those authentic and original stories Miranda uncovered turned out to be fraudulent and recycled lies.

She had been deceived. She had been lied to. She had been abandoned by the stories she had nurtured with such love and care. When she saw her mother suffering from the divorce, from Josie's deception and treachery, Miranda sometimes had trouble keeping herself from gasping in intimate recognition. There is divorce and there is divorce, she told herself. And for me, there is both.

When Felicity said that Annie did not have scandals, she was right about that, too. Annie was a hardworking, even-tempered person who tried to take life as it presented itself without making a fuss. If Miranda was swept up in the waves of successive Lite Victories, Annie was comfortably dug in to her burrow of books. She read the same ones over and over—the classic novels of nineteenth-century England, the minor novels of twentieth-century England. Annie was matter-of-fact, but the facts were never hers. The light of real life, which to Miranda meant the busy melodrama of everyday scandal, never penetrated this soft, dappled world. Miranda sometimes thought of Annie as a kind of desiccated opium addict, stretched out in a smoky, sweet-smelling den with her fictional strangers, cut off from the noisy circus of life, uncaring, inaccessible, eyes closed in someone else's dream. *By the book,* Miranda always said of Annie, trying to describe what she considered to be the literalism of her sister's imagination. Perhaps it was this quality that made it a surprise to Miranda when she discovered that with this divorce Annie, too, was sad and disoriented and, most of all, angry.

'I miss him,' Annie said. 'And I hate him. Hate. Hate. Hate. Loathe. And hate.'

'Life,' Miranda replied, rather triumphantly, 'is wracked by tragic contradictions.'

This was one of Miranda's core beliefs: life was wracked by tragic contradictions . . . that would all come out right in the end. At this moment, however, with regard to Josie's treatment of her mother, she could not bring herself to pronounce the second half of her sentence.

Annie noticed the omission and was about to comment on it when Miranda's cell phone rang. In the past, Miranda would have answered and carried on, with great gusto, a conversation full of personal details from the sordid stories Miranda's authors specialized in. But this time Miranda said, 'I guess that will have to do,' in a tired voice.

'Business?' Annie said when she hung up.

'What's left of it.' Miranda took a deep breath. Failure: it was like having a fatal disease. People

39

pretended it didn't exist, turned away quickly with an embarrassed look of pity, stopped talking when you came up to them unexpectedly. People pretended it didn't exist, and so did she; yet it was always there, the air she breathed.

Annie, apparently sensing some of this, said, 'Sorry,' looking embarrassed in a way that proved Miranda's point.

'Not your fault.'

'Still, sorry.'

Miranda took her sister's arm, walked a few steps that way; then, hoping that was enough reassurance for Annie, dropped it.

*   *   *

In the contested apartment, Betty Weissmann took some satisfaction in finishing a bottle of Joseph's favorite single malt. Some satisfaction, though not much, for Betty did not like single malt whisky.

And where was Joseph now? Off with some woman, no doubt. Some other woman. She had his horrid whisky that tasted like damp and dirt. This other woman, whoever she was, had him. It was enough to make you cry. Betty did not have the energy to cry. She had already cried far too much. She would tie up her belongings in a handkerchief, hang it from a stick, put the stick over her shoulder like one of the three little pigs, and go on the train to the cottage in Westport to seek her fortune. Her fortune did not include a wolf to blow her house down, for that had already been done. But she knew the fortune of an elderly divorcée; she knew her fortune, and it was dark.

I have an idea.

Annie heard Miranda announce that she had an idea the way she heard the sound of traffic. It was ceaseless, and so it barely existed. Annie heard her sister, and she did not hear. She continued mentally adding up the retirement funds that Joseph had long ago put in her mother's name for tax purposes. Betty could take out enough of a distribution to pay for some of her food and gas. Even the new Josie with his brain tumour—there really could be no other explanation for his ugly behaviour—would continue to pay for the AARP supplement to Betty's Medicare. And the car insurance was all paid up for the year. She had checked with Josie's secretary, who, though loyal to her employer, was not unsympathetic to Betty's plight. If Annie and Miranda helped out, Betty might be able to just scrape by.

'Mmmhmm,' Annie said to Miranda.

She would pay for the movers with her tax rebate. A shame to dismantle her mother's beautiful apartment. She wondered how much of Betty's furniture would fit in the little house.

'We'll *all* move to Westport,' Miranda said.

The chairs from the living room would probably work. The image of those chairs in a new setting suddenly made her angry.

'That's my idea,' Miranda was saying.

Annie said, 'Oh, Miranda,' as she so often did.

But Miranda had it all worked out by the time they reached their mother's apartment building, and when Betty heard the plan, she was ecstatic.

'I know you're not serious,' Annie said.

41

'It's so practical, dear,' Betty said. 'You girls sublet your places and make lots of money on them.'

Miranda's cell phone was ringing. She looked at it but did not answer. One of the publishers who were suing her. That seemed to be the reason she had no money, or so her lawyer had tried to explain. Everything was tied up until the lawsuits were settled. She was living on credit cards. She had always lived on credit cards, though in the past she had employed a business manager to pay off the credit cards. Now there was no money to pay the business manager to pay off the credit cards. 'Lots of money,' she said, echoing her mother's words hopefully.

'Mom,' Annie was saying, 'you just called us *girls*. We're women in our fifties. You guys are having one of your fantasies.'

'I'm forty-nine,' Miranda said. 'And I'm not a guy.'

'It will be like the Great Depression, when everyone lived together,' Betty said. 'Oh, I can't wait.'

Annie knew that voice. It was the picnic voice. 'This is not a picnic,' she said desperately.

Betty looked at her, stricken. 'That's what Josie always says.' Her eyes filled with tears.

*   *   *

'A hideous experiment,' Annie said to her son Charlie when he called a few days later. 'Three grown women grafted onto the memory of a nuclear family. Like Frankenstein's monster. There will be mobs of violent peasants. And

42

torches.'

'You don't have to go, you know.'

'If you think you and your brother can get out of taking care of me when I'm old by giving me permission to abandon my mother in this her hour of need, you have another think coming.'

He laughed. 'What about your job?'

'I'll commute. I'll buy a gray flannel suit.'

But Charlie was too young to get the reference. 'Right,' he said uncertainly.

'I can't believe I let them talk me into this,' she said.

'Aunt Miranda could talk anyone into anything.'

*　　　*　　　*

The packing was what delayed them, though at first Betty was willing to leave with nothing but a toothbrush. After all, what was keeping her? What was left?

'Your life?' Annie ventured.

'My life is over.'

'That's very dramatic, Mother.'

'Just some saltines for the trip,' Betty said. 'And a cardigan.'

But one sweater led to another, which led to matching skirts and trousers, jackets, shoes, and handbags. 'And of course I'll need these,' Betty said, gathering photos and several large paintings. 'And something to sit on. And sleep on. And cook in. And plates and the teapot . . . And I'm certainly not leaving the good crystal or the silver . . .'

In the weeks that followed, the three of them met at the Central Park West apartment to tag furniture and sift through linens and pots and pans.

'It's not as if I'm really moving out,' Betty could be heard murmuring. 'I'll bring it back again when all this is sorted out.'

'If I had a backyard,' she said one day, 'I could just bury it until I returned.'

'After the guns stop? In spite of what Cousin Lou thinks, you're not really a refugee, Mother.' Annie was immediately sorry she'd spoken. If her mother could read her tawdry divorce as a heroic wartime thriller, who was she to deprive her of that pleasure? At the same time, though, Annie was exhausted by the giddy self-pity of both her mother and her sister. They seemed to consider this miserable move to be a grand and tragic adventure. Annie envied them, at some level—how could anyone find such heady satisfaction in defeat? But at another level, she had no patience for an attitude that she knew would mean all the decidedly unexciting details, like organizing the mover and ordering packing materials and figuring out how to pay for the unexciting details like the mover and the packing materials, would fall, inevitably, like dead leaves in autumn, to her.

'It's a metaphor,' Betty was saying. 'You've heard of those, Miss Librarian.'

Miranda, who had jammed a straw hat from deep in the closet on top of her head and wrapped herself in a lace tablecloth mantilla, placed herself between the two of them. 'Don't fight. The gypsy family has to stick together.'

'The Joad family is more like it,' said Annie.

And she could envision them clearly, their mattresses lashed to the roof of the jalopy, making their trek along the dusty roads to labour in the

fields of Westport, Connecticut. But she was
mollified now, smiling at the thought, for 'jalopy'
was a word she had always loved.

*   *   *

But even as they packed for their neo-Depression
life together, money was in shorter and shorter
supply for the three Weissmanns. Joseph and Betty
had long ago become accustomed to the bountiful
solidity of the upper reaches of the upper middle
class. They were, by the standards of any but the
rich, rich, and money was a comfort for them,
rather than a concern. Betty's shock, now, was real
and showed itself primarily in a tendency to
undertip.

Things no longer cost what they had when she
was young, which was the last time she had taken
much notice. She had never paid for anything
when living with Joseph. Though not extravagant,
considering her age and her class and her
economic reality, she had been careless: literally
without care. And because she wanted only what
was reasonable for someone in her position, there
had always been enough to buy what she wanted.
Now there was no reason. Or rhyme. Or money.

'You take care of it, dear,' she said to Annie.

*   *   *

For many years, for her entire professional life,
Miranda had delegated the payment of her bills to
her business manager. But now, with the coming of
the scandals and their aftermath, the business
manager had noticed that there was no money to

45

pay him to pay her bills. He had gently informed Miranda of this fact and gone on his way to pay the bills of more solvent clients. Unfortunately, the bills did not leave with him. Miranda gave up her office, but even then the bills did not stop appearing, following her to her home. Finally, Miranda brought this dogged, insistent pile of bills, this reminder of her failure, these dunning, demeaning messages from a life she had lost, to her mother's apartment on Central Park West. She exiled the depressing long white envelopes, unopened, to Betty's little antique desk in the living room, and there they sat, until Annie could stand it no longer and went through them herself.

It was Annie, then, who worried about money. But Annie was far better at worrying in general, and worrying about money was one of her specialities. She did not resent her mother and sister for dumping their financial load on her back. In fact, she felt better when she was organizing them than when she was taking care of her own insistently precarious business, for her finances, always a juggling act, the nonprofit world seeming to take its mandate seriously and to apply it rigorously to its employees, were now more than ever the stuff of nightmares. And nightmares are what Annie had, some while she was asleep, some while she sat at her desk at the library, some on the subway. The worry would rise, like a damp rotten smell, and she would try to quicken her step, to hurry past it. She would talk herself back to the letter she was answering regarding the library's acquisition of a collection of correspondence, or she would amuse herself with a quote from the man she had chosen as her new role model,

Mr Micawber, and the odor of insolvency would temporarily recede. But later, invariably, the ugly stench would creep back into her consciousness: Nick still in college, Charlie in medical school, all those loans—she tried to help them as much as she could—the maintenance on the apartment up 10 percent, her Con Ed bill through the roof, her phone bills—how could there be so many phone bills for one person—and then the cable bill and the Internet, and every time she went out to dinner, could it really cost fifty dollars for pasta and a glass of wine, and as for retirement, did people really save? How? She had always assumed she would inherit a little something that would help her along in her old age, but no more. Old age was now, too, caught up in the stink of financial worry. She was a successful woman in her early fifties and cutting corners the way she had as a graduate student. She had mortgaged her apartment up to its nostrils and had been living off that money and the home-equity line of credit she was able to get. She had always assumed she could sell her apartment as a last resort. That would be difficult in this market, but even if she did manage to sell it, what then? Where would she go? A person had to live someplace. The way her friends filled out Sudoku grids, in an obsessive attempt to make the numbers come out right and thereby exercise and protect their already failing memories, Annie drew her own grids, adding up mortgage and loan payments and maintenance checks, comparing the total to what she would have to pay in rent, trying to take into account the tax deductions she received because of her mortgage. This was how she put herself to sleep at night, too, or how she kept herself awake, adding, subtracting, sighing, twisting, grimacing in the dark.

Then one evening, when she was packing up her own apartment, boxing all her personal items so that the people coming to sublet it could not snoop through her papers, though why they would want to or what of interest they would find there she really couldn't imagine, Annie found a letter from her grandmother, Betty's mother, who had died ten years earlier.

Darling Annie, it said. *Here is a birthday check to celebrate this wonderful day when you turn eleven years old! Use it wisely. Grandpa worked hard so that I would have a cushion to lie back upon. Always remember, dear Annie, these wise words that your grandmother told you: When you have enough money, you can thumb your nose at the world!*

It was signed *Your Loving Grandma*.

CHAPTER FOUR

They made their exodus from New York to Westport on a beautiful August day.

'It will be just like the commune,' said Miranda, who, though her youth had caused her to miss out on the fun of the Sixties by a scant couple of years, harbored a rich nostalgia for the period.

'Right. The one in the French Revolution.' Had she really agreed to this? Although, when Annie allowed herself to do so, she did have to admit that with both boys gone, she was as lonely as she had ever been in her life.

48

The three Little Bo Peeps who have lost their sheeps, she thought. Betty minus Josie, Miranda minus the Awful Authors, Annie minus her children. Three minus everything equalled three zeroes. Three zeroes equalled pathos; emptiness; fear. *Zero at the bone,* she thought. The Emily Dickinson poem made her feel better for a moment. *A transport of cordiality.* Emily Dickinson made even fear feel rich and full and active.

From the backseat, she looked at her mother's profile as Betty drove her old Mercedes along the Merritt Parkway, exclaiming at the beauty of every stone bridge, remembering when this quaint, narrow, twisting road was new and modern, and Annie felt a wave of respect. Her mother was her own poet. Betty didn't need Emily Dickinson to tell her that seeing a snake dividing the grass like a comb was a shiver of mortality and that mortality was a sign of life. Betty could take pleasure in anything, even this exile. She could make her devastating divorce into a picnic, that word that had made her cry. That is what Josie had always said about Betty's excursions into unlikely optimism. 'It's not a picnic,' he would say, his voice full of exasperated love, and he and Betty would look at each other and smile. Annie leaned forward, the seat belt tight across her chest, and kissed her mother's cheek.

Betty made a loud kissing noise in response, but kept her eyes on the road. She and her parents had visited Westport frequently in her youth—whenever Aunt Millie checked herself in to the Westport Sanitarium, a large white mansion on the Post Road that then housed wealthy alcoholics and manic-depressives, both of which diagnoses described Aunt Millie. The sanitarium had been torn down years ago and turned into a park.

'Just terrible,' Betty murmured, shaking her head at the unfortunate transformation as they drove past the vanished sanitarium, now rolling acres of parkland.

Annie raised her eyebrows and made a face, hoping to catch Miranda's eye in the rearview mirror. But Miranda was gazing out the window at what was now called Winslow Park and sighing in sympathetic, wistful appreciation of the lost mental institution. Miranda always sat in the front. She had gotten carsick in the back, ever since she was a child. As a teenager, Annie had wondered once when they were out driving with their parents if Miranda might not have grown out of it.

'I mean, how can we ever tell, if she never sits in the backseat again?' she asked her mother, who had been banished to the backseat beside her.

'That's the beauty of irony, dear,' Betty had said, and Annie never brought it up again.

Now she momentarily panicked at the idea of the months ahead with her sister and mother, then firmly reminded herself that she had finally agreed to the Houghteling Cottage scheme only because she saw that if she did not, the two of them would go ahead without her and live in what they considered genteel poverty until there was not a cent left in either of their bank accounts, at which point they would have to move in with her.

She reminded herself that she still had an apartment, that she had sublet it, furnished, for only ten months. Surely within that time the evacuation to the suburbs would lose its charm for Betty and Miranda.

Betty turned onto a tree-shaded road that eventually led them to the shore. Long Island Sound lay before them in its comfortable modesty, a small, calm stretch of blue. The sky was clear and Long Island, a dark wavy line, was visible on the horizon.

Miranda said, 'It's hardly Cape Cod.'

'We don't have any cousins in Cape Cod.' Her sister had been out to Westport countless times. Did she expect crashing waves and towering dunes?

Still, Annie said in a coaxing voice, 'Fitzgerald lived here. He and Zelda were kicked out of *two* houses in Westport, I think.'

Miranda seemed mollified. 'Two houses,' she whispered, looking at the Sound with new respect.

'Zelda swam at Compo Beach,' Annie added encouragingly, realizing as she spoke that she could quit the Y in New York and save a little money, swim here herself. 'No waves, perfect length, up and down, and you've done your laps . . .'

'Oh, Annie. You and your laps.'

The cottage, on the other hand, was another story. Annie's heart sank when they pulled into the narrow dirt driveway beside the house itself. It was an unpromising sight, a slightly lopsided structure built in 1929, its shingles painted a dull, tired gray. A sunporch ran the length of the front of the cottage, its louvred windows quaint and outdated and yellowed. An overgrown hedge rose on one side of a dirt path leading to the louvred front door. With one corner wedged in the dirt, the rickety gate stood open, as listless as an idling bystander, unconcerned with, unaware of, the ramshackle house. The hard dusty path sidled shamelessly into the patchy crabgrass.

The cottage.

It was a shack, a hut, a garden shed of a thing, stunted and unwashed.

'Oh,' Annie said in dismay.

But her sister and mother were already out of the car and exclaiming with joy. It was so unspoiled! It was so old-fashioned, so perfectly old-fashioned! Think of all the barefooted children who had scampered up and down this path! The commuters in their fedoras, tired and grimy from the train! The two women were beside themselves.

'It's like camp!' Miranda cried.

'Girl Scout camp!' Betty cried in response.

Of course, Annie knew well enough that Betty would have tired of real Girl Scout camp the minute she wanted a hot bath and there was only a cold shower to be had, that Miranda would exclaim over the unspoiled nature of the cottage until the first hot night without air-conditioning. But Annie said nothing. She knew better than to confront her mother and sister when they were waxing poetic together. It would be like stepping into a dog fight. One had to wait, patient and quiet, until they wore themselves out.

Annie sometimes reflected that all those poor publishers who thought Miranda was bluffing or bullying had never understood Miranda's secret, which was supreme innocence. She was a good-looking woman: her face animated; her eyes, tapering at both ends, womanly and remote; and she had a slow, curling half-smile that people around her experienced as a moment of recognition, as if they'd been lavishly but secretly

52

praised. When all was said and done, however, Miranda's greatest strength was a sublime ignorance that things could go other than she, in her benevolent excitement, had imagined them. She didn't worry about what the world thought of her or her tantrums, for the world existed only as imagined by her, and Miranda believed in her imagination the way others believed in God or capitalism: it was a force, and it was a force for good.

Annie, who was acutely aware of how the world viewed her, or at least of how she worried that the world viewed her, often watched her younger sister with wonder. Miranda was so unselfconscious that the older sister was deprived of even the bitter satisfaction of envy. In fact, Annie had always been proud of both her sister's beauty and her guileless, autocratic power.

On the other hand, Annie could not help but notice that her sister was extremely self-involved, and over the years, watching Miranda go through one disastrous love affair after another, she began to suspect that Miranda's preoccupation with herself was a kind of protection. Everywhere Miranda looked, she saw the world she insisted upon. This was her great tautological strength. It had fascinated and frustrated Annie since childhood. How could you ever win an argument with such a sister? How?

She asked herself this question again as they stood outside the cottage. The house hunched over the yard, shabby, uncomfortable, ill-tempered. Its closed windows, dead flies pressed like flowers beneath the heavy wood sills, were bleary, unseeing behind cataracts of grime. Large, smooth plots of pale dirt basked in the sun interrupted here and there by a few straggling, scratchy formations of crabgrass. There were two trees, one an evergreen brown and diseased at the top, the other a gnarled, barren fruit tree. The steps, two cracked concrete squares of faded gray, led up to the sunporch, several missing louvres of its jalousie windows gaping darkly.

*　　　*　　　*

Miranda, for her part, saw a tangle of dark green foliage and pale pink sea roses peeking from the side of the house. The roses were so small and jumbled, their flowers one petal deep, the yellow heart so exposed. Above them, a squirrel rattled a branch. Miranda looked up and watched the squirrel, a fat gray being balanced on delicate little toes. The white clouds of late summer flew by overhead, the sky as deep a blue as a daytime sky could be. She could smell the briny sea. On the chafed lawn, there was a patch of rich green moss in the shade from the house. Miranda took off her shoes and stood on the soft, cool moss. She touched the trunk of the old tree beside her, her fingers stroking the ridges of iron gray bark.

'We will be happy here,' Betty said.

Miranda smiled at her mother. 'We already are.'

Miranda and Betty were still exclaiming at the potential of the peeling hut, Annie's heart was still sinking in silent dismay, when there was a sudden commotion at the front door, which flung itself open to reveal a bald, pink-faced man dressed in bright golf clothes and holding a broom.

Cousin Lou handed the broom to Annie,

apologized about the missing windowpanes, promised workmen and replacements. He then invited them to dinner that night. 'Don't disappoint me.' He shook his head, his pink jowls shuddering with alarm. 'Don't.'

He pointed to the mailbox.

'I ordered it just for you, but look how the idiots painted your name!'

The mailbox was a fat, new, shiny affair, and on both sides, in bold black letters, it said: THE WISEMEN.

*   *   *

They did not go to dinner that night, despite the imploring swing of Cousin Lou's jowls. They waited for the moving van, then began to unpack the boxes. Annie and Miranda had the two bedrooms on the ground floor, their mother the large attic room upstairs.

'My childhood furniture,' Annie said, sitting on the mahogany sleigh bed Betty had gotten her at an auction when she was twelve. 'It's much nicer than my own furniture.' Still, over the years, Annie had acquired one or two pieces she was fond of. Would the visiting French professor and his wife leave cigarette burns on the arms of her chairs? Already, she could not wait to get back to her apartment.

Miranda, in contrast, was quite giddy. 'I feel like we're in a dollhouse,' she said. 'And we're the dolls.'

Annie shuddered.

'It's an adventure,' Miranda said.

'An adventure in claustrophobia.'

55

'You'll see.'

Miranda often said *You'll see.* Annie found it oddly comforting, as if Miranda knew what was coming, knew that everything would be all right, knew how to make it be all right.

'Do you think Mom seems a little shell-shocked?' Annie asked.

'We're our own dolls,' Miranda said, as if she had not heard Annie. 'In our own dollhouse.'

* * *

Upstairs, Betty was staring out the attic window. She could hear Miranda and Annie talking downstairs. The sound was soft and indistinct, but familiar, like a memory. So much seemed like a memory these days. This blue sky with its banks of white clouds was a memory. And this town: leaning against an old black Buick at the station, waiting for Joseph's train, the girls chattering just as they were doing now, that same sky arched high above them; the train chugging into sight, giving its great slow sigh as it braked. Then, out of its door stepped another memory: her husband. Her husband, Joseph.

'Can you see the water?' Annie asked, clumping up the stairs.

'It's beautiful.'

'Oh, look, a sailboat.'

'This is my widow's walk,' Betty said.

It would be worth everything, Annie thought, if her mother could be happy here. Betty's hair, a very pretty auburn created at great expense by an Italian colorist at Frederic Fekkai, was surrounded by a nimbus of light. Annie put her

56

arms around her and rested her cheek on the auburn head. Outside, in the distance, gulls wheeled in the blue sky. 'Don't be sad,' she said.

'Oh no.' Betty patted her daughter's hand to reassure her. 'I'm a merry widow.'

* * *

This, to Annie and Miranda's surprise, turned out to be all too true. In the days to come, not only was Betty merry, but she insisted that she was, literally, a widow.

'Poor, dear Joseph,' she said when they finally accepted Cousin Lou's invitation to dinner. 'God rest his soul.'

Lou raised an eyebrow and looked at Annie. Annie shrugged. 'Mom's a widow,' she said. 'Didn't you know?'

'Don't be fresh,' Betty said, and swept into the living room in her black linen pants and tunic.

Cousin Lou was not one to argue with anyone who was kind enough to accept his hospitality. He took Annie and Miranda, each on one arm, and escorted them into the big living room that overlooked the water. They were on a hill, and their view of the Sound was unimpeded except by the many figures who stood in front of the glass walls. There was an artist and a pianist, a Holocaust scholar, a psychiatrist, a young Internet mogul, several Wall Street people, two surgeons, an architect, and a lawyer—all of them with spouses, all of their spouses with their own careers. Lou introduced all his guests simply by their first names, as if they were family pets, even patting their heads now and then. It was only after he

57

steered Annie and Miranda over to a woman dressed in white and perched on the arm of the sofa who, he reminded them, was his wife, that they learned in great detail the last names and occupations of the guests they had just been introduced to. Annie had half expected Lou to note that his wife was 'like family', but instead, he hurried off and left Rosalyn to nod her rather large head in the direction of each specimen they'd just met and relate in a loud, rasping whisper what that person did professionally.

'They seem very distinguished,' Annie said, sensing that was what Rosalyn required.

'I am drawn to exceptional people,' Rosalyn said. 'It is my vice.' Then she smiled at the absurdity of someone like herself having something as tasteless as a vice.

'They're like family,' Miranda offered.

Rosalyn raised an eyebrow at her. 'One cannot choose one's family,' she said. 'Can one?'

'No,' Annie said drily, noting simultaneously though silently that even when one, that is to say Rosalyn, stood, one was no taller than one had been when seated on the arm of the sofa. Annie smiled at Cousin Rosalyn. 'Families are fate.'

Rosalyn's prominent head balanced rather precariously on what came below, like a blowsy rose on a stem plucked bare of its leaves. The circumference of her head was emphasized by her hair, which was thin but of an intensely hued blond arranged in a helmet of great volume. Annie watched it revolve, slowly, like a golden globe, towards her mother, who now approached them in her beautifully tailored linen.

'Widow's weeds,' Betty explained with a sad

smile when Rosalyn admired her outfit.

CHAPTER FIVE

Frederick Barrow was what Miranda could only call a pleasant-looking man—not, therefore, her type. He had a puckish, friendly face and his hair was thinning, not a distinguished receding hairline like Josie's, just thin, combed back and a bit too artistically long. Miranda was sorry on that score and disappointed for Annie. But, as she loyally pointed out to her mother, what hair he had was silver. And he had kind eyes. They called to mind an old dog's eyes, so dark and earnest, but that she did not say out loud. She reminded herself, instead, that she loved dogs and had often thought of adopting one from a shelter. A shepherd mix. Or a misunderstood pit bull. Immediately after this thought, she felt a rush of warmth for Frederick Barrow, as if he had himself rescued a large abandoned dog that very moment or, an even more compelling alternative, was wagging his tail against the wire confines of his cage, whimpering, his head appealingly tilted to one side, as he waited for Miranda to liberate him from his cramped prison.

In fact, at that moment Frederick Barrow was standing at a podium in front of them reading in a singsong voice that made Miranda sleepy.

'He has kind eyes,' she whispered to her mother.

Thinking really they were mischievous eyes, Betty whispered back, 'A triumph for Annie.'

Miranda wondered if she meant the turnout at the reading—which was enormous—or Annie's friendship with Barrow.

'A feather in her cap,' she whispered, to cover her bases.

A serious, twiggy young man in a hand-knit muffler turned from the seat in front and glared at them, and Miranda was quiet. A wool scarf in the August heat spelled lunatic. Lunatics must not be disturbed.

Readings. If there was an upside to the recent implosion of her career, it was her release from the obligation of attending readings. Yet here she was, back in the saddle, daydreaming, pretending to listen, leaning her head to one side, then the other, to stretch her stiff, aching neck. But this reading was different. It was not for one of the Awful Authors. It was for Annie.

She watched Frederick turn a page. He was dressed in khaki pants and a stiffly ironed blue Oxford shirt with a frayed collar. He wore faded blue boat sneakers. His voice rocked back and forth, a cradle of words, in the treetops, rocking, rocking. She tuned in for a minute to what the cradle contained. Something bleak. Something violent. A nightmarish creature, a Rosemary's baby of snarling prose, rocked softly in the writer's gentle voice. She let the meaning of the words drift past her, soothed by the sound of them, by the writer's sympathetic voice, by his kind eyes.

'Such bright, kind eyes,' she said to Annie when the reading was over.

Annie smiled. She looked at Frederick, seated at a long table signing books. 'He was wonderful.'

She had been wary of meeting him at first. His work, highly regarded by many, was off-putting for Annie, embodying the qualities she disliked in

60

both the Jewish writers of his generation (that showing off masked as neurosis) and the Wasps (the coldness masked as modesty). But Frederick had surprised her, for he was not at all like his novels. He seemed in fact that rarest and to Annie most welcome combination of qualities: both truly modest and truly neurotic.

'We look forward to seeing more of Frederick Barrow,' Betty said.

'Maybe when his next book comes out,' Annie said. 'I'm trying to get Alice Munro for our next reading.'

'Oh, Annie, don't be silly.'

'I know. She probably won't come.'

'Oh, Annie,' Betty repeated, shaking her head. 'You're impossible.'

'Don't be coy,' Miranda added. 'I hate coyness in an adult woman.'

'Do you like it in a young woman?' Annie said, as she was mercifully called away to speak to the volunteers who were folding chairs.

She glanced at Frederick and saw he was surrounded by young women and middle-aged men. An interesting demographic. Where did she fit in?

When the crowd had dispersed, Frederick stayed at the table, sitting on top of it now rather than behind it, talking to two young people, an ascetic-faced woman with incongruously large baby blue eyes, in her early thirties, Annie guessed, and a young man perhaps a year or two younger dressed in expensive casual clothes. Everything he wore looked soft, burnished, delectable: his light cotton sweater—or was it silk—his narrow pants. Annie wanted to touch them, every article of clothing. Even his buttery Ferragamo loafers. Like the lunatic in the audience, he was wearing a scarf, but it was of sheer white cotton lawn.

I do not fit in, that's where, Annie thought in answer to her own question.

Frederick saw her and waved her over.

'This is Gwen . . . and this is Evan,' he said, smiling at the two young people. 'My children.'

Annie tried not to survey them with too obvious curiosity. But she had heard so much about this son and daughter. Gwen had some sort of consulting business she ran from home, Annie remembered. Her husband was a lawyer or a doctor or a banker, she couldn't remember which, only that he 'made a living', as her grandmother used to say. They had two small children, twin girls, who took violin lessons with tiny violins and played soccer in tiny uniforms. Evan had just left one job in public relations for another—Frederick had received that news during one of his dinners with Annie. 'As long as he's not on my payroll,' he'd said when he got off the phone, and Annie, who revered her children and would never have spoken sarcastically about them to anyone but herself, had been a little shocked at his disloyalty, then had quickly chastised herself as a humourless Jewish mother. Frederick had mentioned that Evan's girlfriend, with whom he had just broken up, was a model, something Evan himself immediately inserted into the conversation now, as if both she and the breakup were one of his professional credentials. He looked rather like a model himself, a tall handsome young man, and Annie thought she caught him making a model face in the window's nighttime reflection, pursing his lips, glaring, pulling in his chin just a fraction.

'So you're the famous Annie,' Gwen said with a distinct lack of warmth.

'Dad talks so much about you,' Evan said, and Annie got the impression that, like his sister, he would have preferred that 'Dad' find a new topic of conversation.

'Annie, I was hoping I could take you out to a celebratory dinner tonight,' Frederick said.

'Don't you think you should be getting back, Dad?' Evan said. 'I don't like the idea of you driving so far at night.'

Frederick laughed. 'You guys,' he said.

'It's a six-hour drive,' his daughter said sharply. 'Six and a half.'

'Isn't it lucky I don't have a curfew?'

Even as he said it, Annie could see that although Frederick may not have had a curfew, it would be enforced. She and Frederick were not going out to dinner that night. Children were tyrants.

Felicity had come to the reading to hear her brother, and as Felicity approached the table, her turquoise eyes wide as always, Annie noticed how much Gwen resembled her. Perhaps those eyes remained wide as she slept. Or rolled open like a doll's.

'You mustn't monopolize the star,' she said to Annie.

'No, of course not.'

'I mean, I am his *sister.*' And she gave Annie a meaningful look, the meaning of which Annie could not make out.

Annie pointed to her own sister, as if that would somehow justify her standing by the table. 'There's my sister,' she said, and she waved Miranda over,

63

signaling desperation by the childhood code of tapping her left eyebrow with her right pinky, a gesture distinctive enough for a trained sister to recognize but not quite awkward enough to arouse suspicion.

'Your father has a beautiful reading voice, don't you think?' Miranda said when she was introduced to Gwen and Evan. 'I think this book is extremely powerful. The prose is so vigorous . . .'

The pro forma remarks, into which Miranda was politely inserting as much sincerity as she could muster, would have gone on, but Annie interrupted her with a blunt 'My sister's an agent.'

'Oh yes,' Gwen said. 'We know.' She gave Miranda a cold smile.

'Infamy becomes me,' Miranda said.

'Everything becomes you, beautiful Miranda,' Frederick offered, rather gallantly, Annie thought. '"In thy face I see the map of honor, truth, and loyalty,"' he added in the exaggerated way people do when they are quoting.

'Lovely family, too,' Felicity said, with her pie eyes looking almost challenging. 'But then why shouldn't they be?'

'Where are you off to that's so many hours away?' Annie asked Frederick. She did not even bother to add 'after dinner'. Somehow that was settled—there would be no dinner. No discussion, no dinner, just settled.

'The Cape.'

'Why you want to live there I do not understand,' said Gwen. 'The summer, yes. But winter?'

'Your father is sentimental,' Felicity said. 'Not that it has done him any harm. In the way of real

64

estate appreciation.'

'Oh, I love Cape Cod in the winter,' said Miranda. 'To stand high up on one of those dunes, your bare feet numb in the cold sand, the wind blowing, the crash of the waves . . . It's incredibly romantic.'

'I hope you won't be too disappointed if I tell you that what I like about going up there, especially in the winter, is the quiet. It's so'—he thought for a moment—'so unencumbered.'

Annie turned that unexpected word over in her mind. *Unencumbered.*

'Well, that's not romantic at all,' Miranda said, and her voice was equal parts shocked and authoritative, as if Frederick had suddenly lifted his shirt and showed her a bad case of ringworm, for which she just happened to have the right tube of cream in her purse. 'We'll have to do something about that.'

Unencumbered. Why did that sound so ominous to Annie, so bleak?

'Frederick is done with romance,' Felicity said.

'You think I'm too old?' Frederick asked.

'Oh no, age has nothing to do with it. It's temperament, Frederick. And will.' And she smiled a private smile, her lips pulled together in a cupid bow.

Miranda was saying that she had once gone paragliding on the beach in Wellfleet and suggested Frederick might treat his lack of romance by viewing the dunes from so many feet up; then she drifted off to a cluster of people she seemed to know.

'Why don't you just stay tonight?' Gwen said to Frederick. 'With one of *us*,' she added, glancing at

Annie.

'I'm just a homebody, Gwennie. And I've got some kid house sitter I don't altogether trust this week—I have to get back.'

'In that case, you better leave now,' Gwen said. She gave Annie a challenging look. 'Don't you think?'

Frederick also looked at Annie. 'Maybe you'll come up sometime and see the place.'

Evan said, 'You could get three brownstones in Red Hook for that joint.'

'Hardly that,' Frederick said. 'And you'll just have to buy your own brownstones in Red Hook or wait until I'm dead, because I have no intention of selling the house.'

Evan shrugged. 'I was just making an observation.'

'Dad,' Gwen said. She looked at her watch.

And, suddenly, Annie was alone.

She piled up the six or seven unsold books and thought wistfully of her own children. When would her boys start ordering her around, instead of the other way around?

She saw Frederick trotting back through the door towards her. He took both her hands, then kissed her on the cheek. Their noses bumped as he unexpectedly kissed her a second time on her other cheek.

'I had to thank you,' he said. 'I couldn't leave without thanking you.'

'No, no, thank you for bringing in such a crowd.'

'And don't worry about my driving back tonight,' he added as he walked off. 'I could do that drive in my sleep.'

'That's not too reassuring,' she said. 'The sleep

part.'

'I'll call you,' Frederick said, and he was gone.

*   *   *

Betty watched her daughter from the other side of the room. How serious she looked. Attractive, in a severe sort of way. Betty remembered giving Annie a sweater with sequins, just a few sequins, very tasteful, very chic. The look on Annie's face—it was so pure, such pure dislike. Betty smiled. It was like the time Annie had wanted a cowboy outfit and they gave her a pink cowgirl skirt. It had offended her, even at five. If she had known the word 'garish' at that tender age, she would surely have used it. How Betty and Joseph had laughed that night in bed, embarrassed that they had so misread their daughter, amused by her sickened expression. And touched, too, for just as she had quickly hidden her dislike of the sequins years later, she had even as a tiny child tried to cover her disappointment as quickly as possible. Annie had such a good heart. It must be a burden to be so critical and so considerate at the same time, Betty thought. She was glad Annie seemed so taken with this Frederick Barrow person. He had a twinkle in his eye. Annie could use a twinkle. Poor Annie. She had always been such a grown-up little girl. It had been touching when she was a child, that worried little face watching her heedless, happy sister roar and sob and spin in circles, and it was touching still. Betty watched Miranda now, striding across the room to wrap her arms around Annie. Annie's expression softened. How lucky I am, thought Betty. She felt the damn tears gathering.

67

I'm so lucky, she repeated to herself. But the tears never listened to her these days. Had they ever? It was hard to remember what she had been like before she was like this.

CHAPTER SIX

Miranda lay in her childhood bed and listened to the jingle of cicadas. There must be so many of them to make such a clatter. Cicadas, if she remembered correctly, were the ones that hatched, then rattled, then mated and dropped dead. Miranda felt a stab of sympathy for the noisy insects. It was a pattern she was intimately familiar with. Love arrived; one was lucky enough to feel its warmth; then the season passed, and one shivered in the cold. Still, she had no regrets in that arena, at least. Seasons always returned, and so did love. Love was unchanging, even if the man she shared it with was not, even if she produced no cicada offspring. Love was eternal, even if lovers were not.

She considered how her mother must feel after believing her marriage was eternal, only to find out it, too, had a season, albeit an extraordinarily long one. Was it the same way Miranda felt after each of her own fiery breakups, a desire to move on, to revive the delicious rattle of courtship as soon as possible?

She crept up to her mother's bedroom and stood in the doorway at the top of the stairs. Moonlight came softly through the open window. How pale Betty looked in the blue light. She breathed evenly, a gentle sound just shy of snoring. Miranda realized that her mother was old, an old lady, her skin loose on her fragile bones. And then suddenly, piercingly, Miranda knew that her mother did not feel the way Miranda felt after a breakup, that she did not feel a desire to move on, to rattle and mate and bask in a new season of love. She knew that her mother felt like what she was: an old lady alone in a bed.

Within a few weeks, the little cottage underwent a remarkable transformation. Betty's pale-blue-and-cream-colored silk Persian rug lay across the top of the worn old linoleum of indeterminate color. The creamy silk chenille Queen Anne chairs from the living room and leather sofa from Joseph's library had been arranged in cozy proximity in the small space. Even the curtains from the apartment had been adapted to the little room, which now resembled a Connecticut cottage living room in a 1930s movie.

There were other resemblances to the 1930s that were less welcome. The stove dated from that time. The furnace could not have been much more recent. The dishwasher was from the sixties, but its only function now was to hold up the small kitchen counter. Cousin Lou had offered to update all these appliances, but here Betty had drawn the line on his beneficence.

'It's all so quaint,' she had said. 'And as soon as Joseph, may he rest in peace, sorts out all the legalities, I will be back in my apartment and you can tear this sweet little cottage down . . .'

Cousin Lou winced at the words 'tear' and 'down' in the same sentence.

'Beautify,' Betty corrected herself. 'You will be

able to beautify. No sense in beautifying new appliances, though, is there?'

Betty was very proud of this sacrifice on her part. She wanted to show strength, to reassure her daughters, to reassure the world at large and, perhaps most of all, to reassure herself. Staying at her cousin's cottage as a family guest was one thing. But being given a new refrigerator, like those poor women on *Queen for a Day,* was more than her self-respect could stomach.

*   *   *

On weekdays Annie went into the city, surprised by how much she enjoyed the commute. The train rattled on its suburban rails, filled with men and women, but mostly men, in dark suits. The uniformity of the sober colors, the smell of soap, the soft rustle of the newspapers in the mornings, that hour of fresh, gently rocking, clacking repose; then, ten hours later, the weary, wrinkled, communal escape from the long day of responsibility, the comfortable office dishabille of loosened ties and crumpled white shirts—Annie felt herself part of something, a cell in a great breathing bourgeois creature.

As for Betty, she read books with advice for grieving widows, one of which suggested she decorate a jar and then, with her children, write down happy memories of the deceased on slips of paper and place them inside. To facilitate the decoration of the Memory Jar, she immediately headed to Barnes & Noble to buy a book about decoupage. While there, she saw a book for golf widows and came home to declare that she must

70

take up the game immediately.

'But, Mother, a golf widow is someone whose *husband* plays a lot of golf,' Annie pointed out.

'Well, Josie plays golf,' Miranda said. 'On vacation. It's harder in the city, of course.'

'Exactly,' said Betty. 'May he rest in peace.'

Annie gave a defeated sigh, but the truth was, she enjoyed their company now as she never had before; more, certainly, than she had while growing up. As a little girl, she had not been unhappy, just cautious, adopting a quiet, personal camouflage to protect herself from her more flamboyant mother and sister. It was something she had always felt she'd shared with Josie: they were the ones who created the drab leafy background against which the other two blazed with gaudy color like tropical birds. Annie and Josie were the practical ones, too, the ones who remembered the napkins when Miranda and Betty decided on an impromptu picnic in the park, who thought to bring the umbrella when Miranda and Betty decided to walk across the Brooklyn Bridge on a cloudy day, who packed the map when Miranda and Betty had a sudden yen to see autumn leaves or spring flowers or Hyde Park or the waves crashing onto the beach at Montauk Point. Annie thought fondly of her stepfather for a moment. She almost wished he had died, she realized with shame, for then she would have been able to remember him as he had been, distant but in a quiet, patient, and reassuring way, someone she admired and looked up to and relied on. Instead, he was a living, unreliable, despicable deserter.

'I found the most wonderful jet bracelet at the

consignment store on the Post Road,' Betty was saying, holding out her wrist to her daughters.

Miranda peered at the bracelet. 'Very goth, Mom.'

'Queen Victoria wore jet when she was in mourning for Prince Albert,' Annie said. 'Which was the rest of her life.'

Betty nodded her approval.

'Of course, he was actually dead, unlike other widows' husbands I could name. She started a whole fashion.'

'Well, now everyone wears black already,' Betty said. 'So I don't see what difference I could make. Nevertheless, the bracelet was only two hundred dollars. See how much I'm economizing?'

Annie wanted to shake her mother until her pretty little head wobbled on its aged neck. *We are broke,* she wanted to cry out. *We do not have two hundred dollars to spend on baubles.* But her mother was so wounded, and she *was* trying, in her odd and spendthrift way, to be brave. Annie took a deep breath. She put out the white linen napkins bought years ago in France, if she remembered correctly. 'When the Mitfords' mother needed to economize,' she said, 'she found out how much the laundering of their napkins cost per week.'

Normally Miranda would have commented on two pedantic outbursts in such a short period of time, but she was more indulgent of the Mitford family, awed by the number of memoirs, biographies, and scandals the sisters had generated.

'She thought it was too expensive,' Annie continued, 'so they just stopped using napkins.'

'But think of the cleaning bills for their clothes,'

Betty said, clucking. 'Although they could have used paper towels, I suppose . . .'

Betty and Joseph's housekeeper, a Brazilian woman named Jocasta who had retired last year, had always gotten the napkins snowy white and ironed them into crisply folded rectangles. When they first came to the cottage, Betty had suggested sending them to the dry cleaner, or at least the fluff-and-fold laundry downtown called the Washing Well, but Annie had put her foot down.

'We have a washer and a dryer. It's about the only thing that works in this house, so we might as well use it and not waste money.'

She was, therefore, responsible for the napkins herself. They had acquired a few yellow stains, she noticed, and she certainly was not going to stand around for hours watching soap operas and ironing them the way Jocasta had. She placed the rumpled stained cloths beside her mother's good china. The napkins looked disgruntled, rebellious, like a crowd of dishevelled revolutionaries. Maybe they should use paper towels, after all.

'Wash your hands before dinner, girls,' Betty said.

Girls again. Could you re-create your childhood in a new place at an advanced age and without one of the key players? Annie wondered. For better or for worse, that's what they seemed to be doing. Oh, Josie, what were you thinking, leaving us here to play house, three place settings instead of four? 'The Odd Trio' Miranda had dubbed them, but it was clear from the outset that they were, all three, the fussy one, each pursing her lips in disapproval of the other two, each missing the man who was not there.

'I can't imagine what all the neighbors think we're doing here, three old broads in this ramshackle house,' Annie said as she watched a woman walk a big galloping black dog down the street.

'Oh, they think we're Russians,' Betty said.

'Why?'

'Because that's what I told them.'

Annie pressed her forehead against the window. Russians?

'Refugees!' Miranda said, delighted. 'Cousin Lou must like that.'

'Yes. I said we had all lost our poor husbands.'

'How?' Annie asked.

'KGB, dear. How else?'

*   *   *

Those first few weeks of the Weissmanns' sojourn in Westport had about them both a reassuring and a festive air. The weather was holiday weather— unusually cool for late August, the blue of the sky clear and deep, a few bright clouds rolling by. There were ferocious showers in the afternoons now and then, as if they were in the tropics. Then the rain would pass, leaving the air fresher than ever, the light golden, clean, and rich. In addition, Betty was a wonderful cook in a traditional way that Annie and Miranda both associated with holidays, and it was Betty who did most of the cooking on the old stove. None of them was sure how this had happened—it had never been discussed or formalized in any way. But somehow, Betty was cooking for her children as she had done so many years before. The only exceptions came when the three women were commandeered for dinner at Cousin Lou's. Betty said it was cruel to deny him their company, particularly when he was being so kind about the cottage. She did not say that she was seventy-five years old and sometimes cooking dinner was tiring. Nor did anyone ask.

At one of these Cousin Lou dinners, Miranda was seated next to a tall, serious man, as stately as a house in his dark, smooth suit. He might have been nice-looking if he hadn't seemed quite so formal and hadn't been wearing a bow tie. But he was formal, he was wearing a bow tie, and after releasing the information that he was a semiretired lawyer, he said very little else. Miranda, who liked to listen and was so good at it, tended to interpret reticence as a personal insult. However, she was always willing to give people a second chance.

'What do you do now that you're retired?' she forced herself to ask. 'Or, I should say, semiretired?'

'Fish.'

'Really? Fish has become so stressful.'

He gave her a perturbed look. Has they? he wanted to ask.

'Ordering it, I mean.'

'Ah. It.'

'Aren't you worried about global warming and overfishing and mercury?'

'Oh, I never catch any.'

After this, the conversation refused to take even one more ungainly step, and Miranda, defeated, turned to the person on her other side, her cousin Rosalyn.

'You must be very bored in our quiet little town,' Rosalyn said. She had seen Miranda trudging back from heaven could only guess where with an armful of weeds, a great, tendriled burst of them, surely crawling with bees and ticks, which Miranda then brought up to the house and offered as a bouquet. Rosalyn, who had a horror of Lyme disease, made sure they were thrown away as soon as Miranda departed. Still, it was sweet of her, in her thoughtless, careless way. Poor Miranda. She had to fill up her time somehow after her unfortunate professional downfall. What a scandal that had turned out to be. It was all over *The New York Times,* though it was really just an insular publishing scandal, after all. Nothing for Miranda to get on her high horse about, even with that piece about it in *Vanity Fair.*

Rosalyn had thanked dear Miranda for the buggy weedy bouquets she brought, offering *les bises* with just the right show of warmth—neither too much nor too little. Just because someone was down and out did not mean they should be treated coldly. On the other hand, she could not help thinking that it was inconsiderate of Lou to place his cousin next to her when there was such an interesting woman at the other end of the table, a reporter, younger than Miranda, still in her prime, really, someone at the top of her game professionally, rather than on the way down. Well, she supposed someone had to talk to Miranda. It might as well be the poor hostess. Unpleasant things usually did fall to the hostess. 'Very bored after all the excitement of . . .' Rosalyn paused. She had been about to say 'of your past life.' But Miranda was not dead. She had not even officially retired. She was just washed up. How did one say that politely? She decided on '. . . the excitement of big city life.'

Miranda was gazing in fascination at Rosalyn's hair. Newly tinted a rusty red, it was a work of art, an edifice so delicately, elaborately wrought it took her breath away. How could she possibly be bored with such a hairdo to contemplate?

'You seem to have so much spare time,' Rosalyn was saying. 'I envy you!' she added, feeling in truth only a soft, snug pity.

'Yes, there are so many new things to see here.' Miranda tried to look Rosalyn in the eyes rather than staring at the taut curved wall of hair rising above her ear. 'Richard Serra,' she added softly. Rosalyn's marvelous hair looked like a Richard Serra sculpture. Even the color.

'No, I don't think he lives here in town. Though, of course, Westport has always been such an artistic place.'

*   *   *

When Betty last lived in Westport, there had been a butcher downtown with sawdust on his floor and a cardboard cutout of a pig in his window. There had been a five-and-dime, too. Woolworth's? No, Greenberg's, she remembered now. That was more than forty years ago, yet she felt that if she turned her head quickly enough she might still catch a glimpse of the store's wooden bins filled with buttons and rickrack, of the Buster Brown shoe store next door to it. When she looked at the bank now, she saw the Town Hall it had been. The Starbucks had been the town library, the Y the firehouse. The memories appeared like visions. They laid themselves out like a path to the past.

77

But really they were just a path that led, inevitably, to this moment: Betty Weissmann driving through a town she had long ago deserted, without the man who had deserted her. That's what Betty thought as she parked behind Main Street, facing the river. Her memories all led her here: a parking lot, lucky to get a space.

She got out of the car and locked it. In the days when she had been here with Joseph, she had never had to lock the car. sShe blamed him for this. It had become her habit to blame him for so many things. That's what you get, Joseph—unfair and extravagant blame. A small price to pay for jettisoning your wife, for chucking her out to spin helplessly in the dark, infinite sky of elderly divorce.

A spurned woman has to look her very best when the spurned woman goes into the city to meet with the man by whom she has been spurned. Not to mention the lawyers who helped him. For this reason, Betty decided to buy a silk sweater at Brooks Brothers and a pair of gold knotted earrings at Tiffany's. Her credit cards were useless, thank you, Joseph, but Annie had added Betty onto her Visa for emergencies, and if this wasn't an emergency, what was? Then Betty bought a suit— ideal for a meeting with lawyers, elegant and dignified—at a large store full of overpriced well-made fashionable clothing. She remembered it as, in decades past, a nondescript men's shop. The store had prospered, and the suit she bought there, extremely expensive, was for those who had prospered along with it. She was not supposed to buy clothes like this any more. But spurned women, like beggars, could not be choosers. No one could object to this girding of her loins, she thought, anticipating Annie's voice doing exactly that.

Betty took the train in. When the conductor punched holes in her ticket, she found the old-fashioned mechanical click comforting. The train was creaky, the window bleary. The drive into the city was just too much for her these days. Left cataract needed to be taken care of; she would have to get to that. Right now, it was important to get her hair done. She'd left herself plenty of time. Annie said she would have to stop going to Frederic Fekkai, but Annie, in spite of what Annie thought, was not always right.

*   *   *

Her lawyer met her downstairs. He was very solicitous, she noticed. A slight young man with short curly hair of a nondescript mousy brown. He looked like a mouse altogether, his features small and pointed, his little feet in their little shoes. Only his eyes were wrong. They were pale gray, not mouselike at all. How could this young, pale-eyed mouse, his hair so sad and unimportant, possibly do battle with Joseph, who in his efficient businesslike way had very little hair at all?

She sat at the edge of the dark pond that was the conference table. Across the pond sat Joseph. How impatient he must be. He disliked lawyers, he disliked formalities.

'Please sit down, Mrs Weissmann,' said Joseph's lawyer.

Yes, she thought, Mrs Weissmann. Do you hear that, Mr Weissmann?

She noticed he was wearing new cuff links. That, more than anything the lawyers said, more even than Joseph's coldness and distance, made her sad. Things were happening to Joseph and they were happening without her. Cuff links, barbells made of yellow gold, were happening to him.

'My client is a generous man,' Joseph's lawyer was saying.

'My client is a reasonable woman,' her lawyer was saying.

Joseph's eyes met hers, and in the fraction of an instant before they flicked away, she knew they shared the same amused, unhappy thought: *Both our lawyers are liars.*

CHAPTER SEVEN

The months of struggling against the ruin of her business had taken a toll on Miranda. She had phoned and cajoled and browbeaten and pleaded. She had called in every chit. But there was the stink of failure clinging to the Miranda Weissmann Literary Agency, and neither authors nor editors liked that odor much. No matter what she did or said, she could not seem to keep everything she'd worked so hard to build from washing away like sand beneath her feet.

The appearance on *Oprah* had been the final humiliation. Miranda was defeated at last, and she was exhausted. So perhaps what happened to her was inevitable, especially while she was living in the same house with her sister and mother, eating her mother's cooking, listening to her sister's indolent scolding. Or was it obligatory for someone about to turn fifty? Maybe it was a simple case of pent-up energy—she was not someone who liked to stand still, even if that meant spinning in circles. Whatever the reason, Miranda found herself embracing a new, a second, a rediscovered adolescence. Because her first adolescence, the stormy drama of which she had rather enjoyed, had been marked by a resolution to, whenever possible, examine her soul, Miranda decided in this new iteration to re-examine her soul. It was possible that this time, at least, she might get results.

Miranda determined that the best place to re-examine her soul was on the beach at dawn. It was unfortunate that Compo Beach was so small, perhaps a half mile from end to end. She found that just as she thought she might be getting somewhere, striding along on her re-examination, she would reach the jetty and have to turn back. Then she would be distracted by the sky, turning from purple darkness to its milky violet morning wash, then bursting into bright pink streaks. Each day the sky was a little different, and therefore that much more distracting. Some days she would see an unlikely flock of green parrots in the parking lot, a convocation so odd and busy and noisy that any examination, or even recognition, of the soul was rendered temporarily impossible. And then, just as she was passing the playground, her feet in the cool sand, the salty air in her lungs, gaining just a little ground on her elusive soul, Miranda's cousin's big Cadillac Escalade would pull up and Cousin Lou would roll down the window and holler hello, frantically waving a pink palm, he was just on his way out and wondering if she would like a lift anywhere.

'No,' she would say. 'Thanks so much, but I'm just taking a walk.' *As you see. As we discussed yesterday morning, when you stopped to ask me the same question.*

'Walking!' Cousin Lou would exclaim. 'Such good exercise.' And he and his big black car would purr off into the dawn.

Miranda tried to avoid Cousin Lou as much as possible. It was not that she disliked him. It was not possible to dislike Cousin Lou. He lived to be likeable. But he was not introspective, and Miranda was engaged in a course of introspection that required not only her own attempt to examine her soul but an assumption, typical of her, that, therefore, everyone must of course be examining, if not their own souls, then at least hers. Cousin Lou, however, was not interested in her soul any more than he was in his own. As he explained to Miranda, 'If Mrs H. had wanted immigrant children to examine their souls, she would have withheld the funds required for them to do so.'

After a week or so of these aborted soul-searching walks, Miranda hit on a new idea. Walking on a suburban beach was insufficiently lonely. There were far too many interruptions. She must go out to sea to be truly contemplative. As she realized this, she was watching a yellow kayak slide across the horizon. That was the answer, of course. In a kayak she could be alone, undisturbed. A sea kayak could take her all along the shore. She could explore the tidal areas at Old Mill, at Burying Hill beach, all along the Gold Coast to Southport, where one of her writers, the radio talk-show host who had been fired two months ago for referring to a female African American Cabinet member as Little Black Bimbo, had once lived.

On Craigslist, Miranda found kayaks for sale from the sailing school at Longshore, Westport's public country club, for $395.

'Is that a bargain?' Betty asked. 'I'm sure it must be.'

'On the other hand, hand-me-downs never fit well, do they? Perhaps a new one would be safer.'

'Shouldn't you rent a boat first?' Annie asked. 'Take lessons? You've never been in a kayak in your life.'

'I thought you wanted to save money! Lessons are expensive.'

'Lessons! It's not as if your sister's training for the Olympics, Annie.'

But Betty could see Annie was upset, and at the first opportunity she took her aside and placed her hand firmly on Annie's arm, as she had always done when the girls squabbled as children.

'Miranda needs to search her soul,' Betty then gently explained. 'Now, sweetheart, how is she supposed to do that without a nice new kayak?'

What Betty didn't explain was that she would have paid almost any sum of money, whether she had it or not, to get Miranda out of the cramped bungalow for at least part of the day. It was true that she was happy to spend time with Miranda. It had been a lifetime, it seemed, since she had been able to say good morning to her daughters and to say good night, too. And Miranda was good company. It was a miracle at this age to have her talented, interesting, grown-up daughter there, every day, in the house, to share a pot of coffee, a salad for lunch, a pot of tea in the afternoon. On the other hand, Betty had noticed that it was invariably she who made the coffee, the salad, and the tea. Miranda, once so capable and busy in her life in New York, still so energetic about her soulful walks, was limp and helpless around the house.

Betty would never let her daughter see her concern. Miranda needed her to be strong. But her heart went out to Miranda, and she lay awake at night wondering what would become of her pretty, vivacious, irresponsible daughter, so alone in the world, no husband, no children. And now, no authors either.

She knew Miranda was broke or, as Miranda preferred to put it, 'temporarily unable to access funds', which must be terribly frustrating considering all her success. There was an awful, endless, complicated lawsuit that had frozen all of Miranda's assets. As if they were so many lamb chops, Betty thought, imagining the assets wrapped in aluminium foil and coated with a white film of ice.

Poor Miranda had never been very good with money. Joseph had always been telling her to save more. But Miranda would just laugh and say that money was not the goal, it was the means, then set off on another eco trip, spending tens of thousands of dollars to go someplace whose claim to fame was that it had gray shower water and you had to put your toilet paper in the wastebasket . . . Oh, it was all incomprehensible. If Joseph had been alive, he would have explained it to her, but since Joseph had died so tragically, Betty was left in ignorance to watch with a broken heart as her daughter worried about money. Miranda had never worried about it before, and now that it was all gone, it seemed doubly unfair to have to worry about something she no longer had.

A kayak might be just the thing to cheer her up. At the very least, it would get her out of the house, leaving Betty a moment to search her own soul without having to jump up to make her forty-nine-year-old daughter tuna fish sandwiches 'just the way I like them, Mom!'.

*   *   *

Miranda had gotten a call from her former assistant. Out of the goodness of her heart and a residual, reflexive terror at the sound of Miranda's voice, this young woman was still handling Miranda's health insurance from her busy desk at a rival agency, filing Miranda's claims, and she had called to report on a wayward dental bill. Miranda had taken the opportunity to ask her if she could help arrange parking for the new kayak.

'They must have parking lots for these things.'

The girl—so well trained in her two years with me, Miranda thought with satisfaction—had found a place right at the beach's marina. There was a fee, but what in life did not have a fee of one kind or another?

The new kayak itself was a bright, shiny red. Miranda's life vest was orange, and the black of the clingy kayaking clothes she'd gotten contrasted nicely, giving the whole, according to an admiring Betty, the appearance of a tropical fish.

That semiretired lawyer, the friend of Cousin Lou's, was at the water's edge fishing 'with zero environmental impact', he assured her, showing his fishless basket. She had initially tried to ignore him, but as soon as he saw her struggling with the kayak, he lowered his fishing pole and helped her get the boat into the water.

She shot away from the shore, a streak of color against the slate gray water of Long Island Sound in the early dawn. The wind was cold. Bracing, she thought as she paddled into it, passing Compo Beach. How insignificant the beach looked from the water, even smaller and slighter than from the curve of sand itself. She had Googled some maps of the coast. Coming up was Sherwood Island, which was not an island at all but a state park. She had never been there. But she had driven to Burying Hill beach, the minuscule bit of sand up ahead on her left. There were wetlands there, enfolding several large architecturally uncertain houses that had somehow been allowed to spring up in the last twenty years. She headed her little craft towards the inlet that led to the pretty marsh.

This seems as good a place and time as any, she thought, better than most, to search my soul. But what will I find there? A lint-covered Altoid? Suddenly, alone, slapping among the whitecaps, she recoiled at the thought of introspection. As a girl, she had affected despair and emotional pain in an attempt at depth. Now she had no need of affectations. The despair was real, the pain was real. And depth? It no longer beckoned, that rich, worldly dimension of sophistication, of adulthood. Depth spread itself out before her instead, a hole, a pit, a place of infinite loss.

She thought sadly of her disgraced clients. She had listened to them so attentively for so long. Listening was her gift. She had listened and heard such extraordinary things. And yet she had really heard nothing but tall tales. Was that really a fault? she wondered. To hear stories when people told lies? How brave they had seemed. So much suffering. No wonder they made it all up.

Her arms were starting to hurt. Funny how she had started out so vigorously, hardly noticing the effort of each stroke, as if paddling were as natural to her as walking. Yet she had never kayaked before in her life. She had canoed as a kid at camp. It had been a clunky, achy affair, with a great deal of portage. She remembered it distinctly now as her shoulders throbbed with pain. Her hands, clasped around the little paddle, were stiff and cold, even with the special kayaking gloves she had purchased. Surely the sun would come out soon and warm her up. It was time for the sky to become pale, then to color slightly, then to pale again to a weak blue, then to deepen into the bright daylight sky. She looked ahead. She was facing east, where all this coloring and deepening and brightening ought to have been taking place. No sign of color, no sign of light. Just more clouds, darker clouds. Perhaps she should have checked the weather before heading out. But she had recited the poem Joseph once taught her on a trip to Maine: 'Red sky at night, sailor's delight. Red sky in morning, sailors take warning.' And as there was no red sky that morning, she had believed she was safe.

She concentrated on keeping the kayak steady. The galling picture of the doleful lawyer she had tried to avoid, the image of him coming to her rescue in spite of her snub, kept appearing. Annie claimed he was interesting in spite of his shyness. If Annie liked him so much, she didn't see why he couldn't have come to Annie's rescue. Miranda simply found him dull. As dull as ditchwater. Or was it dishwater? She had no idea which was duller or even why either would be considered dull to begin with. She would have to ask Annie. That was just the kind of thing Annie would know.

She tried to return to the subject of her soul, but was obstructed by an anguished inner dialogue regarding the publishers who had stopped calling her long ago in March and were always 'out' when she called them. One voice within her cried, *After all these years!* The other tried to counter with *It's August—they're all out of town.*

Miranda realized that with all her paddling she had not moved any closer to the marsh. In fact, she was skimming along the coast, past Burying Hill beach, past an enormous house, a mansion, even bigger than Cousin Lou's house, and far older. It was beautiful, stone, in the Tudor style of the nineteenth-century robber barons. It went on and on. The road that ran along the shore was named Beachside Avenue, not very inspired, but accurate. The houses there were separated from the road by great stone walls. On the water side, too, stone walls ran their length, dropping from lush sweeps of lawn down to the crusty little beach below.

Here was another house, not as old, quite hideous really, Palladian style, was that what you'd call it with those awful columns? Yes, but what a view it must have. And its bit of beach curved out in such a way that she might just be able to land there. She really would have to try. The current was being extremely uncooperative. And it had started to rain. She lifted her face to the stinging drops. It was sublime, the cold wind and rain, the physical exhaustion. If she had time, she was sure she could search her soul quite successfully now. She rested her paddle for a moment, breathing in the wild air and the wetness. The kayak swayed and slapped in the dark water between agile, aggressive whitecaps. This is magnificent, she thought, but even as the words came into her head, the sentiment was pushed aside by a realization that it would not be at all magnificent to end up dumped in the water of Long Island Sound or rushing past Rhode Island, which seemed to be her two alternatives, and she began to paddle rather frantically towards the spit of land belonging to the ugly Palladian house. It was tantalizingly close. She was almost there. She was there. But the waves were larger now. They were actually crashing against the beach, against the rocks that jutted out into the water. Not as grand as the waves on Cape Cod, of course, not even close, but quite big enough to keep her from paddling ashore.

And, as it turned out, quite big enough to capsize her. She felt the kayak rolling, felt the smack of the cold water, saw the gray of the sky swivel into the gray of the sea, felt the water lock above her, felt her legs thrashing to free themselves from the red kayak. Her body twisted, her face plunged down into darkness, her arms flailed, she kicked and scratched at the eerie silence. Her feet were caught and useless, her hands farther and farther away, clawing water, her lungs empty, bursting with emptiness.

And then, suddenly, astonishingly, Miranda felt solid human warmth. She felt strong arms reaching around her, pulling her out of the boat, out of the choking water, onto the heavy wet sand, strong arms lifting her up and holding her close.

Miranda sputtered. Miranda opened her eyes. Miranda smiled.

Her rescuer's hair was dripping wet, his long, dark eyelashes sparkling with drops of water. He was as pale as the morning sky, his high, pronounced cheekbones washed with the blush of youthful exertion. She felt his chest heaving. *Oh Lord*, she thought with fervour that bordered on delirium, *I am saved, I am saved!* She imagined herself waving her arms in the air like a congregant at a revival meeting and, amused at the thought of a God with the imagination to drop her into the embrace of an Adonis, Miranda relaxed, enthusiastically, into the young hero's arms.

*   *   *

An hour later, they pulled up into the dirt driveway beside the cottage, which looked even more decrepit than usual in the rain, dripping and homely as an abandoned cabbage. Betty heard the soggy crunch of the wheels in the drive. She went to the window, where with a flutter of expectation she saw a pretty white Mini Cooper. In the passenger seat was the radiant face of her younger daughter. On the roof, strapped by bungee cords, was the bright red kayak. Something had happened!

Betty ran to the door in time to see a handsome young man dashing through the rain towards the house beside her daughter, both of them in pants embroidered with sea creatures—blue whales on his yellow pants, pink lobsters on her ill-fitting brick red pants—and matching pastel green cotton

90

sweaters. When did Miranda buy such odd clothes? She imagined the two of them spotting each other somewhere, kindred spirits, and starting up a conversation about their shared hobby of Extreme Wasp Attire. What a handsome boy he was.

'This is Kit,' Miranda said when they had run into the house and shaken the rain off like two big colorful dogs. 'I almost drowned in that thing.' She pointed to the kayak on top of the little car. 'Kit pulled me out of the water. And took me to his aunt's boathouse. He's visiting her and staying in the boathouse. It's adorable. He was fishing, and he happened to see me go under . . .' She opened her eyes as wide as they would go, threw her arms out in one of her characteristic dramatic gestures, and said, breathlessly, 'Kit Maybank saved my life!'

'Isn't that nice,' Betty heard herself say as she realized that the silly clothes belonged to the handsome boy. It began to dawn on her, in a dull sickening rush, that not only had Something Happened but it had been something of a threatening, dangerous nature. The blood began pounding in her ears, and she could no longer hear what Miranda was prattling on about. All she could understand was that Miranda had been in danger and now Miranda was safe. She was vaguely aware of her arms around her daughter, of holding Miranda in a tight embrace, of Miranda's wet, cold cheeks beneath her lips. She understood, next, that she was hugging Kit, the handsome boy with tiny whales on his pants. She realized, after she had done it, that she had already run to the linen closet upstairs for towels, that she had put the kettle on, that she had poured brandy into an orange juice glass, slopping some on the floor, all the while listening to the pounding in her ears and feeling she was far away, as if she were invisible and weighed nothing at all. Once before she had been invisible and weightless and meaningless in this way, when the girls were very young and had disappeared at Bonwit Teller. Betty had turned around and around, as if the next time she turned they would spin back into view. It was Joseph who found them, both staring at miniature blown-glass animals—giraffes and dachshunds, a rooster and a pig within a pig, all in swirling unnatural colors— lined up in a glass case. Betty found herself now on the floor with a paper towel dabbing at the spilled brandy. She thought of Joseph and the whisky glass she had thrown at him. But Joseph at that moment did not matter. Only one thing mattered. Her daughter had been in danger, and now she was safe.

*   *   *

When she got home and heard what had happened and saw her sister, now in a nightgown, huddled on the couch under a cotton blanket, Annie was tempted to deliver a lecture. She had, after all, warned Miranda not to take the kayak out until she had taken lessons, and just last night she had pointed out that the Sound had been unusually rough lately. 'Small craft warnings,' she had said. 'And your craft is minute.' But looking at Miranda now, so fragile and vulnerable in her flowered nightgown and striped socks, Annie could not bear to say a word that might hurt her. Instead, she sat beside her on the sofa and put her arms out.

Miranda came to her and snuggled in like a little girl.

Annie said, 'It all sounds very dramatic.' She kissed Miranda on the forehead. Did it feel warm? She laid her cheek against Miranda's forehead. 'You have a fever.'

'You don't catch cold from being in the cold,' said Miranda irritably. 'They proved that.'

'You still have a fever.'

Betty began to bustle in earnest now, throwing another blanket over Miranda and attempting to spoon chicken soup into her mouth. 'I read that they did an experiment in Scotland with students. They put their feet in buckets of cold water and exposed them to germs.'

'What happened?' Annie asked.

'Well, I really can't remember. But it sounds so unpleasant. I've never liked Scotland. Here,' she said, putting a thermometer in Miranda's mouth.

'You just gave me soup.' Miranda tried to hand the thermometer back to her mother. 'My temperature will be one hundred and ten after soup.'

'All the more reason,' Betty said firmly. And she replaced the thermometer in her daughter's mouth, where it belonged.

*   *   *

When Cousin Lou came by on his customary evening walk, something prescribed by his doctor for his heart which he converted into a promenade from neighbour to neighbour to chat and invite them to his house for various meals, he discovered Betty fussing over a feverish but contented patient

93

while Annie washed the dishes.

'She was rescued by a young fisherman,' Betty said.

Annie, listening from the kitchen, just able to hear her mother over the running water, smiled to herself. Betty made the young man sound like a Scandinavian in a cable knit sweater crashing about in the Barents Sea.

'By my friend Roberts? Ah ha! I saw him out with his fishing gear this morning. I knew he had eyes for you, Miranda. And now he is your hero. Although I don't think I would call him young.'

'Eyes for me?' Miranda said. 'He was practically mute when I sat beside him at dinner, if that's who you mean.'

'Mute, but not *blind* to your charms,' Cousin Lou said.

'Well, whatever his disabilities, poor man, it wasn't him, anyway,' Betty said. 'It was a young man who spoke very nicely and didn't even need glasses, unless he wears contacts, which is possible, you never know. His name was Kit Maybank, isn't that right, Miranda? A pretty name. Ma-bank. Like a pile of dirt in spring.'

Miranda, the thermometer again in her mouth, nodded.

'Maybank.' Lou sniffed. 'Hoity-toity goity and moity.' He wore his Mrs H. expression, and Miranda steeled herself for a *chechtling* parable, but he just patted Miranda affectionately on the head and said, 'Well, well, never mind. Oh, poor unsuspecting Roberts. Forgotten so soon for young Maybank.'

'Oh, for heaven's sake, Cousin Lou,' Miranda mumbled, the thermometer wiggling absurdly.

'Roberts is old enough to be my father.'

'At least someone is,' Betty said. 'Now that Josie has dropped the ball.'

*   *   *

Miranda went to bed feverish and flushed, her hair flat against her head, her eyes swollen with fatigue. The next morning, however, she emerged from the bathroom brisk and freshly showered, looking and feeling like herself—her pre-*Oprah* self. When Kit Maybank came up the dirt path to the ramshackle cottage, he was not prepared for the radiant woman who met him on the sunporch. He remembered a gasping, pale, wet, older woman from the day before, not this vibrant being with the mocking smile and deep, avid eyes.

After pushing the screen door open, Miranda looked down from her vantage point atop the concrete steps. There was the Adonis, a hank of his dark silky hair falling across his forehead. And there beside him, his little hand clutching the larger hand, was an identical tiny Adonis, a boy of two or three, she guessed. They both smiled at her. Then the child put his hand in his mouth. Miranda watched, fascinated, as his fist twisted until it disappeared completely into the little mouth and the child blinked contentedly.

Kit had returned out of an agreeable feeling of importance and friendly condescension toward the lady he had rescued. But now, facing this surprisingly attractive woman who had darted out the door and given him a long, assured, assessing look, he was, for a moment, as mute as Roberts. Then she looked at Henry, his little boy. He saw the quizzical expression, the swipe of her hand in front of her face, as if wiping away an unexpected drizzle of rain.

'Henry,' he said. 'This is my son, Henry.'

The child, removing his hand from his mouth, said, 'Henry' in a slurred child voice.

'Henry, this is . . .' He forgot her name, then quickly, but not quite quickly enough, remembered. '. . . Miranda.'

She gave a short, sardonic laugh, from deep in her chest, peering down at them from the cracked concrete pedestal. 'How do you do, Henry?' She came down from the steps.

'Henry,' the child said again, throwing a quick glance at his father, as if confirming the fact.

'Mini-me,' Miranda said. Henry was wearing a petite version of his father's outfit: miniature khaki pants, Top-Siders that might have been made for a doll, a madras belt the size of a dog collar, and a postage-stamp-size pink Oxford shirt.

Kit handed Miranda the enormous bouquet of wildflowers he had picked from the meadow behind his aunt's house.

'You're awfully dry today,' he said.

'I try not to drown more than once a week.'

Miranda invited them in. She arranged the flowers in a vase and placed it on the sunporch. 'I love wildflowers,' she said. 'But I should be the one bringing flowers. And burnt offerings.' She put her hands on her hips and tapped her foot, staring at the little boy, who had one small arm wrapped around his father's calf. 'Cookies,' she said.

She left them, and Kit watched her go, trying to ignore her tight, quick, sexy walk. When she returned, she was carrying a plate of cookies in one

96

hand and the pants and sweater he'd lent her the day before in the other.

'This is the only tribute I have to pay at the moment,' she said.

They sat on the wicker furniture in the sunporch and watched Henry eat cookies.

'He's two,' Kit said. 'His mother . . .'

Miranda was suddenly alert. His mother was . . . institutionalized? Dead? She felt a confession coming, a story, a tale of misery transcended . . .

'His mother is in Africa doing research for two months. It wouldn't have been safe to take him. She's an epidemiologist.'

The child sat down heavily on the floor, then popped up and spun around, his arms out, his fingers splayed.

'We're divorced,' Kit added.

She saw him blush. Or was she the one who blushed?

'So I've got him all to myself for a bit, don't I, little guy?' Kit continued quickly. 'With a little help from Aunt Charlotte and her indomitable housekeeper, Hilda. Who might as well be named Mrs Danvers. Henry, what does Hilda say?'

'No, no, no,' said Henry, shaking his finger.

He then ran from one end of the room to the other and came to a sudden stop in front of where Miranda sat.

He climbed into her lap and held a soggy, ragged remnant of a cookie up to her mouth.

Miranda felt the cookie on her lips, like damp, sweet sand. An oatmeal cookie. When they were children, they called oatmeal cookies 'Josie cookies'. She could not remember why. She looked at the big pale gray eyes of the child. His mouth

97

was crusted with cookie detritus. His nails, dug into the cookie, seemed no bigger than five little kernels of corn. She nibbled at the cookie and saw his face light up and held him, suddenly, close to her breast.

'Thank you,' she said softly. 'Thank you, little Henry.'

When Kit was strapping Henry into his car seat, he was aware of Miranda behind him. He turned and saw her, those remarkable eyes aimed right at him.

'I owe you,' she said.

He shook his head, all the time watching her watch him. She took his hand. He heard himself suck in his breath, stirred, and wondered if she heard it, too. She was far too old for him, though he suddenly could not tell how old that actually was. Nor, he realized, did he care. He had fished her out of the sea. He could still feel the weight of her wet body. He quickly turned back to Henry. There was something depraved about even thinking of such things in front of one's son. And yet one did. The sky had cleared overnight, and the late-summer sunlight was deep and slanted and warm. She was wearing some kind of scent. Henry was kicking his feet against the car seat. Bing bang, bing bang.

'You have paid your debt with cookies,' he said.

'No, no. Here's what I'll do,' she said. 'I'll take you out to dinner.'

Her voice was low and straightforward. She was clearly used to people doing what she told them to do. He wanted to do what she wanted him to do.

Henry was singing now. Something from a cartoon show. Kit said, 'Henry, say goodbye to

Miranda.'

An obliging child, Henry waved his small hand. He called her Randa, and she smiled and waved back.

'Tomorrow at seven,' she said to Kit. 'Pick me up here.'

He nodded, watching her walk back toward the dreary little house.

'And,' she added, turning around and flashing her smile, 'make sure to bring your friend.'

CHAPTER EIGHT

The Weissmanns sat, all three together, in the little living room. It was the cocktail hour, a sacred ritual held over from the days of Joseph.

'Look at the size of this baby,' Betty said proudly, holding up an enormous vessel, a glass bottle of vodka the size of a Kentucky jug. 'Costco is a destitute widow's dream.'

'You spent over a thousand dollars there,' Annie said. They all glanced at a newly installed hearth in which a ventless gas fire danced merrily.

'I miss the fireplace ladies,' Miranda said.

'We *are* the fireplace ladies now,' said Betty with a brave smile she had noticed in the mirror that morning and decided to keep.

Annie got up to set the table.

'Don't forget. Set an extra place,' Miranda said. 'Two places.'

'The boys!' Betty said, as if Kit and Henry were brothers, were Annie's children. 'I bought ice cream.'

It was hard to think of Kit as anything but a boy. He seemed to be a very good father, warm and loving, gentle and firm when Henry behaved badly, appreciative the rest of the time. He had the patience of a saint—or a babysitter, Betty thought. There was something easygoing and relaxed about the young man that was extremely charming, but was a grown man with a young son supposed to be so at peace? Betty remembered when she first married Joseph. Annie had been almost as young as Henry. Joseph had not spent all his time playing with the girls. He had been at work, and when he was home, he had agonized about work. Joseph wanted to build a future for his family. That's what he told her at night when they lay in bed, arms around each other, dreaming of all the good things that would someday come their way. Well, Betty thought, here we are in the future, and what good did all of Joseph's planning and concern do them? Perhaps Kit's way was better. The child was his chum, his companion, his 'little buddy'. He always had time for him, except for those occasions when he had to go into the city for an audition. He was an actor, so he never had any work. He did always seem to have plenty of money, however, taking Miranda out to extravagant restaurants and appearing at the cottage with expensive bottles of wine. Perhaps Kit's way was better, Betty repeated to herself. Yet it was hard to accept him as an adult person. He was so intensely boyish, as if not the theater but being boyish were his profession. He seemed to have sprung from Henry's loins rather than the other way around.

* * *

Kit had taken Miranda sailing that morning. She had never sailed much before, but in the last month, Kit had taken her out almost every morning. She preferred sports that actually allowed you to move, like tennis or skiing or, in a pinch, golf. But sitting next to Kit on his Aunt Charlotte's sailboat, his unconscious youth illuminated in the rich autumn light, his skin burnt by the sun and the wind, his pale gray eyes squinting into the benign autumn sun, the sail full and bleached white against the richness of the sky, snapping in the wind, the clouds racing the sailboat across the blue expanse, sitting beside Kit, the sky so deep a blue and so alive on her skin, sitting there, so still, not moving a muscle, yet shooting through the waves, the spray cold and fine, Miranda had rediscovered the joy of speed.

This was not the same as movement, a sensation she knew so well, a sensation she needed and cultivated constantly, clapping her hands, waving her arms, striding purposefully across a room, standing, sitting, crossing and uncrossing her legs. Movement was a language Miranda could speak. But this was something entirely different. This was a rush of excitement, this was the universe's movement, not her own, this was beyond her control. For the first time in years, Miranda was passive, flying through time, hurtling toward her fate, whatever that fate might be.

Henry had been there, too, of course, on all the sails, swaddled in a fat yellow life preserver. That morning he had spent most of the time on Miranda's lap asleep. When he woke, he pointed at an aeroplane, at a seagull, at a plastic bleach bottle

101

bobbing in the water, naming them as God named the birds and beasts of the Bible: plane, bird, bottle. Children are not very discriminating, she thought, seeing his gleeful eyes, and wondered where she fitted into his interests. When he asked her to sing a song, she could think of nothing but 'Puff the Magic Dragon'. But when she got to the part about Little Jackie Paper going away, Henry began to sob.

'It *is* sort of tragic,' Miranda said apologetically to Kit, who took the gasping child and tried to comfort him. 'But who ever pays attention to the words? Except for them maybe being about pot.'

'Really? I never knew that.'

Kit replaced Henry on her lap, and the little boy wiped his face in her sweater. She patted his silky head as if he were a cat, feeling the sweet pressure of his face against her. My little pussycat, she thought, feeling oddly shy, unable to say it out loud.

Kit was still so young that his own childhood was very much alive for him. When he spoke about his family and his youth, his face lit up. Then he gave a relaxed sigh, like someone after a good meal.

Why, he was young enough to be her assistant.

The perfect assistant, an assistant who took over one's life. He poured coffee for her from a thermos. He peeled an orange and passed her bright, perfect sections. He handed her ropes and told her to pull them taut or release them slowly. This, *this* was what she had been searching for in an assistant all these years—a skipper.

Then, reaching across the little boy, who was thoughtfully sucking on a plastic dinosaur, Kit had put his smooth hand beneath her chin. He had moved his thumb softly across her cheek. And she had seen that in spite of his age and his competence, he was neither her assistant nor her skipper. That there was no hierarchy involved in their relationship, none at all.

'I'm so lucky,' he said. He looked down at Henry's shining hair, then turned his pale eyes back to Miranda. 'Always have been.' He smiled, a tight, ironic half smile and closed his eyes. 'And so grateful,' he added. 'So fucking grateful.'

There was something touching about his declaration, as though he knew all his happiness, even his memories of happiness, could be snatched away.

'Lucky to be lucky,' she said, for she suddenly felt lucky, too. Her business was falling apart. Her reputation was ruined. The sky was blue. The wind filled the white sail. A child hummed a tuneless song beside her. She was skimming the water. She was still, motionless, swift.

No, no, bad idea, Miranda, she had forced herself to think then, but of course he had kissed her. He'd opened his eyes, looked into hers and somehow the distance between them, an expanse of sea air and sunlight and decades, had disappeared.

*   *   *

Miranda recalled that first kiss with a private smile. She watched Annie in the kitchen, catching a glimpse of an elbow, an arm, a general bustling beyond the doorway. Annie worried too much. It was very stressful, worry was. Took its toll on your health. Not to mention your skin. She had bought

Annie some La Mer cream, which really did work miracles, but all Annie did was work herself up over the cost. Annie needed perspective. Life was not just about material things. She thought of little Henry. That's what life was about, the little Henrys. Annie had her boys, it was true, but they were grown. She needed someone to take their place, if not in her heart, then at least in her life.

'I wonder how Frederick is,' she called out to Annie. 'You should call him, Annie. Get him to drive down.'

Annie yanked the silverware drawer open. One of the unwelcome side effects of her sister's new fascination with Kit Maybank and his little sidekick was a newfound and frequently vocalized interest in Frederick Barrow. She reached in the drawer. 'Shit!' she said, pricking her finger on a steak knife someone had put in with the forks.

'Don't be so controlling, dear,' her mother said, having no idea what Annie was complaining about but sure it had to do with her totalitarian views of the kitchen. As if Betty had not had a kitchen for over fifty years.

'I cut myself,' Annie said, going into the bathroom for a Band-Aid.

'Don't bleed on the napkins. Although that OxiClean is supposed to be wonderful. And use Neosporin. Cuts heal three times faster.'

Betty had begun watching daytime TV and found it extraordinarily informative and reassuring. There were so many problems in the world she had never thought of, and so many products to solve them.

In the bathroom, her cut throbbing a little in its bandage, Annie stared at herself in the mirror and

104

wondered, not for the first time, what she really looked like. As other people saw her. It didn't seem to mean anything, the way she saw herself, for it changed with her mood. I'm not bad-looking, she decided, as she so often did. Whatever that meant.

Was that what Frederick had seen? A middle-aged woman, not bad-looking, who took very good care of herself, as she would have taken care of a rare first edition? She plucked her eyebrows and had her lip waxed regularly. She used night cream at night and day cream in the morning and sunscreen even in winter. Her makeup was natural-looking, but she never left the bathroom in the morning without it. She swam almost every morning. Her hair was the same natural-looking brown of every other middle-class middle-aged woman who went once a month to have it colored. She was not exceptional, but she was not exceptionable. She was, she realized with a mixture of pride and self-pity, conscientious.

It had been a month since she'd seen Frederick, or even heard from him. Ever since he'd gone up to Massachusetts after his reading. That night, while waiting for his car at the parking garage, he had sent her a text message thanking her again for arranging the event, saying he would miss her and urging her to visit him in Cape Cod. Then— nothing. She was deeply disappointed, but not really surprised. Frederick Barrow was an important person. She was not. There was a reason he was important, there was a reason she was not, there was an order to the universe that kept the important people in their important sphere and the unimportant people living with their mother and sister in a borrowed shack. Still, sometimes an important man like Frederick was in New York City and sought out an unimportant but quite intelligent and pleasant woman like Annie. It had happened before, it might happen again; in fact, she was sure it would happen again in some desultory fashion. It was not enough, but it would have to be enough—to have a friend like Frederick, a friend she saw when it suited him, when he had time, when he was in town.

Annie was used to being alone. There were people who felt they didn't exist if they were alone, who needed to be talking and listening to others all the time. But Annie felt acutely alive when she was by herself, when she was silent, when she was surrounded by silence. She sometimes looked at the books on the shelves in the library and felt a kinship with them, so full, so still, so potent.

Her sister, of course, had always been just the opposite. She had revelled in talk, whether on the phone or in person, her own or that of the couple at the next table at a restaurant—the more people around her, the happier she was. Though she had never entertained like Cousin Lou, she had always taken her clients and their editors out, filling up almost every meal of almost every day—breakfast, lunch, or dinner, the choice calculated using her own internal and complicated formula, a successful author getting dinner, as well as one who had hit hard times. But she did these things, ate these meals, not in a great flourish of hospitality like Lou, but out of fascination. Miranda loved problems. She loved turning problems into stories and stories into gold.

'I am an alchemist,' she would say. 'And a

nightmare.'

Annie knew she herself was neither an alchemist nor a nightmare. Perhaps that was why Frederick had disappeared. Yet she was sure he had liked her. Really liked her. And she was sure she had liked him. She would let her thoughts go no further in that direction. She had liked him. In a way she had not liked anyone in a long, long time. In a way that left her hollow without him. In a way she would push out of her mind.

Back in the living room, she watched her sister thoughtfully perusing a *People* magazine, which, along with all tabloids, she referred to as her 'files'. These quiet days in a suburban Indian summer must be hard for Miranda, Annie thought. Annie was used to being left alone by the world. Miranda was not. But now the publishers had stopped calling. The editors had stopped calling. Even the press had stopped calling. There were, of course, the remnants of the Awful Authors. It seemed as though they unfortunately would never stop calling. They were like foghorns, mournfully hooting from their lonely rocky promontories. No wonder Miranda was so taken with Kit and his little boy. They were young and fresh and untainted by the false disasters Miranda had wasted her life pursuing.

*   *   *

When Kit arrived, he brought a bottle of Maker's Mark and, on the basis of his many years as an unemployed thespian bartender, made them Manhattans. Miranda sucked on the Maraschino cherry. He had actually brought a bottle of them.

The resplendent red, the sweet unreal flavour, reminded her momentarily of Josie, of special nights out and tall glasses of Shirley Temple cocktails.

Henry sat on the floor with a plastic cow and a robot. The cow and the robot danced. Or wrestled. Miranda could not tell which.

Now Kit was talking. But, *mirabile dictu,* instead of telling her his stories, Kit was asking about her own. He wanted to know what she thought about before she went to sleep when she was a child. Did she have wallpaper in her room? What teachers had she loved and why? What was the first pair of shoes she remembered? She sometimes felt that he was rummaging through her life as if it were an attic full of musty antique treasures, but his curiosity was warm and detailed and domestic and endless, and Miranda, so accustomed to listening and waiting and pouncing on the sordid details of others' lives, found herself almost delirious at the intoxicating novelty of hearing her own voice telling her own small stories.

*   *   *

Annie listened to her sister talking about their childhood. Now and then she would add something, or Betty would jump in with a clearer memory. Annie had to admit she liked having Kit and Henry around. On the floor, Henry muttered seriously to his toys and allowed her to stroke his silky hair. Kit had dropped his jacket on a chair and kicked off his shoes and, though just barely suggesting the sweeping piles of shoes and socks and sweaters and electronic gadgets that her own

108

boys would strew around her apartment when they were home, these small gestures afforded her a momentary tender motherly exasperation.

She heard a phone ring from deep inside her reverie and thought for an instant that it was her phone, her call, her sons. But of course it was not even her ring, it was Miranda's.

'Yes,' Miranda was saying in her patient Awful Author voice, at the same time grimacing to the others in the room. 'Oh, that's outrageous! You poor, poor thing. However, that's why you have me. That's exactly what I'm here for.'

'Christ,' Annie said when Miranda hung up. 'Those people. What's he doing, writing a memoir about writing a false memoir?'

Miranda shrugged. 'One of the few clients I have left. You guys have children, I have has-beens. We all do our bit.'

'But look how great you are with Henry,' Kit said. 'The Awful Authors must have trained you well.'

Miranda beamed.

She's beaming, Annie thought, surprised. She was also surprised that Kit knew the family name for Miranda's clients. It seemed so intimate, somehow. And Kit and Miranda had known each other such a short time—a month? Although they had been together almost constantly during that time. She watched Miranda turn her smile to Kit, not her seductive manipulative smile, but this open, unstudied, happy, beaming smile. Kit, clearly dazzled, blinked at Miranda as if she were a bright light and he a stunned bunny.

This can only end in tears, Annie thought.

This can only end in tears: the words parents

used when their children became too exuberant. She reminded herself that Kit and Miranda were not her children. Even her children were no longer her children. They were all grown up. Soon enough they would have their own children. This small boy on the floor who had brought back so many memories was closer to a grandson than a son. She felt suddenly very old and curled up next to her mother on the couch, murmuring, 'Mommy,' as she laid her head on Betty's shoulder.

We are old, she thought. Miranda is old. Miranda must not become a desperate old cougar.

Then again, who was she to say what Miranda should be? Who was she to say what was desperate? That way lies tears, but who was she to say that tears were wrong? You couldn't protect anyone, not even Miranda. Particularly if they did not want to be protected. Particularly from a handsome, attentive young lover. If lover is what he was. A handsome, attentive young lover might, at any rate, take Miranda's mind off the Awful Authors. The Awful Authors were not the victims they had been cracked up to be. They were charlatan victims. It must be galling to a connoisseur of imperfection like Miranda. They were fakes, reproductions, costume, paste. If she could not have authentic victims, then at least she deserved an authentically ordinary, healthy person like Kit Maybank, a man with a real life—if you could call auditioning a real life—to take her mind off all those counterfeit people chronicling their counterfeit lives.

Nevertheless, this could only end in tears.

Frederick was a real man with a real life, she supposed. He worked, and he doted on his children and grandchildren. He woke up in the morning and breathed air blown in from the sea. That was really all she knew of him. Except that he had come up to her apartment one night. He had followed her into the narrow hallway. He had pushed her roughly against the wall, a hand on each of her arms. He had kissed her and pressed against her and surprised her with his urgency, to which her response had at first been the unworthy thought that he had perhaps taken Viagra. Was it just kicking in or about to wear off? Was that what this was all about? 'Erections lasting more than four hours . . .' The TV commercial flashed through her mind—then her thoughts got gorgeously foggy and she pulled him even closer and they staggered like teenagers to the bedroom.

Annie smiled at the memory. Frederick had spent the night, his clothes scattered across the floor. He had carefully turned off his cell phone, though, probably hiding from those children of his.

CHAPTER NINE

Betty marveled at the new houses that seemed to lurch out of the ground at ever-decreasing intervals, each one bigger and in a more complicated interpretation of a greater mixture of historical styles than the last. Each new house had a garage with three doors, behind which were three cars, which explained, she supposed, the constant traffic in the town. She drove her own car slowly and disapprovingly to the supermarket and wandered stupefied through the wide aisles. When she marvelled at the size of the supermarket, at the abundance of produce and the gigantic cereal boxes of every brand imaginable, Annie told her she was like a Russian refugee in 1983, and she might just as well have been a refugee, that was how foreign she felt. In New York, she had fought her way through the cramped aisles of Zabar's and Fairway or stopped on the corner at the little produce market to pick up some flowers. The bags were delivered, and the doorman kept them for her if she was not home, bringing them upstairs when she arrived, carrying them into the kitchen. Here, she pushed an oversized shopping cart to her car, struggled to get the bags into the trunk, struggled at home to get them out of the trunk and into the house. She enjoyed her shopping trips when she set out. The supermarket spread before her as a place of boundless opportunity, something new and vast and exciting, the way the prairie must have looked to the first settlers of the West. But by the time she got home, Betty was tired and defeated and longed for her old life.

My old life, she would think. And then she would muse on the irony of the phrase. She was young in her old life. She was old in her new life. It didn't add up. She wished she had a doorman.

She never let her daughters know how she felt. What would be the point? Annie went off swimming at the beach in the early morning. Miranda took walks in thunderstorms. They seemed to have adjusted to this country life very well. She would stay in Westport for the time being, for their sakes.

It was not easy. She was not a youngster just starting out. It had not been easy for her in

Westport when she was a youngster just starting out, so how had anyone imagined it would work this time? Lou had meant no harm, of course. But Joseph, Joseph of all people, should have known better than to consign her to a cottage in a town with traffic but no place to go.

In New York, Betty and Josie had often entertained when they were younger, and even in the last few years they would invite old friends to dinner. More often than not, though, they would meet their friends at restaurants. There were always new restaurants in New York about which to read, at which to make reservations a month in advance, in which eventually to overeat and overspend. Restaurants had taken the place of movies, which had all become so violent and crude, and children, who had all grown up, in the social lives of the Weissmanns and their circle. Betty wondered where that circle was now. They had perhaps circled around Joseph, for they had certainly not drawn their wagons around her. There were a few close friends—the Harveys and the Littmans—who called regularly and tried to make dates with Betty. And there were her friends from college, Judith and Florence. Nothing changed those friendships, which were intimate and deep and existed still, as they had for decades, almost exclusively on the phone. But Social Life, as Betty once knew it, was gone. The restaurants in Westport were dull and overpriced. There was no movie theater, even if she had wanted to see a film and could have found a friend to accompany her. There was nothing to do, no one to do it with, and she wouldn't drive at night, so on top of everything else there was no way to get there. She

113

daydreamed about the buses in New York with their interesting bits of poetry or quotes from George Eliot, their ads for Con Ed or the Bronx Zoo. How civilized and communal New York seemed from the vantage point of this lonely land of cars and crows and Lanes and Drives and Crescents.

'Oh, it's so peaceful here,' her friend Judith said when she came to have lunch and go to the Westport Playhouse with Betty one day. They walked along Main Street, peering into shop windows. 'You can see the sky! All the stores we have on Madison Avenue, but on this quaint little street. A theater, too! It's got everything New York has, really.'

In some perverse way this was true—the play turned out to be just as dreadful as most of the theater in New York, the shops were frequented by the same loud, slender mothers as the ones who shopped in the city, the styles were too young for Betty, just as they were on Madison, the sky was the same gray swathe high above.

'Very cosmopolitan little town,' Betty had answered her friend in her most chipper voice. But Westport struck her as neither cosmopolitan nor little. In fact, it did not even strike her as a town. It was large and spread out and bustling and provincial.

'If you have to be in exile, Betty, you could do worse,' said Judith, who was no fool and had known Betty such a long time.

Betty smiled at her. How lucky she was to have friends who understood what she meant rather than what she said. 'You're absolutely right,' she said. But as they drove out of the parking lot onto the Post Road, she could not help adding, 'Look at this traffic!'

* * *

Cousin Lou's latest event was a particularly large dinner party in honor of Rosalyn's father, Mr Shpuntov. Mr Shpuntov had changed his name to Sherwood many years ago, on 24 October 1929, to be exact, Black Thursday. He was eighteen years old on that day, and fearing the Jews would be blamed for a stock-market crash as they were blamed for every other disaster, Shpuntov looked into the future and saw himself as Sherwood.

But as Sherwood né Shpuntov got older and began to forget more and more, one of the things he remembered perfectly was his old name. He had stopped responding to Sherwood about a year before. He disliked younger people calling him Izzy, thinking it impertinent, and as there was never anyone present who wasn't younger than his ninety-eight years, he prevailed. Shpuntov he had been, and Shpuntov he became.

Mr Shpuntov was seated between Betty and his son-in-law, Lou. His daughter, her hair coaxed into its stiff, elaborate swoops and valleys, sat across from him.

'My father and I were just marveling at the farmers' market phenomenon here in Westport,' Rosalyn was saying to a woman sitting beside her.

'That man has a terrible comb-over,' Mr Shpuntov said loudly to Cousin Lou, pointing his chin at his daughter. 'Comb-overs . . . never liked 'em myself.'

'That's *Rosalyn,* Mr Shpuntov,' Cousin Lou

whispered nervously.

'Dad has a theory about farmers' markets,' Rosalyn continued, in a louder, determined voice. 'Don't you, Dad?'

'He looks ridiculous,' Mr Shpuntov said, glaring at his daughter.

Rosalyn glared back.

'I would like to make a toast,' she said suddenly. She stood up. 'To my father, who has come to live in our house. We hope to make his waning years happy and comfortable.' She bowed to Mr Shpuntov. 'To your waning years!'

'What's he say?' Mr Shpuntov asked.

'Hear, hear,' said Cousin Lou quickly, at top volume. 'Hear, hear!'

Hear hears echoed down the table, drowning out Mr Shpuntov.

Waning years, thought Betty. Oh dear. I don't like the sound of that. Poor fellow. 'Never mind,' she said to the old man. 'You're as old as you feel.'

'Why is that old woman talking to me?' Mr Shpuntov said to Cousin Lou. 'I'm as deaf as a post.'

It was Lou who had insisted on taking his father-in-law into the house. The old man had been living with his girlfriend, a younger woman of eighty-two. But she had died suddenly of an aneurism, leaving Mr Shpuntov and three unruly dogs in an apartment in Queens. Rosalyn suggested a home, and Lou assumed she meant their own. When she realized his mistake, it was already too late: the arrangements were much too far along and, more important, much too public to countermand. Mr Shpuntov moved into the big house in Westport and was assigned a bedroom and an attendant.

(The dogs, thank God, had been taken in by the deceased girlfriend's son—there had to be some limits, after all. Though, with regard to Lou and his hospitality, Rosalyn had yet to discover what they were.) And so a permanent place was set for the old man at Lou's long table. Rosalyn attributed opinions and bons mots to him, and he, increasingly petulant, wondered aloud why the skinny old man with the comb-over kept badgering him.

'*Beautiful baby*,' Lou had begun singing, winking at Miranda.

Miranda was sitting next to Kit, the beautiful baby in question. At the other end of the table was the pensive Roberts in a sprightly yellow bow tie. Lou now made some comment about September and May and romances in those lovely but different months. He seemed to amuse himself by casting Kit and Roberts against each other as rivals for Miranda's affection. Annie thought her cousin was remarkably indelicate on this matter. Still, she could understand where he got the idea—her sister was so beautiful, so lively these days. Annie's heart went out to Roberts. He caught her glance, and his mouth twitched into a slight, tentative smile.

More and more, she'd found herself engaging Roberts in conversation, as if it were her duty to compensate somehow, to provide some small diversion for the spurned lover by offering him her less glamorous attention. He was, indeed, difficult to talk to at first, shyly answering questions with monosyllables that made any continuation of conversation on that topic almost impossible. But as she spent more time with him, Annie observed that he grew more comfortable, and as he grew more comfortable, Roberts grew interesting and surprisingly amusing.

'How come people call you by your last name?' Annie asked him. 'Why does everyone just call you Roberts?'

He smiled modestly. 'It's kind of a rock-star thing.'

*   *   *

The weeks passed and the days began receding, becoming shorter and darker, drawing themselves in, curling in on themselves like sleeping animals. Crows dozed among the turning leaves. Fatter and fatter credit card bills arrived in the Wisemen mailbox, but still Betty and Josie had not ironed out the wrinkles in their separation, still Annie heard nothing from Frederick Barrow, and still Kit spent almost every day, and evening, with Miranda.

Kit joined Miranda on her morning walks, with Henry, sleeping or singing or whining from an olive-green backpack, coming along for the ride. They walked slowly and watched the sky expand into the silver light, and they talked.

After the initial days of questioning Miranda, Kit had begun at last, as expected, to talk about himself. Miranda dutifully prepared herself to listen, as she always listened to everyone, waiting for the confidences she knew would come.

But instead of describing sexual abuse at boarding school or stepfathers who beat him or a sordid struggle with crack cocaine, Kit talked about his happy boyhood in Maine, the walks through the woods digging up rare wildflowers with his parents and brothers and sisters; the evenings on the rocky beach splashing and digging for clams in the frigid water. The picture of this group of beautiful human beings—for surely they all looked like Kit—plunging headlong through the verdant Maine woods beneath the cheerful songs of warblers or standing windblown knee-deep in the surf made Miranda long to be in Maine herself. The smell of the pines. The breeze hurrying the bright white clouds through the infinite blue of the sky. It was true that Miranda could smell pines perfectly well right where she was, and that the breeze was hurrying just the kind of bright clouds through exactly the infinite blue sky she imagined right there on Compo Beach, which was probably what made her think of pines and clouds and infinity in the first place, but still she longed for Maine, the land of Alex Katz and E. B. White.

'I thought lobster at a bar mitzvah was totally normal . . .' Kit was saying.

Miranda smiled at him. She looked at Henry, asleep at the moment, his pink mouth pressed into his father's shoulder. She listened intently to Kit, not hearing him. What a luxury his stories were, like a vacation. No tortured memoir here, no Lite Victory. Just tender reminiscence. She had never seen eyes like Kit's, she thought. His best friend, Seth, he was saying. His words passed over her like a silky breeze. Bright, pale gray eyes as deep and translucent as air—look at them—the lashes thick and dark, above and below, like a horse's lashes. His eyes were as dramatic as the eyes of a silent-film star. Oh, she could go on and on about Kit's eyes. *At Seth's bar mitzvah,* Kit said. Bar mitzvah, Miranda thought, trying to pay attention. Seth's bar mitzvah. She was probably the same age as

Seth's parents. But surely she was better preserved than Seth's parents, whom she envisioned as a weathered couple in matching track shoes and kelly green fleece jackets. *Appetizers of oysters and chopped liver*, said Kit.

Henry woke up, and Kit put him down on the sand. Miranda and Kit stood together and watched Henry dig a hole. It seemed to Miranda that this must be the most beautiful time of the year, the air cool, the light soft and clean.

But I'm too old, she thought, and Kit's too young.

Then Kit took her hand and put it to his lips.

Now, *Kit*'s parents, of course, were *older,* she remembered, definitely older than she was, Kit very presciently being the youngest of four children, each three years apart. And how well they all got along, the three of them, she and Kit and Henry.

Miranda dropped suddenly down on one knee and patted some sand into a pile. 'Castle,' she said.

Henry nodded vigorously. 'Yes,' he agreed. 'Castle.'

Miranda wondered what life would be like with this small, busy person at her side, day in and day out, waking her in the middle of the night with a bad dream and a soggy diaper, banging a gummy spoon on the kitchen table, crying in wild, piercing simian shrieks in the grocery store while grabbing at boxes of cereal. When Henry cried, his face crumpled so immediately, so completely. He was not crying now, though she was sure he soon would be, and for some reason she could never have anticipated—an ice-cream cone dropped yesterday, suddenly recalled; a filthy cigarette butt

120

found in the sand and confiscated; the sand itself, suddenly deemed itchy and hostile; the wind, the sound of the waves, a gull swooping low? It could be anything, it would be something. But right now Henry was sitting on his heels poking holes in the wet sand with a stick. The yellow light held him in an embrace. His face was serious and beautiful.

She felt a hand on her hair and looked up. It was Kit, smiling down at her. She had almost forgotten he was there.

*   *   *

Once, Miranda asked Kit why he didn't return to his apartment in the city or move into his Aunt Charlotte's big house.

'I know this place is adorable and picturesque and all,' she said, looking around at the boathouse. There were three rooms, all painted a glossy nautical white—a living room containing two Adirondack chairs, a rag rug, a tiny two-burner stove, and a half-size refrigerator; a small bedroom with a maple dresser and a brass bed from the time when people were apparently shorter and thinner; and an even smaller room with an ornate and old-fashioned crib. 'But it's all sort of built for hobbits.'

'Or Henry.'

'But even little Henry needs screens. What do you do, pull out a mosquito net at night? Do you have a fan? Do you have heat? It's not winterized, is it? I hope you have hot water. You do, don't you?'

Kit laughed and nodded.

'But seriously, wouldn't you two be more comfortable in that big rambling mansion? . . .

121

Manderley,' she added in a Thirties movie voice, suddenly self-conscious, worried she had crossed some sort of line.

'Aunt Charlotte would like nothing better, believe me, and I love Aunt Charlotte to death, and I'm really happy to stick around for a while to help her out with a few things before Henry and I go back to New York, but live with her? In the same house? No, thank you. And don't worry, my little homemaker. We not only have hot water, we have heat, don't we, Henry?'

That night when she returned home, Miranda told her mother and sister about this conversation.

'No screens? Feh,' said Betty.

Miranda imagined Aunt Charlotte as someone like Big Edie from *Grey Gardens*.

'I lean more towards Miss Havisham,' said Annie.

But they were never able to discover which one was closer, for none of them, not even Miranda, could ever think up a reason to meet the reclusive Miss Maybank, and Kit never offered to introduce the old lady.

*   *   *

On the days Kit needed to go into the city, he left Henry with Miranda.

'Now, don't let your friend take advantage of you,' Betty said, thinking of the talk show she'd seen about grandmothers stuck raising the toddlers of young, irresponsible parents. She was not technically Henry's grandmother, and she liked the little tyke well enough, but if there was one thing she had learned from the many therapists adorning television's daytime couches, it was the need for boundaries. She had grown up thinking one was supposed to transcend boundaries in life, but it appeared she had been wrong.

Miranda laughed. 'No, no,' she said. 'This is just what the doctor ordered.'

And it did seem to do her good, the days spent on the beach searching for shells and sticks, digging saggy tunnels and building uneven, lumpy mounds. Her life in the city, her love affairs, even her work, seemed to fade. The agony of failure rose up and clutched at her still, but less often, with less force. She woke in the morning eager to get out of bed, to bathe with the lavender soap that Henry said smelled like tea. She and Henry had tea parties, just like the ones she had had as a child, with the exception of the fireplace ladies, who were invited, Miranda told Henry, but could not attend due to a previous engagement. She told him all about the fireplace ladies. He nodded sagely and poured his tea, which was really apple juice, on the floor, watching the puddles with scholarly absorption. When she gave him bubble baths, he took the plastic measuring cups and bowls provided for him and imitated her ritual of tea preparation. She was touched, to a degree that surprised her.

Sometimes she would sit Henry atop the ceremonial cannons at the beach and listen to him talk. He would tell long tales about a fox named Higbee.

'And then?' she would say, not paying attention, closing her eyes against the dying autumn sun and the sharp wind, her arms around Henry's waist, her shoulder against his leg. The joy of not listening—

why had she never tried it before?

Henry's voice was like music, a pretty little piccolo, the chant of a boy in his own boys' choir. No wonder people had children, she thought. A child replaced art and work and culture. A child, so small, so loud, took up all the time, all the energy, all the love. It was so easy: just give in, just let your life be ruled by this simple and tender embodiment of need. No choices, no decisions except those that related to one person, one little demanding Napoleonic person. She felt relief flood through her body: being with Henry was so clear-cut, so obvious, so essential, so undeniable and absolute.

When the stories got too boring even to ignore, Miranda took Henry down and they walked slowly home, stopping to examine the offerings of low tide—mussels, the abandoned, upturned armature of a horseshoe crab, a white pebble, a tangle of russet seaweed, a smell of salt and brine and smooth, sparkling muck.

*   *   *

One evening, Annie caught sight of Kit on the train coming home from the city, pushing the strands of boyish hair back from his face, smiling a rather dazzling smile. Seated in the back of the train car, she watched him walk past her, down the aisle, and she saw heads swivel to look at him, one, then another, as he passed by. He actually turns heads, she thought, amused. Annie could understand it. He was a magnificent creature to look at, a peach ripening on a branch. Annie caught herself noticing his strong young arms beneath his shirt. Even his wrists looked young and manly to her. For years, Annie had been aware of the physical beauty of her sons' friends. They would come and stay during college vacations and sleep piled in their rooms like a pack of dogs, then wander into the kitchen shirtless and sleepy, their hair tousled, their torsos long and smooth as ancient Greeks'. They would blink and stretch and eat, unconscious of their beauty, of the limber physical eloquence of youth. Annie had anaesthetized any simmering physical response as quickly and thoroughly as possible. But you could admire them. In fact, how could you help but admire them?

Remembering those shaggy morning parades of boyish beauty, Annie found it natural to fall into a state of admiration for the handsome young Kit, and would have felt no unease if Miranda had done the same. But Miranda's reaction to Kit was not what Annie expected. First of all, Miranda rarely spoke of him, never extravagantly extolled the virtues that would later be cataloged as vices. Nor did she call him on the phone at short, regular intervals. She did not buy him absurdly expensive presents. She did not loudly announce her intense happiness, at last!, to salesgirls and crossing guards and the man behind the meat counter at the grocery store. This one time, Miranda did not fall impetuously in love, announcing that here at last was the one and only man for her. She did not spend every waking minute with him for four weeks and then weep her eyes out when she discovered that he was a fundamentalist, a lush, a Republican, whatever it was that rose up and disappointed her. This time, Miranda, depressed and disoriented by the collapse of her life of

125

the past couple of hard-earned decades, had apparently not had the energy to throw herself into one of her accustomed ferocious love affairs. Her relationship with Kit was different, more even, more peaceful, more plain. Miranda seemed happy, which made Annie happy. But there was something worrisome, too. For who'd ever heard of a temperate Miranda? Without her cloak of extravagance, Miranda seemed so unprotected. She had let down her guard: her gaudy, frenetic, romantic guard. Which meant, Annie thought with dread, that anything could happen now.

CHAPTER TEN

The first time Kit and Miranda made love, it was late in the afternoon, two days after they met. Henry was asleep in his crib. The light was golden, saturated, and the white curtains on the windows fluttered noisily in the breeze that swept in from the water. Miranda felt the same arms around her, the Adonis arms, the hero arms that had lifted her from the tossing sea. She laughed out loud, thinking what a fool she was to cast her soggy rescue in such epic terms. When she laughed, Kit told her she was beautiful, that he had found her floating in the ocean and that he would keep her, finders keepers, it was only fair. She allowed herself to disappear, to dissolve into his arms. It was a conscious, almost frenzied release. This was another kind of freedom, this letting go. All responsibility, all aspiration, all disappointment, all of life before that moment was left far, far behind.

126

He undressed her, and she felt her jeans and her sweater, her bra, each bit of clothing slip over her skin. He undressed himself, too, slowly, sure she was watching, she noticed, stringing it out.

They spent almost every afternoon like that, she reeling from the heady emotional simmer: her own fierce, demanding extinction, beneath which rested a calm, solid sense that she was as safe as houses.

When Henry woke up, she would leave Kit asleep in the boathouse and take Henry for a walk on the beach. Tide pools glazed the smooth dark sand, and silver flakes of mica reflected the setting sun. When it rained, they squatted in their slickers and watched the raindrops disrupt the surfaces of the shallow beach puddles. They held hands and spoke in undertones. Miranda had never been religious, but she thought that she could worship Henry with fervour and joy. She thought, I already do.

*   *   *

Cousin Lou was not religious, either: he claimed that he would not like to insult the memory of his benefactress, Mrs H., by worshipping any god but her. This sacrilegious declaration made both Rosalyn and Betty squirm, but Annie and Miranda laughed every time he said it. In spite of his irreligiosity, however, their cousin could not give up an occasion for a large gathering, and he planned to have thirty for dinner on Rosh Hashanah. The three Weissmanns were invited, as were Kit Maybank and Henry. Among the other guests were a woman Cousin Lou had recently become acquainted with at the Westport YMCA

127

pool during free swim who turned out to be a distant cousin of Rosalyn's; Lou's accountant, Marty, with Marty's large family of several generations; a fellow Lou knew from the golf course who had invented a folding six-foot ladder that was only three-quarters of an inch deep; a plastic surgeon who was always very popular at dinner parties for his willingness to put on his reading glasses and take a closer look; the psychiatrist and his wife; the lawyers; the judge; the metal sculptor; a retired factor from Seventh Avenue; and a former cultural minister of Estonia Lou and Rosalyn had met thirteen years earlier at a spa in Ischia.

When Rosh Hashanah came, a bright, clear, unseasonably warm day, none of the Weissmanns went to synagogue. It had not been their custom for many years, and Betty particularly did not want to this year because, she explained, as one so recently widowed, she could not stand the spiritual strain. So the three women sat on the sunporch and enjoyed the warmth and read the newspaper until, around two o'clock, Kit's white Mini pulled into the driveway.

'They're awfully early,' Betty said, eyeing the child in the car seat and wondering if her quiet day was about to be invaded.

Miranda gave her mother a look and went to the car. She could barely contain her excitement. She had just gotten a pair of Crocs that were identical to Henry's own tiny pair of rubber clogs. They were not the kind of footwear she would have ever considered before, not even to wear on the beach, but when she saw them in the store, she imagined Henry's amazement, his pleasure. They were still in the box. She couldn't wait to show him.

She opened the car door and reached in to unstrap Henry.

'No,' Kit said, putting a hand out as if to protect the child. 'I mean, we're not staying. I mean, we're going.'

'But dinner isn't until seven. You can hang out here. Or if you have stuff to do, just leave Henry with me. We have important things to discuss, don't we, Henry?'

'Going on a airplane,' Henry said. He clapped his hands.

'An airplane?' Miranda said, clapping in response. 'When?'

'Today!'

'Wow! Is the airplane going to take you to Cousin Lou's for dinner?'

He shook his head with vigour. His lower lip pushed out. His eyes screwed shut. And he began, like a thundercloud that blows in with a sudden downpour, to wail.

'Baby,' Miranda said, squatting beside the car, reaching in through the open door to stroke his hair. 'What's wrong? What's the matter?'

Kit had twisted up his own handsome face uncomfortably. He looked around him, as if searching for reinforcements, then bit his lip, then said, 'Look, I'm sorry, Miranda. But we do have to get going . . . Henry, hush, it will be okay . . .' He dug in his jacket pocket and pulled out an old, half-eaten Fruit Roll-Up. 'Here, Henry. Now stop crying, okay, buddy?'

Henry sucked sadly on the scrap of red fruit leather.

Miranda continued to stroke his head. 'My poor

little boy,' she said softly. 'What was all that about?'

Henry kissed her wrist as it passed near his lips. The pressure, so gentle, like a butterfly's wing, seemed to travel through her entire body. She took his free hand and held it against her cheek. This, she thought, is all there is. This little hand. In mine.

Miranda then had a sharp, clear, overpowering vision of holding Henry on her hip while she . . . well, not while she cooked. No, but while she entered a restaurant. With Kit beside her. She saw them feeding the child bits of California roll, without wasabi, the way Henry liked it. She could feel the bedtime sheets, too, pulling them up as she tucked Henry in at night, could feel his soft, warm breath on her hand as she stroked his cheek. The sweaty, wet sweetness of his body, soggy diaper and all, when he woke up—she clutched that against her; the echoing crunch of Henry eating cereal—she could hear it. Every night, every morning. Then, in a year or so, he would go off to preschool and make wobbly little friends his own age, and she would walk him there, holding his hand, slowing her pace for him, lifting him up when he got tired. Truck, he would call out, pointing at the garbage men rumbling by. He would want to grow up to be a garbage man, and she would look at him proudly and think, You are perfect, Henry. You are perfect, and I belong to you.

When Kit spoke, now standing beside her, she turned a beatific face to him.

'Hmm?' she said. 'Sorry . . .'

'I said we really do have to catch a plane . . .'

130

Miranda tilted her head, like a dog, a trusting and innocent dog who has been given a confusing command.

'Plane?' she said, looking up at Kit.

'Listen, I just wanted to say goodbye. It's so sudden and crazy. And I wanted to apologize about tonight . . .'

'Wait,' Miranda said. 'What?'

She'd thought for a moment that Kit said he had to catch a plane. Henry's fingers were now splayed out in the air in front of him. She watched them, marveled at them. They were like some glorious, exotic insect. A new species, one she had discovered.

'I got a part,' Kit said.

Miranda thought she heard 'I've got to part,' and wondered why Kit said 'I' and not 'We,' but then realized what he meant. 'Part?' she asked.

'Look, I just found out.' Kit was kicking the dirt of the driveway nervously. 'It's a real break. I mean, it's nothing, it's tiny, but it's work.'

Work, Miranda thought. Work is good. Say something nice. But she felt panicked. Work was what she had loved once. Now she loved Henry. And maybe, just maybe, Kit as well.

'Work!' she said.

Betty observed the threesome from the porch. She thought how much they looked like a family. Perhaps, somehow, against all odds, this improbable arrangement would work for Miranda. If only Miranda could find some kind of domestic peace at last. Betty waved hello to Kit and, followed by Annie, descended the cracked cement steps onto the patchy stubble of lawn.

'Hello, Kit!' they called. 'Hello, Henry! What

brings you here so early?'

'A part!' Miranda said, trying to smile. 'Kit got a part.'

'Oh well,' Kit murmured. 'Small part . . . Independent film . . .'

'Kit and Henry are going away,' Miranda said in a bizarre singsong, as if she were addressing Henry, or were insane. 'On an airplane.'

Betty was visited by the swift, looping nausea she'd had when Joseph announced his departure. She saw Miranda's expression, she heard the loud crashing echo, felt the chill, the vortex. She had been married to Joseph forever, Miranda and Kit had known each other for a month or so. But however long it had been or however short, did it matter? Did it ever really matter? No, Betty thought. A broken heart is a broken heart.

'How long will you be gone?' she asked, though she thought she knew. He had that look about him, that I'm-not-sure-how-long look, that look of goodbye.

'I have to go to L.A. . . . I don't really know how long,' Kit said. He turned back to Miranda. 'Look, I'm so sorry about tonight . . . I mean, I'm sorry period.'

Miranda took Henry's hand again. 'L.A.' She wanted to explain to Kit that L.A. was too far away, that even a short trip was interminable, that one day would be one day too many. She wanted to explain that she had had a vision of their lives together, she wanted him to understand what she had just discovered, that her heart had found a home at last.

Instead, controlling her voice as well as she could, she asked if Kit would like to leave Henry with her. 'Won't that make it easier for you? I mean, if it's a short time . . .'

Kit drummed his fingers on the roof of the car. 'Look, Miranda, I don't know how long it will be. And his mother will be back soon, so she can get him, right?'

His mother. Miranda held Henry's hand against her cheek, pressing it there, absorbing the touch of each small finger.

'I'm really sorry about all this . . .' Kit was saying. 'I'll miss you, Miranda. We'll both miss you.'

'Hey, don't be sorry,' she forced herself to say. 'A part in a movie! It's great, Kit.'

'Yeah.' He shrugged and looked miserable.

'What?'

'No "what". It's great.'

'Jesus, cheer up, then. Right, Henry?' She leaned farther into the car and pressed her face against Henry's. He made kissing, smacking sounds, then pushed his sugary lips on her cheek. 'I love you, Henry,' she whispered.

'I love Randa,' he shouted.

Miranda stood up. She felt off balance, disconnected from the little car, the man in front of her, her mother, her sister. How silly of her. They were just going away for a while. She had no claim on either of them. Visions were dreams. Dreams were fiction. Fiction was lies. 'Break a leg,' she said to Kit with her big public smile.

'Yeah. Thanks. Well, I'll call you.' He gave her a quick hug. 'I really will.'

Betty noted the 'really'. She reached out for Miranda's hand and squeezed it.

Miranda pulled her hand away. 'I'm fine.'

'Randa!' Henry cried with sudden desperation

133

as they pulled out of the driveway. 'Randa! Randa!'

'Oh God,' Kit was saying. 'Not now, Henry, please.'

Miranda waved and called goodbye to Henry, who waved a chubby hand as his father reached back and shoved a pacifier in his mouth.

Miranda stood in the driveway beneath the dying pine tree. Her smile faltered, sagged into heavy, slack resignation.

'I realize he just found out and he had a plane to catch. But, boy, that was so sudden,' said Annie.

'We'll miss Henry,' Betty said. She could not bring herself to say anything about Kit. 'Cute little fellow.'

Miranda said simply, 'They're gone.'

Betty tried to ignore the visceral, light-headed wave of empathy. Emptiness was so unexpectedly heavy, so solid and massive. So pervasive and muffled. So hateful. 'Well,' she said, trying to shake herself out of it. 'We all must have boundaries, and we all must learn to separate. All the therapists on television agree on that. Anyway, the boys will be back soon. And L.A. is not very far away, is it?' The clatter of her own voice rang unconvincingly in her ears. 'Not in this day and age.'

'That's true, Miranda,' Annie said.

'Oh Christ, what do you know about it?' Miranda snapped. 'Either of you?'

*   *   *

When they arrived for Rosh Hashanah dinner at Lou's big house overlooking Long Island Sound, Miranda was quiet and subdued. She had barely

134

spoken a word to her mother and sister since the departure of Kit and Henry. Annie was surprised Miranda had even agreed to come with them. There had been a moment when, after coming out of her room dressed and made up and looking beautiful, if a little grim, Miranda's hand had gone to her forehead and her eyes had closed and Annie had braced herself for some sort of histrionic display. But Miranda had merely pushed her hair back, opened her eyes, and said, 'Oh, let's get it over with.' Perhaps with the real difficulties that had befallen them, Miranda had finally grown out of her stormy theatrical fits. Annie decided to take Miranda's passivity as a good sign. Yet when she stole a glance at her sister's face, colorless, expressionless, she almost wished Miranda would give a good rant, would fume and tear out her hair.

'It won't be as much fun without little Henry here,' Annie said, looking around at the crowd of senior citizens, most of whom continued to refer to themselves as middle-aged. She did miss the presence of the little boy, but she also meant to convey some kind of sympathy—although Miranda did not always appreciate sympathy from her sister, usually interpreting it as pity or criticism. 'I'll miss him.'

'You have your own children.'

'Well, yes, but . . .'

'But nothing,' Miranda said savagely, then turned on her heel and stalked off, leaving Annie and Betty nonplussed and, both, somewhat embarrassed.

A knot of people were already gathered in the living room and engaged in fervent conversation. The surgeon had complimented the cultural minister of Estonia on breaking away from the Soviet Union thereby escaping socialized medicine, because just look at Canada, to which the lawyer responded that Canada had no privacy laws. At this, the woman from the YMCA pool said that if you have nothing to hide, privacy should not be an issue. The metal sculptor pointed out that you could still live a bohemian life in Montreal, what with cheap rents and government grants, even without privacy and a falling U.S. dollar, to which the surgeon replied that a government grant would not be much solace if you had to wait six months for a knee replacement by a doctor who spoke only French, which caused the inventor to lament that French President Sarkozy's flamboyant behaviour was perhaps not as good for the Jews as he had at first hoped.

'President Bling-Bling,' Cousin Lou said, savouring the sound of the words.

'Oh, Betty!' cried Rosalyn. Seeing her cousin and suddenly reminded by the word 'bling', she waved her wrist with its heavy gold-and-emerald bracelet. 'What do you think?'

'Beautiful. Beautiful.'

'Not too much? I don't want to look gaudy. The economy is so bad, it could be offensive. I try to be sensitive to these things.'

'They're cabochon, that tones it down.'

'I'm a limousine liberal,' Lou said. 'Why not be comfortable?'

'You were always an iconoclast, dear,' said Rosalyn, patting his arm indulgently.

There was very good wine. Rosalyn had tried, in the early years, to economize by serving lesser wines to the constant flow of guests, but Lou had prevailed.

'But they're here every night,' Rosalyn had said.

'And so are we,' Lou had explained.

Rosalyn bowed to what she understood to be self-interest, but in fact Lou would have served his guests good wine even if he'd been a teetotaller. He enjoyed raising a glass of the good stuff with his guests, however, then raising another. On this Rosh Hashanah night, he held his third up to the light to watch the liquid cling to the sides as he gently swirled it. It has legs, he thought happily. Like a play that is a success. Like a showgirl. Like a table. Lou loved the English language. English was part of his American identity, and so he cherished it. He had been told that when he left a message on an answering machine, you could hear his German accent, but he dismissed that information as complete nonsense, making sure however, from that moment on, if someone did not pick up their telephone themselves, to hang up and try again later.

'Beautiful,' he murmured now, meaning the wine, its legs, the word 'legs,' legs of all kinds, the room, the people in it drinking wine, and always, the view of the water, over which an enormous harvest moon rose in slow, round orange motion.

Annie, seated on a low bench, also looked out at the moon and wondered what Frederick was doing.

'Why is he always talking to me?' Mr Shpuntov was saying in a loud angry voice. 'Why does he bother me?'

'He's your *daughter*,' Cousin Lou yelled into his ear.

Miranda, pacing nervously in front of the picture window, did not hear Mr Shpuntov or

137

Cousin Lou or Rosalyn's cry of 'Good Gawd!' Kit was gone. Henry was gone. Her little pretend family had driven away in that miniature car and boarded a plane for Los Angeles. She clenched her hands and opened them, clenched them, opened them, unaware that she was doing so. We could still be a little pretend family, she told herself. Kit could return in a week, two weeks. It was a small part, he had said so. Of course, it could be a small part that popped up frequently. He might be there for months. Who would take care of Henry? It was outrageous. A form of child abuse, really. Poor Henry, locked in a hotel room with some undocumented babysitter yakking in a foreign language on her cell phone. He would never learn to speak properly at this crucial juncture in his development. She had been online for hours last night reading about the progress of a two-year-old's speech. She would have to call Kit and explain it all to him. She checked her watch. They would be on the plane now. She hoped Kit had taken Henry's car seat on the plane and strapped him in. It was so much safer.

Miranda sat down with a small internal groan and began chewing on her thumbnail.

Betty wished Miranda wouldn't bite her nails. It was unattractive, and she was such a beautiful girl.

'That little Henry and his father were very taken with your sister,' she said to Annie, who was slumped on a bench. 'Are very taken, I should say. I wish they hadn't rushed off like that. It's lovely that Kit got some work, but Miranda seemed to be settling in to such a nice routine with them. Sit up straight, sweetheart.'

'Mmm,' Annie said. Frederick's children were

138

not very taken with her, she thought. Though they clearly revered him. Perhaps that was why they seemed so possessive. Or did it have to do with their mother? Annie never asked what had become of Mrs Frederick Barrow, but she did wonder. Had she died recently? Or was she, like Betty, dumped and destitute? What had she been like? What had she looked like? Did they still see each other? Or did he carry flowers to her grave and lie on the grass beside it and whisper to her? It was difficult to picture any of it, as she knew nothing at all about the wife and not much more about Frederick, but she pictured the two of them anyway, blurry, indistinct, far away.

It was therefore a shock when she saw her mother rushing enthusiastically away from her towards the door, through which walked a very real and sharply drawn Frederick, the very same Frederick Barrow she had been thinking about, who had just entered the room with the stern young woman Annie recognized as his daughter, Gwen, as well as a man who must have been her husband, and two little girls in matching velvet dresses.

It is too hot for velvet was Annie's first irrelevant thought, remembering many sweaty holiday dinners from her childhood. Rosh Hashanah is always too hot for velvet.

The night air swept in through the door with Frederick, Gwen, her husband, and the two pink little girls in cherry red velvet, the damp breath of the shore following them across the room like a ghost.

'New blood,' Rosalyn whispered hungrily as she hurried toward the newcomers. She frequently

139

experienced a sense of world-weary ennui with her husband's guests. Like many a collector of pottery or butterflies or vintage handbags, Rosalyn cared far more for the act of acquisition than she did for the guests in her extensive collection. Lou provided her with an ever-expanding list of names to remember and occupations to place in her own mental hierarchy, for which she was grudgingly grateful. But this new acquisition was, uncharacteristically, all her own. She had found Gwendolyn Barrow herself at a dreary evening of incomprehensible art and clannish New Yorkers at which the two bored women had fallen into a friendly discussion of Pilates versus Gyrotonic, Rosalyn coming down heavily, if such a slight and narrow person could be said to be heavy in any way, on the side of Gyrotonic, a view to which Gwen revealed she was just coming around. The two women bonded, and Rosalyn rather recklessly invited her new friend to Lou's Rosh Hashanah.

'Gwen!' she said, 'Welcome to Westport! And who are these elegant young ladies you've brought with you? They cannot be Juliet and Ophelia?' Gwen and Rosalyn had met just the one time, and Rosalyn congratulated herself on remembering the names of the twins. Her father might be lazily indulging himself in senility, she thought, but she could still hold her head up. 'It's not possible, they're so grown up . . .' she continued, her immense face tilting towards the girls.

Juliet and Ophelia looked up at her with expressions that suggested they would rather have met the fates of their famous namesakes than be standing in Rosalyn's living room beneath the looming face of Rosalyn. Then Juliet and Ophelia

140

began to cry, their little lips quivering a moment in unison before twisting into twin grimaces. They wailed in chorus, and their father squatted down and spoke earnestly to them, his face serious but deferential, as if they were tiny ambassadors from a tiny foreign land.

From her post near the glass doors to the terrace, Annie saw the family's entrance, felt the damp air. Her heart beat faster, and the heat of emotion spread across her face. She concentrated on her glass of wine, the liquid black as a deep, round pond. She waited for Frederick's voice, and when it came, beside her, saying just her name, it sounded soft and rich and aromatic.

'Your voice is like wine,' she said, looking up and smiling. 'It really is, Frederick.'

'Not demon gin?' he said. He took her hand and they stood for a moment, a very heady moment for Annie, her blood coursing through her, drowning out the sounds around her. But Frederick must have heard something, for he glanced quickly, self-consciously, at his daughter across the room, and the spell was broken.

He dropped Annie's hand awkwardly, said, 'What on earth are you doing *here*?' then looked around him as if he weren't sure what he was doing there, either. 'What a wonderful surprise!'

'Cousin Lou is my cousin,' she said.

'Cousin Lou is everybody's cousin, isn't he? Gwen heard all about him from his wife. They're great friends, I gather. After one meeting. Gwen is a terrible snob, but she's very taken with Rosalyn. Is Rosalyn a terrible snob? It's the only thing I can think of to explain this sudden friendship.'

Annie couldn't help laughing. 'But Lou's really

141

my cousin,' she insisted. 'Not by blood exactly, but he really is family.'

Frederick nodded enthusiastically. 'Right! Just what Gwennie told me—everyone is "like family".'

Annie gave up, adding only, 'Anyway, I live here now.'

'Oh, I remember now . . . the cottage, your cousin . . . So Cousin Lou is your cousin and you live in his cottage.'

She wondered if he was thinking of her apartment, of her bedroom, of her bed. If he was remembering.

'We live just down the hill.'

'By the beach, right? That's fantastic. My house is by the water.' He looked suddenly uncomfortable. He tapped his mouth unconsciously with two fingers. 'My house . . .'

'Your house . . .' she said, the way you would to encourage a child who was trying to tell a story.

'Hmm?'

'Your house? The water?'

'My house,' he said again, more to himself than to Annie. 'My house by the water. Dark and treacherous . . .'

'Your house or the water?'

'. . . Darker and more treacherous by the day . . .'

'You sound like my sister!'

'Yes, but she finds darkness and treachery beautiful.'

'And you?'

'I find it dark and treacherous . . .' He trailed off, then said, suddenly, with a rather forced grin, 'Well! Enough of that. So you're here because you live here, and I'm here because Gwennie met

142

Mrs Cousin Lou at the Whitney. They're bosom buddies.' He smiled, more pleasantly now. 'That's an expression that doesn't really work any more, does it? Pity. It conveys so much if you're a man's man of a previous century. I can't quite carry it off.'

Annie felt herself relax. She liked him, she just did. Whether Frederick wanted to remember what had happened between them or not, she did remember, and she would continue to remember— why not remember something so pleasurable? But that did not mean she would look back. At her age, she found that it was better to keep her eyes facing forward.

'Isn't Westport where Peter DeVries lived?' Frederick asked. 'I miss his presence. How does that happen, I wonder? His books still exist, they're still just as wonderful as ever, but he has no presence. Do you know what I mean?'

Annie said she did know what he meant and wondered if what he really meant was: When will I have no presence? Frederick was sixty or thereabouts. Was he feeling that shift, too, the way she was? The cresting of the hill? Down, down, down we go from here . . .

'Lucy lived in Westport,' she said, shaking herself from what was threatening to become full-blown melancholy. 'On TV after Little Ricky was born. The Man in the Grey Flannel Suit lived here, too.'

'And now you: Annie Weissmann.'

'An unbroken line of unrelated people.'

Annie began to enjoy herself. She described the nostalgia her mother and sister had expressed for the local lunatic asylum.

143

'And my sister almost drowned in a kayak and was rescued by a young actor,' she continued. They proceeded to discuss kayaks and boats in general for a while, the conversation then veering inexplicably to a shared appreciation for the actor James Mason, whom they both occasionally confused with Dirk Bogarde.

'I was once thinking about that scene, that wonderful, ghastly scene in *Death in Venice* in which Gustav von Aschenbach's makeup begins to run,' Frederick said. 'Then, days later, I realized that the entire time I had been picturing the makeup running down James Mason's face.'

From across the room came a shout: 'Dad!'

It was Frederick's son-in-law. Annie felt a stab of pity for Frederick: his son-in-law called him 'Dad.'

I often think about Gustav von Aschenbach when I put on my own makeup, she thought, though she might have said it aloud, for Frederick stared at her.

'Dad! There you are,' said Frederick's daughter, arriving beside them with her husband and little girls. 'Oh, hello,' Gwen added hastily to Annie. 'You're the librarian, aren't you? Ann, is it? How nice to see you here of all places.' Gwen was holding one daughter who chewed dreamily on a cracker.

'Of all places,' Annie repeated.

'This is Ron, my son-in-law, and this small person,' Frederick said, reaching for the child, 'is Ophelia.'

Annie shook Ophelia's sticky hand. 'Pretty dress,' she said.

'Hot,' said Ophelia.

Betty was watching the little group with interest. She was happy that Frederick had come to see Annie. Had Annie invited him? It was not like Annie to go out of her way in quite such a public manner, to show her hand. She must really like the novelist with the sparkly eyes and mellifluous voice. If my children can be happy, I will be happy, Betty thought, squaring her shoulders, though what she felt was the same simmering anger and confusion as always.

'I heard about Joseph,' a man next to her said.

She tried to recover herself and remember who he was, gazing with fascinated revulsion at his meaty lips while the general conversation of the people standing around her washed over them.

'Marty,' Betty said, finally remembering the man with the liver-colored lips was Cousin Lou's accountant. 'Hello.'

'I'm so sorry about what happened,' he said.

He was eating a piece of dark orange cheese. She noticed it left a narrow oily trail on his lip, like a snail.

'You need a good lawyer, Betty. A shark. I'll give you a name.'

'Talk to Annie, Marty dear. I'm in mourning.'

'Yeah. They say that's one of the stages, right?'

'I don't believe in stages,' Betty said.

'It's not a religion, Mom,' her younger daughter said, coming up beside Betty. And because Marty looked a little hurt and her voice had accidentally emerged with a far too haughty timbre, Betty forced herself to smile at Marty and his odious snail-slimed lip.

'Thank you,' she said, taking his hand, administering a short shake and releasing it, as if she were in a receiving line. 'Thank you for your kind words.'

'Shark,' he said, repeating the kind word as he went away.

'Dear God,' Betty said.

'Who was that?' Miranda asked.

Roberts was a step or two behind her.

'Lou's accountant. He said I needed a shark divorce lawyer.'

'A forensic accountant is more like it,' Roberts said. 'I'm sorry,' he added when Betty did not reply. 'None of my business.' And he hurried off.

Forensic accountant. As a recently converted and loyal member of the daytime television audience, Betty had seen numerous reruns of numerous crime shows and wondered if a forensic accountant was a CSI for divorces. A divorce was surely a kind of death: a murder, in fact. It was the memories, so stubbornly happy and lifeless and useless, stinking with decay, that lay in a putrid heap like a rotting corpse. If only the memories *were* a corpse, Betty thought, and could be buried under six feet of clotted dirt. But they never *really* died, did they? They wandered through her thoughts and her heart like scabby zombies. A forensic accountant could never find the murderer if he couldn't even discover the dead body. It was better on television. 'I like the one with the bugs,' she said out loud.

'What?'

'I don't like the one with the sunglasses.'

'What are you talking about, Mother?'

'Television.'

'I have a migraine,' Miranda said. She stared at Frederick Barrow's granddaughters and felt angry.

146

Betty put the back of her hand on her daughter's forehead. 'Do you have a fever? Do you want to go home? Do you have that medicine? The kind you roll onto your forehead? Maybe you'll feel better if you lie down.'

Miranda pulled away from her mother's hand.

'Who is that young woman leading Frederick away from Annie?' Betty asked. 'Is that his little doxy?'

'That's his daughter, Mother.'

'Well, thank God for daughters,' Betty said, giving Miranda's arm a squeeze. 'But, I mean, really.' And she departed, pulled open the sliding glass door, and stood in the dark, moist air to brood in peace about Joseph and his irreconcilable differences.

*   *   *

At the same time that Betty retreated to the outdoors, Miranda saw Roberts coming toward her again. She gulped down the rest of her Scotch and headed for the bar to refill. Doddery old lawyer— was everyone here two years old or a hundred and one? Roberts wasn't really doddering, to be fair: he had a steady gait; he was tall and straight and had the pleasantly browned, pleasantly leathery skin of someone who spends a lot of time outdoors. He was rather distinguished-looking. A thin beakish nose, the kind that could be acquiline and English or acquiline and Italian or just Jewish. And he had a pretty mouth. Betty had pointed that out—how his mouth was soft and so different from the rest of his face. But Miranda was in no mood to appreciate his handsome mouth or relative good

147

health. Her head was throbbing and her heart was breaking.

Roberts stood beside her and refilled his wineglass. Seeing no escape, Miranda gave a wan smile.

'Is everything all right?' he asked. 'Your mother . . .'

'She's in mourning. It's very tiring for her.'

'I like your mother. She's kind of indefatigable. But I suppose even she has to give in now and then. Age is exhausting sometimes, exhausting if you hold it at bay, more exhausting if you give in. My mother used to say you have to be brave to get old.' He stopped, as if his flow of words surprised him as much as it did Miranda. 'Not that your mother is old, of course,' he added. 'I was thinking more of myself.'

'Oh, you're as young as springtime,' Miranda said politely, though she was thinking he had to be seventy if he was a day. And how dreary of him to speak about aging, as if it were synonymous with living. The image of Kit, young and shining with curiosity and hope, his vibrant child at his side, shot into her thoughts almost painfully.

Roberts laughed. 'I've seen a few springtimes, anyway,' he said. 'You, on the other hand, look wonderful. I heard what happened that day you went out kayaking, and I admit I was worried about you. I feel a little responsible. I never should have let you go out on such a rough day.'

Miranda wondered if the semiretired lawyer had taken a wee drop too much. Never had she heard such a flow of words emanate from his, admittedly—give the devil his due, as Josie always said—lovely lips. 'You're so sweet,' she said, thinking, Go away, geezer, please. 'But first of all, you couldn't have stopped me. No one can stop me, I'm an absolute nightmare. And, as it turned out, it was a lucky day after all. My kayaking adventure brought us a new friend—Kit Maybank. Have you met him? Kit rescued me from certain near-death. He's an actor. He was supposed to be here, but he just got a part in a film and had to leave. He's extremely talented.' She found that once she mentioned Kit, she had a hard time leaving the subject. 'He has a child, a beautiful little boy named Henry . . .'

'Ah,' Roberts said in his quiet voice.

'Henry,' Miranda repeated, almost belligerently, as if Roberts had snubbed the boy. 'Henry looks just like his father.'

Roberts mumbled something inaudible and retreated into his customary silence.

*   *   *

As they filed into the dining room, Frederick held one of his rosy granddaughters on his shoulders. The little girl began drumming on his head and singing in a high wail that carried surprisingly well across the large room, then was seated beside her sister, the two of them lolling in their chairs, their heads tilted back, their tongues hanging from their mouths.

Annie was on the other side of the long table, towards the head, sitting in what she hoped was quiet, self-contained dignity. She could sense Frederick across from her, near the foot of the table, but she did not look up to see. If he had not been intimate when they spoke, he had been warm.

149

But at the arrival of Gwen and her entourage, he had become suddenly quite solemn and had melted away with them as if he had never been there at all.

'You shouldn't have,' she heard him say, and looked up to see one of the girls—Annie could not tell if it was Juliet or Ophelia, or Medea, for that matter, she thought irritably—press a honey-soaked piece of challah into his hand.

Miranda came up behind him and pointed to the empty chair beside Annie.

Annie quickly looked away.

'There's a seat beside Annie,' Miranda said shrilly to Frederick. 'Go, go!' She put her hand in the small of his back and gave him a little shove.

What is wrong with her? Annie thought, coloring.

What is wrong with him? Miranda wondered. *Carpe diem, carpe, carpe, carpe!* she wanted to cry out. She felt quite heroic, facilitating her sister's romance when she herself was so leaden and alone. She had checked her cell phone several times, retreating to the powder room to do so, but Kit had not so much as texted her. Of course, he was still on the plane, she knew that, but that did not make her sense of abandonment any less painful. She would have thought he could send her just a few words from the airport before he left, or email a picture of Henry strapped into his seat. She longed to check her phone again, but would have to wait until they were sitting down. Then she would surreptitiously remove it from her jacket pocket, hold it on her lap, and glance at it, the way Annie's boys were always doing, the way she had done when she still had a real life with real work.

The thought of her smashed career came back, after leaving her alone for the last few peaceful weeks, searing and bitter, rising like bile. Furious, she nudged Frederick again. If she had lost everything and everyone, then at least Annie should have her novelist.

Frederick hesitated, then murmured that he ought to stay close to his granddaughters, and slid into the nearest chair. Juliet and Ophelia, the smocking of their red velvet dresses now smeared with a layer of golden honey that was studded with yellow challah crumbs, smiled at Miranda and licked their fingers.

In the background Annie heard a man's voice, a singsong voice mottled with static. It was Rosalyn's father, Mr Shpuntov. He was in his room now, his words reaching the dining room through the intercom that had been installed to keep track of him and was kept on at all times.

'He sold bananas,' said the voice. 'Hung them in the basement to ripen. Have you ever seen bananas in the Bronx, Mr Eight-o-seven? A basement full of bananas in the Bronx . . .'

Mr Eight-o-seven? Annie looked at her watch. Ah. Mr Shpuntov was telling stories to the clock.

*   *   *

'It was wonderful seeing all of you ladies,' Frederick said to Annie and Miranda and Betty at the end of the evening.

Miranda looked at him scornfully.

'Oh dear! Mother!' she then said. 'Mr Shpuntov is drinking the dregs.' And she purposefully dragged her mother off to stop Rosalyn's father in

151

his procession down one side of the table and then up the other, raising half-finished glasses of wine to his lips and draining them.

But she saw, as she relieved Mr Shpuntov of a goblet, that Frederick had not lingered to exchange an intimate goodbye with Annie as Miranda had hoped. He had simply nodded his head, said, 'Well, bye,' turned on his heel, and walked out the door to wait while Gwen held up the girls, one by one, to be kissed by Cousin Lou.

'What was wrong with Frederick?' she asked Annie as they walked home.

'How do you mean?'

'How do I mean? You know perfectly well how I mean. He was so odd and cold and standoffish.'

'Frederick was perfectly pleasant,' Annie said. But in her room, later, she silently echoed her sister's words: What was wrong with Frederick?

CHAPTER ELEVEN

The mornings came later, and the air grew colder. The beauty of Westport shrank and drew back from the eye. What had been lush and green was stalky and irrelevant. Where the roads had been lined with trees swaying in the breeze there were now just bare, rigid trunks. Behind them, stripped of their leafy veils, colossal façades of houses meant to look like mansions were revealed to resemble nothing so much as the better chains of New England motor inns. Annie surreptitiously phoned the professor subletting her apartment to see if he might want to leave early, which he did not. Betty stood for hours staring out her bedroom window, her widow's walk, and mused bitterly that she was neither walking nor a widow, yet there she was, in Westport, in purgatory. And Miranda? She was quiet, quieter than the other two had ever seen her.

Miranda knew she was making a sullen spectacle of herself, but she didn't seem to be able to stop. It was very much like having a tantrum—she felt that herself. There was that same fatigued momentum. But she could not talk to either her mother or her sister about Kit and Henry, and Kit and Henry were all she could think about. Sometimes she felt herself storing up affection for them, hiding it, protecting it, like a squirrel burying nuts. It was a kind of treasure, this burrowed cache of emotional heat and urgency. Other times, she felt herself losing them, as if they were long dead and she could no longer remember their features.

What the hell had happened? She felt again the shiver beneath her hand as Kit drew back, on the day he left, like a horse who'd been spooked.

*   *   *

Annie's emotional schedule took on an almost heartening regularity: days of work, nights of worry, mornings of icy aquatic contemplation leading nowhere. On one of these faded, dun-colored mornings, Annie was slapping through the icy water of Long Island Sound, engaged in her morning swim. The clarity of the cold, the obscurity of the dark water, the sincerity of true solitude: these were things she cherished. As she lost herself in the rhythm of her exertion, as she exhaled into the freezing water, then turned her face to the sky and gulped in the dawn air, she worried about money and her mother's manic widowhood and Miranda's sullen silence; then, what she always somehow came around to thinking about was Frederick. She recalled his appreciative laugh at some remark she had made, the remark itself lost, the laugh clear and ringing in her memory. His eyes, dark and mischievous, looked into her eyes, and they were full of feeling. Or were they? Had she misread his eyes, his feelings? Had she gotten it so wrong? No. No, in spite of the fact that he had not called, in spite of his cool treatment of her on Rosh Hashanah, in spite of this, in spite of that, Annie was somehow sure she had been right about him. Of course, it made no difference. Right or wrong, the facts remained the same: he hadn't called, he had treated her with mere civility the last time they met, he was as far from her as if he had never had any feelings at all.

Miranda had stopped teasing her about Frederick, which was both a relief and a morbid confirmation of her own conviction that the affair was indeed over. But Miranda was so uncommunicative about everything lately. Her new reticence was just as showy as everything Miranda did, Annie thought irritably.

*   *   *

Inside the cottage, Miranda sat in the kitchen, her arms resting on the table. She held a large orange in her hands. She stared at it.

'Honey,' Betty said, shuffling in and standing behind her. She watched her daughter listlessly roll

154

the orange back and forth from one hand to the other. 'Honey, maybe you need a hobby.'

Miranda laughed. 'A nobby?' It was part of a joke Josie used to like, about retirement.

An old man who's just retired to Florida asks another old guy, 'How do you stand it? After two days already I'm bored.'

'Simple,' says the guy in a heavy Yiddish accent. 'I have a nobby.'

'A nobby?' says the first old man. 'What's a nobby?'

'A nobby, a nobby—like collecting stemps.'

'You collect stamps?' the first one asks.

'Stemps? No. I keep *bees.* In mine condo.'

He takes the newcomer up the elevator, into his condo, takes a shoe box from the closet, and lifts the lid. 'There!'

'But they're all dead! This is just a box full of dead bees! What kind of a beekeeper are you?'

'Hey,' says the guy. 'It's just a nobby.'

'Want me to keep bees, Mother?'

'If it would make you happy,' Betty said. She paused. 'Would it?'

'I'm okay,' Miranda said, and turned back to the orange, making it clear the interview was over. The citrus scent drifted up. She waited for the thud of the newspaper on the muddy drive, then went out to lift the gritty blue plastic bag and carry it inside. By the time Annie returned in her lumpy wet suit and showered and dressed for work, Miranda had riffled through all the sections.

'I wish you wouldn't always crumple it up like that,' Annie said, picking up sheets of the *Times* and smoothing them out.

'Just get another paper at the station if you don't

155

like it.'

'Typical.'

'Of what?'

'Now, girls,' Betty said abstractedly. But her heart wasn't in it, and Annie and Miranda, sensing it wasn't, scowled at each other like spoiled children until it was time for Miranda to drive Annie to the station. They left their mother staring blankly out the window, holding a coffee mug against her cheek, where her sinuses hurt.

'I'm sorry,' Annie forced herself to say when they got in the car. 'It's just a newspaper. I'm too old to act like this.' She did not add that Miranda was also too old. 'I've lived alone too long.'

'You?' Miranda said. 'What about me? Talk about living alone too long . . .'

Annie felt sororal rage rising. Was she not even able to apologize, to apologize so delicately, without it becoming a competition? *'Green,'* she said in retaliation, when the traffic light turned and Miranda did not instantly gun the engine.

Miranda dropped her sister at the station, roared off in the noisy old Mercedes to the parking lot at Compo Beach, then walked along the road in the gloom until she reached Burying Hill beach. She did this every day. It would have been easier to drop Annie at the Greenfield Hill station, which was so much closer to Burying Hill, but she did not want Annie or anyone else to know where she was headed. She stared eastward, in the direction of Kit Maybank's aunt's house. It made her feel closer to Henry and Kit somehow, as if they were just around that rocky bit of coast ahead. She had called Kit several times. Once, she even spoke to Henry. Then Kit stopped answering her calls.

156

Miranda had emailed him and gotten a quick, apologetic note in response—so busy, just impossible, soon . . . Of course, she had not heard from him again. It was as if Kit, and so Henry, had dropped off the face of the earth, her earth at least. She wondered who was looking after Henry. Kit had said one of his college roommates had a nanny who had a cousin. This didn't sound reassuring to Miranda. Poor Henry. She had offered to come to L.A. to look after him, but Kit had not really taken her suggestion seriously. And so they were gone, beyond her reach, out of earshot and out of sight, and she was here gazing eastward in the early November drizzle.

'Hi,' someone said, coming up beside her.

Miranda jumped, hoping for a fraction of an instant that it was Kit, then stared at Roberts as if she didn't recognize him.

'Sorry. I didn't mean to startle you. But it's really starting to rain. Can I give you a ride home?' he asked, looking back at the beach's parking lot and seeing Miranda's car was not there. 'Or did you paddle here in your trusty kayak?'

Miranda did not smile. She could not summon the social will on this her private, solitary walk. She just managed to mutter a thank you and decline the offer.

'I like to walk,' she said.

'Okay,' said Roberts.

After that morning, she would occasionally run into Roberts, who also seemed to like to walk. He never presumed to join her, for which she was grateful. He would pass her, going in the other direction, or come upon her as she stood silently admiring some sombre moment of landscape. And

157

he would incline his head in greeting. No more. Yet even that she found intrusive and jarring. Although she knew she was being unreasonable, she often varied the time of her walks in order to avoid him.

It did not help that he found his way to the cottage now and then for dinner. He's certainly made himself at home, she thought as she came in one evening and found him mulling wine in the kitchen.

'Doesn't the house smell delicious?' Betty said.

Annie threw Miranda an anxious glance. She hoped her sister would not insult Roberts. He stood at the stove looking so proud of his concoction. She moved toward him protectively, and stood beside him, as if her presence could shield him from the cold indifference of her sister.

Miranda sniffed the sweetened air and could not help but smile.

Relieved, Annie took a mug from Roberts. She wondered why Miranda thought he was so old. He was probably in his mid-, possibly late sixties, she realized. His face was creased, but not from age. It was a hearty, weather-beaten face. Miranda's aversion to him was a mystery to Annie. And an irritant. He was so much more suitable than Kit Maybank. It enraged Annie that Miranda was mourning so ostentatiously for someone who had treated her so badly.

*　　　*　　　*

'Roberts is such a lovely man. And, by the way, I am very disappointed in Kit Maybank,' Betty said to Annie that night when Roberts had gone and

Miranda was out taking a final solitary walk. 'Has she heard from him at all?'

Annie shrugged. Miranda had certainly not confided in her. 'Maybe he'll come back for Thanksgiving to spend it with his aunt. But, Mother, I don't think we should make too much of this friendship. I mean, Miranda has her enthusiasms, that's what makes her Miranda, but she's about to turn fifty, for God's sake. She can't just keep pining for, well, you know, a kid half her age.'

'You're so literal-minded, Annie. She isn't pining for *Kit*. I mean, really! She's not a teenager.'

'That's what I just said. That's my point.'

'You and your points,' Betty said indulgently. 'Anyway, it's the child she wants. I would have thought that was obvious, poor thing.'

Not for the first time, Annie wondered at her mother's acuity. And at her own lack of it.

*   *   *

Ever since they had come to Westport, a little over three months ago, Miranda and Annie had been avoiding Josie's calls. At first, when they were still willing to speak to him, they had tried to point out the error of his ways. He had answered that this was how things had to be, in a tone of such firm resignation that he might just as easily have been saying it was God's will.

'The roof leaks,' Miranda screamed into her cell phone. 'There are mouse droppings on the sunporch.'

'You've beggared our mother, your wife,' Annie yelled into her office phone. 'Have you no shame?'

'Josie, you have to help her,' they both pleaded. 'If you really understood what was going on, you wouldn't do this. Please let Mommy come home.'

After a while they realized that Josie did not want to understand what was going on, and they stopped calling him. They stopped answering his calls, as well. It had been months since either of them had heard his voice on anything but an answering machine.

Then Betty informed them that there was a standing lamp in the apartment that she absolutely had to have. Annie pointed out that there was no room in the cramped and cluttered cottage for another lamp. Miranda said Josie had probably sold the lamp anyway. But a few days later, Miranda and Annie found themselves driving their mother's old car into the city to pick up the lamp. It was Annie who had finally agreed to call Josie at his office to arrange the time.

'Josie? It's Annie.'

'I know it's you, honey. How many people call me that?'

Annie thought she heard a catch in his voice. Do not weaken, she told herself.

'I've been calling you,' Josie said, his voice hurt.

'I know.' She glanced at the three pink memos with his name on them sitting on her desk.

'Well, never mind. Now you've called me back. How are you girls? How's your mother?'

'Look, I just need to get into the apartment. Mom wants the standing lamp from the bedroom.' Annie hesitated, then said, 'From *her* bedroom.'

There was silence.

'Josie?'

'Okay. Right. I'll have Ozzie bring it down for

160

you. Any day you say.'

Ozzie was the handyman. Annie wondered if Ozzie missed her mother.

'That's okay,' she said. 'I have a key. I just wanted to let you know.'

'Mmm,' Josie said. 'Well, actually, I had the locks changed.'

Annie said, 'What?' but she had heard him.

'It just seemed prudent,' he said.

'Jesus, Josie.'

'I know.'

'Prudent? Jesus.'

Then neither of them said anything. And neither one hung up.

'I'm sorry, honey,' Josie finally murmured. 'I'm so sorry.'

Annie was in her office. It was a small room in the back of the building on the ground floor. There was a window that faced a wall covered with ivy. The window needed to be washed. Her back was aching. She hadn't gone swimming in a week. It was getting too cold, even with a wet suit. Maybe tomorrow she would go to the Y. She thought these things, noticed the shaft of thin city light that slanted in through the window and landed on her desk, but what she really thought was *Oh, Josie. Josie, how could you?*

'When are you coming?' he asked.

'Saturday.'

'Right. Okay.'

'Okay.'

'Okay.'

Annie thought, This is the man who brought me up, the man who was a father to me.

'Look, have dinner with me, okay?' Josie said.

'You and Miranda?'

Annie was about to say no when he added in a truly pathetic voice, 'Please?'

*　　　*　　　*

Now she and Miranda were driving into the city to pick up a useless lamp and have dinner with a useless father-manqué.

'I hate him,' Miranda said. 'Why are we doing this?'

'Beats me. I weakened, I guess. His voice . . . it was heartbreaking.'

'Hmmph.' Miranda crossed her arms and held them against her chest, pouting. 'I think men are big babies.'

'Infantile grandiosity. I've always liked the sound of that. Rolls off the tongue.'

'But real children aren't grandiose. They're actually grand. Look at Henry, for example.'

Annie pictured Henry on the floor of the living room, four adults gazing adoringly at him as he pushed a car in circles. She remembered, too, a moment later in that same day. Henry had fallen asleep with Betty on the couch. Kit and Miranda, returning from a walk, had just come up the battered cement steps, leaving the door from the outside to the sunporch open. Annie was at the window facing the sunporch, picking dead roses from a bunch Kit had brought them a week earlier, and she was just aware of them, in the corner of her vision. They stood, one on each side of the door. Kit put out his hand and touched Miranda on the shoulder, a gentle, single, petting motion, like the soft swat of a cat. And they had both

162

laughed softly and privately.

Annie wished she had not witnessed this scene. It meant that much more worry. She had always worried about Miranda. Even when Miranda was riding high, Annie had kept an eye on her younger sister. It was a remnant of childhood—a wariness of her sister, who demanded so much and seemed to devour the bulk of their parents' attention. It was also a source of power for Annie, a self-protective self-importance that translated into an almost prim protectiveness of Miranda. She had understood this even as a little girl. If Annie did not look after Miranda, what other role was there for her? Only resentment, and resentment was such an uncomfortable sentiment. Annie loved Miranda, found her impossible not to love, and very early on she had discovered a way to love her with dignity: worry.

Such good friends, Annie told herself when she saw Kit and Miranda that day from the sunporch. Friends, she thought again, trying to convince herself. And then, unable to hold out against her own eyes, the admission: lovers. She'd felt suddenly envious of Miranda and sorry for her all at once.

But as soon as Kit and Miranda came into the living room, it was as if the handsome young man at her side vanished. Miranda stood before the sofa, her face, that lively, determined face, shifting, suddenly and beautifully. A transformation, Annie thought at the time. Peace, she thought. Miranda at peace. And she had followed her sister's gaze, an almost palpable emanation of simple, complete happiness, to its destination, a small child, blinking, sucking his thumb, his pretty mouth

163

curling in a smile around his little fist.

'How is little Henry, anyway?' Annie asked now as they drove against the shimmer of the setting sun.

Miranda said nothing.

Perhaps she had not heard. Annie glanced at her silent sister, profiled against the window, her sunglasses hiding her eyes.

Impassive, wordless, Miranda turned to face the window and the passing prickly November woods beyond.

Annie did not repeat the question.

Josie was meeting them at a tiny bistro they had all liked 'when the family was intact', as Miranda put it. 'He could have chosen a more neutral place.'

'I don't think he wants to be neutral.'

'Fat chance,' Miranda said.

'That he can be or that he wants to be?'

'I don't know, Annie. Why do you always have to make so much sense? You know what I mean.'

And Annie, after a moment of reflexive annoyance, had to admit that, yes, she did know exactly what her sister meant.

Josie had not yet arrived, but their table was ready, their usual table; he must have requested it, for the restaurant was busy. They sat and waited, neither of them sure what her feelings were. Then he walked in, and they were overcome by waves of love, embarrassment, and penetrating anger.

He looked older and younger at the same time. What is that about? Annie wondered. She had not seen him in months, and here he was, her Josie, smaller somehow, grayer, thinner, but his step was so jaunty, the way he moved his arms, so light and

164

carefree. How dare he be carefree when her mother could barely walk beneath her load of care?

'I miss you girls,' he said.

'Whose fault is that?' Miranda said.

Joseph stared at his two daughters, his little girls. Miranda sat with crossed arms, her lower lip jutting out, the way she had when she was truly a little girl. She glared at him, which was on the whole less unsettling than Annie, who did not even look at him. Oh, what had he done? His whole life was gone, just like that. Betty was gone, Betty and her picnics. It had been their joke, that she turned everything into a picnic. She turned everything into an outing, even a trip to the motor vehicles bureau to turn in the license plates of their old car. Oh, we'll go together, she had said. Let's go to the one downtown! We'll take a walk along the water, see the ships like the tourists. It's not a picnic, he had said, as he so often did. They could have had such a nice old age, an old age full of unlikely picnics. But picnics were old-fashioned entertainments, and he wasn't ready for his old age. Felicity had reached down a firm young hand and fished him out of that murky bog.

'I don't think it's legal to lock Mom out of the apartment,' Annie said. 'And if it is legal, it's not ethical, Josie. It really isn't.'

'But your mother agreed to it,' Joseph said. 'I discussed it with her.'

'I beg your pardon?' Annie was really shocked. Betty had never mentioned it.

'What possessed her to do that?' Miranda said. 'And why do you want the locks changed anyway? It's not like we're going in there to ransack the place. The place that is her home, by the way.'

'Oh,' Joseph said vaguely. 'It's just protocol. Anyway, I'm living there, and I need my privacy. I'm entitled to my privacy, aren't I?' He looked at them, hurt.

'Well, you're entitled, anyway,' Miranda muttered.

'I just want to have a nice dinner,' he said. 'That's all. A nice dinner.'

They had always come to this restaurant for their birthdays, ever since Annie was ten years old and Miranda eight. It was a grown-up restaurant, and they were each allowed a sip of wine.

'A bottle?' Josie said. 'White, right?'

Yes, white wine, Josie, Annie thought. They would come with their mother and settle into their seats, order their pretend cocktails with jolly red cherries floating on top. Then the doors of the restaurant would fly open and there would be Josie, his overcoat and briefcase, artefacts from that exalted, distant place, the office. And he would bring Annie a bouquet of anemones for her birthday, white roses for Miranda. The waiter would fetch a pitcher of water, and the flowers would adorn the table, bright and important.

What would Josie do this year? Send flowers? Forget that he had ever gotten the anemones and roses? Either way, it would be heartbreaking.

Next to Annie, Miranda sighed, wiped away a tear. 'Fuck,' she said softly.

The food came and the girls picked at their *moules frites*.

'That's your favorite,' he reminded them. He felt sick and barely touched his steak. He ordered another bottle of wine and wondered what he

166

could do to make them understand. It was something that had just happened. One day he had been laughing at one of Betty's comments, walking to Columbus Avenue to get Tasti D-Lite with her, the next he was so in love with Felicity he could hardly speak. He had fallen in love in a way he could barely credit, a heart-pounding, urgent, hopeless way. If they really loved him, these daughters of his, they would rejoice for him, rejoice with him. I am reborn, he wanted to cry out. He wanted to drink champagne and celebrate. He wanted Miranda and Annie to join him in a toast. A toast to life. His life.

But he looked at the girls, and he saw he would have to drink that toast alone. They loved their mother and he had hurt her. But he loved their mother, too. That's what they didn't get. He noted that it was much easier for him to say, even to think, that he loved her when he referred to her as 'their mother', rather than Betty, but he did love her, their mother. He would always love their mother. But things change.

He sighed, and both girls glared at him. Well, he didn't really expect them to forgive him. Not in this lifetime. They were hurt, they were angry. Fine. He got it.

'I understand that you're angry,' he said. 'I'm not a fool. And I'm not perfect. I understand that, too. But I love you both, and I'll always be here for you.'

His voice was shaking with emotion. There were tears in his eyes.

Annie shook her head in disbelief. Was he kidding? 'You threw our mother onto the street,' she said loudly. 'With no money. None. Do you

167

understand that, too?'

Joseph looked nervously at the surrounding diners.

'Look,' he said, lowering his voice. 'There are steps. Steps you take. You know . . . in a'—he lowered his voice even more—'divorce.'

'You can't even say the word? Divorce. Divorce, divorce. Ugly cruel mean-spirited divorce. There. Okay? Clear?'

Annie's face was hard and furious. Joseph glared at her. She had always been so sensible, a calm, rational person—like him. But being reasonable obviously had a cold side to it, too.

Miranda, on the other hand—there had never been anything reasonable or cold about her. She was a flurry of impetuous emotion. She understood love. So he tried his other daughter, he tried Miranda: 'It's just unavoidable, honey. I can't help it. It doesn't mean I don't love you both.' He attempted a conspiratorial smile. 'It will all work out in the end.' That was Miranda's saying, her mantra.

'You think so?' Miranda said.

She pushed her chair back violently as she stood up.

The wrath of women, he thought. There was a downside to heat, it seemed, as well as cold. They could all go to hell. He watched Miranda's napkin, which she had thrown from her lap, falling like a white gliding gull. He heard the clatter of Annie's chair echoing Miranda's. He heard his daughters' footsteps. A waiter's hand reached down and whisked the napkin off the floor. When he looked up, Miranda and Annie were gone and he was alone.

One morning shortly after the disastrous dinner with Joseph, Betty waited until both Miranda and Annie arrived at the breakfast table before surprising them with the news that she had received an offer from Joseph's lawyer the evening before.

'You mean our dinner with Josie did some good?' Miranda asked. 'I knew it would!'

'Thank God,' Annie said. 'It's about time he stepped up to the plate.'

'Yes,' Betty said. 'Of course, I can't possibly accept it.' She shook her head sadly. 'Generous as Joseph is being . . . Well, it's just that he's offered a settlement of three hundred thousand dollars.'

'Oh brother,' Annie said.

'Over ten years.'

'That's a joke, right?' Miranda said. Then she added thoughtfully, 'Except you still have the apartment. That must be what he's thinking. You could sell it and invest, what, three million dollars? Even in this market. And live really comfortably. Not the way you've been living, but . . .'

'Oh no, dear, the three hundred thousand dollars paid over ten years would be his payment for my share of the apartment. Now that is a decent return on my five-thousand-dollar investment, I guess, although it has been almost fifty years. However, there's an argument to be made for it, I'm sure. But I just don't feel comfortable having Joseph live there with that woman.'

Annie and Miranda stood dumbfounded.

169

'That woman?' Miranda said after a long, uncomfortable silence. '*What* woman?'

'Vivacity?' Betty said, looking thoughtful. 'Something like that. Joseph's middle-aged young woman. Capacity! That's it.'

Miranda and Annie never did learn how their mother found out about Felicity. She never mentioned the incident. She had said her piece, made her decision, and the subject of how she learned of the intruder need never be raised. It had been a shock to her when she had called Joseph at the apartment the night before and the woman who worked in his office answered. Betty had recognized the voice—it was quite distinctive, a high, strong voice still carrying a trace of Boston. She saw the woman's face in her imagination, a pale, heart-shaped face with sharp but not unpleasant features and big, unnerving, round blue eyes. She heard the woman's confusion when she recognized Betty's voice. And she knew. She had known all along, she realized. She had known all along.

'Is Joseph in?' she asked.

'Joe!' she heard the woman call.

Joe. It was as if Joseph had cut off not only half his name but half his life. Her half.

'Betty!' he said. 'What a surprise.'

'I won't do it, Josie,' she said, using the children's name for him.

'Won't do what?' he asked.

But she knew he understood.

'Life is not a picnic,' she said. 'You were right about that.' And she hung up.

CHAPTER TWELVE

In the following weeks, it was as if the spirit of the three women had faded with the leaves. It rained day after day, and with the bad weather, the cottage began to feel as small and damp and rundown as it was. Miranda forced herself to make useless phone calls and write useless letters to people in the world of publishing who would have preferred to forget she ever existed. Annie slid into an ennui of routine, terrified that the order of this methodical, meaningless existence would turn out to be her future as far as the eye could see. Betty tried to cheer them up by claiming they were all suffering from cabin fever, a term redolent of the pioneering West, yet even she had to admit the days were long and tempers were short in the Weissmann household. She ordered an infomercial triangular sponge on a stick called the 'Point 'n Paint' and began to slather her bedroom walls a modish but vaguely funereal gray.

It was at this time, when the weather was dismal and the sky dingy and mean, that Cousin Lou and Rosalyn made their yearly migration to Palm Springs, bringing a peevish Mr Shpuntov along with them. Betty and her daughters stood in the light rain beneath their umbrellas as the Cousin Lous, as everyone called that family, followed a large number of suitcases into the Escalade and decamped for the dry, sunny heat of California, where Lou and Rosalyn had a house on a golf course.

'The desert beckons,' Rosalyn said from the car

as her cousins stood in the driveway beneath their umbrellas. She threw the three women a magnanimous kiss. 'We must follow the sun!'

'That's French for "So long, suckers!"' cried Cousin Lou.

Mr Shpuntov, his voice harsh and unnaturally high, said, 'What's going on? What's going on here?' He was in the front seat beside the ancient driver, a retired police officer, who would bring the car back and lock it up in the garage. The retired police officer's hand trembled as he adjusted the rearview mirror. Annie wondered if it wouldn't be safer to let Mr Shpuntov drive.

'You'll have to visit,' Lou was saying.

'Of course, our house there is much smaller,' Rosalyn quickly added.

'Always room for family,' Lou said, and the car backed down the long driveway.

The Cousin Lous planned to be gone until April. To her surprise, Annie found that she missed them. The dinners at their house had often been tedious, it was true. And after a long day at work and a bumpy commute home, making small talk was the last thing she wanted to do. She looked forward to getting into her pajamas and watching *American Idol* or *Project Runway* or the show about the family with dwarfism. Annie had never been a social person, and over the years she had gotten used to filling up the blanks of her evenings. But surprisingly quickly she had also gotten used to Lou and Rosalyn's dinners. Now her cousins were gone, and the nights in the cottage were long and disagreeable. She stayed in town to have dinner with friends once a week or so, but she didn't like to leave Betty and Miranda too much.

172

Her mother and her sister both seemed so fragile, so bare, stripped of everything that had given them joy, like two gray brittle branches rattled by the wintry beach winds.

*   *   *

In New York, Joseph walked from his apartment to the office in the morning, from the office to the apartment in the evening, every day just as he had always done, except now, Felicity walked beside him. She was such a vigorous woman, breathing in the cold air with such determination, exhaling like a thoroughbred about to thunder down the track. Just standing next to her on the elevator thrilled Joseph. His routine was no longer routine. The elevator man who had gathered him up from his apartment for decades now gathered him up with this sturdy little blonde by his side. Good morning, Mr Weissmann, the elevator man said, as he always had. But it was all different now. All new. Good morning, Miss Barrow, the elevator man added.

Felicity had formally moved into the Central Park West apartment a few weeks before Betty's call. On her first proprietary tour, she saw that the sofa from the study and the chairs and coffee table from the living room were gone and said, 'I hope all that furniture won't be a burden for poor Betty, out there in her cozy little hideout.' She walked through the rooms noting empty spaces and lighter patches on the walls that told of former household treasures now relocated to Connecticut. 'So much *stuff*,' she said. 'Material things . . . people get so attached . . .' She wandered into the kitchen, opening and closing drawers. 'Still, I *don't* think taking the silver was a good idea. There's absolutely no security in those little beach places.'

They had come straight from the office, and it was six o'clock. She pulled out the bottle of Scotch and thought, I am giving Joseph his drink in our apartment. She filled a glass with ice. 'Lucky Betty, living in a resort,' she said as she handed Joseph his drink. She rubbed his tense, tired shoulders. 'A permanent vacation. Not like us wage slaves!' Then she laughed and settled in next to Joseph on the living room sofa, which Betty had, remarkably, left behind. That beach cottage must be the size of Versailles, she thought, judging from how few things remained in the apartment.

'Here we are,' Joseph said. He put his arm around her. Here we are, he thought uncomfortably. Here we are.

'Home at last,' said Felicity. She turned her round blue eyes to his.

Unblinking, Joseph thought. He kissed her head. She was a tough little nut. 'Here we are,' he said again, more cheerfully.

*   *   *

'She started out being pretty reasonable,' he told Felicity the night Betty called. Why had Felicity answered the phone? he wondered. It made everything so much more complicated.

They sat at the dining room table eating Chinese takeout with plastic forks. Felicity, still a little shook up after hearing Betty's voice, eyed the bare wood floor (hadn't there been a gorgeous Oriental here?) with grim neutrality.

'Of course, now that she's found out about us,

174

all bets are off,' he said.

'Betty ought to be happy that you're happy,' Felicity said. 'After all, *you're* happy that she's settled in such a snug little cottage with her loving daughters by her side. She owes you that much, after all these years. It's true she's become difficult, but she can't be completely unfeeling.'

Joseph poured himself another drink and breathed in the perfume of the Scotch, so familiar, yet so full of promise. He remembered the glass Betty had thrown at him, the golden liquid pooled on the floor, the heady alcohol vapors floating up through the angry silence. Betty could indeed be difficult. He patted Felicity's hand.

'We'll get some new silver,' he said.

'Oh no, that sort of thing is not important to me at all. Though why she needed the silver *and* the Dansk stainless, I have no idea.'

'Wedding present from her parents, I think.'

Felicity, on consideration of this information and where it might lead the surprisingly nostalgic Joseph, consoled herself with the knowledge that although she could not erase the fact of his wedding to Betty and the existence of those in-laws, the in-laws were by now dead and, regarding the nature of their gift, Joseph was, at least, not sure.

'Here,' she said, and she shoveled more sesame noodles on his plate. 'You finish these up, darling.'

*   *   *

Betty, meanwhile, spoke to the divorce attorney frequently—daily, really—and though she told Miranda and Annie very little of what transpired,

175

her phone conversations were so long and so loud, conducted in Betty's fluty voice of determination, that they were able to piece together a few things. Because Betty would not agree to Josie's terms, Josie would not go ahead with the divorce, leaving Betty in a kind of limbo, legally and financially. She, therefore, had to sue for divorce herself on the grounds of abandonment. This she seemed, surprisingly, to relish. She quit her painting, sparing two of her bedroom walls the sad gray color. Daytime soap operas and talk shows still blared from the TV, but Betty no longer sat on the couch to watch. She established herself formally at her desk each morning and pored over the most recent papers her lawyer had FedExed. She provided herself with a large collection of exquisitely designed folders and file boxes. She referred lovingly to her Case with nearly Dickensian reverence. Because of the Case, she explained, she could no longer do the cooking or the marketing, she was much too busy. In fact, she seemed to have little time left even for eating, living on saltines smeared with almond butter.

*   *   *

'I feel like I'm buried alive,' Miranda said one morning.

'Better than being buried dead,' said Betty, looking up from her papers. She smiled encouragingly, hoping to cheer Miranda up. Miranda occasionally executed a round of unanswered phone calls, she read the odd manuscript that some memoirist in the boondocks who had not heard of her disgrace still sent in. But she was fading, detaching, disappearing in front of their eyes. All for that young actor? Betty wondered, then answered her own question. No, not for him. For a dream, a dream most women her age had already dreamed and either lived or forgotten. Why had it taken Miranda so long? she wondered.

Then she noticed that both her daughters were staring at her.

'What?'

'Buried alive better than being buried dead?' Annie said. 'Hardly, Mother.'

'Oh, wait until you're my age.'

'God, I hope we're not still in this dump when I'm that old,' Miranda said.

'Amen.'

Betty looked stricken.

'Not that you're old,' Miranda quickly added.

Betty was old and she knew it. That was not the issue. She put both hands down on her pile of legal documents. 'Are you so unhappy here, girls?' she said. Her voice was earnest now. 'I feel terrible. I thought the change would be so good for you. I'm so sorry, my darlings. I know you came out here for me, and I'm so grateful, but look what it's come to. Oh dear. I've completely disrupted your lives, and for what? I'm afraid I've been very selfish. But I honestly thought . . .'

'No, Mom, it's great, it's fine,' Annie interrupted. 'It's so beautiful here, it's almost like a vacation for us.' She made a face at Miranda— Come on, agree, make Mommy feel better, hurry up . . .

But Miranda was sulking, staring at the floor. 'Well, I'm glad *someone* is enjoying themselves,' she said. She rose from the table, gave Annie a sour look, grabbed her coat from the closet, and headed towards the door.

Annie examined her hands. They were clasped tightly. She wanted to use them to murder her sister.

'I'll go with you,' she called. Her voice took on a tone she recognized from child-rearing days: rage altered by the alchemy of necessity into enthusiasm. Perhaps outside in the air she would somehow be able to speak to Miranda, really talk to her. 'A walk!' she said, in consequence. 'What fun!'

'A picnic,' Betty muttered darkly. 'Everything a picnic.' And she turned back to her documents.

They walked to the end of the little street, and there before them stretched Compo Beach. The sand was brown and coarse, the sky blowing layers of dark clouds above the rough gray water. There were a dozen or so people out, couples mostly, with their dogs.

'Miranda, talk to me.'

'I'm going crazy here, that's all. Crazy, crazy, crazy.'

Three grown women, three independent, bossy women in a tiny ill-equipped house? Three unhappy women . . . Annie was about to expound on this, to say how natural it was to go stark, raving mad, how temporary this situation was, please God, when the sun suddenly appeared through a crack in the slate sky.

'My God,' Annie said, stunned by the beauty.

'My God!' Miranda echoed her. But she was not gazing at the illuminated gash in the clouds. She was staring at an approaching figure outlined by the sudden glare. The figure was waving.

'Oh, Annie,' she cried. 'It's him! It's Kit! He's back.'

'No, I don't think . . .' But Miranda was already running towards the man.

'Miss!' he called, his voice muted by the wind and the slap of the waves. 'You dropped your scarf!'

Miranda stopped, all the energy drained from her form: it wasn't Kit, after all.

Then, abruptly, she squealed with joy. 'Nicky!' she cried. 'It's Nicky!'

But Annie, recognition of that unexpected voice coming upon her headlong, was already running to throw her arms around her younger son.

'If it was anyone else,' Miranda was saying, 'but it's not, it's you, oh little Nicky, you're gigantic . . .' And she was hugging him, too, all three of them jammed together as the wind whipped the sand around them.

Annie was so happy she felt ill. Her son had been away for more than six months, and now he had come home to surprise her for Thanksgiving.

'Of course, there's the, um, plane fare,' he said later when they were sitting on the couch together. 'I kind of put it on the credit card . . .'

'Don't you worry,' Annie said. He could have put all of South Africa on her credit card at that moment and she would have paid the bill somehow. How? she thought for an instant, but such a fleeting instant, for then she rested her head against his shoulder and forgot credit card bills and money and everything but the familiar smell of his skin.

'I'm sorry you had to bounce from the

apartment, Grandma.'

'Bounce,' Betty said. 'I like that. I bounced.' She smiled.

Nick looked around him at the little living room. 'It's very . . .' He paused. 'It's very cozy here, that's for sure.'

The mood of the cottage had changed completely with Nick's arrival. The Costco fire cast a yellow glow on the small room. The tea Betty had poured was fragrant and hot. Nick's voice was young and loud as he laughed and told his traveller's tales and made them laugh with him.

'You knew he was coming,' Annie said suddenly to her mother. 'You did, didn't you?'

'She did,' Nick said. 'She planned the whole thing.'

'How could you keep it a secret, Mom?'

'I have many secrets,' Betty said. And Annie realized that she did, that her mother to whom she condescended, at whom she rolled her eyes, her mother whom she adored and admired even as she felt the superiority of a younger generation towards her, this woman whom she thought she knew so well had secrets, had an inner life Annie knew nothing about.

Within its corny hearth, the gas fire from Costco flickered; the teacups clattered musically on their saucers. Outside, a crow cawed from somewhere in the silver sky. Miranda observed her nephew, the large male movements, the deep voice, his cough, loud and rough. He stretched his legs out, and she had to climb over them to get past him.

'I remember you when you were a little boy,' she said, so softly he almost didn't hear her. She stroked his hair thoughtfully. 'Just a little, little

180

boy.' There were tears in her eyes.

'What's up with Aunt Miranda?' Nick asked Annie later. 'She seems a little emotionable.'

Annie laughed at the word, then said, 'She's missed you, that's all,' and Nick, in the blissful narcissism of youth, nodded his understanding.

*   *   *

Thanksgiving was a frenetic and happy event in the little household. Charlie came in from Chicago, and Annie was so flooded with feeling that she recognized for the first time the drought she had been living through. It was difficult for her to resist pulling her sons onto her lap. They were affectionate boys, always had been, but they were now so old, she reminded herself. She waited, as if they were yearlings in the forest, for them to come to her.

Betty went all-out for their Thanksgiving dinner. 'I haven't cooked turkey in so long, it seems,' she kept saying. 'I wonder why.'

'You wonder why it seems that way, or you wonder why you haven't cooked one in so long?' Annie asked.

'Oh, Annie,' said Betty and Miranda.

'Oh, Mom,' said the boys.

'I don't know how you did it with this stove,' Annie said to redeem herself.

'I got the recipes from Martha. On her show. I liked some of the recipes from Lydia better, and that girl with the awful voice had a few that seemed interesting. But I wanted to be loyal.'

'To Martha?'

'She's been through so much. And she used to

181

live in Westport.'

'So did the star of *Behind the Green Door*. Maybe we should rent it on DVD.'

'One of my favorites, dear,' Betty said.

The others stared.

'Katharine Hepburn,' Betty continued. *'"The calla lilies . . . Such a strange flowuh"* . . . *She* grew up in Westport?'*

No one corrected her. She was so happy cooking her dinner, serving it on her good plates, clearing the table with the boys.

'Now for our traditional Thanksgiving family walk,' she announced after Annie and Miranda had done the dishes, and though they had never in anyone's memory ever taken a walk on Thanksgiving before, they got their coats and scarves and gloves and followed her out to the beach.

Charlie and Annie walked hand in hand, a little behind the others.

'Grandpa Josie called me,' he blurted out, darting a questioning look at her.

Annie said only, 'Did he?' in as neutral a tone as she could muster, but she was furious. How dare Josie go behind her back?

'He just wanted to stay in touch. You know, with the divorce. He said he didn't want to lose us, me and Nick. I didn't mention it in front of Grandma. Because, well, obviously I didn't. He called Nick, too. Is that okay, Mom? I mean, it seemed to be really important to him. He said how much he missed us and . . . everyone. He sent me a check for my birthday, too, which I actually thought was really nice.'

Annie looked out at the dark water and the

north shore of Long Island, a darker strip just visible below the gray horizon. The air was cold and clean. No! she wanted to cry out. It was not really nice for Josie to call you and make you feel sorry for him and give you money and buy more sympathy when Betty has no money at all. Your sympathies and loyalty lie elsewhere, Charlie, she wanted to say, shaking him by the shoulders.

'I used the money for my ticket home. To see you and Grandma,' he added.

'That seems only fair,' she said at last. Protect your child, Annie. Protect him from vanity and greed, from reality—the reality of his grandfather. Nevertheless, she blurted out, 'He's a bastard.'

'I know,' Charlie said softly. 'I know, Mom.'

'I'm glad he feels responsible to someone,' Annie said. 'Do I sound bitter? I am. But it's hard to be bitter about someone you love. So you don't have to be bitter. That will be my job.'

'Mixed message, Mom.'

'You bet.'

'What about you?' he asked after a while. 'Are you doing okay? Living here and everything?'

He had stopped and taken both her hands, and now gazed at her earnestly. She thought how handsome he was, how kind his expression was, how lucky she was. 'Well,' she said, in a rush of gratitude—someone to confide in!—'it's pretty hard sometimes . . .' But even as she spoke she noticed that though Charlie had asked because he was concerned, he expected her, as his mother, to make that concern go away, the way she had soothed him after a nightmare. 'But we're doing great,' she quickly said.

He looked relieved.

'We haven't all been together since Miranda and I were children.' Then she remembered that in those days there had been another person present. Perhaps she could expunge Josie from her memories the way her grandmother had scratched out all the dates scrawled by a younger incarnation of herself on the corners of her snapshots. 'And I really do like the commute. Gives me a moment of repose.'

His face cleared of any worry now, Charlie began to give her an animated description of his latest run-in with one of his professors, a tyrant, a bully, an incompetent, and an hysteric. Annie listened to the soft breeze of his complaints and felt refreshed. Her children were home. They slept for five nights on AeroBeds in the living room. She could hear them whispering to each other at night, laughing their deep laughs. Their beard hairs clogged up the sink downstairs. They had more lotions and creams for their skin than she had. They left the foil packaging of their contact lenses, each one with a tiny pool of liquid in it, on the side of the sink. Their clean clothes lay twisted on the floor with their dirty clothes. Annie wanted to lie down among their stuff and roll like a dog in carrion.

And then, one morning, with a short but ruthless storm of searching and washing and folding and tripping over cavernous bags, they were gone.

That night as the three women sat in the flickering light of the fake fire, Miranda said, 'Nobody here but us chickens,' and threw her head back dramatically.

Annie made a halfhearted chicken noise.

'Let's sing,' Betty said. 'That will cheer us up.'

Annie laughed. 'You haven't tried that one in a while, Mom.'

CHAPTER THIRTEEN

When Nick and Charlie left, the household sank into an even deeper state of misery than it had been in before they showed their young faces. Betty rustled through her papers as if she were preparing a well-padded nest. Miranda had taken to leaving shrill messages on answering machines of former colleagues.

'Aren't you sort of burning your bridges?' Annie said. 'I certainly hope so.'

'She's being proactive,' Betty said. 'That's a sign of self-esteem, you know.'

Each day the shower rail separated a little more from the wall of the bathroom. Each night Annie lay in bed and tried not to think of their finances. That was how she began to divide her days: first the aluminum disk pulling away from the dull pink tile, bit by bit, while she showered (she swore she could see it moving), then the rush of panic in the shadowy nighttime room.

'We're running out of money,' she ventured at breakfast.

'I was never good at money,' Miranda said. 'Obviously.'

'Joseph always took care of everything,' Betty said, shaking her head sadly. 'Well, those days are gone.'

And so they both, each in her own unassuming way, assumed Annie would somehow take care of the finances.

Her sublet apartment, unlike her current roommates, was rolling up its sleeves, putting its shoulder to the grindstone and earning its keep. But there was still Charlie's medical school and Nick's college tuition, only partly paid for by loans. It didn't leave Annie much. Her mother had even less, with any eventual divorce settlement a long way off. Miranda, meanwhile, saw only an occasional royalty check from her once popular and now disgraced authors, but even her tithe, as she called it, was withheld while the legal cases worked themselves out. She appeared to have otherwise run through every penny she had ever earned.

Sitting at the table trying to make a budget, Annie said, 'There's very little coming in and there's way too much going out.'

The other two nodded, then continued to read the newspaper.

When Annie said it again, louder, Miranda patiently explained that writing down all their debts did not miraculously supply the family with more money. The point of a budget was not to miraculously conjure up more money, Annie answered. The point was to figure out realistically how much they could afford to spend. Betty said she thought it would be far more practical to have more money, miraculously or otherwise, and Annie gave up, sitting with her pencil and her calculations in lonely, resentful silence.

That night, as every night, the bills rose up in her memory and haunted her. She turned in her bed, twisted in the sheets. The thin moonlight came in through her window. It was cold and

186

white, like a marble tomb. She was hot and flushed and alive with worry.

Her anger and frustration with her mother and sister, however, were just bits of sand caught in the wind of her true rage. That was saved for Josie and, now, Felicity as well. Annie still could not believe that the person behind all their suffering was Frederick Barrow's sister.

'And to think Rosalyn invited that treacherous family to Rosh Hashanah,' she said one evening as they sat glumly before the faux fire. 'Maybe that's why Frederick was so weird.'

'You said he wasn't weird,' Miranda muttered.

'Well, he was.'

'Listen,' Betty said abruptly, 'I'll just have to get a job.'

'What are you going to do, Mom? Greet people at Walmart?'

Betty leaned toward her, suddenly animated. 'Is Walmart as nice as Costco?'

*   *   *

It was therefore with great relief that the three women accepted an invitation to visit Lou and Rosalyn in Palm Springs.

'It's our fiftieth wedding anniversary,' Rosalyn said when she called. 'Can you believe it?'

Betty congratulated her coldly.

'Against all the odds,' Rosalyn said.

'And how is your father?' Betty asked to parry the indelicacy. 'How is Mr Shpuntov?'

'The desert agrees with him.'

Betty imagined a towering dune nodding polite assent to Mr Shpuntov.

'Well,' she said more cheerfully, 'that's something, then.'

'Now, Betty,' Rosalyn said in a pedagogical tone that got Betty's back up whenever she heard it. It was Rosalyn's docent voice. 'Now, Betty, listen, and don't be stubborn. Lou and I both miss you and the girls.'

Betty walked out to the sunporch. There was no sun, just weak, struggling light. The sky was overcast and dull. It had rained the night before and the trees were still dark with wet. She was cold on the unheated sunporch. There was nothing to do there, nothing to see, nothing even to hear, no birds or passing children. She stood suspended in a winter void, only the damp cold and the musty smell of old carpet penetrating the deprivation.

'We miss you, too,' she said. And perhaps the girls did miss Lou and Rosalyn now and then, she really didn't know. As for herself, she missed only one person.

'We want you all to come out here for Christmas. Our treat, of course. My father was saying the other day that in all his years he had never seen people who were so generous to their friends, but you know us, Betty—that's just the way we are. And I don't want you to start giving me excuses about why you can't come. A trip will do you good, Betty. Lou and I are worried about you. Even my father mentioned it to me just the other day. Sitting there in that hut, of course you get what you pay for, no disrespect to the landlords. Ha! I make myself laugh. But there you are. No one to talk to. Except your daughters, of course. How lucky you are to have daughters. Still, I manage very well, don't I, even without children?

Lou and his Like Family. I have to laugh.' And she did.

Betty, who had not been listening but had heard the words lucky and daughters, said, 'Oh yes,' in an absent voice.

'Now, don't you Oh Yes me, Betty Weissmann. I know what you're thinking. You're thinking we're just making this generous offer because we feel sorry for you, and I can understand that, I really can, but you have to believe me, it's *mostly* because we love you and want what's best.'

Betty moved back to her desk, but she did not look at the mound of papers and bright folders piled high upon it. She was staring at the television set. There, on the soap opera she favored because it was set in a seaside town not unlike Westport, if Westport were inhabited by spies, terrorists, gangsters, and swinging wife-swapping millionaires, which who was to say it wasn't, there on the screen, in the soap opera's popular new art gallery hangout, stood a handsome dark-haired young man facing another handsome blond young man. There was tension, visible tension between them. And tenderness. And longing. Betty had seen that expression before. She had seen Kit Maybank look at Miranda like that. Only now Kit Maybank was on television in an art gallery standing before a reproduction—she supposed it had to be a reproduction—of a Keith Haring (her friends Arnie and Maureen bought one years ago, she hadn't understood it at the time, but it certainly had appreciated) and his, Kit Maybank's, hand shot out and grasped the hand of the other handsome young man, the one with blond hair, and Kit Maybank stepped forward and the other

189

young man stepped forward and Kit Maybank was in the other young man's arms and the other young man was in Kit Maybank's arms and with the Keith Haring reproduction as a backdrop they were kissing, passionately, with their mouths gaping, as people always seemed to kiss on soap operas.

'Oh my God,' she heard Miranda gasp from the doorway behind her.

'Betty?' Rosalyn was saying into the phone. 'Betty, are you there?'

'I can't believe it!' Miranda said.

'Now, Miranda, it's just a role,' Betty said.

'Betty?' Rosalyn said again.

'Oh, I'm sorry, Rosalyn. Miranda's young man just kissed another young man on television.'

'What young man? Kit? Kit's gay?'

'Just on TV.'

Miranda, moving closer to the TV, said, 'Kit's in Los Angeles!'

'Los Angeles?' Rosalyn said, overhearing Miranda. 'I hope he got his marriage in before they changed the law.'

'Kit's married?' Betty asked.

'Kit's married?' Miranda said. She grabbed the phone from her mother. 'Kit's married?' she asked Rosalyn.

'He is? Well, you live long enough, you see everything.'

*   *   *

On the plane ride to Los Angeles, Miranda gazed impatiently out the window. Although all of them were thrilled to be liberated from what Miranda called cottage arrest, it had still not been easy for

190

her to convince the other inmates to make the trip. It was a challenge, but Miranda had always liked a challenge in the good old days before her life had collapsed, and this one had energized her. It was a pleasure to have a goal again, to work her mother and sister the way she used to work publishers and editors. She snapped back into that alert, predatory sentience of her occupation not with pleasure so much as exasperated fondness—this was something she knew, an old fawning pal. She had been forced to campaign using both subtlety and aggression, sweetness and sour-tempered sarcasm. Of course, she had prevailed. She could not recall a time when she had not prevailed within her family. Betty had hesitated, not relishing the role of beggarly relative in two different geographical locations. But she had caved fairly quickly. The holdout, as usual, was Annie.

'They're paying for it, so you can't use that as an excuse,' Miranda said. 'The library is giving all of you a forced two-week unpaid vacation, so you can't use *that.*'

'Go by yourself,' Annie had said. 'If you want to go so badly.'

Only when Annie found out that neither Charlie nor Nick could make it to Connecticut for Christmas did she give in.

'I'm sorry we won't get to see them,' Miranda said to Annie.

But she wasn't sorry. She was exhilarated. The nose of the plane was pointed towards the West Coast. Somewhere on that coast were Kit Maybank and Henry Maybank. Somewhere between Los Angeles, where Kit now lived, and Palm Springs, where he spent his weekends in a rented house he

191

shared with a friend. She had read all about him on a soap opera fan blog. Kit's disappearance made sense to her now, his silence. He was not on a little independent movie at all. He was a soap opera regular. No wonder he had been so uncommunicative, so distant. He who had dreamed of Shakespeare was now playing Zink Lattimore, gay graffiti artist. Poor Kit was mortified, that was all. That was why she hadn't heard from him. He had hoped to slink away into daytime TV obscurity, leaving her with her exalted vision of him, with her memories intact.

'Funny about memories,' she said to Annie, who had, as usual, volunteered to sit in the middle seat.

'Useless author trivia,' Annie said. 'That's the kind of memory I have: today is Rex Stout's birthday. For example.'

'What street did his detective live on? It seemed an odd address even at the time,' said Betty.

'Thirty-fourth Street. 918 West Thirty-fourth Street, sometimes 922, 904. Once it was 918 *East* Thirty-fourth Street. It was always the same brownstone, though.'

'You were always like that, even as a child,' Betty said, patting her arm proudly.

'*Memories*,' Miranda said irritably. 'Not memory.'

'Memories are like fish,' Betty said. 'Isn't that the expression? After three days they stink.'

*   *   *

A layer of white clouds lay beneath them, occasional openings affording quick glimpses of the United States with its crop circles and ribbons

192

of rivers and faded, flat winter landscape. Annie looked past her sleeping sister at the greasy window and the blue sky beyond. That she had agreed to follow Lou, Rosalyn, and Mr Shpuntov to Palm Springs was still sinking in. But there had been no resisting Miranda. Miranda was more animated than she had been since Kit Maybank left Westport. Annie assumed Miranda and Kit had been in touch. Were they getting back together in some way? She wondered if that was a good thing. Her sister smiled dreamily as she slept, forehead on the window, white billowing clouds beyond. Yes, it would be good. If it made Miranda happy, it would be good. As for Betty, although she hated to fly, although her relationship with Rosalyn could charitably be called prickly, although she loved having Christmas in her own house, once she had given in to Miranda, she had taken up the cause like a true convert. Christmas in the desert! Palm Springs! So mid-century! So Rat Pack!

'J. Smeaton Chase lived in Palm Springs,' Annie had offered. 'He wrote a book about it.'

'Celebrities, etc. ?' Betty asked.

'No. More like cactuses, etc.'

*　　　*　　　*

When they arrived at the airport, they picked up their rental car. It was the only expense they would have for their entire two-week stay. Cousin Lou had insisted on paying for the plane tickets. They had refused until Rosalyn explained that he would use frequent-flier miles that were about to run out.

'Don't be proud,' she said. 'It is no longer

193

appropriate.'

Betty was too proud to respond.

Now she drove along the windy highway, the little Ford Focus shaking from side to side. Her daughters had each offered to take the wheel, saying what a long flight it had been, how tired she must be. Meaning, of course, how old she was. It was an ugly road, but the sky was vast and blue, the malls gradually gave way to cactus, and the snowy mountains crept closer and closer. Betty tried to enjoy the view as the car shuddered through a forest of tall white windmills.

'Wow,' Miranda said. 'Try tilting at those.'

They pulled up into the driveway of a one-story house among other one-story houses. Its roof was shaped like a nun's hat, wings swooping up on either side. Standing at the front door were two men: Rosalyn's father, Mr Shpuntov, and Roberts, the semiretiree.

Annie rolled down her window and called out a hello.

'Huh,' Miranda said. 'Codger talk, poor old souls.'

'*Your* soul certainly isn't old,' Annie said. 'Infantile perhaps, but not old.' While my soul is quite thoroughly middle-aged, she thought.

'There is no soul,' Betty said suddenly, with unexpected force. 'Everyone knows that.'

*   *   *

Roberts and Mr Shpuntov had indeed been indulging in codger talk. Mr Shpuntov found it warm for December in the Bronx, while Roberts agreed that the dry, bright winter heat was not

194

usual for the Bronx at this time of year and left it at that. Then the old man lurched towards the door and began violently ringing the bell. When his daughter answered, he barked out a cross 'Who's there? What do you want here? Go away,' then slammed the door in her face, muttering something uncomplimentary about Jehovah's Witnesses.

Roberts paid no attention. He had turned his back on the shouting and slamming and was striding over to the white rental car. He gave a short wave and a quick flicker of a smile. He did not smile much, but when he did, his face was animated. Annie noticed, to her surprise, how strong he was—his arms in their short-sleeve polo shirt were surprisingly thick for such a tall, slender man. As he carried all their suitcases into the house, she gave Miranda a poke in the back.

'What was that for?'

Annie shrugged. She really didn't know. 'You underestimate Roberts,' she said.

'Oh, that again,' Miranda said, shaking her head and walking off into the house.

But you do, Annie thought. You're unfair. Roberts is pensive, a man of calm surfaces and immeasurable depths, while all you notice is the chop and spray of windswept waves. It's a pity. For both of you.

'Are you staying with Cousin Lou and Rosalyn, too?' Annie asked him when they were all inside.

'No, no. I have a condo here. Just down the street.'

'You people move in a pack,' Miranda said, laughing.

Roberts smiled. 'All the old snowbirds. Yes, we

195

do. Not much imagination, I guess.'

'You ladies will stay in the guesthouse,' Rosalyn said. 'Your mother will stay in the house with us. That way you will *all* have your *privacy*.'

She managed to say this in a way that suggested both that the daughters wanted urgently to get away from their unpleasant mother and that the mother wanted urgently to get away from her unpleasant daughters.

'We are indebted to you and will be happy wherever you put us,' Betty said with narrowed eyes.

'It's beautiful here.' Annie looked out the windows. Across the street was a pink stucco house with an incongruous rich green lawn. Beyond it, the desert, purple in its shadows, reached out to the snow-capped mountains.

In the back of the house, a large patio surrounded two sunken areas, one containing what seemed to be a kind of outdoor kitchen with refrigerator, grill, and bar, the other centered on a fire pit. Beyond that was a pool, a golf course, and then more mountains and the wide Western sky.

'We practically live outside,' Rosalyn said proudly, seeing Betty staring out.

'No, but look at that scrawny dog,' Betty said. 'Just sunning himself on the golf course. It's so sweet.'

'Lou!' Rosalyn cried. She began waving her arms. 'Shoo! Shoo! Lou! The coyote!'

The animal rose lazily to its dainty feet and loped away across the green, turning its head once or twice to look back at the small, wildly gesticulating woman.

'You did it!' Lou said proudly. 'My little frontier

woman. You bow to no coyote!'

But within seconds they beheld another reason for the coyote's rapid departure: a golf cart, its fringed canopy bumping jauntily, carrying two girls, rattling across the exact spot where the coyote had lain.

'Oh, look!' Rosalyn said. 'It's Crystal and Amber!'

For a moment Annie wondered if Rosalyn had spotted mineral deposits in the rocky mountains above them. Then she realized she was referring to the golf cart girls. They were both in their twenties, tanned and fit and wearing shorts, their identically pretty bellies exposed below tiny stylish polo shirts. They resembled each other so much they had to be sisters, but one, the younger, was dark and bright, her eyes sparkling with certainty, while the older had a fair, indefinite smoothness. Neither was beautiful, but they both conformed to the rules of fashion and gave off a vague sense of beauty anyway, like a fire that burns bright but has no heat.

'Did you see the wolf?' the older one, who was Crystal, said. 'Oh my God, I was freaking *out.*'

'It was a coyote,' said Amber. 'Don't you ever watch Nat Geo?'

'Well, whatever,' said Crystal, her face glowing with excitement.

Amber and Crystal were in Palm Springs house-sitting. They did not call themselves house sitters, though. They were 'home sitters', they said. Rosalyn had met them on the golf course and they had 'adopted' her. Accustomed to standing by as people made a fuss over her husband as he made a fuss over them, Rosalyn had, not surprisingly, grown fond of the two girls. They had arrived now to take her around the golf course and drop in on any neighbors who happened to be sitting out on their patios having cocktails.

'Don't the neighbors mind?' Annie asked. 'I mean, if you're not invited?'

The girls looked at her as if she were the middle-aged librarian she was.

'Oh, Annie, don't be such a stick in the mud. You're in Palm Springs now! You're on vacation,' Rosalyn said, climbing aboard the golf cart and waving gaily as it trundled off across the bright green turf.

Annie waved back, chastened. She and Miranda proceeded to the guesthouse, a little miniature of the main house. Miranda was almost giddy with pleasure. She spun around the small patio facing the mountains.

'I love it here!' Miranda shouted. 'The sky. The mountains. The froufrou minimalism of the houses. The lawns in the desert. The coyotes on the golf course. It's so wild and dowdy at the same time. I just love it!'

She stretched out on a chaise. 'Sun!'

'Don't get a burn,' Annie said, more because she felt it was somehow expected of her than because she worried about the late-afternoon rays.

But Miranda, eyes closed, just shook her head and smiled.

*　　　*　　　*

Annie sat outside that night missing her children. Christmas holidays without them were a sickly, hollow time. She had spoken to them earlier, using

198

the computer and seeing their faces, distorted by the angle of their laptops. Nick had wanted her to send him the shampoo he liked and more contact lenses. Charlie was too old to ask her to do long-distance errands. That was a blessing, but it made her sad, too. Everyone grew up, it seemed. Except perhaps Miranda.

Annie went to the bathroom and held up her traveling magnifying mirror and gave a few desultory plucks where needed, then went back to the bedroom, where Miranda was in bed intently studying something on her laptop. The room was cool, and outside, the world ended in abrupt black night. Annie moved closer, but Miranda moved her cursor across the screen and the windows swept themselves away, leaving behind nothing but an expanse of digital blue.

So, Annie thought, Kit Maybank? Maybe Henry would appear in the morning and moo like a cow and quack like a duck to the amazement of his elders. Miranda and Kit could walk and talk and admire the sunset, bound by the little boy between them, swinging from their hands. Or not. Miranda had confided nothing to Annie. For all Annie knew, she had met a new suitor online and was going to meet him at midnight in Joshua Tree National Park. Probably turn out to be a serial murderer. Oh God . . . Annie looked over at her sister, safe in the next bed, to reassure herself. I wonder, she thought, if Miranda ever worries about me.

*　　　*　　　*

The next day, while Mr Shpuntov napped in his

199

room, his uneven snores broadcast through the house by a baby monitor, Betty sat on a comfortable mid-century chair trying to read a mystery called *Return to Sender* she'd found in her room. It was bright midmorning, but the wall of windows was protected by an overhang of the swooping roof and the living room had a welcome dimness, a soft contrast to the harsh daylight on the other side. The book was frustratingly dull. Most mysteries are, she thought. The mystery of her marriage, for example. She could turn the years over and over again in her mind and they still added up to happiness that had been shredded suddenly and inexplicably into ugly scraps of pain. She sighed, more loudly than she would have liked, for Roberts, who had just come in, looked concerned and sat beside her.

'You're worried,' he said.

'No. Not really. That would involve hope.'

'Oh dear.'

'I just don't understand. Maybe the end of a marriage is like God, and we are not meant to understand.'

Roberts nodded in apparent agreement. 'My wife died ten years ago. I don't understand that either. I miss her every day. Do you miss your husband?'

'Yes. Every minute. It's easier when I pretend he's dead. I'm sorry—that must sound so callous to you. But if he's alive, if he's alive and behaving like this . . . well . . . And he always prided himself on being such a decent man . . .'

Roberts said, 'Sometimes people need some guidance, don't you think? Even decent people, and especially people who think they're decent.'

Betty liked the tone of his voice. Not hysterical and fuming like her daughters, not cautious and pessimistic like her lawyers, not numb and beaten down like her own inner voice. Even talking to Cousin Lou, who advised her on some of the real estate aspects of her Case, was trying—his hearty reassurance, so touching, so enraging. Roberts's voice was quiet and determined, as if it were on its way somewhere, someplace it needed to be. He asked her a few questions about her lawyers, about the disposition of the Case. Betty had never discussed her Case with someone who understood the law before, except her lawyers, of course, but they seemed to find the law a constantly surprising series of impediments, as if they were crossing rocky desert terrain for the first time and had forgotten their shoes.

'What fun this has been!' she said. 'Odd how a little kvetching can cleanse the soul.'

'Well, let's just see what happens,' Roberts said with a smile. 'Let's just see what happens with the late great Joseph Weissmann.'

She smiled back at him. 'Let's just see,' she agreed.

Cousin Lou came into the room then, his voice booming, 'All hands on deck! All hands on deck!' And only when all the inhabitants, including his bewildered father-in-law, had gathered around him did he continue. 'Tonight I celebrate fifty years of wedded bliss.'

Rosalyn clapped her hands like a girl.

'I am pleased to include all of you, my family, in this great celebration of love.'

Annie glanced at her mother and then at Miranda to see how well disposed they were to such a celebration. Betty looked resigned, Miranda tense.

'So, I invite all of you to join us—'

'And Amber and Crystal, of course,' Rosalyn interjected.

'And Amber and Crystal, of course,' he said, bowing to his wife. 'I invite you to join us at the country club's Seafood Night.'

'Seafood in the desert!' Rosalyn said. 'We've got it all.'

'Do we wear costumes?' Annie asked with a worried face, for she was remembering Western Night at the boys' day camps when they wore bandannas and boots with their shorts and T-shirts.

'You eat heaps of seafood piled on silver platters,' said Cousin Lou.

'It's all endangered and full of mercury,' Miranda said.

Miranda had been agitated and rather sour since she woke up. The eagerness of the past few days had bloomed into something else altogether, like algae. She was so volatile. It was hard to keep up. Betty put her finger to her mouth to shoosh her.

Annie frowned at her sister. Now as usual she would have to work that much harder in the civility department. 'Seafood!' she said. 'Who doesn't love seafood?'

Roberts looked from Miranda to Annie and back again. 'There you go.'

Annie thought, Poor, poor Roberts, not for the first time that day, either.

Betty said, 'Yum yum,' and went back to her book.

That afternoon, when Rosalyn returned from

another golf cart 'booze cruise' chaperoned by Amber and Crystal, several glasses of wine the merrier, she collapsed onto the sofa and confided to Betty that she had harbored some doubts about Crystal and Amber at first, thinking they were not exceptional enough for her. After all, what had they done in their lives? They moved from house to house like gypsies, first looking after a house on the East Coast, then the West Coast . . . It was hardly a recommendation for an extraordinary acquaintance. But then she had gotten to know them, and they were extraordinary, indeed. Just the nicest girls you could imagine, full of fun . . . They had taught her a delightful game involving Ping-Pong balls and plastic cups of beer . . . 'Amber is a massage therapist, you know. She's not licensed yet, still studying. But, Betty, she has a gift. I mean, it's amazing. My sciatica? Gone! It's almost as good as having a doctor in the family.'

The extraordinary girls, meanwhile, after dropping off Rosalyn, had turned the golf cart in the direction of the guesthouse and pulled it up to the edge of the patio there.

'Hello!' they cried. 'Hello in there!'

Miranda and Annie both came to the sliding glass door and stepped out. Annie, having just come out of the shower, was wrapped in a towel.

'We wanted to give you a real Palm Springs welcome!' the older one, Crystal, said. 'Of course, we're not really from here. Only old people are really from here, and even they are from other places, it's a very unique spot, but since we're officially here and staying in such a super house, the pool is totally unique, a waterfall . . .'

'Two,' her sister Amber said.

203

'That's what I said. A waterfall, too.'

'There are two waterfalls, Crystal.' She turned to Annie. 'I've trained myself to be very observant, sensitive to my surroundings. I really have to be.'

Annie pulled her towel closer around her. Please be sensitive to my dripping hair, she thought hopelessly, and let me go inside.

'She's a healer,' Crystal said

Miranda, who had not said a word, now gave a slight, rather dismissive wave and disappeared inside. Again Annie was left to hold down the obligatory chitchat fort. She wondered what would happen if she, too, decided to have no patience.

'That's excessive, Crystal,' Amber said, laughing. 'I'm just a regular old student of massage therapy.'

'No, that's not true,' Crystal insisted loyally, impervious to her sister's embarrassed glare. 'She works in so many modalities. Like chakra balancing and Inca shamanic healing . . .'

Amber rolled her eyes. 'Annie so doesn't want to hear about all that. Anyway, we just wanted to welcome you. We just love your cousin Rosalyn. She's a total hoot.'

'That's really nice of you,' Annie said. It was nice of them, actually. And there was something open and jolly about them. If only they would go away. 'I gather we'll see you at Seafood Night.'

'Sometimes there are spottings,' Crystal said. 'I live for spottings. We saw Orlando Bloom once. And of course Barry Manilow. On Cape Cod, we saw Gwyneth. That was really unexpected. I hope we have a spotting for you tonight. You must miss the spottings in New York. I mean, there can't be many good spottings in Westport now that Paul

Newman is gone.'

Annie, surprised that Crystal seemed to know so much about where she lived and where she had lived, said nothing.

As though she sensed that her sister might have caused offense, Amber quickly added, 'Phil Donahue! Don't forget Phil Donahue.'

'Who is Phil Donahue?' Crystal asked.

'I told you, you have to watch the History Channel, Crystal.'

The girls then reversed the golf cart with much waving and excited demands to meet up later, and they were gone.

*   *   *

That night, as they walked to the clubhouse, across the deepening green of the evening grass, as smooth as a carpet rolling out before them in the dusk, Rosalyn strode ahead, her silver leather jacket shining in the evening gloom.

'What if the coyote comes back?' Betty said.

'He only comes to that spot to bask in the sunlight, poor fellow,' said Roberts, who was also with them. 'He's there almost every day. A man of habit.'

'That I am,' said Mr Shpuntov.

Seafood Night was the first of several Nights at the country club. The clubhouse was a circular modern affair, all curves and brass railing, like a cruise ship. By the time they got there and claimed a big oval table by the windows overlooking the darkened golf course, the first round of oysters and clams and shrimp had already disappeared, leaving only big silver platters of shaved ice on the buffet tables. But new trays quickly appeared, and then lobster and crab as well.

'It's like a bar mitzvah,' Miranda said mournfully, remembering Kit's story of his friend Seth.

Annie had always wanted a bat mitzvah, but Betty thought they were vulgar and Josie thought all religious ceremonies were primitive, so Annie had waited until college to study Hebrew. That had been her prime reason for wanting the bat mitzvah. Her parents thought she wanted the party and the presents. But it was the lure of a dead language. To speak a language that had begun so long ago—it was like knowing a secret. She had taken Latin in high school for the same reason. Both her sons went to Hebrew school, though neither seemed excited by learning the secret language. Nevertheless, when they turned thirteen they chanted their Torah portions and took their places in the ranks of Jewish manhood. Betty and Josie didn't seem to mind a bit. Funny about grandparents and their grandchildren.

'I wish I had grandchildren,' Annie said as they settled around the big round table.

'Yes, you do wish that,' Betty said, smiling.

'You're too young,' Miranda said.

'Anyway, my kids are too young.'

'You're too influenced by Palm Springs,' Rosalyn said. 'You just want to retire with the rest of the oldies.'

'Oldies but goodies,' Lou said, kissing her.

The room was filled with the elderly, it was true—women with leathery brown skin and skinny arms and legs, men with bellies and big, red, veined cheeks. How crisp they all looked and prosperous in their white slacks and bright tops. Betty knew she was elderly, too, but still she felt left out of the relaxed affluence of this group. She was elderly and she was poor. How had that happened? She longed to join these athletic oldsters, to belong among them, and at the same time she despised them with their preposterous desert lawns and short-sleeve shirts and fringed golf carts. She was wearing black, and she was glad of it.

There were others in the dining room, younger people walking down the wide, curved ramp from the upper level entrance to the tables with their white cloths, young men and women carrying plates laden with oysters and lobster and asparagus salad.

'The gays,' Rosalyn whispered. 'They keep the place going. The rest of us are dying off,' she explained. 'New blood. I always like new blood.'

There was a three-piece band on a small raised platform, a keyboardist, guitarist, and drummer. They began to play 'YMCA', and Annie had to agree with Miranda that it was the very image of a bar mitzvah.

'One of the New Bloods is coming our way,' Miranda said.

'Nice boys. They like to dance,' said Rosalyn.

And, indeed, the young man asked Rosalyn to dance.

'They know the husbands don't like to,' Cousin Lou said, watching his little wife glide around the parqueted dance floor. It was then that the Weissmanns noticed that each of the other couples were also made up of one scrawny, elegantly decked-out older woman and one fit, elegantly decked-out younger man.

Miranda turned away from the dancers. The anomaly of their ages did not make much of an impression on her. Cousin Lou might tease her about the vast expanse between her age and 'young Kit's', but she in no way identified with the sinewy old birds being waltzed around by their youthful partners. She was going to be fifty, but even fifty, gargantuan and massive, seemed vague and distant, like the mountains outside—looming, jagged, threatening, inevitable great humps of stone and earth made soft by the pastel light, made invisible by the dark, made irrelevant by miles and miles of suburbs and dust. It was difficult to imagine a young man being so very much younger when you could never quite see yourself as old. She ordered a martini, drank it, and ordered another.

She perused the room, patient, alert.

Somehow, she knew he would be there. She couldn't have told you how, and like so many premonitions, this one could so easily not have been true, in which case she would have forgotten that she ever had had a premonition. But she did have one, and it was sure and accurate; she was a sybil, a prophetess, a seer, for there, marching down that ridiculous brass-railed red-carpeted gangplank, was Kit Maybank.

She downed another drink. He was here, as she had foretold.

'He's here,' she said to Annie, casually.

'Hmm?' Annie followed her sister's gaze. 'Oh my God, so he is.' She raised an arm and waved heartily in the direction of Kit, but Kit did not see her. 'I *thought* that's why you were so cheerful the past few days.'

208

Miranda had not taken her eyes off Kit. Nor did she make a motion toward him. 'Yes.'

A number of young men clustered around him asking for his autograph. 'Jesus, I didn't realize soap stars were such big deals,' Annie said. 'Must be all those gay kisses.'

'Yes,' Miranda said again.

She still hadn't moved. Annie wondered if she was too tipsy to get up. She waited, but Miranda stayed put.

'Miranda, what's going on?' Annie said. 'Are you okay?'

'Oh yes.'

'Seafood Night. How funny. Did you know Kit was coming here tonight?'

'Oh, I knew.' She began to examine herself in the butter knife, then looking resolutely over the glint of the blade at her sister, as if daring Annie to contradict her: 'I had a premonition.'

'Wait . . . you and Kit haven't been in touch? Except by premonition?'

But Miranda was no longer listening to her sister. The musical trio had begun to bang out a rendition of 'Love Shack'. Miranda could see the top of Kit's head across the room. She rose to her feet. Everything would be fine now. It was a wonderful world, a world full of premonitions and seafood and bar mitzvah music, a world in which you could walk across a dance floor, dodging old ladies and young pansies, and rest your hands on a man's shoulders and lean forward and give him a friendly kiss on the head and watch him turn toward you in a flutter of confusion and then smile.

Smile awkwardly.

And stand up and shake your hand.

And say, 'Miranda! What are you doing in Palm Springs?'

In a cold, cautious voice.

'Kit!' She heard herself laugh nervously. Kit released her hand. She noticed the hand, free, pale, floating in the air like a bird. It flew to her face. 'It's so good to see you,' she said. 'Where's Henry? I hope I get a chance to see him, too.' She was speaking too fast. She took a breath.

'Henry?' Kit said, as if they were talking about some acquaintance.

Again she laughed nervously.

'Henry's with his mother.'

'Oh.'

'So that's that,' Kit said.

'Oh,' Miranda said again. Little Henry. Little Henry had a mother.

'Henry?' asked the woman sitting in the chair next to him. She turned her beautiful face to Miranda for a second. Not quite as young as the others at the table, she thought. Why was she so familiar? College? An editor? Then Miranda thought, She is an actress. A famous actress.

Kit bent his head towards the woman and smiled as if to say, Nothing, nothing.

Miranda glanced around for an empty chair she could pull up. She saw Kit's fingers curl around the back of his own chair protectively. She caught his eye, about to be amused, to make a joke about stealing his chair, but his expression told her this was not a funny moment. His face was rigid with effort. Effort at what? He took a breath, slanted his head away from her; his eyes flickered shut, open, shut, back toward her. Something was very wrong. Something was very important. She had a premonition.

Kit took the hand of the famous actress and drew her to a standing position.

'Miranda Weissmann, I'd like you to meet Ingrid Chopin . . .'

Miranda smiled and held out her hand and felt the woman's cool fingers as Kit finished his sentence, '. . . my fiancée.'

The woman smiled back at her, a gorgeous, ravishing, impersonal smile, then gracefully withdrew her hand. Miranda's hand was suspended in the air. Kit was saying, 'Well, it really was lovely to see you.' Later, she noted the past tense, the dismissal. Now, as if she were operating in slower motion than the rest of the room, she noted only that she had already opened her mouth, about to speak, the words all assembled, ready to go: *God, I'm so happy for you, all your success . . . and now this wonderful news . . .*

But those words, like people loitering in a line, were pushed aside by other words, nasty pushy little words that could not wait their turn.

'You little fuck,' she said.

It must have been quite loud, for heads turned.

She was aware of her own stillness, standing as if posed, as if thinking, her hand now again lightly resting on her cheek. She began to pivot slowly away, then pivoted slowly back again. I forgot something, she thought. There's something I forgot. She moved the hand that had been resting on her cheek, lifted it high in the air, then brought it across Kit's face with a loud whack. That was better. That was much better. As she walked deliberately away, her face shone above the room as white as the cold moon.

211

'Oh Jesus,' Annie said when she heard Miranda shout at Kit. 'Oh Jesus,' she said when she saw Miranda give him a crack across the face.

'What, dear?' her mother asked, turning from an animated conversation with Lou. 'Is something the matter?'

'No, no,' Annie said, standing to block her mother's view.

Roberts, who had clearly seen the contretemps, looked up from his chair at Annie standing above him, a pained expression on his face.

The band broke into a rousing rendition of 'That's Amore'.

'Oh, I love this song,' Betty said. 'Where's Miranda?' she added, looking around.

Miranda was standing very still beside a glistening cliff of oysters, weeping.

Roberts hopped to his feet. 'Would you like to dance, Betty?' And he swept her safely away into the tightly packed crowd of couples.

*   *   *

Kit had whispered to his astonished fiancée, given a bemused smile to his table of gawking friends, and then walked quickly after Miranda, his head lowered the way men walk when they're being arrested. When he reached her, he put his hand on her shoulder. She was crying without moving a muscle, as if she were not personally involved with the tears at all, standing quietly while they made their way of their own accord down her cheeks.

'Miranda, I'm sorry. I should have told you. I know I should have. It's just that things happened so fast. And what you and I had together . . . it was

212

so much of the moment, wasn't it? But still, I know I should have, well, warned you. But it's been a total whirl.' He gave a swift little boyish smile. 'I'm going to be in her next movie. Did I tell you that?'

Miranda shook her head.

'You know what that means to me, you of all people. You understand me so well, Miranda. A feature film? After all these years?'

The tears had stopped. Miranda neither spoke nor moved.

'I'm sorry,' he said again.

They were blocking the mountain of ice ornamented with its large silver oysters in their large iridescent shells. Several people approached, shifted their feet a bit, then gingerly reached around them to scoop oysters onto their plates.

'I love oysters,' Miranda said.

'I know.'

She shrugged.

'I'm so sorry, Miranda.'

'I know.'

*   *   *

Miranda's progress towards her own table was slow, violent, and almost magisterial, her stride measured and regal, her head held high as she pushed aside stray chairs that lay in her path with unthinking, clattering nobility. Annie saw the other diners turning their eyes away, trying not to stare. When she reached her own chair, Miranda kicked that aside, too. It tipped, fell listlessly on its back, and lay with its legs sticking up. Miranda, silent and ashen, was trembling.

Annie took her sister's hand, as much to prevent

213

her from making a further scene as to comfort her.

'Darling, what's happened?' Betty said, returning with Roberts from the dance floor. 'Are you all right?'

'Food poisoning,' Annie said. The first thing that came to mind. What a Jew I am, she thought, seeing a tray of clams go by.

'Seafood in the desert,' chirped Rosalyn. 'It's unnatural. Just what my father was saying.'

Her father wagged his finger at her. 'It shouldn't stink of herring,' he said.

Roberts and Annie took Miranda back to the house in Amber and Crystal's golf cart. Miranda got into bed and fell asleep almost immediately. Annie came back to the main house to find Roberts smoking a smelly cigar outside by the pool.

'Does this bother you?' he asked.

Annie shook her head, but he put it out anyway.

'Thank you,' she said.

'Bad habit.'

'I didn't mean the cigar.' She stared up at the bright pulsing stars. Why had she allowed Miranda to talk them into coming to Palm Springs? Why had she allowed Miranda to talk them into going to Westport in the first place? Why did she ever listen to Miranda about anything at all? Her job as the reasonable older sister was to protect Miranda, not to indulge her.

'I'm a lousy sister,' she said.

'I don't think this really has much to do with you,' Roberts replied softly. 'You can't do everything, Annie.'

Then the others trooped out from the house through the sliding glass doors, noisy with wine and dancing.

'My housekeeper's nephew was killed by a coyote,' Rosalyn was saying. 'In Mexico, crossing the border.'

'They attack people?' Crystal said. 'Oh my God, Amber . . .'

'Not the *animal* coyote. Don't you watch CNN? God.'

'How is my baby?' Betty asked Annie, looking around for Miranda. Her voice was a little thick.

She must have had quite a few glasses of wine. Just as well, Annie thought. 'She's better. She went to bed, though.'

'You won't believe who we saw,' Rosalyn said. 'At Seafood Night, too!'

'Zink!' cried Crystal. 'We saw Zink! Kit Maybank, the actor! He's even better-looking in person. I can't believe you know him. Did you see who he was with? Ingrid Chopin? He's moving up in the world. I knew he wasn't gay. In real life, I mean.'

'She's about ten years older than he is,' Amber said.

'She is not. Jake Gyllenhaal just dropped out of the project she's doing. Maybe Kit Maybank will be her co-star.'

'This is so Palm Springs,' Rosalyn said happily. 'I expect Frank Sinatra and Peter Lawford to come through the door any minute.'

'Well, there *is* someone coming,' Lou said. 'But it's Mr Shpuntov. Not the Rat Pack exactly.'

'Just the rat,' Rosalyn muttered.

Roberts gave a short laugh. 'Plenty of rats to go around out here.'

'There are rats everywhere,' Betty said, thinking

215

of Joseph.

'So,' Annie said. 'And how *is* our friend Kit?'

'I wish Miranda had been there. He must have been so confused to see us all out of context. I told him Miranda went home with a headache—I didn't want to say food poisoning, it's so unappetizing, and there they all were looking so healthy and sporty and glamorous . . .'

'What did he *say,* though?'

'He didn't say much of anything.'

'Do you think he's shy?' Crystal asked. 'A lot of actors are shy.'

'Rats are shy, too,' Annie said.

'I just don't care for rats,' Betty said, and the party broke up.

Annie watched them trail away, her mother to bed; Mr Shpuntov escorted to his room by the attentive Cousin Lou; Rosalyn off to make sure all the windows were locked against the local coyote; Roberts, shooting her a quick but piercing look of concern, to make his long-legged way down the street; and Crystal to bounce towards the golf cart. Only Amber was left, lingering by the door.

'Pssst!' Amber said, waving Annie over, looking furtively around as she did so, then repeating the comic-book sound: 'Pssst!'

Amused, Annie walked the three steps to her side.

'Yes?'

'We have to talk,' Amber whispered.

'We do?'

'Tomorrow. Ten a.m. Fifth hole. Come alone.'

'But what . . . ?'

'Tomorrow,' Amber hissed, then squeezed Annie's arm with sober urgency and was out the

216

door.

*   *   *

Miranda's breathing rose and fell with an easy regularity that belied the crumpled figure arranged across the bed in a tangle of legs and arms and sheets, an arabesque of despair. Alas, this was a world in which a kind and generous and fiery woman could not love in peace. It seemed neither fair nor natural. Then again, when had Miranda ever chosen to love in peace? Miranda found peace banal.

Annie allowed herself to imagine a peaceful love. Two people in a bed. Lovemaking had taken place, of course, wonderful lovemaking. But that was a while ago. That morning, perhaps. Now it was night. Two people, their heads propped up on pillows. They each read a book. Now and again, one would glance at the other and smile, reach out, perhaps, lay a hand on the other's hand.

Perhaps that was banal. But how luxurious, then, was banality! thought Annie, who had spent so many nights alone in her bed with just the book. To love enough and be loved enough, to love and be loved in such quantities, such abundance that you could squander whole nights in simple companionship—that was a richness she could hardly fathom.

The man in the bed next to her in her imagination was Frederick Barrow, of course. He turned to her with that almost amused blaze of desire, as if he had surprised himself with his own need and intensity, and he took hold of her arms, pinning her to the bed, as he had done in the dark

217

in New York, the smoke detector blinking overhead.

Women in love, Annie thought as she climbed into bed. She gave a rueful smile, thought how little she liked D. H. Lawrence, wondered what Frederick thought of him and if she would ever have an opportunity to ask him. An owl hooted outside the window. Another owl answered it. Annie realized she had never heard an owl in real life before. Was this real life, though? Sometimes her life struck her as a mistake, not in a big, violent way, but as a simple error, as if she had thought she was supposed to bear left at an intersection when she should have taken a sharp left, and had drifted slowly, gradually, into the wrong town, the wrong state, the wrong country; as if she returned to a book she was reading after staring out the window at the rain, but someone had turned the page. The owl hooted again, one owl. It was a beautiful nighttime sound, and she fell asleep.

*   *   *

In the morning, Cousin Lou wanted to take them all out for pancakes. Annie could not imagine how she would escape and be able to keep her secret assignation with Amber until Miranda refused to get out of bed.

'Should I stay and keep an eye on her?' Annie asked her mother. 'I think maybe I should.'

'Poor bunny,' Betty said, kissing Miranda before she left with the others.

If Miranda looked like a bunny, it was the road-kill variety, Annie thought. Overnight her lithe frame seemed to have become merely angular,

218

skeletal. Her cheekbones appeared to have sharpened, to jut coarsely from a gaunt face, while her eyes, her remarkable eyes, sagged with apathy where they once had curved, enigmatic, playful.

'Oh, just please go away,' Miranda said to her.

'I'll take a little walk?'

Miranda gave a barely perceptible shrug.

*   *   *

Annie was no golfer and had to Google the country club and study a diagram of the golf course in order to figure out where the fifth hole was and how to reach it from Lou and Rosalyn's house. It was uncharacteristically hot for December. She walked along in the crisp winter sun, the desert outline distinct, legible against the hard blue sky, and wondered what Amber could want.

She did not have long to wait to find out. At the crest of a little green golf hill, as prominent as a general on his magnificent stallion, Amber sat in the yellow golf cart surveying her domain.

The general wore a pink floral-print blouse; nevertheless there was something warlike about the girl's bearing. She dismounted and strode over, her carefully tapered eyebrows drawn together in a purposeful frown. 'You're the only one I can trust,' she said.

'Thank you,' Annie said uncertainly. She wished she had worn a hat. She put up a hand to shade her eyes. 'Can we sit in the golf cart? Out of the sun?'

Amber nodded gravely and led the way to the cart.

'Now,' Annie said, noting Amber's determined little frown. She thought of her heartbroken sister,

219

her heartbroken mother, her own heartbroken self, and she felt a rush of sympathy for this girl, whatever the problem might be. She put her hand on Amber's tanned arm. 'What is it?'

Another golf cart, bearing an older man and woman, puttered by. The couple were pretending to argue, laughing and pointing their fingers at each other.

'We have a friend in common,' Amber said.

'We have several.'

'I mean *another* one.'

The grass shimmered in the light. Annie waited. Amber had beautiful hands, a short shapely manicure. Annie looked down at her own blunt nails.

'Do you know Gwendolyn Barrow?' Amber asked.

'Gwendolyn Barrow?' What could Frederick's daughter have to do with Amber? 'Well, yes, I've met her. Once or twice.'

'What do you think of her?'

'I don't really have an opinion, Amber. As I said, I met her just a couple of times. Do you know her?'

'No, not her, but I know someone very close to her. And I know *him* very well.' She pursed her lips and gave Annie a sly look.

'Oh,' said Annie. 'You're friends with her brother Evan?'

'No, no, not Evan,' Amber said. '*Freddie.*'

Amber had rather humid eyes, Annie noticed. Big, moist brown eyes. Like an animal, a hooved animal. 'Freddie?'

'The *father.* Frederick, Freddie.'

Annie willed the blush away. 'Ah, *Frederick.* Yes,

220

I know him. I didn't realize you did, too.'

Amber pulled her mouth again into the little simpering smile. She tilted her head and, from that angle, caught Annie's eye. 'I know him, all right,' she said.

Heat radiated down from the canvas roof of the golf cart. The clarity of the air was unrelenting. Even billowing clouds looked hard, sharply outlined against the blue sky.

'I knew I could trust you. He speaks so highly of you.'

'Does he?' Annie felt Amber watching her, scrutinizing her, looking for clues. She breathed as regularly as she could and looked Amber in the eye. Freddie, indeed. 'Well, I think very highly of Frederick, too.'

Amber bit her plump lower lip and nodded. It was a proprietary gesture, an acknowledgement that others might well admire what was hers. She offered Annie a piece of gum from a blister pack and, when Annie refused, popped three pieces into her own mouth. The smell of artificial fruit, which Annie associated with air fresheners in public bathrooms, wafted over from the gum.

'How do you know Frederick? If you don't mind my asking.'

'Oh no, I totally don't. It's one of the things I really need to share with you. So, Crystal and I were home-sitting for him. He has this gorgeous home in Massachusetts. On the water and everything. But then Crystal was at this seminar.'

Amber stopped and looked uncomfortable.

'She's a student, too?' Annie asked. She had no idea where this private meeting under the blazing sun was going, but she wanted to move it along.

'Crystal? Yeah. She's going for her certificate to be a life coach. And so she was gone, right? And then Freddie came back unexpectedly, and well, it just sort of happened.' She paused and assumed a dreamy expression.

Annie listened in a fog of abstracted fascination. She could scarcely understand the words formed by Amber's pretty lips, much less believe them, yet of course she heard and of course she knew it was absolutely true. Frederick, her Frederick, though he was hers only in her imagination and her memory, her Frederick and this girl. 'I'm not sure why you're telling me this,' she said as politely as she could. Although she was quite sure of one reason. Amber was staking her claim, planting her flag, and at the same time doing a little reconnaissance of the enemy lines. You really are a general at war, Annie thought. But I am not your enemy. I'm the war-torn village, the smoking rubble abandoned by all but the crows.

'It was such a coincidence when I saw you here! I feel this heavy burden, in more ways than one, believe me, and there you were. It just seemed so perfect. Like, ordained almost. I super hate having this secret.'

'But why is it a secret at all?'

Amber gave a bitter sigh. 'His family.'

Annie almost laughed. Yes, they would be a problem.

'I've never met them, right? But I can tell already that Gwendolyn is very possessive. Very, very possessive. And controlling. Freddie practically told me. And the son—he just wants Freddie in New York. They both do.'

'But there's nothing wrong with wanting to be

close to your father.'

'They just want him at their dinner parties to impress their friends. Believe me, I know the type. He's a celebrity, you know. In that world, anyway. You have to have an artistic sense to get what I mean. Have you ever read any of his books?'

Annie nodded.

'Oh. Well, I haven't. Yet. They're not my thing, instinctively, if you know what I mean, but they're very impressive. I mean, he's won prizes. His children treat him like a trophy.' She laughed: '"Trophy Dad"! I never thought of that one before.'

Annie did not laugh. She wondered if the night Frederick came home unexpectedly was the night of the library reading. I had to thank you, he'd said, coming back to her. I'll call you, he'd said. No wonder he had never called. This girl had been there, at his house, waiting for him like a girlish spider. Annie gave Amber a new appraisal—the perfect, slender curves, the young vibrant skin, the almost pretty face, the general overwhelming aura of youth and health and life. And how astute Amber turned out to be, as well. Trophy Dad. Yes, she was dead on about that, this formidable bimboesque person.

'Those kids of his take him for granted. They're after his money, too, trust me. And free babysitting. I've seen it before.'

As Amber seemed to have finished, Annie parted her lips in preparation for speech, but what was there to say? What was there, even, to think? Frederick was the man who turned to her in bed and recited all of Sonnet 116. Frederick was the brother of the woman who had stolen her mother's life. Frederick was the lover of this coy yet oddly earnest girl.

'They would never approve of me,' Amber resumed, very agitated now. 'I'm only twenty-two years old!'

More like thirty, Annie thought uncharitably. Either way, she was far too young for Frederick Barrow. She could just picture Gwendolyn's tight, suspicious face at the sight of Amber and the panda tattoo on her arm. She felt suddenly sorry for Amber.

'But, I mean, he *is* a grown man,' Annie said, finding her voice at last. 'He certainly doesn't need his children's approval to have a'—she stumbled, looking for the right word—'girlfriend,' she said.

'But don't you see?' Amber took both of Annie's hot swollen hands in her own young smooth ones. 'It's different now. I mean, because, you know, we're engaged.'

Annie did a double take. She couldn't help it.

'You and Frederick are engaged?'

'We *are*. You see . . .' Amber leaned close to Annie now and whispered shyly in her ear: 'I'm pregnant.'

CHAPTER FOURTEEN

Beneath a garish blue sky, Annie made her way quickly across the synthetic golf-course terrain. It was unimaginable, this story of Amber's. She, at least, had never imagined it. In what world could Frederick, her Frederick, even Felicity's Frederick, be the father of Amber's child?

224

In this world, this very one, the one with clean-shaven lawns and exaggerated sunlight. It was unimaginable, and yet it was true. Like so many stories, the stories she never read, the stories Miranda liked so much. Palm trees spread out before her, their tall, curved trunks and symmetrical spray of fronds, such platitudes, like cartoons, like doodles, like a neon sign.

Frederick was going to marry Amber.

Annie had been so careful these last months to view her relationship with Frederick in the clearest light of the clearest day: he was drawn to her, he liked her; he was a man who had lived alone for a long time and seemed to like it that way; his children wanted him unencumbered by a wife, by a rival for their affections, their control, their inheritance; his wide-eyed sister had torn apart her mother's life. Annie had shone the light of reality on what she knew was an unlikely match, Annie Weissmann and Frederick Barrow. She had talked to herself and explained the situation in all its unpromising detail. She had also, she now knew, fallen in love.

Perhaps, she thought, it would be more accurate to say that *love* had fallen, fallen like a log in her path. And she had tripped over it. Still, she'd landed on her feet, hadn't she? In an attempt to illustrate how much better suited for sorrow her sister was than she, Miranda sometimes dismissively declared that Annie always landed on her feet, like a cat. Annie sighed and thought of a cat's pretty little feet, so dainty and treacherous. She did not feel like a cat. Her feet did not feel like a cat's paws. They felt flat and enormous and abused, the dead feet of an old and weary waitress.

The tears came. They evaporated in the heat. They reappeared. They disappeared again. Everything dies, Annie thought. Even tears.

Pregnant. She repeated the word to herself several times, but she could not connect it to Amber and Frederick. Funny, she thought, since it was a word that embodied, literally, the connection between them. Among them, she corrected herself. Among the three of them: Amber, Frederick, and the proto-baby. But try as she would, all she could really imagine and understand, each time she silently uttered the word 'pregnant', was the memory, the reality, of her own pregnancies: the humid, overheated, swollen fleshy physicality of it; the weight of her belly pulling down and straining, simultaneously, horizontally, in its taut width; the vast dense fatigue; the fear, the pride, the terror, the joy, the extravagant joy. She had stretched herself out on the couch and read *War and Peace* both times, a different translation with each pregnancy. Yet she had never read *Anna Karenina*. Odd. But was it so odd? She had started *Anna Karenina* numerous times, and with each attempt had been flooded with a startled anxious concern for Anna and her comfort that made her close the book in panic. She didn't want to know what she already knew.

She suddenly missed her children. She missed them as the young men they were and as the babies they had been. The soft wavy hair that had become coarser with age, the little dirty hands that had grown big and clean, the eyes that looked out from their manly faces, eyes that were the same eyes she had looked into when each one was first placed, blue and scrawny, on her exhausted belly.

226

For the first time that she could remember, Annie felt alone, truly and desperately alone. Even when her husband had disappeared and she had been left to fend for herself with two little boys, there had been the two little boys. Now they were gone, too. They loved her and called her and sent her emails and would still snuggle up to her to be petted when they were in the mood, but they were men, and though they would always be at the centre of her life, she was no longer at the centre of theirs.

She imagined Frederick coming home to his house, a house he loved and longed for. Perhaps it was that very night he left her at the library and his children urged him to stay in the city with them. He had driven and driven in the highway's nighttime of passing headlights and blank horizons. He had stopped for coffee, certainly. Maybe a doughnut, too. Then back in the car, his knees a little stiff, squinting at the windshield. When he finally pulled into his driveway, with what joy and relief he saw his little house, or his big rambling house, or whatever size house he had, with what joy and relief—a surge of emotion. I'm home, he thought. At last, I'm home. And then there, in her tiny jersey shorts and camisole, getting herself a late-night snack or pouring yet another glass of wine, there was Amber, a beautiful young woman in his kitchen smelling of the bath she had just taken, her skin glowing with youth and health. And she would have greeted him with so much warmth. And poured a glass of wine for him. And then they would have gone out onto the porch and listened to the sea as it swished up onto the sand. The stars would have stared down

227

at them, or they would have watched the clouds rush across the face of the moon. He would throw out some lines of Shakespeare, she would be thrilled. He was so happy to be home. And part of that home was the pretty home sitter, someone so comfortable, so natural, in his kitchen, on the arm of his Adirondack chair on his porch, the arm of his Adirondack chair in which he was sitting while she kneaded his shoulders with her strong, young healer hands. And then, on the arm of his Adirondack chair, his own arm would notice her bare thigh against it, and the thought of comfort would fly from his mind, swept out by another thought, a new thought, an unexpected thought, but one he could not now unthink. And his hand would move to the suggestive curve of her leg, and he would take the suggestion and move his hand higher. And, with a little moan, the home sitter would slip into his lap, at home . . .

Annie, to her horror, could, and did, envision every movement of this New England soft-core courtship.

Turn the page, she told herself. Better yet, close the book.

*   *   *

Miranda had waited until her sister, that hovering, omnipresent figure of concern, had finally gone off for a walk. Then she sat up in bed. She opened her computer.

There he was.

He had stopped wearing pants with whales on them. He wore jeans in the picture, like everyone else, and a designer army jacket, like everyone

228

else. He even had on the obligatory Hollywood hat, a small brimmed straw hipster hat with a ribbon band. And the red string. She hadn't noticed that last night. The red fucking Kabbalah string. Beside him was the actress, Ingrid Chopin, a slight, dark woman with a voluptuous chest and a dazzling smile. Her long hair tumbled like wild vines onto her shoulders. She was irresistible, Miranda could see. She was at least forty, though she passed for thirty-five. A less-older woman, but another older woman nevertheless.

What does she have that I don't have? Miranda asked herself. Let me count the ways.

She pushed the laptop away. She returned to the position Annie had left her in, a tight fetal loop of enraged humiliation. Her arms, extraneous things, coiled around her. Her thoughts raged. You moron, you cretin, you thick-headed, gullible old bag. You thought you would have a little family with a little white picket fence, you and your handsome hero and your innocent little child friend. But you have nothing. Your life is a mess. A folly. A blank. You will not be spending your waning years with your attentive husband and adoring little boy. You will be alone, ranting, in a cardboard box in Riverside Park. White picket fence? Your home will be spattered by the white excrement of pigeons. Your life is empty. A shoe box. A few dead bees.

'It's just a nobby,' she growled into the pillow. 'It's just a fucking nobby.'

*   *   *

Annie slunk from the blazing outdoors into the

bedroom, hoping somehow to be alone, but there was her sister, knotted up on her bed, embalmed in air-conditioning. For just a moment, Annie thought of confiding in her. She would sit on the side of the bed and tell Miranda how profoundly let down she was, how fatigued and defeated, how beleaguered, how disappointed. She would sink back into the bed in her misery and stare at the ceiling, and Miranda would lie beside her, and they would talk and talk and talk until Frederick and Amber were dismantled, torn into smaller and smaller pieces, bits so small and tattered and insignificant they just floated away.

Miranda opened her eyes, said, 'Jesus, Annie. Go away,' and closed them again.

Rebuffed, rejected before she had said a word. Annie felt the heat she had just left and the chill of the room coursing through her. It was all too much. It was all too little.

'Why are you just *lying* there?' she said.

She poked Miranda's shoulder.

She was suddenly, finally, thoroughly angry, so angry the blood came rushing to her head. Poor little Miranda, poor ever-suffering Miranda. 'It's pathetic! Get up!'

Miranda sat up, her hair stuck to one side of her face. 'What is your problem?'

'What's my problem?' Annie was almost dizzy now, a blind ferocious nausea of fury and disillusionment. 'That's a first.'

'What the hell is that supposed to mean?'

'It means you're a diva,' Annie said. 'It means you're a self-important diva. Do you even notice that other people *have* problems?'

Miranda looked stunned, then the color began

to creep up her neck. '*Since* you bring it up, at least I don't try to control everyone else's life like you.' Her voice darkened with strangled tears. 'Why don't you get a fucking life of your own?'

Now they began to fight the way they had as girls—nasty, vicious, both of them crying. It went on like this, ugly and loud.

'I'm tired, okay?' Annie sobbed. She wiped away tears with her hand. 'Stupid,' she said. 'Damn.' She drew her arm across her eyes. 'Tired. Tired of figuring out the money while you buy boats and Mom buys Chanel suits. Tired of being the grown-up . . .'

'Whoa! And you call *me* self-important?'

'*Miranda is upset, Annie, so we can't possibly take you to ballet class* . . . You and your theatrical breakdowns devoured my childhood . . .'

'Ballet class? You mean where you stomped around wearing an undershirt under your tutu? With *sleeves* . . .'

'I was *shy.* I was *cold.*'

'You *stole* my troll.'

'*You* stole it from Debby Dickstein. *I* gave it back. I was just trying to help.' Annie's voice veered into the hated high register of female weeping. 'That's all I ever do. I try and I try . . .'

'Yeah? Well, instead of being such a martyr, why can't you just leave me alone to mind my own business?'

Annie shot her sister a venomous look. She said, '*Business?* That's a good one.'

Miranda was suddenly still. There was no sound but the hum of the air conditioner. She said softly, 'Fuck you, Annie. Fuck you and your worries and your budgets and your cramped little life. Fuck

231

you, fuck you, fuck you.'

Annie, watching herself in disbelief, threw a lamp at her sister, a white lamp shaped like a giraffe, the giraffe's head popping up over the white shade. The giraffe bounced on the bed, lay there peering sideways.

'Amber is pregnant,' she said. 'Frederick is the father.'

Watching Miranda's eyes widen, Annie thought, So *there*.

'Oh, Annie . . .'

'So fuck *you,* fuck *you,* fuck *you.'* And Annie left the room, slamming the large shivering glass door behind her.

*   *   *

The next day was Christmas. Miranda had tried to speak to Annie, to tell her that yes, Annie was right, Miranda was a melodramatic monster who appropriated every emotion she could get her hands on, that she was selfish, that Annie was selfless and good and suffered in silence and could she ever forgive her? But Annie refused to listen.

They both did their best to conceal the estrangement from their mother. Betty, thankfully, seemed more dislocated than usual and noticed nothing. She waited for Roberts with the rest of them in the living room. He was going to take them all, including Amber and Crystal, to a secret place he knew, a cave in a canyon, shady and cool, looking out on cactus and brush, an easy walk from the road. There would be a picnic with cherry pie and apple pie and pumpkin pie. And there would be a turkey and a goose. It was Christmas, after all.

'And every good Jew knows what is required,' Rosalyn said.

Annie, ashamed of her outburst the day before and so even angrier at Miranda, thought back to their childhood Christmas trees. There were little wooden Santas on skis, glass balls whirling with color, reindeer, teddy bears in red stocking caps. 'Now remember, girls,' Josie would say as they danced around the tree, hanging the ornaments from its fragrant branches. The *Nutcracker Suite* played on the stereo. 'Remember. This holiday celebrates the birth of a man in whose name an entire religion has persecuted and murdered our people for thousands of years.' He would look at them sternly. 'You understand that, don't you?'

'Yes, Josie.'

'Good! And knowing that, why should we let them have all the fun, right?' And he would break out into an enormous grin, and the sisters would dance like ballerinas, their arms stretched above them, spinning and spinning until they fell, dizzy and exhilarated, onto the floor.

'Where is Roberts?' Betty asked now. 'I feel just like a kid. I want to get on the road!' In fact, she wanted to get on a plane and go home. The memories of so many happy Christmas mornings were unbearable in this strange, empty place with its sunshine and rocks. But she could not spoil Christmas for her daughters. She clapped her hands and smiled at them, remembering the children they had been and would always be to her.

Annie forced herself to smile back at her mother. Betty was still wearing black, today a black sweater with a lavender gray scarf, but lavender was a color the Victorians used for light mourning, right before they reverted back to their normal clothes. Could this be a sign? Was Betty coming out of her distracted depression? Perhaps this trip had at least been good for someone.

Annie sat down on the corner of the couch, brooding. She assiduously avoided eye contact with Miranda. She hated the bright sun, unsparing and ugly. She hated the mountains. Cousin Lou offered her a mimosa. She shook her head. She closed her eyes. She was waiting for Amber to arrive as if anticipating a blow.

Then, a rustling, a shift in the couch cushion. She sensed someone next to her, someone leaning against her, someone so familiar she might just as well have been a part of Annie.

'I miss Josie,' Miranda said, her head now heavy on Annie's shoulder.

'"Why should they have all the fun,"' Annie said softly.

The heavy head nodded. The fight had come to an end.

*   *   *

Roberts never did appear. He called on his way to the airport. He had sudden, urgent business in Connecticut. He was sorry. The Christmas outing had to be cancelled.

In the general commotion following this announcement, Mr Shpuntov spilled a glass of water, pointed a crooked finger at Rosalyn, and said, 'So, Mr Plumber! You took your time getting here.' He turned his finger to the wet carpet. 'Leaky roof, torrential rains. What next?'

'We'll miss our Family Jewish Christmas picnic?' Cousin Lou was saying, dismayed.

'A plumber on Christmas?' Rosalyn said to her father. 'Now, that would be a miracle!'

'Come on, mister,' he replied brusquely, 'get to work, get to work now.'

'Oh, what's the big deal?' Miranda said. 'It's only a picnic.'

'Life is not a picnic.' Betty spoke in a dull singsong, as if she were reciting the multiplication table. 'Once again.'

*   *   *

They spread the picnic food out on the dining room table, then assembled in the living room with their paper plates on their knees. Annie sat on an isolated chair to protect herself from any further intimacies with Amber, but Amber simply sat on the floor at her feet.

'I hope I didn't, you know, upset you,' Amber said quietly. 'You know, about my secret.'

'Upset me?' Annie listened to her voice, relieved that it was level and neutral. 'Why would you think that? After all, I'm not your mother. Or Frederick's mother, for that matter.' She affected an astonished laugh, but when Amber did not confirm the absurdity of either of those scenarios, she sobered immediately.

'Still,' Amber said, 'I don't know. You seemed kind of pissed. No, not pissed. But like critical? Or cold? That was the vibe I got, Annie, to be honest. I mean, maybe you guys had a flirtationship or something. Of course, I know there was nothing *really* going on. But I just wanted to clear the air.

Because I felt badly. Like, had I been too personal or whatever.'

'You have no reason to worry, Amber.'

Did Amber get the point? Oh yes, Annie thought she did. Just as Annie had gotten the point: whatever might have happened between you, which of course could not be much, because here I am carrying his baby, as they say on the soaps, whatever happened, it didn't really happen at all.

'God! Total relief!'

'It must be pretty tough, walking around with that kind of secret.'

Amber gave a little laugh of agreement.

'Especially since it can't really stay a secret,' Annie added, enjoying the touch of cruelty in the remark. 'I'm sorry the family part is so awful,' she said, to compensate. 'His kids *are* pretty proprietary. But, you know, Amber, even if they weren't, it's always hard—a new member of an established family.' Not to mention two new members, she thought. Poor Amber. Fireworks ahead. 'Oh well, I guess you won't be the first stepmother in the world.'

'Stepmother?' Amber looked confused. 'Oh, *them*.' A bitter laugh. 'Right. He's so devoted to them.'

She said the word 'devoted' as if it were a disease Frederick had caught from his children.

'I mean, he's always having to go into New York to see them, to stay with them. God, he can't be away from them for more than a few days. I sure as hell don't spend that much time with my father. And I wouldn't want to, either. Couldn't pay me to. We fight like cats and dogs, me and him. Wait till

236

he hears about this. That should be fun on a bun. But what the fuck.'

'What the fuck,' Annie repeated.

'Freddie is so scared Gwen will hijack his grandchildren once he tells her. Like he'll have time for grandchildren, with his own baby? I don't think so. But tell him that. Well, he'll just have to get used to the situation, I can understand that. God bless. He hasn't been in this position in a long time, right? That's what my trainer says.'

'You told your trainer?'

'Well, not in so many words, but they feel things, they can just tell. And I had to let her know I was pregnant.' She lowered her voice when she said 'pregnant', the way people sometimes do when they say 'gay' or 'black' or 'cancer'.

'So I know it will take a while, and if I didn't know how he really felt, I guess I would be really insecure and defensive. But since I'm so sure, I can totally wait.' She paused: assessing, Annie thought. Then, seemingly satisfied with Annie's studied neutrality, she continued: 'And if I really thought he wanted me to, I would get an abortion, you know.' She straightened her spine and let her chin jut out prettily. 'I would do anything to make him happy.'

'But he didn't want you to?'

'Oh my God, no. He asked what *I* wanted, isn't that *so* totally Mr Frederick Barrow? And did I want him to get in touch with a doctor he knew, and of course he would pay and everything, but when I said that he had no obligation at all to even recognize his own child as his own, because after all we're all children of the planet in a way, you understand what I mean, I know you do, well, he

237

wouldn't hear of that. He's an honorable human being. And of course, he was just looking out for me, because I'm so young and everything.'

Poor Frederick had gotten himself caught in a web spun of his own thread, part manly sexual adventure, part manly honor. Annie could see that there was no way out. She tried to conjure up the anger of the day before. He was old enough to know better, he was irresponsible, there was a completely innocent life at stake, hadn't he thought about that, hadn't he ever heard of contraceptives, was he so out of control? But really all she could feel now was pity. He had made a mistake and he would pay for it for the rest of his life.

'There you are!' Mr Shpuntov yelled out, spotting Rosalyn. 'Highway robbery. I should have been a plumber, I tell you.'

'You *were* a plumber,' Rosalyn said drily. 'For fifty years.'

Miranda watched Cousin Lou lead Mr Shpuntov into the dining room. She sat as far from everyone as she could. She ate her goose and her duck and her apple pie. She drank eggnog. She offered Annie the occasional sheepish smile, which Annie returned in kind. She participated in the lighting of the Hanukkah candles. Poor Hanukkah, she thought as she did every year, as if it were a bird with a bent wing she'd found on the sidewalk. It was the third night of the holiday. They had completely forgotten the first two.

CHAPTER FIFTEEN

Frederick's house, gray-shingled, late-Victorian, had been in his family for almost a hundred years. He and his sister, Felicity, had both grown up in the warren of oddly shaped bedrooms and parlors and pivoting stairways. When their parents died suddenly (Arthur Barrow in 1980, Mary the year after), the house was all they left behind. It seemed fitting—two sickly, cranky, frail old people, stranded in the wrong era, leaving behind a house as sickly, cranky, frail, and outdated as they had been, a wood-framed earthly shadow, a leaky memorial. On the day of their mother's funeral, Frederick and Felicity had gone back to the house to accept the condolences of the surprising number of people who attended the funeral. Felicity had prepared sandwiches the night before—small, ceremonial, and now quite dried out. She took the tray out, set it down on the mahogany dining table that had always reminded her of an outsized coffin, then returned to the kitchen. She found her mother's big 'festivity' percolator, the one dragged out for Thanksgiving and Christmas and Easter dinner, turned on the faucet, and tipped the percolator clumsily into the sink.

The ancient pipes hemmed and hawed, then sputtered to life. She heard a toilet flush, loud, surprised, exasperated. A family of squirrels had gotten into the attic and worked their way down the walls. With their tiny, verminous claws, they scratched out muffled, secret sounds. Felicity had never liked the house. She disliked the fog, the mournful foghorns, the sound of the ocean, the smell of the ocean—its filthy odor of rotting seaweed and rotting shellfish. She hated the smug insularity of the summer people, and she hated the mirrored smug insularity of the year-round people. It had not been until she made her college escape from Cape Cod to Manhattan that Felicity experienced what felt like fresh air. In New York, she felt as though she could truly breathe for the first time.

She filled the percolator and turned the water off. The pipes gave a strangled sigh. The house was constantly sighing. Structural self-pity.

She had tried to talk Frederick into selling the house even before their mother died. But he was stubborn in his flimsy, easygoing way. 'I love this house,' he said in response, as if that were a response.

Felicity lugged the percolator out to the dining room and plugged it in. A spark flew from the electrical outlet.

The house's revenge, she thought. Trying to kill me before I can kill it.

But later, she realized that this had been exactly the spark she needed. The spark of an idea. For there she had stood, looking at the frayed cord of the percolator in her hand, at the yellowed plate that surrounded the outlet, at the wood floor that creaked even when no one stepped across it, as if it were a ship struggling through the sea, and the idea, so simple, so obvious, hit her.

She took Frederick by the arm and guided him back into the kitchen.

'You love this house,' she said.

Frederick produced one of his looks, the clear

240

dark-eyed expression of a rogue trapped helplessly in his own sincerity, the look that drew so many women to him.

'I'm agreeing,' she said. 'Christ. I *said, You* love this house, okay?'

'Okay.'

'And *I* don't *want* this house.'

He sighed and said, 'Felicity, it's the day of the funeral. Can we . . .'

'Buy me out,' she said. 'It's so simple. Buy me out.'

Frederick gave her a fair price, or so she thought at the time. She'd immediately invested the money in the stock market and had done fairly well with it. Still, as time passed and she thought it over, the whole thing didn't seem quite fair. It was almost, well, not exactly shady, but . . . Over the years, the house had increased in value far more than her stocks had, and that value had then fallen far less than her stocks'. If Frederick sold it now, he'd make a fortune. And wasn't half that fortune really, by rights (maybe not by law, but by rights), hers?

'Well,' she was often heard to say to Frederick, '*you* certainly got a bargain.'

'Well,' she said to Joseph as they settled into the guest bedroom that had once been her parents' bedroom, '*he* certainly got a bargain.'

The whole family had gathered in the house for Christmas. Gwen, her husband, Ron, and the twins had adjoining rooms on the second floor. Evan was across the hall from them in the smaller bedroom next to Felicity and Joseph. Frederick's room was on the ground floor. He had long ago converted the east parlors, front and back, to his own use—

241

the front parlor with the bow window was where he worked, the back parlor his bedroom. It was there that he stood at the window this Christmas morning watching the insipid winter dawn.

Felicity, lying in bed with a frown on her face, was also looking out the window.

'Joe,' she said.

Joseph gave a round, trumpeting snore, followed by a series of liquid burbles.

'Joe,' Felicity said again. She turned and pushed his shoulder gently, then more forcefully.

'Sorry,' he murmured. The snores retreated for a moment, then came back in force.

Felicity got out of bed, as she had gotten into it, hating the house. The tiny chambers, the sea pounding in her ears—it was like being buried, impotent and rotting, forced to listen to that mocking, immortal sound. And now the snoring. Buried alive with the sea and a snorer. She put on a robe and slippers. Impossible to heat the house. And still it was worth a fortune! She creaked down the stairs.

Frederick heard her. Her tread was instantly identifiable—a quick, sharp step. He met her at the bottom of the stairs.

'Coffee?' he said.

'You're up awfully early.' She raised an eyebrow at his rumpled corduroy pants and moth-eaten sweater. He really was absurdly affected.

'I'm not sure I ever went to bed.'

'Bad conscience?'

To Felicity's surprise, her brother seemed to start.

'What?' he said sternly. 'What do you mean?'

Felicity laughed. 'I'm not sure, Frederick. What

242

did I mean? I obviously meant something or you wouldn't look like a dog who's been in the garbage. Have you been in the garbage?'

Frederick considered confessing. Yes, he would say, I have been in the garbage. I have strewn garbage everywhere, and now I must live with it, great stinking mounds of my own garbage, chronic irreversible garbage that I richly deserve and would settle into like Job without complaint, except that it involves an innocent being, a poor wee soul about to be born into a loveless faux family, God forgive me.

'Coffee, yes or no?' he said.

They sat in the kitchen, steam from their mugs rising in the faint wash of white daylight.

'Joe seems like a nice guy,' Frederick said. The bland remark expected of him. But Joe did seem like a nice guy. Annie had never told him any particulars about the ongoing divorce, nor did she have to—he had only to look at Betty the two times he'd met her to understand. He had seen a hundred such women, a thousand. They flocked to his readings, to the workshops and classes he sometimes taught. They were an identifiable class of citizens, America's lost souls, like the lost boys of Africa, but they were not boys, they were women, older women, still beautiful in their older way, still vibrant in their older way, with their beauty and vibrancy suddenly accosted by the one thing beauty and vibrancy cannot withstand— irrelevance. Yes, Joseph seemed like a nice guy. And he had done what even nice guys do. Frederick would have liked to feel outrage toward Joseph Weissmann. But he did not dare. His sympathies, he realized sadly, must lie with Joseph now, for they were compatriots, fellows in the fellowship of heels.

'He's a new man,' Felicity said. 'Thank God.'

'You didn't like the old one?'

'Don't be stupid, Frederick.'

'Well, you showed great foresight, seeing the new man in the old one.'

Felicity gave him a short, searing smile. 'We fell in love. He needed me.'

'And there, providentially, you were.'

Felicity blew her nose. 'This house is freezing.'

'I like his daughter. Annie. That was a nice gesture, Felicity, getting us together for that reading.'

'Oh, that. I thought it might soften the blow. At least you're good for something.' She patted his arm affectionately. He was quite a bit older than she was, but he was so unworldly. This frayed wool sweater business, for instance. She picked at a loose thread.

'And what's the other daughter's name?' he said.

'*Step*daughter. And even so, the man is absolutely devoted to them. As if they were, well, you know, his real daughters. Indulged them, spoiled them. But you just have to be firm as they get older. Strong. When it matters. I think he sees that now, poor, sweet, generous man. Of course, it's all very painful for me, in particular. The stepmother and all.'

'And all,' Frederick agreed absently.

*   *   *

The day after Christmas, Crystal and Amber were to fly back East. Their Palm Springs home-sitting

244

was over, the house on the golf course reclaimed.

'Like two Gypsies, you girls,' Rosalyn said with envy. 'Or two birds, migrating here and there. Always on the wing.'

Annie entertained the unworthy thought of an albatross. Didn't they stay aloft for a year at a time? Among other things.

They were returning to an earlier home-sitting location: the house on Cape Cod. 'We feel so at home there,' Amber said. She glanced at Annie. 'It's such a beautiful old house.'

'A little too old if you ask me,' Crystal added with a snigger.

'But no one did ask you, did they, Crystal?'

Nor me, Annie thought as she waved goodbye to the two young women. The yellow golf cart trolled off among the verdant golf hills, its fringe giving a jaunty shake in the desert breeze.

*   *   *

'My new home,' Amber whispered to Crystal as they drove their rental car up the driveway. '*Summer* home, I should say. No way I'm living here all year around.'

Felicity was the first to hear the car.

'Who's that, I wonder.' She drew aside the curtain.

'Oh,' Frederick said as nonchalantly as he could, 'some friends. Coming to stay for a few days. The girls who sometimes house-sit for me.'

'Your house sitters?' Evan said. 'At Christmas?'

'When *we're* all here?' Gwen said.

'Well,' said Frederick, 'I wanted you to meet them.'

Evan and Gwen looked at each other.

'Are you trying to fix me up or something, Dad?' Evan said. 'Because, really, I can find my own girls, and I mean, your loser house sitters?'

'No, Evan, I am not trying to fix you up, believe me.'

*   *   *

'It's so nice to meet you,' Amber said when Frederick introduced the sisters to his children. 'Freddie talks about you all the time.'

'Freddie?' said Evan.

'She means your father,' Crystal explained confidentially.

Frederick said, 'Never mind, never mind. Here's my sister, Felicity. And this is her friend Joe.'

'Freddie?' Evan was saying in astonishment to his sister.

The sisters moved into the attic bedroom and, they pointed out, would make themselves at home, no one needed to bother about them, since the house was practically their home; after all, they had spent so much time home-sitting in it.

Amber knew she had a high hill to climb, and she knew, too, that the going would be tough. She squared her pretty shoulders. Might as well get started at once. She had exaggerated only slightly to Annie: there had definitely been talk of marriage, or at least living together. But it was clear to her that she would have to neutralize Gwen and Evan first.

'What a great home,' she said to Gwen. 'So much history. I found a picture of it from, like, over a hundred years ago. On the Internet. It took me weeks, but . . . Here.'

She had actually called the town museum and talked to an archivist who emailed it to her a few days before. She handed Gwen the copy she had printed out on thick matte photographic paper.

Gwen looked pleased in spite of herself. 'Thanks.' She examined the photo. 'I've never seen this one. It looks so bare, doesn't it?'

'Your family obviously did a lot with the grounds.'

Gwen nodded. 'The rosebushes.'

'Heirlooms.' Then feeling a little more comfortable, Amber said, 'Speaking of heirlooms, did your dad ever get that bathtub drain fixed? I reminded him about it a thousand times. That dad of yours, head in the clouds, right? Artists, right?'

Gwen looked at her blankly.

Amber, sensing she had gone too far too fast, tried to shift into reverse. 'Such a beautiful old tub. With those claws? I brought some new bath salts. Perfect for that luxurious antique tub. I got them on a professional massage-therapy website. They're organic. They even have hemp in them.' She bent down and unzipped her bag, pulling out a jar. 'Would you like to try them?'

'No,' Gwen said, her voice cold again. 'I have no interest in hemp, thank you very much.'

'I do,' Evan said. 'Just not in my bath.'

'Oh yeah?' Crystal said. 'Well, I have some really good weed . . .'

And so it was Crystal, not Amber, who chiselled the first real social chink in the Barrow family wall. Amber felt the victory had practically been handed to Crystal on a silver platter, and that it wasn't such a very big victory anyway, and she watched with a

247

mixture of pique and gratification as Crystal and Evan retired to the back porch.

CHAPTER SIXTEEN

The winter blew through Westport, hard and fast, as if it were a season in a hurry, ready to get the whole messy business over with and move on. There was just one big snowstorm, which dissolved in the bright yellow sun of the following morning, and one ice storm that brought with it a townwide loss of power as branches fell to the ground, hundreds of them, sheathed in frozen rain, heavy and ornate as French mirrors. Some gray skies hovered, some wind blew through, a fair amount of rain fell. And then, suddenly, in February, deep blue heavens and gentle breezes and mud.

When the Weissmanns returned from Palm Springs at the beginning of January, the snow had just come and gone and the ground was oozing. Betty decided to take up online poker in an attempt to supplement the family income. Annie and Miranda had forgiven if not forgotten what each had said to the other and were on precariously good terms, but Annie tried to spend as much time as possible at the library. Even there, however, she felt the need to escape. When she could no longer stand the part of her job that required her to speak to board members and ask bibliophilic rich people for money, she would retreat to the library's attic and putter. She told the staff she was looking for artefacts, and she did discover a discolored letter from George

Washington in a frame with cracked glass, as well as the first volume of the two-volume first American edition of *Sense and Sensibility*. But the main reason she dug through piles of broken chairs and abandoned space heaters was to be alone. It had become an aching, physical need. The beach in Westport, where once she had felt so free, now seemed to her to be teeming with the presence of other human beings: they were behind her in their houses, they were across Long Island Sound in other houses, they were a mile away on I-95, whizzing past her in cars. They flew above her, back and forth, in planes in the sky. They were even buried beneath her, or close enough, deep and silent, in the earth. Wherever she went, they followed. They spoke to her on telephones and wrote to her on computers. They sang from radios and hailed cabs and demanded she hold the elevator. It was not their fault, of course, they were only doing what people were meant to do, yet she found herself despising them.

But in the attic, there were just the things people had discarded, not the people themselves. A bulky electric typewriter. A framed diploma from Barnard College for Mildred Peacock Winship, 1927. Engravings, photographs—it was like picking up seashells. She was alone, blissfully alone. Who *was* Mildred Peacock Winship? Perhaps she had been a devoted member of the library's staff, a middle-aged unmarried person who typed and filed, collected her meager paycheck, and went home to a big frame house in the Bronx to make supper for her aging parents. Perhaps she was a trustee who had bequeathed to the library thousands of dollars as well as her treasured editions of Emerson and Hawthorne. Annie thought vaguely that she should find out. At the same time, she blessed Mildred Peacock Winship, for, whoever she had been and whatever she had done, she was now, blissfully, absent.

The attic was safe. It was quiet and remote. Like me, Annie thought. She was walking to the subway after a particularly tiring board meeting.

'Aren't you just so bwack and bwown?' a woman cooed to a dog tied to a parking meter.

When Annie emerged in Grand Central, a homeless man holding a battered coffee cup said, 'Hello there, beautiful lady,' and she was wondering whether to smile politely without making eye contact or just hurry past, when she realized he was talking to the woman behind her. On the train, she walked through the first couple of cars looking for a seat facing forward. She spotted a likely prospect—the back of a single well-groomed female head sticking up from the three-person bench—but when she got up to the female head and was about to heave her bag onto the middle seat, she saw it was occupied by a small child.

There was an awkward moment when, even as she drew back her bag, determined to avoid what could only be a very loud and very dull young companion on an evening when she wanted peace and solitude, she caught the mother's eye and wondered if she had already somehow committed herself to join the duo and if it would now be insulting to this doubtless doting parent to continue on her way. But even as she quickly and decisively decided in favor of insult over boredom and annoyance, the child in question spoke.

'Annie!'

And she looked down at the boy, focused, and recognized Henry.

Annie put out her arms, and Henry jumped to his feet and, standing unsteadily on his seat, gave her a hug. She saw the mother's face over his head. Henry's mother. It was instantly and unquestionably apparent. Not just the full cheeks or the set of the eyes. But that look, that proprietary mother look. 'Oh, you must be Henry's mother,' Annie said quickly, holding a hand out. 'I'm Annie Weissmann. A friend from Westport.'

Henry was looking around. 'Randa?' he asked.

'Are you Randa?' the mother asked. 'He talks about you quite a bit. I'm Leanne.'

Annie sat down and explained that Randa was her sister, Miranda.

'Miranda's at home,' she said to Henry.

The woman was blond, her hair short and straight, her narrow eyes a faded blue. She wore no makeup, and Annie could see at once why she didn't bother with it—her skin glowed, smooth as a child's. She seemed a little older than Kit, however. Well, Annie thought, returning her friendly smile, the man ran true to form in the age department, that seemed clear.

Henry climbed over his mother and pressed his face against the window. He stared at the passing lights and sang a jumbled version of the alphabet.

'You were in Africa?' Annie said, trying to make conversation that somehow did not touch on Kit Maybank.

'We're staying with Aunt Charlotte now. She needs some looking after. And the house is huge.'

'Yes, I've heard that,' Annie said, then fell into

251

an uncomfortable silence, for how else would she have heard that except from Kit?

Henry unglued himself from the window to watch the conductor punch holes in his mother's ticket but not in Annie's monthly pass. Annie explained that she was a commuter, then explained what a commuter was.

'You go on the train *every day*?' he asked, his eyes wide with awe and envy.

'Two times.'

'*We* saw dinosaurs,' he said a little defensively.

After that, conversation flagged until they neared the station at Westport.

'We don't get off until Greens Farms,' Leanne said as Annie started putting on her coat.

'Right. Of course. Your aunt's house is so much closer to the Greens Farms station. I like that station. And the little old-fashioned post office there. Kind of my favorite place in Westport.'

Leanne laughed.

'I want to go to Randa's house,' Henry said.

'You never met Aunt Charlotte, did you?' asked Leanne.

'I want to go to Randa's house.'

Annie shook her head. 'No. Never did.'

'No. She and Kit are not exactly on friendly terms, so you wouldn't have.'

'But you're obviously on good terms with her.'

'Oh yes. She's a bit of a gorgon, but we love her, don't we, Henry?'

Henry sucked silently on his fist.

No wonder Kit had lived in the run-down boathouse. But what had he done to alienate his aunt? What had his ex-wife done to keep the confidence of her in-law? Annie wished she had

252

time to pursue this interesting conversation. Of course, it was none of her business. But gossip so rarely was.

Henry continued to want to go to Randa's house, now in a loud singsong chant. Annie wondered if she should respond. She knew Miranda would be overjoyed to see Henry. But perhaps Henry's mother would not be overjoyed to drop her son off at the home of her ex's ex. It all seemed very complicated.

'I want—'

'Okay, okay,' his mother said, clapping a hand over Henry's mouth. 'Listen,' she added suddenly to Annie. 'You'll all come for tea. Yes. Perfect.' She released Henry's mouth and dug in her purse. 'Here.' She thrust her card at Annie with a dazzling smile and an almost military sense of authority. 'It's settled.'

Annie laughed. Leanne reminded her a little of Miranda.

*   *   *

While Annie was rumbling home on the commuter train to Westport, Frederick was rumbling toward New York on the Amtrak train from Boston. Amber and Crystal were not with him. They had taken his car a week earlier. Amber was accompanying Crystal to Great Barrington, where they were house-sitting (Frederick could not bear to pronounce 'home-sitting' even silently in his thoughts), then they would both continue on to the city to meet Frederick. They were all staying with Felicity and Joe in Joe's big apartment on Central Park West, although Felicity didn't know it. Amber

253

and Crystal were going to be a surprise. Frederick chuckled, imagining his sister's face. They could all go to hell, he decided. He asked very little in life, really. Just to sit in his office and listen to the sea and write his books. Why was there always so much fuss?

His head back, Frederick closed his eyes and tried to concentrate on something other than the fuss. He had to write a book review and tried to compose his opening sentence, but the novel he was reviewing, a stark and painful allegory set in Las Vegas, was, finally, boring. Everything, he'd discovered, was boring as you hurtled towards the abyss. Fear, hopelessness—it turned out they were unequivocally dull. He decided to take up smoking again as soon as possible.

Amber and Crystal had spent the day shopping, starting on Fifth Avenue, ending up at the Time Warner Center at Columbus Circle. They were meeting Frederick for drinks at Gabriel's, on the other side of Sixtieth Street. They perched on their bar stools, their shopping bags clustered around their feet. They ordered Cosmopolitans and waited.

'I feel very artistic,' Crystal said.

'Don't you mean sophisticated? There's nothing artistic about shopping, or even cocktails, to be honest.'

'*Pardonnez-moi.*' Crystal contemplated her pink drink. 'Hey, should you even *be* drinking? Doesn't it cut off their placenta or oxygen or something?'

'It's *my* placenta,' Amber said. But then she saw Frederick pushing open the door and slid the drink away from her.

'Hey, Daddy-o,' she said, standing and

254

embracing him.

'You really have to stop calling me that, Amber.'

'Silly,' she said, kissing him.

He smiled. 'Ready, girls? Once more into the breach?'

They gave him a quizzical look.

'*Henry the Fifth,* dear friends.' He was insufferable, he knew. And rather enjoying it. And entitled, too, to a little self-indulgence. Think what was ahead. My God, think what was ahead. He took out one of his brand-new Marlboros.

'No smoking, sir,' said the bartender.

Ah yes. No smoking in restaurants. How could he have forgotten? But then, he hadn't smoked in thirty years, so perhaps he could be forgiven. He slid the pack back in his pocket. 'Well,' he said. 'All ready for another stab at my children?'

Stab, Amber thought. Yes, she was ready for that all right.

They arrived just at eight. Gwen and Ron lived in a two-bedroom apartment on the third floor of a brownstone on Bank Street. Frederick was a little out of breath from the stairs when Gwen answered the door. The cigarettes he'd smoked on the street had not helped.

'Oh!' she said. 'Look who the cat dragged in. Amber and Crystal. I'm afraid I wasn't expecting you.'

'"Unbidden guests are often welcomest when they are gone,"' Frederick said. '*Henry the Sixth.*' He bowed. I'm on a roll, he thought. If only Shakespeare had written *Henry the Seventh.*

Gwen stepped back, viewing him with a puzzled frown. 'Are you drunk?' She could think of no other reason that her father, so polite, so

255

gentlemanly, would show up on her doorstep for
dinner with two uninvited guests and then stand
there and insult them. 'You look pale. And you
smell like cigarettes.'

He was about to take out the red pack and
proudly show her the depths to which he had sunk
when Amber said, 'It's the steps. He needs to do
some aerobic exercise. I tell him to go to the gym,
but you know how he is.'

Gwen did know how he was. But she did not like
it that Amber seemed to know, too.

*   *   *

As they set two extra places, Evan said, 'Hey there,
Freddie.' He shook his head and laughed, then
turned to Crystal. 'So, how's the home-sitting
industry?'

'You sit on homes?' one of the twins asked.

'I am a student.'

The girl looked disappointed.

'Life coaching, right?' Evan said. 'Do you have,
like, a whistle? Gatorade?'

'I'd say you could use some coaching yourself,
sir. In manners.'

'I could use a lot of things.' He held an
imaginary joint to his lips and inhaled.

Crystal laughed.

'Evan!' Gwen said. 'Jesus. There are children
here.'

'I'll say,' Crystal said.

Evan pursed his lips in a pout. 'I was just kidding
around.'

When shall I tell them? Frederick wondered.

'Amber, why don't you sit here, next to

Ophelia?' Gwen pointed to a small stool wedged beneath a corner of the table.

'What a quaint little stool. Shaker?' She had been reading up on antiques.

Gwen nodded reluctant agreement with the intruder.

Should I tell them before they eat? Frederick wondered. That will ruin their appetites. After they eat? Then they will feel ill.

'What fun!' Amber had settled herself on the stool. 'Don't I look like a little milkmaid, Ophelia?'

'Juliet,' the child said petulantly, and gave Amber a kick.

Suddenly it was Frederick who felt ill. The bravado that had started in the bar deserted him. He looked at Gwennie. She had grown up to be a snob, it was true. But she was only protecting what she thought was important. She had been officious even as a child. He had always found it touching, her need to make hierarchical order out of a chaotic world. And Evan, so sarcastic and obnoxious these days. Perhaps he would outgrow it. Whether he did or not, Frederick knew he would always adore him. He watched his son torturing Crystal, playing with her like a cruel cat. Good luck to you, Evan, he thought. Those mouse sisters are cleverer than you think.

'I'm sorry Joe couldn't be here,' Ron said.

'The economy.' Felicity spoke as if the economy were a traffic jam. 'Just terrible. I just barely made it here myself. But then I'm just a VP, and of course my part of the business is going so much more smoothly than the rest.'

'I'm glad you're here,' said Frederick, 'all of you. Because I have something of an announcement to make.'

'That's funny,' Gwen said. 'Because so do I!'

All eyes turned to her.

'I'm pregnant!'

Frederick and Amber exchanged a look as everyone congratulated Gwen and Ron.

'Now, what was your announcement, Dad?' asked Ron.

'Nothing,' said Dad. 'Nothing that can't wait.'

*   *   *

At the apartment on Central Park West, Amber was sharing a room with Crystal, not Frederick. She had been shocked the other night when Frederick almost announced her pregnancy and relieved when Gwen's news made it impossible.

'They have to get to know me better,' she explained to Frederick. 'But when they do, you'll see. They'll love me. In spite of themselves.'

And so, to Frederick's surprise, it came to pass.

'Gwen, would you mind if I took the girls to the Met today? There's a toddler tour of the European paintings . . .' 'Oh, Felicity, you have managed to make this apartment both grand and yet so personal. You really used a decorator? It feels so organic to your personality. You must be a fabulous manager . . .' 'Gwen, did you hear Juliet singing the Dora the Explorer song? Have you considered voice lessons?'

Amber was blatant, brilliant. Frederick watched with amazement as the flattery did its work on his prickly daughter and pricklier sister. If Amber had been rubbing her hands together and muttering how 'umble she was, she could not have been more

258

obsequious. 'I'm sorry—*what*? You made this dinner *and* you worked all day?' she said to Felicity. 'If that handsome boss of yours were ever foolish enough to let you go'—and here she simpered at Joseph, who smiled foolishly back— 'God, you could so get a job as a chef. I mean, who am I to even say that, just your grateful, useless houseguest, but I can't help it—you should try out for *Top Chef.* You're totally what they're looking for, totally telegenic.'

And on and on it went, this sycophantic barrage. Amber went to Dumbo and found trendy baby blankets and bibs for Gwen. She appeared at Joseph's office with a basket of designer cookies and gave them to Felicity, then helped her pass them out to the employees, all the while giving the impression that it had been Felicity's idea.

'I went all the way to Red Hook for them,' she told Crystal that night in a whisper. They lay side by side in twin beds.

'Why? There's bakeries all over this neighbourhood.'

'But they never leave Manhattan, these people. Red Hook is totally exotic. So that makes it like I made this big effort.'

'But you did make a big effort.'

'You have to invest in your future, Crystal. Don't you ever watch Suze Orman?'

Perhaps it was the massage that finally turned the tide of Amber's Barrow fortunes, for, as it happened, she was a truly gifted massage therapist, just as her sister had claimed. She offered frequent and free sessions. It was more than either woman could resist. Evan became a regular visitor at the big apartment on Central Park West, too, making

259

faint noises of physical discomfort and twitching his shoulders (once bringing his latest girlfriend, a dancer, as well) until Amber picked up the hint and offered her help.

Both Gwen and Felicity were accustomed to a certain intimacy with the people who tended to their personal and cosmetic needs. The hair cutter, the colorist, the manicurist, the personal trainer—these were all members of a nether-world of women with whom they never would have thought to socialize, yet trusted as confidantes. Amber benefited from that familiarity and comfort. She fitted herself into the family as someone not quite an equal, and so not a threat, but she was not quite a servant, either.

Gwen began to ask Amber to join her for lunch, to go on shopping trips for maternity clothes. Amber stood in for Ron as her coach a few times at her birthing classes. They even went away for a weekend to a spa. Crystal accompanied them sometimes, but she was in hot pursuit of an insurance broker she'd met at a club.

'Crystal, he's very bridge-and-tunnel, okay? Just don't bring him around the Barrows'.'

'Why? You don't think they would like him?'

Amber laughed.

'Yeah, I know,' Crystal said. 'Hey, have you noticed that Evan pays a lot of attention to me? I think he might be hot for me.'

Amber rolled her eyes. 'Dream on. Anyway, you're better off with the B&T guy.'

'Yeah. We go to really good clubs. Of course, you don't care about clubs any more, being engaged.'

'True,' Amber said. 'I have priorities.' Then:

'Which clubs?'

CHAPTER SEVENTEEN

On a warm spring day when even the hard, cracked earth surrounding the cottage offered itself up as welcoming and full of promise, Miranda received the news that she was officially bankrupt.

The call came from her lawyer in the mid-morning sunlight as she sat on the concrete steps with a cup of coffee. Her cell phone rang, an artificial chirp, a vibration in the back pocket of her jeans.

'Hello, Brian.'

'Hello, Miranda,' said her lawyer.

Silence. A robin raised its head from a patch of crabgrass and turned one bead of an eye at her.

'Bad news?' she asked.

'Sorry, Miranda.'

'The Miranda Weissmann Literary Agency is now in bankruptcy, officially?'

'Again, I'm terribly, terribly sorry.'

'So it's over?'

'Well no. I explained this all to you. You still have creditors. Any money you earn from previous properties . . .'

Miranda stopped listening. It was over.

'Thanks, Brian. Thanks for all your help.' She hung up and stared, dry-eyed, at the robin. When she was a child, she used to draw robins with bright blue bodies and bright red breasts. But robins were really brown. Their breasts were not red, they were rust-colored. She had never really thought about the discrepancy until just this moment. Where had she gotten the idea that robins were royal blue and red? Some amalgamation of children's book illustrations? Robin redbreast. English robins had red breasts. Bluebird of happiness. Bluebirds were blue. She had never seen either in real life. *She is too fond of books. It has turned her brain.* Well, well. Real life. Time to start a new real life. Time to start over.

She waited for the great flood of self-pitying tears. If I don't pity myself, who will? she thought. If not now, when?

But she didn't cry. She felt only impatience. Time to start over. Off we go. Get a wiggle on. Yes, but as what? She stared unseeing at the brown-and rust-feathered robin. And as whom?

*   *   *

There was a pot of tea at the tea at Aunt Charlotte's, but little else. A few crackers. A small piece of sweaty cheese. Betty was glad she had brought the cake from Balducci's. The goyim, she had explained to the girls, do not feed their guests; it is not their custom, and we must respect the customs of other cultures, but that does not mean we have to starve. She always kept saltines and Life Savers in her bag in case of a blood sugar drop, but she did not think she ought to haul either out at a tea party, even if there had been enough to share. The cake, on the other hand . . . no one could object to guests bringing a nice crumb cake. Miranda and Annie had laughed at her. But now, as she watched Miranda attempting to cut a strip of the rubbery cheese and put it on a limp cracker,

262

she felt vindicated.

Charlotte Maybank seemed pleased with her cake, too. She was a woman of about eighty, small and birdlike except for her teeth, which were rather prominent. She had awaited their arrival in the living room, laid out, quite literally, in a new automatic recliner that looked bulbously incongruous among the eighteenth-century furniture.

When presented with the white box tied up in red string, she activated the chair's controls, which whirred importantly until her head was an inch or two higher. Then she eyed the cake greedily, her teeth bared in a smile. 'Well, well. You know, I think I'd better take some cake now, Leanne,' she said as if the cake box were a bottle of pills. She handed the box to Henry's mother. 'I could *use* a piece of cake.'

'Keep up your strength,' Leanne said, heading for the kitchen, a smile hidden from her aunt.

'Surgery,' the old woman said to her guests. She motioned her guests to a hard, slender, bow-backed sofa and two wooden arm chairs facing her.

'Oh,' Annie said, 'I hope . . .'

'Successful,' the old woman said, cutting her off.

There was silence then.

'These are lovely,' Betty said finally, running her hand along the arm of the chair she sat in.

'Want them? Leanne!' the woman shouted, waving a taut little arm towards the kitchen. 'Leanne!'

Leanne appeared, followed by Hilda, the ancient retainer, the same old woman who had opened the door for them, carrying a tray. Miranda thought she saw Leanne give her aunt an ironic salute as she approached, but she might just have been pushing the hair from her eyes. She had fine, reddish-blond hair, not at all like Henry's black glossy locks. And yet, there was something, something so Henry-like about her. Miranda smiled as she watched Leanne move across the room, wondering what it was. Her hands? The set of her shoulders, just a little rounded? Maybe. When Leanne caught her staring and smiled back, with a questioning look and slightly tilted head, Miranda quickly averted her gaze to a large painting of some sort of hunting dog. But she had found the answer to her question. The smile. The tilted head. The expression of curiosity.

'Leanne,' the aunt continued, 'this charming person admired the Hepplewhites. Make sure she bids on them.' She turned back to Betty. 'When I'm gone. The whole place, you know: up for grabs, on the auction block, *when I'm gone.*' She shook her finger at Betty. 'Mind, I'm not gone yet.'

'Hardly,' Leanne said, handing her aunt a plate bearing a thick slice of cake.

'The dishes, too,' the old woman said, tapping her fork on the dessert plate, which was exquisite, Betty noticed. But really, Betty had her own chairs and plates. She didn't need this woman's household goods. And where would she keep them, anyway? So little room in the cottage as it was. And of course, even auctioned, these pieces would go for a pretty penny. She began thinking what a lovely phrase that was, 'pretty penny', only vaguely aware of the aunt continuing her catalogue: 'Forks, knives, spoons . . . the whole shebang. Get out your checkbooks, ladies.'

Roberts joined the tea party towards the end. It

was not the first time the Weissmanns had seen him since Palm Springs, but it was unexpected to see him in the big house on Beachside Avenue.

'All this time I didn't realize you knew the Maybanks,' Betty said, thinking back to what now looked, in retrospect, like coldness to Kit.

'Roberts is very discreet,' Aunt Charlotte said. 'He handles all my affairs.'

'Not quite all, unfortunately,' said Roberts.

'He'll be the one auctioning off those chairs, won't you, dear?'

'I sincerely hope not, Charlotte.'

Miranda sat on the other wing chair, Henry curled on her lap. She rested her cheek on his head and breathed him in. She had been feeling so ragged, so disoriented, for so long, a woman without a country, and now she was bankrupt as well, but what did any of it matter? Here was Henry, returned like Odysseus from a long, long journey.

When Henry's mother offered her another piece of cake, Miranda said, 'You look so much alike.' She glanced from Henry's mother back to Henry. 'Even though . . .'

'Even though he looks just like Kit?' Leanne ruffled Henry's hair, accidentally grazing Miranda's cheek. 'Sorry,' she said, pulling back her hand.

Miranda caught her breath. The closeness of Henry, the touch of the woman's hand, a gentleness meant for her son mistakenly shared with a stranger—she felt somehow moved, on the verge of tears.

Leanne smiled, looking more like Henry than ever, and moved away.

Really, Miranda, you are becoming absurder and absurder, as Josie used to say.

'What's the matter, dear? Don't like cake?' It was the old woman.

Miranda forced herself to smile. 'Me? Oh yes. Love it.'

'Eat up, then,' Aunt Charlotte said, her hungry eyes on Miranda's untouched slice of cake. 'Can't make an omelette without breaking eggs.'

*   *   *

A month or so after the tea party, Lou and Rosalyn returned from Palm Springs. Lou appeared the very next day, knocking on the door of the Weissmann cottage. He wanted to extend a personal invitation to a welcome-home party.

'All of us together again,' he said happily. 'What an occasion!'

Annie was embraced by her enthusiastic cousin, from which position she contemplated the prospect of socializing once again enveloped by Cousin Lou's capacious family bosom. In addition to all the people she did not know very well, there might easily be those she wished she had never met—Amber, for example, and Gwen. Would they be at this party? Perhaps they would bring Frederick. Perhaps Frederick would bring his sister, Felicity . . .

'It's a big tent, your family,' she said when Cousin Lou released her.

At that moment, Miranda burst through the door, followed by Henry and his mother, Leanne.

'Cousin Lou! You're back!' Miranda threw her arms around him.

'You're looking well,' he said. The last time he had seen her, she had been so drawn. Withdrawn as well. What a surprising language English is, he thought, not for the first time. *Drawn. Withdrawn.* He would have to *draw* her out and see what this was all about! 'Roses in your cheeks.'

Miranda smiled. Why, Miranda is irresistible, Lou remembered suddenly. But she had recently been so, so . . . negligible. That was the word for the Miranda of Palm Springs. Moody, absent, quiet, irrelevant. But here she was with her old funny, suggestive smile—half a challenge, half a reassurance. He hadn't seen that smile in a long time. He sighed with pleasure. He liked people to be happy.

And yet, how could she smile? He'd heard she'd gone bankrupt. Rosalyn said her business had been dissolved. She had nothing, absolutely nothing.

The thought of bankruptcy made his stomach drop.

What a brave woman she was, putting up a strong front.

She was looking in the mirror. 'Hey, I do have roses in my cheeks.'

Henry examined her cheeks in his solemn literal way.

'Hello, Henry,' Lou said, 'remember me?'

Henry ran back to the other woman who had come into the room. He wrapped his arms and legs around her leg, then stared at Lou with an expression of menacing confusion.

'This is Henry's mother, Leanne Maybank.'

'Maybank,' Betty said. 'It *is* such a pretty name. Every time I hear it.'

'It is, isn't it?' Leanne said. 'But that's not really

why Kit took my name.'

'Maybank?' Miranda said.

'Your husband took your name and kept it after you split up?' Cousin Lou swayed from side to side, clearly agitated.

'Lovely name,' Betty said again.

'It's a new world, a new world,' Lou continued. He emitted a series of unhappy grunts: 'Uh, uh, uh. Sometimes I think I'm getting old.'

'He just really didn't like his own name.'

'Why not?' Annie asked, fascinated by this piece of news. 'Was his last name Carson or something?'

'Well . . . yes.'

Kit Carson: there was an appreciative silence.

'He grew up in Wyoming,' Leanne said after a while. 'I guess that's why his parents thought of it.'

'Wait, how old was Kit when he moved to *Maine*?' Miranda asked. 'He told me so much about growing up in Maine. Really, it made me jealous. All those brothers and sisters, the clambakes, the wildflower gathering. Keeping honeybees . . .'

Leanne gave her an uncomfortable look. 'He told you that?'

Miranda immediately regretted her words. She was aware that she occupied a delicate position with regard to Kit and Leanne. Her bitterness towards Leanne's ex-husband must be kept under wraps. She had discovered a long time ago that no one can attack an ex-husband or wife except the ex's ex. You can agree, but you cannot initiate. She had learned this over the years, though she had never really understood it. On the other hand, any positive comments or happy memories about the ex were equally off limits. There was nothing one could say that would not somehow offend the injured party. So one kept quiet. Particularly if one had slept with the ex. Particularly if one valued the friendship of the injured party more every day.

Miranda's friendship with Henry's mother was a revelation to her. She had never had a best friend before, not as an adult. And even as a child, there had always been Annie first and foremost. As she got older, she had friends, lots of friends. But that was the point—there were so many. And then there were the men. So many men. Now there was just this one woman in this suburban town. It was so different here. She was different, too.

Bankruptcy—the bright line between her old life and her new one. To her surprise, her reaction to bankruptcy had not been depression or anger but an overwhelming, sometimes disorienting sense of freedom. She was free of her success, free of her failure. She was . . . she suddenly remembered a word Frederick had used: she was 'unencumbered'.

She found herself tenderly protective of this new incarnation, consciously thinking of it as a slender green seedling, perhaps because she had begun gardening a little, an experiment in her new self, fascinated by the arbitrary bits of green that appeared in the yard. At Charlotte Maybank's house on Beachside Avenue, there were gardens galore, and she had begun to spend time in them, weeding and pruning, constantly consulting her laptop, as well as the old gardener who came once a week, to make sure she did not inadvertently kill an unfamiliar infant flower. She also took care of Henry when Leanne went to New Haven to the library to work. When Leanne stayed home to work, Miranda played with Henry, gave him his nap, made lunch for the three of them.

'I feel like I'm taking advantage of you,' Leanne said.

'You can give me advice if I ever suffer an epidemic. In exchange,' Miranda said, then remembered her mother's warning about Kit taking advantage of her and laughed.

She had begun to cook dinner at the cottage sometimes, too. It was easy to cook, she discovered. Not to cook well, necessarily, but to cook. You read the directions and followed them. How soothing it all was. A teaspoon meant a teaspoon, no more, no less.

She began pulling together a résumé, which both depressed her and invigorated her. She researched headhunters and began to write the letters she would send out.

'But I was born to be a nanny,' she said.

There were evenings when Roberts appeared and Leanne would be locked up with him and her aunt discussing business. Then it fell to Miranda to give Henry his bath. At other times, Aunt Charlotte would want Leanne to attend to her at bedtime, and Miranda would gratefully accept the job of getting Henry to sleep. 'That one'll go,' Charlotte would say, pointing to a portrait as Leanne helped her up the stairs. 'On the auction block for you!' In his bed, Henry would point at his stuffed animals and say, 'On the auction block for you! What's an auction block?'

When both their charges were asleep, Leanne and Miranda would sit in the living room and drink. They both liked to drink. Sometimes they polished off a bottle of wine, sometimes they drank bourbon, sometimes gin. They drank and they talked. But they had never discussed Kit. It was an unspoken agreement.

And now Miranda had stupidly mentioned Kit's tales about his childhood. All those sweet and intimate conversations Miranda had had with Kit about his sunny youth—of course, Leanne would resent that.

'Maine, huh?' Leanne said. She seemed as though she had more to say, but she gave a disgusted little sigh, no more.

'Maine? Maine has nothing we don't have right here in Westport,' said Cousin Lou. 'Forget about Maine. You come to our party, too . . . After all, you're Henry's mother . . . you're like family . . .'

* * *

'The Season', Annie said wearily after the third dinner in a row, 'has begun.'

Betty often begged off this new rash of meals, waving her daughters out the door with a sense of relief. 'Find nice, rich husbands,' she would always call after them, just for the pleasure of hearing their ritualized outrage. Then, at last: privacy. Alone to rest, to order interesting inventions that were advertised on TV. It had begun with OxiClean, which even Annie admitted worked wonders. But since then Betty had gotten a fleece blanket with arms, which you wore like a backward robe; a portable steam cleaner; and a wonderful brush that worked for both dogs and cats and came with a free bonus attachment that cut off burrs and tangles.

'But we don't have a dog,' Annie said when it arrived in the mail.

271

'Or even a cat,' Miranda added.

'Unpredictable times, my darlings,' said Betty. 'Unpredictable times.'

She turned the TV on now and found the channel that reran soap operas. She liked to watch Kit sometimes. It excited her that she knew someone who was on television. She wouldn't have admitted it to her daughters, however. They were so cavalier about things like that. Growing up in New York had done that, she thought. Nothing impressed them.

'But it's wrong,' Kit was saying to his handsome lover.

Wrong, Betty thought. So much was wrong in this world. Why did those two beautiful, healthy young men worry about a little thing like a kiss? She remembered the first time Joseph had kissed her. It was as clear as if it had happened that morning. It had been on a morning, too, but so long ago. They had met at a party a week earlier and he had asked her to come to see an exhibit at the Metropolitan. She couldn't remember what the exhibit was. Spanish paintings, perhaps? Afterward, they had gone for a walk in Central Park. Her children, her babies, were home with the teenage girl from the apartment next door. She remembered wondering if the girl was ignoring them, talking on the phone with some pimply boyfriend instead of playing dolls and peek-a-boo. That wouldn't be so bad, she had thought, as long as the girl didn't let them drown in the bathtub somehow . . . Then, suddenly, Joseph had taken her hand and led her to a thicket of trees and bushes. She heard the traffic on Fifth Avenue; she heard a dog barking and a mother telling her

272

children not to go too far ahead of her, a siren in the distance, a squirrel scurrying through the leaves, or was it a rat . . . And then Joseph looked down at her with half-closed eyes and kissed her.

Her heart fluttered even now, remembering. She had fallen in love with him the first time they spoke at that awful smoky downtown party. Sometimes people are mistaken when they fall in love at first sight, or even second or third sight. But I was right, Betty thought. Pity he had to ruin everything.

She turned off the TV and sorted through some papers. When the phone rang, she saw on the caller ID that it was her lawyer and eagerly picked it up.

'How's my Case?'

'You won't believe this, Betty, but I think . . . well, I think we're making progress! Suddenly Joseph Weissmann's lawyers, who refused to even refuse my calls, are calling and asking for meetings to "clear this all up".'

Betty felt a sickening surge of relief, sickening because it forced her to acknowledge how frightened she was, how precarious, how vulnerable. Then, a blind flash of rage. Then, oddly, a pang of sorrow for Joseph.

'I don't know what happened. Maybe you've just successfully waited Joseph out. Not all women have the resources to do that,' the lawyer said. 'They settle because they can't buy groceries.'

'Joseph would never do that,' Betty said.

'Only because you haven't let him. You can thank your family for that.'

Joseph is my family, she wanted to explain.

'We did it, we did it!' Miranda cried, dancing

273

around the cottage, when she told them the news.

'Maybe!' Annie joined in. 'Maybe we did it!'

Betty found the possibility of victory painfully anticlimactic. What on earth were they dancing for? She looked around the little cottage, at her furniture and rug, her paintings and vases, and tried to remember them in their original setting. If she really went back to her apartment, would she miss the cottage? She wasn't sure. She hoped so. She didn't like to think of these past months as wasted. But for her, there was no joy in the thought of return. Living alone in the apartment would be like drifting on an ocean in a tiny boat. Nowhere to go, and no real hope of getting there.

CHAPTER EIGHTEEN

On one of the afternoons when Leanne was working in the library of the big house on Beachside Avenue, Miranda and Henry were searching for worms on the lawn in back. Long Island Sound stretched out before them. The sky was a vibrant blue and the wind was brisk. Aunt Charlotte had recovered enough from her surgery to be steered outside in a wheelchair. She was wearing one of the fleece blankets with arms that Betty had ordered from TV. 'The second one was half-price,' Betty had explained to an outraged Annie. Then she had given it to Charlotte Maybank, who wore it at all times, inside and out.

Henry curled his fingers in the bright grass and damp sod. The earth was dark and rich, almost black. A pink worm slithered out from the trench he had carved.

'Look!' he said.

'We can go fishing,' Miranda said.

Henry's brow wrinkled. Miranda knew by now that this was the cloud before the storm.

'The worm will die,' he said in the tremulous voice that preceded a wail. 'The fish will die . . .'

Miranda quickly picked up the worm and took Henry's hand. She placed the worm in his palm. She said, 'See that brown part? That's dirt. It eats the dirt and then the dirt comes out the other end and the dirt that comes out is better for growing things.'

'Worm poop,' Henry said, mollified.

As Miranda breathed a sigh of relief, she saw Roberts coming out of the house and walking down the flagstone path toward them. He wore his habitual dark suit. His shoes gleamed in an old-fashioned way. He looked even more grave than usual.

'Roberts?' she said, standing up. 'Everything okay?'

He gave Miranda a halfhearted wave, turned to the old lady and said, 'Charlotte, we really have to talk,' then began to wheel her inside.

'Housewares, durable goods, knickknacks . . .' Charlotte Maybank's wavering voice came back to Miranda on the wind. 'Oh yes, they'll all have to go!'

Later, Miranda asked Leanne if anything particular was up. 'Roberts looked pretty spooked.'

Leanne pursed her lips, then gave a quick shake of her head and said, 'Just my aunt's nonsense. You know how she is.'

On top of the dunes, Frederick stood with his bare feet in the cold sand. He was thinking about the night he gave the reading at the Furrier Library in Manhattan. He could picture Annie Weissmann, her eyes shining, a little imperfectly hidden smile of pride on her personable face. Cape Cod in the winter, his daughter had said with disdain. Annie's sister had said something nice but odd, some nonsense about paragliders, but also something about her feet in the cold sand. Gwen had never understood things like feet in cold sand. Neither, it appeared, did Amber. He leaned into the wind coming from the water. It was almost strong enough to hold him up. He felt it against his face, in his hair, on his scalp. His hands were red and cold. He never wanted to move. With the hollow rumble of the waves and the wail of the wind in his ears, embraced by the gusts of sea air, his feet planted, aching in the cold of the packed sand, Frederick felt safe from the life he led and alive in the life he truly lived. He stood on the edge of the dune until the light began to dim. His joints were stiff. He was refreshed.

When he drove home, he got a call on his cell.

'Where have you been?' Amber said. 'I've been calling for over an hour. I thought you had a heart attack or something.'

'I hope you're not disappointed. I was on the beach. I left the phone in the car.'

'Listen, we're staying in the city a little longer. You don't mind, do you?'

Amber and Crystal had stayed on at Joseph's apartment, even after Frederick came back to the

Cape. It had been over two weeks now. It seemed to Frederick that Amber had become quite indispensable to his sister and daughter, a kind of in-house house sitter. She ran errands for them. She babysat for the twins, took them to puppet shows and to the paediatrician. Felicity often asked Amber to run out to the market, to the butcher. They all three (Crystal seemed to bow out of a lot of these activities) would take the little girls to the park and then cross to the East Side to go shopping. Frederick tried not to think about any of them too much. He spent an hour or two each morning walking on the beach, then worked, then took another walk in the evening, then drank himself to sleep. He was a solitary person and was not unhappy with the way things were, only with how they would be.

*   *   *

'Daddy?' Henry said, pointing to the television screen. Kit was against a brick wall, a look of horror and fear on his face, a gun to his head. Henry started to cry.

'Baby, it's not real,' Leanne said. 'It's make-believe. That's Daddy's job—pretending.'

Henry sobbed and wailed, his little body shaking.

Betty said, 'Get a cookie. Get the child a cookie.' It had never worked with the girls when they were little, but you never knew. Did they even have any cookies?

Leanne and Miranda took Henry into the kitchen and sat him on the counter.

'I'm really sorry, Leanne. My mother should not

277

have been watching that while you were here.'

Leanne was opening cabinets. 'Where do you keep your cookies? Don't worry about it, Randa. Right, Henry? Mommy and Randa are right here. And Daddy is just fine. So try to shape up, sweetheart,' she said to Henry, kissing his forehead.

'I don't have any shape ups left in me,' he sobbed.

Miranda opened a cabinet and stared at the boxes of whole-wheat pasta, the saltines, the can of chickpeas, and the jar of almond butter. 'How about sort-of peanut butter on a cracker?'

Henry nodded solemn agreement.

'Good,' she said. 'And don't cry about Daddy. He'll come back from the TV and see you really soon, right?' She looked at Leanne. 'Right?'

Leanne shrugged.

'Right,' Miranda said. 'I know he will. Let's call him. You know, you can call him up on the telephone and you can see him at the same time talking to you on the computer.'

Henry ate his cracker while he contemplated that.

'Okay,' he said finally.

Leanne looked relieved. 'Thanks,' she said to Miranda.

'It's so difficult sometimes with Kit in California.'

'I understand. It's all been so painful and awkward.'

Leanne nodded. 'I guess.' She stroked Henry's hair.

Miranda watched Leanne's hand. How easily it shaped itself to that beautiful head. She felt a confused stab of jealousy and looked away.

'Painful subject,' Leanne said very softly.

Miranda took a deep breath. She exhaled slowly. It was going to rain. She gazed out the window at the putty-colored sky. Then she said what she had wanted to say for a long time, a simple sentiment, a statement of friendship and solidarity, but it had until now always seemed so presumptuous. 'I'm so sorry he made you so unhappy.'

There was an awkward pause, and then Leanne said, '*Me?*'

'Well, me too. And I know how weird it is coming from me, but when your husband leaves you . . . I mean, look at my poor mother . . . You feel so abandoned. So hurt . . .'

Leanne was staring at her. '*Kit* didn't leave *me*,' she said.

'More?' Henry asked, pointing to the crackers.

Miranda spread more almond butter on another cracker, then absentmindedly ate it herself.

'More *please?*' said Henry.

'*I* kicked *Kit* out.'

Miranda picked up Henry and set him on his feet on the floor. 'Go ask Betty if she wants a cracker, okay?'

She licked almond butter off her fingers as he scuttled away.

Finally, she said, 'Ah.'

In an irrelevant echo, a crow outside gave a hoarse caw.

The faucet dripped hollow, portentous plunks.

'Also, about Maine?' Leanne said at last.

'Look, I'm really, really sorry I mentioned that. I know it was awkward. I mean, even if you left him,' she added. She got up and tightened the taps, first

279

the hot, then the cold. The dripping continued. 'It's a tricky subject. Especially between you and me.'

Leanne produced an uncomfortable laugh and turned away.

'Okay, I know it's unlikely, our friendship.' Miranda felt almost elated, declaring friendship, just like that. 'Bizarre that Kit brought us together . . .'

'Henry brought us together,' she heard Leanne say.

Miranda had never really discussed Kit with anyone, but now she found herself compelled to talk about him to the last person in the world she should. 'I guess I just needed you to understand about Kit. Because you're the only one who really can.' She heard how ungainly she sounded, on and on in an inappropriate, breathless rush, yet she couldn't stop. 'All those stories from Maine, they meant so much to me; I was just so happy to be around someone who had such an idyllic childhood, especially after all my Awful Authors and their gruesome stories of childhood, which all turned out to be fake anyway; it was just so comforting, and inspiring, actually, to meet someone normal, someone who didn't have anything to hide, whose childhood was so real, and so real to him . . .'

As she was speaking, Leanne leaned towards her across the table in an almost menacing posture. After every few words she would try to interrupt Miranda, but Miranda stumbled on. She felt like a broken-down racehorse who has to reach the finish or his heart will break. It was suddenly urgent that she explain herself. 'My whole career was built on cheesy lurid tragedy. Cheesy lurid tragedy that turned out to be *fake* cheesy lurid tragedy. Think how that felt. It felt like shit, okay? So think how refreshing it was to talk to someone who grew up in a family full of love and fun and birds and wildflowers . . .'

'Jesus!' Leanne said. 'Stop! I can't stand it anymore. Love and fun and birds and wildflowers? I'm going to puke. Christ almighty . . .'

Miranda did stop. She became very serious. In a firm voice she said, 'Look, whatever Kit did to me, or to you, it's crazy the way we never mention him. I've been worse than you, I know. But I was wrong, okay? We should be able to speak honestly about Kit.'

'Honestly? About Kit? Really? Okay. For starters, Kit did *not* grow up in Maine,' Leanne said. 'Okay? Got it? He's never even been to Maine. And he didn't have any brothers or sisters. Not a one. He was an only child, okay? And his father? Left when he was two, never showed his face again. The mother? The mother was a drunk who barely knew he existed . . .'

Miranda sat down heavily at the kitchen table. 'Gosh. Really?'

'It's a performance, Miranda. Kit *pretends*,' Leanne said. 'That's what he does.'

Leanne was on a tear now—how Kit had usurped her Waspy name 'because he's a snob, do you get that? Because it made him sound East Coast Waspy'; his pretensions in dress and speech; his irresponsible spending on clothes and cars and boats they could not afford in order to impress his friends; the grandiosity; the selfishness, the lying— always, first, last, and in between, the lying. 'You

281

found him boyish. I get that. But there's another side to boyish when the boy lives off credit cards he can't pay, when the boy is thirty-five years old and has never had a job . . .'

'He's thirty-five? He said he was thirty.'

'Too old for you?' Leanne gave Miranda a sharp look, then her face softened into affection. 'Poor Miranda.'

Maybe it was the gentleness of Leanne's voice, maybe it was simply the last straw, the final example of her own inability to see what was in front of her, but the tears, the bankruptcy tears, the Kit tears, the self-pity, stupidity, whirling queasy exhaustion tears were coming; she could feel them welling up, weeks', months', worth of tears. 'Not very good at telling fact from fiction, am I? No wonder I went bankrupt. I'm such an ass. Such a fool . . . How pathetic . . .'

Oh, she was feeling sorry for herself now. The shrill insistence of her voice—that always came first. That was the warm-up. Soon the games would begin in earnest, she thought, the Olympic tantrums, the dramatic flinging of arms, the cries of despair. Leanne had never seen her in full sail.

Leanne stood up, moved towards Miranda. 'You like a happy ending, Miranda. Nothing wrong with that.'

'Except they're not real,' Miranda said, her voice rising, tangled in the words. 'There are no happy endings.'

Leanne stood beside her now. From her chair, Miranda pressed her face against Leanne's waist and began to sob. Leanne held her close and stroked her head until the storm subsided.

Embarrassed at her outburst, Miranda tried to

282

laugh. 'Drama is draining,' she said.

Leanne sat back down, tilted her head, like Henry.

Miranda reached out and poked her cheek. 'You're real, right?'

With a little grimace, Leanne said, 'I'm not very good at pretending, if that's what you mean.'

There was a heavy, tense moment of silence between them.

Leanne reached across the table and took Miranda's hand. 'Not for very long, anyway.'

As Leanne's fingers closed over Miranda's, there came a jarring sound, a little shout from the doorway, a sudden shrill 'No!'

Miranda jumped. Leanne pulled her hand back. They both turned to the door.

Henry stood there staring at them.

'We were just . . .' they both began, then stopped. They were just what?

'No!' Henry said again. 'Betty says *No,* she does not want a cracker.' He turned and ran back to the living room calling, 'I told them! I told them!'

Miranda noticed the top of the almond butter jar on the table. She automatically began to screw it back on.

*   *   *

At Cousin Lou's, the dinners had become somewhat less elaborate. There was a downturn in the real estate market, which did not affect Lou too much. He had made his bundle, as he liked to say, thinking of a package shaped something like a baby, wrapped in cloth and cradled in his arms. He had made his bundle and taken it out of real estate

283

some years ago. Unfortunately, he had put the helpless little bundle into the stock market, and though it lived, it suffered, and so did Lou's parties, causing some of the hangers-on to let go. Annie was glad to see that Roberts was not one of them. It did pain her, though, to imagine what he felt when he saw Miranda so often, for he saw her at the Maybanks' house on Beachside Avenue as well as at Lou's. He turned up frequently at the cottage, too. People should not retire, she thought. They should not even semiretire. Obviously Roberts had nothing better to do than follow Miranda around.

But Annie was glad to see him for her own sake. He was quiet and restful as a companion. Annie could sit beside him at dinner, notice the elegance of his long, slender hands as he held a glass or passed her the salt, and still never leave her own thoughts, which were so sad, but somehow almost dear to her. Thoughts of Frederick. Poor man. Foolish man. Poor, foolish, weak man. She could not help but worry about him. They had heard nothing, though, not a word, not about Amber or a marriage or a baby, not about anything. Even Betty had stopped mentioning him, stopped insinuating that there was anything between him and Annie. As for Miranda, she had, at Annie's insistence, never mentioned Amber, Frederick, or the pregnancy again. She had been, briefly, more gentle with Annie, which Annie found both touching and cloying. But now, thankfully, Miranda was off on a cloud as usual.

Off on a cloud as usual, though the cloud itself was new, different. No man, no love affair, no histrionics. Just . . . friendship? Babysitting? A

284

tremendous amount of amateur gardening, certainly. The front yard was all dug up. She had become like some Victorian companion or maiden aunt. Annie did not understand any of it. But Miranda was happy, and that was all that mattered. Although how she would earn a living now that her agency had really disappeared altogether, Annie had no idea. Perhaps she could hire her at the library. The library that was cutting staff . . .

'I saw your sister today,' Roberts was saying. He had brought her a glass of wine, and they stood before Lou's big windows. The moon was exceptionally bright. They could see the Sound spread out beneath it. 'She was weeding at the Maybanks'.'

'Maybe they'll hire her as their gardener.'

'I don't think so. She was digging the weeds up very carefully and putting them in a basket. She plans to replant them. In the woods.'

'Miranda likes to rescue things.' She sighed.

'So do you,' said Roberts.

They were silent. The wind was driving silver clouds across the face of the moon.

Annie thought, What a polite man he is.

Roberts swirled the wine in his glass. 'Miranda's lucky to have you.'

'Oh, *what* is Miranda going to do?' Annie said, half to herself.

'And what is Charlotte going to do?'

It was only as she walked home in the moonlight that she wondered what he had meant. Perhaps all that talk about putting the ancestral portraits on the auction block was true.

'Roberts is there so often,' Miranda said that night when Annie recounted her conversation.

'How much business can they have?'

'He's here a lot, too,' Betty pointed out.

'I'm sure he goes there to see you,' Annie said.

'Maybe Henry is his love child,' said Betty.

*　　　*　　　*

On one of springtime's bright afternoons, Betty stood in the kitchen of her bungalow and watched a small yellow-and-black bird flitting through the new leaves of a maple tree. Birds were meant to be free, one always heard that. Because they could fly. She remembered Rosalyn comparing Amber and Crystal to birds because they flew from nest to nest, but what did that really mean except that they had no home? Free as a bird. But how free were you if you were required to fly up and down the coast of the same continent, year after year, just as your father and mother did before you, just as your sons and daughters would do after you? That bright little bird—a goldfinch?—was not free at all. It was just another prisoner. With no home.

Betty laughed to herself. How macabre she had become. A pretty bird on a pretty day! She should be outside in the fresh air marveling at all of nature's wonders, not condemning innocent birds to the diaspora. She put on her sneakers, a jacket, her dark glasses and wide-brimmed sunhat, took a deep breath, and ventured forth.

The waves were uniform and hushed, each gentle white hiss followed by another. She saw some sea glass, a nice large piece, beautiful muted green, but she was too stiff to bend down and pick it up. In the distance she could make out the white sail of a little boat. Perhaps that was Miranda, out sailing in that peculiar Charlotte Maybank's boat with Henry and his mother. Betty had warned her to wear a sweater under her jacket. It was so breezy, and the sun was deceptive. There was still a chill in the air. A few years ago, Betty would not have thought of a sweater. She would have thought only of the exhilarating snap of the sail. She would have been on the boat herself. But those days were gone. Perhaps she would drive downtown and get a cup of coffee at Starbucks. Annie would not approve. Annie thought Betty should make coffee at home and bring it with her in a thermos, but where was the fun in that? Soon the concession would be open at the beach and Betty would be able to get coffee there. It would be summer again, and children would descend on the sand, their mothers, on cell phones, trailing after them laden with beach chairs and buckets. Now, though, there was only a man with an Irish setter whose coat gleamed in the sun. Perhaps she would get her hair colored to match the dog's. She could ask the man for a hank of dog hair and bring it to her colorist.

Slowly, Betty walked back to the house. She had made it a home, with the help of her girls. She had always made a home for them, one way or another, and they for her. But they couldn't live with her forever. They were grown women. And so was she. She wondered if and when she would be going back to her apartment. A woman alone. Homeless as a bird.

She felt awfully tired. Her head began to hurt. Her neck was so stiff. Her head was pounding now. She saw the little cottage and wondered if she would be able take the steps necessary to reach it. One step. Two. She counted. Ten. She was at the cracked concrete stoop. The pain in her head shot into the sky, exploded there, hurtled back down at alarming speed; and again, like the little waves. Step. Step. Thirteen, her lucky number, for she had reached the couch in her house. The couch was beneath her. The pain in her head screamed out loud. There was no one to hear. No one, Betty thought, except me.

* * *

Miranda was the one who found her and called 911. She and Leanne had not sailed that day. First they had called Kit using Skype and watched Henry chat with his father. Miranda had worried a little over how she would respond to seeing Kit again, even if it was only through a video chat on a computer. Leanne told him she was there, and he looked a little taken aback, then recovered and said in his typically jaunty way, 'A conspiracy. Don't believe everything you hear.'

Miranda thought, No, I guess not, but she said nothing, stood out of range of the camera, and watched.

He was just as good-looking as ever, she thought, though his manner, so easy and free, now struck her as fraught with new meaning—it was as if Henry were his nephew or younger brother, a little kid he liked, for whom, however, he had little or no responsibility.

'I was scared,' Henry said about seeing a bloody Kit held at gunpoint on TV.

'It was catsup,' Kit said. 'Isn't that funny? Catsup all over Daddy's face?'

Henry thought that was funny. Then: 'Come

home,' he said.

'Okay, buddy,' said Kit. 'I will! As *soon* as I can.'

Leanne, standing behind Henry, gave Miranda a significant look.

'I saw that,' Kit said. 'Listen, I'm working, okay? That's what you were always on me about, so now I'm working, okay?'

'Okay,' Leanne said. 'Fair enough. Sorry.'

Kit sulked for a moment. Was he really thirty-five? Miranda wondered. She looked at Leanne. How old was Leanne? It had never occurred to her to ask or even to wonder.

'As a matter of fact, I have to leave for work right now, okay? It's like an hour drive to the studio . . .'

Henry threw his father a kiss, and the screen went black.

'How old are you?' Miranda asked suddenly.

'Thirty-eight,' Leanne said. 'Why?'

'Eight,' Henry said, holding up all his fingers.

'I'm forty-nine,' Miranda said.

Leanne tilted her head thoughtfully, then said, 'So that's all right, then.'

She lifted Henry up, gave him a twirl, and said they should go on an adventure, a bike adventure to Devil's Den.

They pedaled along the winding, hilly roads that led to the nature preserve in Weston. Henry was strapped in his seat behind Leanne. Rushing down a hill, Miranda passed the other two, stood on the pedals as she had as a child, and coasted. Speed, she thought, is the glory of going forward.

'Bankruptcy definitely agrees with you,' Leanne said, laughing, when they reached the bottom of the hill.

The papers from the lawyers had arrived the day before. 'Belly up,' said Miranda. 'That's me.'

Henry looked curiously at her belly.

'I'm free,' Miranda said.

They followed the steep path to a leafy spot closely sheltered by tall skinny birch trees. Miranda put her hand on the white trunk of one of them. 'The most beautiful tree.' She felt a surge of emotion, this same surge she felt so often now. Maybe it was menopause.

'I wonder if I'm starting menopause. Everything makes me want to . . .'

'What?' Leanne asked.

Miranda threw herself to the ground and rolled in the leaves, breathing in the damp of spring, the dust of last autumn. She lay on her back staring up at the blue sky just beyond the lacy canopy.

'Everything makes me want to weep with happiness,' she said. Would that it were menopause, she thought. She could sweat it out and emerge in a few years a calmer person with somewhat brittle bones. But this? This calm, deep satisfaction? *This* was madness. This sharp, painful sense of joy, of gratitude that felt like an inhalation of fresh, cool air. This soft exhalation that felt like peace.

Leanne swept a leaf from Miranda's face.

Peace? Miranda bit her lip. If peace burns, this is peace, she thought. If peace makes you tremble, this is definitely peace. If peace is feeling calm one minute, tortured the next, if peace is war, then, then, and only then is this peace.

She stared up at the canopy of leaves, the sun drifting down in dappled warmth. Why couldn't she just have a friend like everyone else? Maybe

Annie was right—she was just a drama queen, couldn't live without it.

'Randa?'

She turned to Leanne and opened an eye. Oh, what a mess. 'Yeah?'

Leanne twisted a stick in her hands as if she were about to start a fire. 'Oh, nothing,' she said.

Miranda rolled onto her back again. Leanne had called her Randa.

Suddenly a large little face hung over Miranda, its cheeks streaked with dirt.

'*Now* you're belly up,' the little face explained.

When Miranda got back to the cottage late that afternoon, she found her mother writhing in pain on the couch.

'I can't turn my neck,' Betty whispered. 'My head is exploding. It keeps exploding.'

The EMTs were volunteers. She recognized one—a blond girl she sometimes saw running on the beach. She followed the ambulance in the Mercedes, though later she had no memory of the drive.

'It's meningitis,' Miranda told Annie over the phone.

'*What?*'

'No, it's okay, it's not the kind that kills you.'

'Just the kind that makes you wish you were dead,' Betty whispered from her hospital bed. 'Please stop talking, darling.'

But she did not want to be dead at all. She wanted to go back in time, not very far, not to when she was young, not to when she was still happily married to Joseph, just back to that afternoon before she went for a walk on the beach, to that moment when she stood looking out the

291

kitchen window and saw the goldfinch fluttering through the maple leaves. She had been so unfair. She wanted to go back in time, to look out her kitchen window, to see the movement of the little bird, the flash of yellow and flash of black, as it rustled among the leaves, and she wanted to apologize. To the bird. It had been a pretty bird on a pretty day. She should never have doubted either one.

'I will never take another day for granted,' she told Annie the next day when the antibiotics had begun to take effect and the pain had lessened, 'and neither should you.'

'Have you suddenly seen God?' Annie asked.

'Goodness, no. Why, have you?'

When Annie called Josie to tell him that Betty was sick, she had to fight off an irrational sense of I-told-you-so justification. How awful to celebrate your mother's pain because it shamed someone, even if that person deserved to be shamed. Yet when she said to Josie, 'Mom is in the hospital with meningitis,' she felt a distinct shiver of satisfaction.

CHAPTER NINETEEN

Betty came home after six days, but she was very weak. After a few days in the cottage, she was even weaker, and Annie and Miranda took her to the doctor's office, each holding an arm.

'What a fuss,' Betty said. 'I just need rest.'

But the doctor said she had caught a staph infection when she was in the hospital, and he put her on heavy doses of various antibiotics.

She insisted on getting out of bed each morning, however, and her daughters would settle her, in her sunglasses, on the living room couch when it was chilly and on the sunporch chaise, in her sunglasses, when it was warm. The sunglasses helped with the headaches.

'You look very glamorous,' said Cousin Lou on one visit.

'It's my own private sanitorium.' Her legs were covered with a blanket, a cup of broth in her hands.

Lou caught sight of the broom in the corner, grabbed it, and began to sweep absentmindedly.

'How is Mr Shpuntov?' Betty asked.

'He hit his caregiver yesterday.'

'Uh-oh.'

'She hit him back. So that was fine. I wonder when the word went from caretaker to caregiver.' He stood at the foot of Betty's chaise. She looked chalky and thin—her wrists protruded from her sweater, tight veined sinews. 'How are you?' he said, suddenly serious.

Betty said, 'I never hit my caregivers. Or my caretakers.'

Annie came out with her mother's pills.

'Do I, Annie?'

'Hardly ever.'

'Sit down, Lou,' Betty said. 'It's very pleasant, just sitting. I had no idea I would like being a patient so much. I highly recommend it. I think I have found the career at which I excel. Of course, I am still a widow. I won't give that up.'

'Multitasking,' Annie said. She was worried. Betty really did seem to like reclining on her chaise, staring out at the trees and the sky. She was dreamy and faraway, preoccupied.

'There's a goldfinch here,' Betty was telling Cousin Lou as if it explained everything. 'A goldfinch I see when I'm very quiet and patient.'

Roberts came that evening and brought bunches of daffodils for Betty.

'This one is for you,' he said, handing a stem to Annie.

He came almost every day now. Poor man, Annie thought. Miranda was hardly ever there, yet he sat so patiently, entertaining Betty with stories of some of his greediest clients and their twisted estates, often staying for dinner.

'Do you miss it? Do you mind being retired?' Betty asked. 'Because we can get another chaise and you can come to my sanitorium. It keeps me busy.'

'Oh, I keep my hand in. I have a few clients still.'

'Like Charlotte Maybank? She seems very excited about her posthumous financial dealing.'

Betty expected Roberts to smile as he did when regaling her with the eccentricities of clients and the absurdities of cases over the years. Instead, he set his jaw and said nothing. Betty said, 'Sorry. None of my business.'

Annie often came home from work to find them sitting in silence, the lengthening day casting a pale light on their faces. How tiny and frail her mother looked in her wispy black outfits beside Roberts, who was tan, almost ruddy, a tall, lean man in a tall, lean suit.

His face would crease into a smile when he saw her. He would rise from the invalid's side and lean over to kiss Annie's cheek. She would compliment his bow tie. And they would have cocktails.

'Miranda didn't pick you up at the station?' he asked on the first of these evenings, when Annie arrived alone.

Poor Roberts, she thought. 'No Miranda. Just us chickens tonight, I'm afraid.'

'Ah.' He took a martini from her. 'Did you walk from the station? You know, I could always come and get you, Annie, if Miranda's busy.'

Annie smiled. Gallant Roberts. Very old-school. Like me, she thought. 'I dropped Miranda off after she picked me up. At Leanne's. But how thoughtful of you.'

He nodded. 'Miranda's been a blessing to Leanne. Charlotte is a handful. But . . .' He paused here, then said, 'Well, Charlotte's been going through so much.'

Miranda was not coming home until much later, so Annie didn't ask him to stay for dinner. He joined them anyway.

Lonely, she thought. Not like me. What was the opposite of 'lonely'? The word to describe someone who could not stand to be around people? 'Togetherly'? 'Loneless', she decided. Yet she found that he was one of the few people she did not feel like running away from. No hiding in the attic from Roberts. In fact, he rather reminded her of an attic, the air soft, the light filtered, the contents dusted with recognition or obscurity or gentle surprise.

*   *   *

Felicity decided to treat the girls, by which she meant Gwen, Amber, and Crystal, to lunch at Café des Artistes. Amber was such a . . . she smiled . . .

295

she had been about to use the word 'treasure', as if Amber were an exceptional maid of long service. There *was* something a little servile about the girl, in an ambitious way that Felicity recognized. Crystal was a silly nonentity, but Amber . . . even with her aging teenager slang . . . there was something about her. She was so attentive, and yet one felt the steel behind her acquiescence. She reminded Felicity of . . . Felicity. Which intrigued her. And then, all those free massages. Felicity was the envy of her friends.

She had never been to Café des Artistes, but it was an Upper West Side institution, and as she planned on becoming a proper Upper West Side institution herself, she thought she and Café des Artistes should meet. She had made a reservation for 1.00, and she left the office with plenty of time to get there, even with traffic. Taking cabs was a new luxury, taking cabs even when the subway ran directly to her destination. Her life had changed in many small ways like that, she thought with satisfaction. She had worked hard for these little luxuries, worked hard at the office, worked hard at making Joe happy. She did not begrudge either the office or Joe her sweat equity, she loved both her work and Joe, but sweat equity it was, and now she was getting her returns.

She walked into the richly dim restaurant, and a courtly man led her to her table. The silver glistened, the napkins and tablecloths were stiff and formal and white, like dress shirts, she thought. She looked up at the murals. They were famous, she knew. Redheaded women, nude, swinging from vines. Those redheads never had to work in an office, she thought. They didn't have to

296

save and save to buy a boxy one-bedroom apartment in an unfashionable building in a huge unfashionable complex that might just as well have been in New Jersey as on the Upper West Side of Manhattan. Felicity pursed her lips, then smiled. The fleshy naked women in the old-fashioned paintings would be scrawny ancient crones by now. Not to mention dead.

*　　*　　*

Rich soil for a rich house, Miranda thought, digging in the rose garden behind the Beachside Avenue house. House? It really was a mansion, there just was no other name that fit. It had been built as a show of wealth, not as a shelter. The rose garden had been neglected for years, but the tendrils and vines still crawled vigorously over the trellises. Miranda pulled at the weeds. Henry was taking his nap inside, Leanne was working on the paper she would soon have to present at some epidemiology conference. Miranda, who had no paper to write, no nap to take, was weeding. She did not know how to garden. But she could weed. Anyone could weed. Even a failure, even a bankrupt, even a woman who was silently, odiously betraying her best friend.

Miranda had fallen in love so many times, each of them a dizzying ascent of need and a sickening drop of disappointment. But this was Leanne, Henry's mother, her new friend, this person to whom she confided everything. Except one thing. The most important thing.

How odd, how private, how intimate to keep quiet about your feelings. Miranda cherished her secret. It sickened her, literally, leaving her breathless and queasy, but she somehow didn't mind. She reveled in her misery. Ironic, this Romantic extravaganza all bottled up inside.

It began to rain, hard. Perhaps she would catch pneumonia and die. That would be very Romantic.

Miranda had read plenty of books about women falling in love with women. They were a niche part of her business, a popular sub-genre, a little out-of-date now but very big in the nineties. She had sold two of them herself, one to Knopf, a huge advance, quite a coup, she had to admit. The women discovered their real selves, etc. Could no longer live a lie, etc. She had felt some sympathy, yet the whole business had always seemed so unnecessary, extravagant even. An act of excessive imagination, if not sheer will. She had been far too busy falling in love with unsatisfying men to think very much about it, much more than: What would be the point?

You're the point, Miranda thought. Now I know.

She watched Leanne, dry and warm and shuffling papers inside. The rain fell dramatically, and the Long Island Sound waves, waves that had caused so much mischief months ago at this very spot, splashed behind her. She didn't really know how she had gotten from there to here, and she didn't really care. As long as she could stay.

From her vantage point of rain and rose stalks, Miranda saw Roberts enter the room and speak to Leanne. She saw Leanne run her hands through her hair, a gesture of despair. Roberts was showing her a sheaf of legal-looking papers. Leanne threw her head back, staring at the ceiling. She stood and made helpless, questioning gestures, her arms wide and flailing. Her hands became fists, and her mouth opened and closed. Miranda walked through the rain to the window. She gestured weakly at Leanne: Should she come in? Leanne, shouting and waving the papers at Roberts, did not even see her, and Miranda slogged her way to the car and drove to the station to wait for Annie.

*   *   *

Felicity marched through the same downpour. The trees in Central Park, budding but black in the rain, rattled their branches ominously. The doorman held his umbrella for Felicity, and she walked beneath it with as much dignity as she could muster under the circumstances. She was soaked, her mink coat matted and limp, a sad family of vermin drowned and slung across her body. Her hair was drenched, her umbrella blown inside out and abandoned long ago. She had been walking and walking and walking. Her shoes were ruined, of course. In the elevator she could smell the wet fur, musky and animalistic, reeking like a dripping dog.

'Joe!' Her shoes squelched on the marble she'd had installed in the entrance hall. 'Joe!'

He came out of the kitchen looking warm and unruffled, a glass of Scotch in his hand. In general, she approved of his meticulous clothing, his careful grooming, his unchanging habits. Now his smooth comfort infuriated her.

'Can't you see I'm soaking wet?'

He took her coat and held it away from him. 'Towel?' he said, walking towards the bathroom. He wondered if he would always be supplying towels for hysterical women. At least Felicity had not thrown a glass of good whisky at him the way Betty had. He had just phoned Miranda. He called every day. She hung up on him every day. The girls did not bother to hide their contempt for him. But he had to find out how Betty was. Meningitis. Betty rarely got even a cold. How had she gotten this terrible infection? Somehow he knew it was his fault. Miranda and Annie obviously felt the same way. At least she was out of the hospital now. They never let him speak to her. He was sure Betty would want to talk to him if they let her. After all these years together. But they were no longer together, Annie had reminded him. She has cut the cord, Annie had said. She's recuperating physically and emotionally. Do you want to make her feel worse? Are you that selfish and self-centered? I don't care how guilty you feel, she had said, you are not going to upset my mother.

'It's Frederick,' Felicity was saying, squelching behind him.

He pulled an enormous white bath towel from a shelf. 'Here, darling.'

'I'm speaking to you! Didn't you hear me? Frederick!'

The wet coat hung heavily at the end of his outstretched arm, dripping. He dropped it in the bathtub, half expecting damp revengeful minks to rise up from its folds. He hated that coat. Why was she wearing it in April anyway? If Miranda had ever seen it, she would have been furious. Of course, she was furious anyway. He threw the towel around Felicity's shoulders. 'What about Frederick, darling?'

'He's *marrying* her. That . . . girl.'

300

Joe put a smaller towel on Felicity's head. She looked like an angry nun. 'Which girl? The one who was here? Which one? I couldn't really tell them apart. Are you sure? Neither one of them seems at all like Frederick's type. And they're just children.'

'Hah!' said Felicity. 'There you have it. *Children.*'

'Well, it's better that he's marrying a girl than a boy, isn't it?'

'No, don't you see, they're going to *have* one. She's pregnant, or so she claims. I don't believe a word of it. She's not showing at all. Of course, how could you tell, she's always going to some gym. I told him to demand a paternity test. Gwen is beside herself. Think how she feels! After all she's done for that girl. And me! I let her live here!'

Joseph held the glass of Scotch to his lips. He could see Betty on the couch in her crumpled bathrobe, a fury. The glass had hurtled through the air. The perfume of the Scotch had hung around him like a cloud. The apartment had been a battleground. Now it was just an apartment. Felicity shuffled ahead of him, draped in terry cloth. He would have to tell her soon, he knew.

'And Frederick!' she said, her words drifting back to him, muffled by the towel around her head. 'How he could do that to his own daughter. Is he from Alaska? That's where they'll move, no doubt. That's what they'll tell us next. And don't even ask about Evan—he's beside himself. He's furious. It's so humiliating for the family. I mean, Frederick is a public figure. Everyone will know. I'm so upset, I walked home. But when it rains it pours, and it poured, and I'm soaked. Thank you,' she added, turning into the kitchen, rubbing her hair with the towel. 'That little golddigger.'

'Where is she, anyway?' Joseph said, glad to be able to postpone his own news. 'She didn't come home with you?'

'Oh, she'll never set her scheming little foot in this apartment again.'

He put the kettle on and poured some whisky and sugar in a mug. 'Sit down,' he said gently. He took a lemon out of the refrigerator, cut it, squeezed it in the mug. When the water boiled, he poured it into the mug and handed the concoction to Felicity.

She breathed in the fumes. 'Just what the doctor ordered. We'll have to change all the locks.'

'Yes,' Joseph said. 'We will definitely need to do that. Or someone will.'

At his tone, Felicity stopped sipping from the mug. 'What?'

'I just got the final word from the lawyers.'

Felicity stood up, very straight within her nun's habit of towels. 'Yes?'

'The apartment is Betty's.'

Felicity took a moment, then said, 'Fine.'

She sat back down, drank a little more of her toddy.

This was the part of her Joseph loved, he realized. The hard part. The unyielding part. Felicity was strong. She was not always entirely human, he had discovered. But she was always strong.

'I've always wanted to live downtown anyway,' she said. 'The West Side is so over.'

* * *

In the Museum of Natural History, beneath the dinosaur, where she and Crystal had taken refuge from the rain, Amber held her cell phone in one hand. With the other she pinched her sister's arm as punctuation to every other word. 'It's all her fault, Frederick. Everything was going so well,' she said into the phone, administering three pinches.

'Ow . . . It just slipped out, Amber . . . Ow . . .'

*   *   *

The day before the rainstorm, Betty had gone to the doctor with a bad cough. She hadn't wanted to, but when Annie got home from work and heard her, she had called the doctor and made the appointment without even asking Betty, treating her like a child, and Betty did not have the energy to argue.

'I don't like the way you sound,' the doctor had said.

I don't like the way *you* sound, thought Betty. He was a young man and condescending. But at least he didn't call her dear and talk very slowly and loudly the way some of them did.

'But she just has a cold,' Miranda said when the doctor insisted on putting Betty back in the hospital. No need to make a big deal out of it. And everyone knew that people got sicker in hospitals. Especially older people.

'Don't get sundowner's syndrome,' she said that night when she and Annie left Betty to the ministrations of the harried nursing staff. 'Wash your hands a lot.'

'I already have a staph infection, darling.'

303

'See?'

Betty had sent them off with a thrown kiss, a coughing fit, and a wave.

'*American Idol*,' she'd gasped urgently, pointing at the TV.

They looked back at her when they reached the door. She was small and pale and wracked with coughs. Tubes ran into and out of her. She fished her wallet out of the bedside drawer. She dialed the phone, glancing up at the 800 number flashing on the television screen to get it right.

'Oh God, not again,' Annie said.

A young man on the TV commercial mopped up a puddle of cola with a miraculously absorbent cloth. 'Wowsham!' he said.

The next day, the day of the rainstorm, Betty was still in the hospital. Miranda had spent most of the day there, then taken a break to pull up weeds and breathe the uncontaminated air blowing off the Sound.

Now, as Roberts and Leanne enacted their unhappy pantomime behind the window, Miranda picked Annie up at the station and drove straight to the hospital. She said nothing about what she had seen in the rain. They spoke only of Betty.

'She was fine this morning,' Miranda said. She heard how lame this sounded. 'She ate some toast and applesauce.'

When they arrived in Betty's hospital room, they hung up their wet coats, and their mother waved them closer, one on each side of the bed. 'Sit here, and you here,' she said. Then she held them close.

'I love you,' she said softly, tears welling up. 'I love you both so much.'

Annie and Miranda caught each other's eye

across their mother's back.

'We love you, too,' they both murmured. But, what the hell is going on? said their tone.

'It's over,' Betty said at last, after a considerable embrace and hushed sniffling. 'It's over.'

'What?' Annie asked, standing suddenly. 'What's wrong? What did the doctor say?'

'The divorce. The *divorce* is over,' Betty reassured her.

'You're not getting divorced?' Miranda asked, a stupid smile spreading across her face.

'Oh, darling, of course we're getting divorced. That's the point. Josie has to give me a divorce now. The forensic accountant figured everything out.'

'What forensic accountant?' Annie asked. 'What are you talking about?'

'His name is Mr Mole. Isn't that perfect? I knew he'd help the minute Roberts told me his name.'

'Roberts?'

'Roberts and Mr Mole arranged everything. Josie has to give me our apartment. He has to give me some of our assets, he has to behave like a mensch. It's all settled. I knew he was a mensch. He always said so, after all.'

Annie sank back onto the bed. 'Jesus,' she said, letting out a sigh of relief. Then: 'Some mensch. What Yiddish dictionary do you use?'

'We won!' Miranda said. 'Finally. We really won?'

'I'm supposed to go into town tomorrow to sign the papers. But . . .'

'They'll let you come home tonight, and we can drive you in,' Annie said.

Betty laughed. 'You practically pronounced me

dead, and now you want me to hop out of bed and go to meetings? Anyway, they will not let me out tonight . . .'

'But . . .'

Betty coughed, then pointed to her chest. '. . . Pneumonia or some such thing . . .'

Annie rushed out of the room in search of the doctor, who was nowhere to be found, of course. Pneumonia or some such thing? She had saved that minor piece of information for a parenthesis? Her mother was infuriating. Annie wanted to shake her and her pneumonia. She wanted to shake someone, anyway. The doctor would do. She listened to the page: *Dr Franken, Dr Franken, please call in . . . Dr Franken, Dr Franken . . .'* Her mother called him Dr Frankenstein. He was not much older than Annie's son Charlie. *Dr Franken, Dr Franken.* Hospital pages always sounded so ominous. The blood was pounding in Annie's ears.

'You have power of attorney,' her mother was saying when she went back into the room to wait for the doctor. 'I want both of you to go in and sign the papers for me.'

'Oh, Mom, that can wait. Let's worry about your health now . . .'

'You can worry about two things at once, Annie,' Betty said, smiling. 'I've seen it firsthand. I want you to go in.' She paused. She reached out and held Annie's hand in her own left hand, Miranda's in her right. 'I want you to go,' she said.

Dr Franken, Dr Franken, said the page.

'I want that rotten, selfish, dirty bastard to face *you*,' Betty said. Her eyes were fierce. '*Both* of you.'

Miranda and Annie stared at their mother.

'He owes you that,' Betty said. 'Rest his soul,' she added gently.

* * *

The doctor appeared eventually, a youngster in a white coat. Betty's staph infection had gotten worse, he said. Pneumonia . . . intravenous antibiotics . . . couldn't possibly go home . . . at her age . . . lucky to have survived the meningitis . . . at her age . . . at her age . . . at her age . . .

Annie had mechanically taken notes. When she tried to decipher them when she got home, she said, 'Just words. A bunch of meaningless words. All I really heard was *at her age*. She's not even that old. That little punk doctor.'

She lay down on Betty's chaise.

'Don't worry, Annie,' Miranda said in a worried voice. 'She'll be okay.'

It was the first time Annie could remember Miranda comforting her. It terrified her. Things must be very bad indeed.

Miranda called Leanne, who promised to call the hospital and see, doctor to doctor, what was really going on.

'She'll go in and see her in the afternoon, too, when Henry's napping. Hilda can keep an eye on him.'

Miranda seemed so proud, Annie thought, as if Leanne's generous behaviour reflected on her somehow. 'That's great,' she said, and Miranda beamed.

Then Annie called Cousin Lou's house to see if Rosalyn could go to the hospital in the morning.

'Oh, she can't possibly, she'll drive your poor

mother crazy. No, God, no. I'll go, though. I'm more soothing, aren't I? I cheer people up. I'll go. Rosalyn is much too nervous right now. This business has been a terrible strain on her.'

'What business? Mom in the hospital?' Leave it to Rosalyn to turn this into her own malady.

'No, no. Those two girls from Palm Springs. It's gotten all topsy-turvy.'

Annie almost moaned. She did not care about Amber and her antics right now. She did not even care about Frederick. What was done was done. She cared only about her mother.

'One of them seems to have run off with that Barrow fellow,' Cousin Lou was saying. 'Gweneth is mad as a wet hen . . .'

Where did her cousin ever come up with that colloquial American expression? Annie wondered irrelevantly.

'Rosalyn has been on the phone with hysterical women all day. She's devastated. And with a baby coming . . .'

Annie said, 'Cousin Lou, I'm sorry Rosalyn is in such a state, but can you go to the hospital tomorrow morning or not? I kind of have to know.'

'What am I? Family? Or family? First thing in the morning.'

CHAPTER TWENTY

The meeting took place in an office with a view of the Hudson River. Miranda stared out at a motionless barge roosting in the river's fawn-colored water.

'Garbage scow,' she said. 'Poor old garbage scow.'

Josie's lawyer looked up irritably from his papers. Josie laughed.

'Only you would feel sorry for a garbage scow,' he said gently.

'Don't patronize me.'

Josie looked genuinely shocked. 'Miranda . . .'

The door opened and the forensic accountant, Mr Mole, entered, a fat man who looked as if he should have been named Mr Toad of Toad Hall. Behind him, to Miranda's surprise, loped Roberts, a briefcase in his hand.

'You turn up in the oddest places,' Annie said, but for once Roberts, with his lanky formality, seemed a perfect fit. He slid into a chair at the head of the table, folded his long fingers together, and gazed out comfortably over his pale blue bow tie.

'Shall we begin?' he said.

'*Semi*retired,' Miranda said half to herself.

They signed the papers in silence, the ballpoint pens scratching.

'Now,' Josie said, smiling, 'I told you girls I would be generous!'

Annie looked at the man who had been until very recently her father, and she knew that sometime in the future he would be her father again. Not because she forgave him. It was not her place to forgive him, really, he hadn't divorced her, and anyway, she didn't forgive him, her place or not, and she never would. It was not that she would forget, either, although she supposed she might, one so often did, with years and years to fade the colors of memory. But it was for neither of those reasons that Josie would somehow leech back into her heart. It was because she loved him.

She just did not love him right now.

'Oh, Josie,' she said sadly, and she stood up to give him a lingering embrace, taking in the feel of his fatherly cheek, his fatherly soapy smell. 'You really have been a complete shmuck.'

'Lunch?' he said rather pathetically, turning from Annie to Miranda and back again.

'We have to get back to our ailing mother,' Miranda said, 'who will now at last have a decent roof over her head.'

Joseph nodded. 'Thank God,' he said. 'Thank God we finally worked out the details.'

'Thank forensic accountancy,' Miranda said, giving him her most defiant glare, a narrowed-eyed face he knew so well from her growing up.

How could they understand how relieved he was to have Betty properly cared for? But look at them, so fierce, so loyal to their mother, so strong.

'You're good girls,' he said.

Silence.

'Your mother deserves this,' he added. 'She's a remarkable woman. A fine human being.'

Miranda burst into tears, threw herself into Josie's arms, then snarled, 'I hate you,' and ran out the room.

'Well, bye,' Annie said, following her sister, and the meeting was over.

*   *   *

They shook hands with Mr Mole and thanked him.

'Oh, don't thank me,' he said. 'I would do anything for my old friend Roberts.'

310

Roberts offered to drive them home, and as they walked to the car, Miranda stepped into a deli to get a bottle of water.

'Thank you,' Annie said. 'I don't know how to thank you for what you've done.'

She took his hand and, without thinking, kissed it.

His face creased into a huge smile. Then, noticing his hand lingering by Annie's lips after she had let it go, he coughed, retracted it, straightened his tie, said it was all Mr Mole, all thanks to the magical Mr Mole.

'Mole is pretty much the best forensic accountant in the country,' he continued as they pulled into the traffic of the West Side Highway.

'Well, he must have done a great job if he got Josie to change his mind,' said Miranda.

'Oh, he didn't have do anything at all. It was just the possibility. Just the thought of having Mole go over your books—it gets people to reevaluate their positions, shall we say.'

'Thank you again,' Annie said. 'Thank you for Mr Mole.'

Roberts colored a little. Annie could see the back of his neck grow pink.

'Thank you,' Miranda repeated. 'Thank you with all our family heart.'

They rode in silence for a while. The sun was behind them. The trees glowed with the clear spring light and tender spring leaves.

'I guess we won't be neighbors any more,' Annie said after a while. 'It's back to the city for the Weissmanns.'

She saw both Roberts and Miranda start.

'Let's get Mom out of the hospital first,'

311

Miranda said after a while.

'Well, whenever this exodus occurs,' Roberts said, 'I will definitely miss you.'

Annie caught his eye in the rearview mirror. She looked away.

'Yes,' he said. 'Yes, I will.'

A few weeks earlier, Annie had found herself wondering idly what Roberts's first name was and had consulted a Westport–Weston phone book from 1993 that sat on a shelf in the kitchen. She had leafed through the thin gray pages until she reached the Rs. About halfway down the second page, she found it.

Mr and Mrs Phineas Roberts, the phone book entry read. She had smiled at the first name. No wonder. Mr and Mrs Phineas Roberts. *Mr and Mrs.* A couple, an entity. She had not been able to get that listing out of her mind for days. She wondered if he ever had.

*   *   *

After visiting Betty in the hospital and telling her about the meeting, about Josie's bubble of self-regard, about Mr Mole, who looked like Toad of Toad Hall, and then hearing from their mother, between coughs, about the way Roberts had quietly, quickly, and entirely on his own come up with and executed the plan of frightening Josie with Mr Mole's prowess, Miranda dropped Annie off at home and drove to Charlotte Maybank's great pile on Beachside Avenue.

'Miranda!' said Leanne, when the maid led her into the living room. 'I'm so happy to see you.'

She didn't look happy at all, curled in the

embrace of the sofa, a half-empty bottle of Johnnie Walker on the table beside her, a glass in her hand.

'How is your mother? She was asleep the whole time I was there. Henry's asleep, too, you know. I know that's why you're here—to see Henry. But he's asleep. Aunt Charlotte is asleep, too. I'm not asleep, though. So you're stuck with me, I guess.'

She held her glass out.

Miranda could not tell if Leanne wanted her to take a sip from the glass or to pour more into it. She took it from her friend's hand and gently set it down beside the bottle. 'I came to talk to you, Leanne, not Henry.'

'Me? Poor me. That's nice that you came to talk to poor me. Did you know I am poor? Poor me is poor? I was always poor, but now I'm broke, you see, and so is Aunt Charlotte, who was always going to leave everything to me, so I never really worried too, too much about being poor, because I'm a doctor and I can always earn a living, so how poor is that, but going to Africa to study epidemiology, that doesn't bring in a lot of money, although it does make you realize that when you're poor here, you would be rich there, but Aunt Charlotte has never been to Africa, so she can hardly be expected to understand that . . .'

As Leanne rambled on, Miranda paced up and down the room. She knew she should be trying to comfort her. This was a financial tragedy of major proportions, she gathered. She should sit down beside Leanne and say soothing things. Instead, she walked to the windows, then back to the door, then to the windows again, and said absolutely nothing.

'Poor Aunt Charlotte is finally poor now, just as

she always thought she would be, and now we really will have to auction the portraits and the chairs and the silver spoons, but she thought it would be death duties, that's what she calls them, total affectation, and now the death duties will come while she's still alive, crazy old thing. Well, at least she'll be able to see her fantasy come true, that's one way to look at it . . .'

Finally, Miranda got hold of herself. She had come here to say something, not to listen, not to sympathize. But disaster had struck. What she had to come to say would have to wait. Leanne was in trouble. She needed Miranda. Miranda would speak to her, patiently, gently, discover the parameters of the disaster, offer advice and hope. 'What the hell happened?' she snapped. 'What the fuck are you talking about?'

'Don't blame me,' Leanne prattled on. 'I told her not to trust him, I told her not to give him a penny, and she didn't, she says—not a penny.'

'Give who a penny?' She saw just how far gone Leanne was. She moved the bottle to a distant table, then came back and sat beside her. 'Who?' she said again, curious now, impatient. *'Who?'*

'No, not a penny, not one penny,' Leanne was saying. She shook her head triumphantly. 'Not *one* penny—*every* penny.' She took no notice of Miranda. 'Not to him, she says. No, not to him, just into an investment he told her about, a nice, safe fund, a friend of his on Wall Street, and he would take only a finder's fee sort of thing, which would all be used for Henry, anyway, and not from her, but from the fund manager . . .'

A light dawned. Miranda, with foreboding, said, 'Kit?'

'And it was a *closed* fund, but he could get her in, this friend of his. The manager's nephew could get her into this closed fund. She never could resist anything exclusive, the idiotic old bat.'

'Leanne, get up.' Miranda pulled her to her feet. 'You're kind of hysterical, right? So take a deep breath or something.'

'She wouldn't let him stay in her house, even to take care of Henry when I was away, locked him away in the boathouse like Mr Rochester's mad wife—and now it's all gone up in flames. She couldn't bear him, thought he was a fraud, and then suddenly she gives him all her money, and then suddenly, more suddenly, it's gone. It's all gone . . . I was away for six weeks, and look what happened . . .' She grabbed a pillow and threw it.

Miranda wondered if this was what she was like when she ranted and raved.

'Stop it!' she said. 'You're acting just like me!'

She grabbed Leanne. Leanne struggled. Just for a minute. Then collapsed, sobbing, in Miranda's arms.

Miranda buried her face in Leanne's hair. 'That's better,' she said.

'Better that I'm sobbing?' Leanne said, her voice muffled in Miranda's shoulder.

'Better for me. I can hear myself think.'

'Go to hell.'

'Let's take a walk, okay? Outside. Fresh air.'

'Fresh air,' Leanne repeated dully.

They walked to the water's edge, then up and down the little beach. There was a moon, a sliver of a moon low in the black sky.

'Sober yet?' Miranda asked. But it was she who felt drunk. Drunk with confusion, with need, with

315

impatience.

'Yeah, yeah. That's where you met Kit.' She pointed to the spot on the beach Miranda had shown her. 'The financial wizard.' She took a deep breath. 'What am I going to do?' she said softly. 'What am I going to do with her? Maybe she'll die before she has to move out, before she realizes what's happened.'

'Maybe.' Miranda tried to listen, but it was difficult for her to focus. She had come to the house that night with a purpose. It had taken all her resolve to drive up the long driveway, to ring the bell, to follow Hilda into the living room. And now, a catastrophe. 'I'm sorry, Leanne,' she remembered to say. 'I'm really sorry about all this.'

Leanne kicked at a pile of shells. 'Why are you here anyway?'

The moon was sharp above them, a slash in the velvety black sky. The smell of the sea hung in the cool air. Miranda threw a rock into the water. She stared stupidly at Leanne. She took Leanne's hands in hers. She felt Leanne tremble. Miranda looked at her in surprise. Leanne moved a step closer. Miranda wondered if she was trembling, too. Yes, she was. She was trembling, too. She watched herself from far away, from another life, and thought, This is it, it's all over, over a cliff, feet still running, thin air, high above the hard, jagged earth.

'I wanted to talk to you,' she said again. But she didn't talk. She let her fingers move across Leanne's lips, the top lip, the bottom lip. She let her hand move across Leanne's cheek, past her ear, until she held Leanne's head cupped in her hand. She let her hand pull Leanne's head towards

her. She let her face move in to Leanne's face, let
her lips press against Leanne's lips.

CHAPTER TWENTY-ONE

Betty died the next week. The infection had gone
to her heart. The cottage, so small, loomed huge
and empty around Annie and Miranda. The sky
lowered.

*   *   *

Miranda wandered from room to room in the
cottage in the night, the moonlight tinny and weak.
She made her way up the stairs. She remembered
the night she had stood at the top of the steps and
watched her mother sleep. The night of cicadas.
There were no cicadas now.

Her mother had been so small and pale.

She looked at the bed, her mother's bed, empty
of her mother.

'Oh, Mommy,' she said out loud.

Or was it Annie who had said it? Annie was
somehow beside her. They were lying in their
mother's bed clinging to each other.

'Mommy,' they said. 'Oh, Mommy, Mommy,
Mommy.'

*   *   *

'Now, you see?' said Felicity. 'You have provided
for your stepdaughters very generously.'

Joseph said, Yes, that was true. Betty had left

317

them everything. The apartment and the settlement would all go to Miranda and Annie.

'As it should,' he said.

'Well, should, could, would—it's all thanks to you. Thanks to *you* and your sense of what's right and just, Annie and Miranda are heiresses now,' Felicity said. 'God bless them.'

Joseph nodded. His girls would be very comfortable, it was true.

'I'm so glad I was able to be supportive of you and your relationship with them. Family first, I have always said.'

Even so, he asked Felicity not to accompany him to the funeral.

'Family first,' she had repeated rather severely, but Joseph did not answer. He poured his own drink that night and took it with him into his study and closed the door.

*   *   *

Annie and Miranda took a break from crying for a cup of coffee. Annie noticed the coffeepot in her hand, the cups she put out, the good ones, the ones Betty liked. She tipped the pot and the coffee flowed in an arc to the cup. Why? she wondered. Why did the coffee bother? The phone rang. It was a cousin from Buffalo. She gave the information: *Tomorrow. Riverside. My apartment after. Yes, thank you so much. She really was. I know you do. I love you, too.* Her coffee was cold.

'We're orphans,' Miranda said. She began to cry again.

Oh, Miranda, must you? But Annie cried, too, and held her sister tight.

318

They had done nothing that morning but call people on the phone, informing, arranging, crying. They had slept all night curled together in Betty's bed.

They drank their coffee and sat quietly, worn out.

'I'll sort of miss this place,' Annie said after a while.

Miranda scratched her head with both hands, pulled her hair violently away from her face, made a peculiar half-sigh, half-groan, and said, 'I'm staying.'

And then she told Annie.

'And Leanne felt the same way for months, but she didn't say anything, either, because, really, it's, well . . .'

'Embarrassing?' Annie was shocked. Did things like that happen, just like that? 'Just like that?' she said. 'Just like that?'

'You think I should have done an apprenticeship? Yes, just like that, just like that, the way any change happens, any realization, any . . . well, any falling in love.'

'I don't do things just like that,' Annie said. 'I do things gradually.'

'Good. Then you can fall in love with a wonderful woman gradually.'

'Oh, Miranda, you know what I mean. It's just . . . well, I'm surprised, that's all. And I guess I feel a little betrayed.'

'It's not like I joined the Confederate Army.'

'And I'm worried, too,' Annie said. 'I mean, is this another one of your stunts? Because, Miranda, there's a little boy involved.'

A dreamy look came over her sister's face.

'Henry,' she said.

'You're not doing this just to get to Henry, are you? That would be really sick.'

'You know what?' Miranda said, giving her a kiss. 'For once, you don't have to worry about me, Annie. You really, really don't.'

Annie wondered if that could ever be true. She said, 'I guess I'm really happy that you're happy, Miranda.

'Mommy knew,' she added after a while.

'Knew what?'

'About Leanne, I think.'

'Maybe.' Miranda drummed on the kitchen table nervously for a few seconds, her lips pursed, tears running down her cheeks. 'Maybe. She knew a lot.'

Miranda and Leanne had decided to stay in the cottage together with Henry. 'And guess what?'

'What?' Annie was worn to the bone with surprises. What could really be a surprise except death, always a surprise, that inevitable surprise?

'Leanne and I are getting married.'

'Oh, for God's sake, Miranda.'

Miranda smiled. Innocent. Ingenuous. Enraging.

'I thought you didn't believe in marriage,' Annie said. 'What, you only believe in gay marriage?'

'I believe in this marriage.'

The simple sincerity of her words, the naïveté, struck Annie. She could almost feel her mother's finger poking her back, her whispered *Go on, be nice, you know how your sister is . . .*

Miranda held up an unopened box of saltines for Annie to see.

'Her crackers,' Annie said.

320

They had a good cry, a noisy one in which they held each other and rocked back and forth like old men at prayer, then reverently, wordlessly, opened the box and ate crackers with almond butter spread on them.

* * *

When Miranda told her that she was staying on in the cottage with Leanne and Henry, Annie did wonder what was to become of Aunt Charlotte. Would she have to go on the auction block along with her chairs?

But Aunt Charlotte was going somewhere much more pleasant, and close enough for Leanne to see her every day. She was moving in with Cousin Lou.

'You can't do this,' Rosalyn had said when she heard Lou's plan. 'You hardly know the woman. This is not an old-age home, Lou.'

But Lou was adamant. To take under his wing a woman who, it turned out, was the fourth cousin many times removed of Mrs James Houghteling was something he could not resist.

'Like family,' he said with relish.

Mr Shpuntov, followed by his attendant, shuffled past them, headed for the kitchen.

'And a friend for your father,' Lou said.

'Lou, for God's sake, what are they going to do together? Play handball? This really is the limit. Beyond the limit. We don't even have enough room.'

'We will,' he said. 'Once we move into that lovely old house in foreclosure on Beachside Avenue.'

'The Maybank house?'

'The Maybank house. The house I just bought.'

*   *   *

The funeral home was not far from the Central Park West apartment where Joseph and Felicity were still living. They were not scheduled to move out until the following month, and he had offered to have people back to the apartment after the funeral.

'Betty would have liked that, I think,' he said to the girls.

'Betty is dead,' Annie said.

They were going to Annie's apartment instead. The French professor had returned to Paris the week before.

'Well! If Annie's got her place back, and Miranda is staying in Westport with her bankrupt lesbian lover, maybe we should buy our apartment from them,' Felicity said when she heard this, remembering how the Cape Cod house had appreciated. 'I'm sure they'd be reasonable. I mean, it's all in the family, after all.'

'Maybe we should not,' Joe had replied.

And so Felicity returned to her search for a downtown loft with a doorman.

*   *   *

Betty had died young enough to have a full house at her funeral, Joseph thought as he entered the funeral home. He wondered if he would have the same opportunity, and felt a bit sorry for himself, believing as he did that he would die so old that none of his friends would be alive to attend

322

the service. He recognized everyone—couples, widows, widowers, second-marriage couples, grown children, grown grandchildren. So many people from his life with Betty. They all greeted him with a mixture of grief and curiosity. *How was he taking it?* they wondered. *Not well,* he wanted to answer. *My Betty is gone. I let my Betty go.* Instead, he gave a stoic smile and a warm handshake here, a lingering and meaningful meeting of the eyes there, a hearty hug, a brave kiss. I let my Betty go, he thought through his tears. And she is gone.

Lou said nothing to Joseph, just gave him a handshake, then grabbed him in a tight hug. Rosalyn asked about Gwen.

For a moment Joseph could not think who Gwen was.

He saw Annie and Miranda. He noticed how like Betty they looked, though they looked so different from each other. Annie's boys were there. They left their mother's side and came to his. They called him Grandpa Josie.

The girls followed. They cried in his arms.

Everyone is here, he thought. And no one.

*   *   *

Frederick Barrow came to Betty's funeral, too.

'I hope you don't mind,' he said to Annie, embracing her. 'I know it's awkward—Felicity and all. But your mother was a wonderful woman. And . . .' He paused. 'So are you,' he said, pausing again, then: '"Life's but a walking shadow."'

Annie tried not to cringe. Cringing at a man expressing his condolences, even with a slightly insensitive quote from *Macbeth,* was ungracious.

But surely one was allowed to be ungracious on the day of one's mother's funeral? One was certainly numb. One alternated between vacant silence and bitter tears. One quibbled mentally with quotations. One laughed. One was utterly out of control. And one cringed.

Well, so what? she thought. My mother is dead. Why doesn't everyone go away and leave me alone without my mother?

Frederick ducked his head, almost shyly, then lifted it. His eyes sparkled. 'It's been a while, hasn't it?'

Was it possible that Frederick was flirting with her, on the day of her mother's funeral? She made a motion to move away. He took her hand. 'Annie,' he said hoarsely, 'I mean it. I know now is not the time. I'm truly sorry about your mother. But I also wanted to tell you that I know I haven't been . . . well, I haven't exactly behaved the way I would want to . . . but I'd like to pick up where we left off . . . try again . . .'

There was Josie staring blankly into the distance, standing alone. Why was he alone? Where was Betty? Where is my mother? Annie wondered. I want my mother. The room was too warm. Frederick wanted to pick up where they'd left off.

She withdrew her hand. 'How is Amber?'

'Amber?' he said dismissively. 'Amber's off on her honeymoon.'

Annie backed away in confusion. Amber was on her honeymoon. Frederick had taken hold of both her hands. They might have been dancing. She watched Miranda sobbing on Charlie's shoulder. She wanted to sob on Charlie's shoulder. But

324

Amber was on her honeymoon. 'On her honeymoon? By *herself*?'

'Of course not by herself,' Frederick said, obviously annoyed at the interruption to his earnest declaration. 'She's with Evan.'

'*Evan?*'

'Ah, Evan, my wayward son . . . But "let me not to the marriage of true minds admit impediments . . ."'

Annie clapped her hands on her head. Perhaps Frederick was insane. That had never occurred to her. The marriage of true minds indeed.

Frederick laughed. He couldn't help it. She was the picture of bafflement. '"Confusion now hath made his masterpiece!"'

Macbeth again? she thought automatically, then: 'But Amber and *Evan* . . .'

'*Quite* a scandal, you're right.'

'Jeez Louise.' Annie thought: Frederick, whatever your missteps, in spite of them, because of them, you must be reeling. I am reeling. Are you reeling, too? She wanted to sit down. She tried to focus on Frederick. 'Are you okay? I mean . . .'

Frederick thought for a moment. He pursed his lips in a small, private smile, shook his head slowly, and said, 'Truly? I think it's a match made in heaven. Those two will give each other a run for their money.'

'But what about . . . well . . . the baby?'

A short, ugly laugh, though Frederick was no longer smiling. Annie was sorry she'd asked. Just to satisfy her curiosity? What if something awful had happened, a miscarriage, say? And what if there was no miscarriage? Your own son raising your baby, his baby brother? Very *Tobacco Road*.

Frederick said, 'The baby, eh?' He looked at her closely. 'You mean Gwen's baby, of course.'

Annie said nothing. Her mother was gone. She had no mother.

'Gwen's baby is due next month.' He gave her a sharp look with those eyes. No twinkle this time.

Annie forced herself to smile. 'Well!' she said. She supposed she would never know exactly what had happened. But there was to be no Frederick Jr, of that she was sure. How liberated Frederick must have been that his mistake turned out to be a mistake. She imagined him discovering the news—an abortion? A simple lie?

Whatever Amber had done or not done, had said or not said, Annie realized suddenly that she didn't care.

'Things don't turn out the way we expect sometimes.' Her voice held more meaning than she had anticipated.

Frederick raised an eyebrow.

'Things end,' she said. 'Don't they?'

'Pity,' he said.

He kissed her cheek, back to his good humor, unruffled by the messy lives of others, even his own children's, even, especially, the mess of his own life. He smiled. Frederick's smile was magnetic, she could still feel its pull. But it was a magnet that had a switch, a convenient toggle to turn it on and turn it off. Frederick was always safe, drawing to him only as much as he wanted, giving back only as much as he wanted to give back, a self-sustaining, self-sufficient circuit, a private Marxism of the soul. Frederick could afford to have a twinkle in his eye.

Will he say *Comedy of Errors*? Annie wondered.

'A veritable *Comedy of Errors*,' he said.

Annie thanked him silently for the 'veritable'. It would sustain her when she mourned his absence. For she mourned his absence even now, as he stood before her.

'I have to go,' she said.

*   *   *

Annie held her sons in her arms, first Nick, then Charlie, and felt their broad, manly shoulders shake with sobs. She stroked their heads, her hands absorbing the shape, the warmth. How could she stop? She clung to them. During the funeral ceremony, she sat behind them, refusing to take her eyes off them. She remembered them as children, tiny children, asleep on the big bed in Betty's apartment, Charlie clutching his rabbit and a stale bagel, Nick in a basket. Betty sat upright between, looking first at one, then the other. For hours.

Miranda sat down beside her, took her hand.

Roberts sat quietly on her other side, his long legs tilted off to one side.

'I will miss her forever,' Annie said. Her children's heads were beautiful. She could see them through her tears.

'Forever,' Roberts said. He put his arm tenderly around her and drew her close. 'It's true. You will.'

As the cantor chanted his wailing ancient words, Annie cried loudly, as loud, even, as her sister. Then she rested her head on Roberts's steady shoulder and cried some more.

ACKNOWLEDGEMENTS

I am happy to have this opportunity to again thank my editor, Sarah Crichton, for being so good-humored and patient; and my equally good-humored and patient agent, Molly Friedrich, for being so utterly unlike Miranda Weissmann. Thank you also, Adam and Liz, for reading; thank you, Barbara, for giving me a place to read; and thank you, Janet, for reading and reading and reading.

CHIVERS
LARGE
PRINT
–*direct*–

If you have enjoyed this Large Print book
and would like to build up your own
collection of Large Print books, please
contact

Chivers Large Print Direct

Chivers Large Print Direct offers you
a full service:

- Prompt mail order service

- Easy-to-read type

- The very best authors

- Special low prices

For further details either call
Customer Services on (01225) 336552
or write to us at Chivers Large Print Direct,
FREEPOST, Bath BA1 3ZZ

Telephone Orders:
FREEPHONE 08081 72 74 75